Echoes Beyond the Shadows

by

Alan Thereault

Echoes Beyond the Shadows
Cover design by Alan Thereault

First Author Edition: October 2025
Printed in the United States of America

Published by Vanishing Point Press

Content Advisory
This novel contains depictions of violence, trauma, psychological manipulation, coercion, interrogation, and the use of strong adult language, including explicit profanity. These elements are integral to the story's espionage setting and are presented with care and responsibility. Reader discretion is advised.

Author's Note

Espionage has always fascinated me—not for the covert missions or coded tradecraft, but for the quiet betrayals that happen in rooms without windows, and the fractures they leave behind.

Echoes Beyond the Shadows grew out of that fascination. It is a story about what remains when loyalty splinters, when truth is weaponized, and when the institutions designed to protect us turn inward and begin to consume their own.

The idea of **Oblivion**—a deniable, black-tier intelligence network operating beyond oversight—emerged from a single question:

What if the greatest threats were not foreign adversaries, but the ghosts we created ourselves?

In a world of fractured truths, synthetic memory, and eroding trust, that question no longer feels distant or hypothetical.

This book lingers in the psychological weight carried by those who live behind masks, and the cost of surviving in a profession where trust is not a lifeline, but a liability. James Rourke is not a super-agent. He is a man who believed in the system, until he learned what lived behind its shadows. Sometimes the echo you hear is not a warning, but a residue—something left behind.

If you have ever wondered what lingers after the mission ends—what survives erasure, silence, and denial—this story is for you.

—Alan Thereault

For Anastasiia,

Through every shadow I pursued,
you remained the constant light I never doubted.

This story is reborn between the lines—
because you noticed what the world overlooked.

[Oblivion Archive // Archive Index]

File Reference: **Ghosts of Oblivion**

Access Level: Classified – Eyes Only

Ghost and Flame: Shadow Fall

[Origin Record — Identity, Intimacy, Weaponization]

Echoes Beyond the Shadows

[Continuity Record — Aftermath, Silence, Institutional Erasure]

Inheritance of Signal

[Convergence Record — Escalation, Persistence, Succession]

Gravity of Signal

[Persistence Record — Life Inside Inevitability]

When Infinity Divides

[Succession Record — Continuity Beyond Meaning]

Additional records remain sealed.

Archive structure may change without notice.

Prologue

Snow pressed against the concrete walls, drifting fine as ash—a world already burning in silence.

Kyra pressed her palm against the steel, fingers shaking where blood had dried between them. On the other side of the glass, James's silhouette blurred in the strobes. She couldn't hear him, but she knew the shape of his voice, the shape of his hand, as if both were written into her.

I never broke, she mouthed—and in her silence, it was him she meant, him she carried as vow and fire.

The lock thundered shut. Kyra closed her eyes. For one stolen instant, she let herself imagine her sister's laugh, the warmth of tea, and James's gaze—the only thing that had ever made her believe in tomorrow.

She smiled into the silence.

[OBELISK SYSTEM LOG | OBSERVER: SIGIL-3]

Fragment recovered: "Tell her I never broke."

Status: variance dismissed. Archive complete.

And in the silence that followed, the words lived on as echoes beyond the shadows, fragments carried further than flesh.

ACT I – THE MAKING OF GHOSTS

Some ghosts are made in silence.
Others are sharpened in fire.
When names are erased,
what remains is not absence—
but echo.

CHAPTER 1: WIESBADEN
Wiesbaden, Germany | Yesterday

Listening to the city with one ear and holding his pace to a quiet rhythm in the other, James ran with a balance that came from repetition, rather than thought. The music regulated pace, nothing more. He never allowed himself the comfort of full immersion, not here or anywhere.

Wiesbaden moved around him in damp, controlled gray. Rain had passed more than once before dawn, leaving the pavement dark and reflective, the buildings holding the cold along their surfaces. Tires whispered across wet asphalt. A tram ground somewhere beyond the next block, its sound bending through the narrow streets before dissolving into distance.

A faint scrape reached him from behind, subtle and easily absorbed into the background if he had allowed it to be. It didn't belong to the rhythm of the street or align with the spacing of footsteps around him; it didn't belong.

He did not turn.

His right calf tightened a fraction, the muscle reacting before the thought did.

Turning would have made it legible.

Instead, he adjusted his stride by a fraction, extending it slightly before drawing it back in, altering cadence without changing his pace. The shift was small enough to vanish inside normal movement, but precise enough to force correction from anyone trying to match him.

He counted the spacing without looking: one breath, then another, then a third, waiting for something to resolve that never quite did.

Nothing resolved cleanly; the sound thinned, then disappeared, folding back into the larger noise of the city. For a moment, it could have been nothing at all.

Then a breath followed, closer than before, not wind or distance but something with weight behind it.

He shifted direction without signaling, slipping into the narrow gap between a bakery and a shuttered florist. The alley compressed everything immediately. Sound tightened. Space reduced. The air changed. Warm yeast rolled out from a vent above him, thick and alive against the damp cold, carrying with it the faint sourness of old rain trapped in brick.

If someone followed, they would have to commit.

He slowed just enough to listen, letting his pace fall into something that could be mistaken for fatigue rather than intention. The alley held still. No footfall answered his. No movement corrected for his change.

He stepped back out onto Wilhelmstrasse and allowed the city to absorb him again, folding into its movement without resistance. Commuters moved in loose patterns, purposeful without urgency, each carrying a direction that did not intersect with his. Uniforms blended with civilians, NATO presence dissolving into routine until it became background rather than signal.

That was where mistakes lived.

He passed a pharmacy window and caught the reflection without focusing on it, letting it come to him the way it needed to. Movement registered first—his own outline cutting through the glass, then the shapes behind him resolving in fragments.

A coat crossed the reflection—dark, wet, unremarkable.

He kept his pace and let the reflection go.

Five seconds later, the same coat appeared farther down the block, moving in a direction that did not align with the flow.

The timing was wrong, the placement was wrong, and there was no bag, no destination, no visible purpose.

He stopped at the next storefront and bent into a stretch, using the motion to hold the reflection longer without drawing attention to it. The glass held only passing movement now—umbrellas, shoulders, the shifting density of the street.

The coat did not appear again, and that absence carried more weight than the sighting itself.

He straightened slowly, rolling tension out of his shoulders, letting his breathing settle into something that read as ordinary. Not relaxed—never relaxed—but consistent enough to avoid drawing a second look.

The city resumed around him, then, without warning, it shifted.

Not visually or in a way that could be pointed to or named, but something structural, a presence where there had been none a moment before.

She stood beneath a café awning across the street, brushing rain from her hair with a motion that carried no excess. There was no adjustment for appearance, no hesitation in the movement. It existed only to remove water and restore control.

Her head remained lowered, though not in a way that suggested distraction. It was angled, positioned to allow her to take in more without appearing to take in anything at all.

She was working. She wasn't guessing.

A drop of rain ran from her sleeve to her wrist, and she didn't brush it away.

James did not look at her directly. He let the reflection carry her instead, the glass flattening the scene just enough to make the details clearer. Her attention moved without fixing. Not scanning—assembling.

She shifted her position by inches, testing the way her silhouette fell against the lamppost behind her. The shadow distorted across the pavement, lengthening under the sodium light, then tightening as she adjusted again. She watched the change indirectly, reading the way it altered her exposure without needing to see it directly.

She was not measuring space; she was measuring risk.

And she was measuring it against something already known.

Most people would have missed it.

To James, it was clear enough to remove doubt; it was tradecraft.

His pulse remained steady.
He didn't like how easily it stayed that way.

She never looked at him directly.

Not once.

There was only a slight adjustment in her posture, a turn of the shoulder that acknowledged his position without granting him presence. It was enough to make it clear he had already been placed inside her awareness.

He was not being watched; he had already been accounted for.

That distinction settled deeper than it should have, carrying with it the faint impression that this moment did not begin when he noticed her, but earlier—somewhere else, under conditions he had not witnessed.

Breaking off now would confirm he had seen her; staying would concede initiative.

Neither option offered clean ground.

So he crossed the street.

He did not alter his pace or his breathing, allowing the movement to read as nothing more than a runner cutting inside for warmth and coffee.

The door opened to a wash of heat and scent: wet wool, bitter espresso, old wood saturated with years of conversation that lingered without resolution. A tram bell cut sharply across the street outside before fading into the rain.

She had already chosen her seat.

Against the wall, both doors in view, with a mirror behind the counter reflecting the room in a way that allowed her to see without appearing to look.

It was exactly where she would have been.

One of the few positions in the room that did not require adjustment once occupied.

He ordered tea he had no intention of drinking and crossed to her table.

"Taken?" he asked.

Her eyes passed over his face without settling, tracing the line of his posture instead, the position of his hands, the space behind him.

"It is now."

He sat.

The decision to do nothing was deliberate, and he treated it that way. The chair angled slightly off-center. His coat remained buttoned. The bag stayed close enough to move without reaching. His hands rested where they could be seen, his shoulders relaxed without opening the line of his body.

She read all of it.

Not directly, never directly.

Her attention moved across him without settling. Hands first. Then posture. Then the distance between them. Then the reflection behind him.

His face did not matter; it never did.

What mattered was the structure beneath it—the way he occupied space, the way he held stillness without tension, the way his attention moved without revealing its path—and the speed at which she processed those details suggested she was not discovering them for the first time, only verifying that they matched expectation.

Up close, the details sharpened further. A small pin at her lapel— a lark. Not decorative. Placed.

Not for him, not exactly, but for someone who would understand what it meant to place something in the open and trust that it would be read correctly by the one person it was intended for.

He ran through the possibilities without settling on one. Agency alignment was suggested, not confirmed. The reflection work pointed toward military training, but not within the constraints of standard operations.

Something deniable, designed to exist in the spaces where attribution became inconvenient.

Something that implied the decision had already been made.

The server moved behind them, clearing a table. She waited until the motion passed before leaning in slightly, compressing the space between them without making it obvious.

"Special Activities Detachment," she said quietly. "HUMINT."

The words arrived clean, without hesitation.

"Off the reservation if you ask Langley."

Her mouth shifted, the suggestion of a smile forming and disappearing before it could fully register.

"They think only they can touch the Russians."

She leaned forward.

"Some of us know better."

He let the beginning of a smile form, more reflex than intent, then allowed it to fade before it committed to expression.

"The Army's good at acronyms," he said, his tone light enough to pass as casual. "This one sounds like an inside joke."

She lifted her cup, watching him over the rim without ever quite meeting his eyes. The motion was unhurried, controlled in a way that suggested she was less interested in the act of drinking than in the space it created between them.

She offered no correction.

No confirmation.

The silence that followed carried its own weight. It was not uncertainty; it was allowance, an acknowledgment that he could continue playing at not understanding for as long as he needed to, so long as he understood that she saw through it.

"You working now?" he asked.

"Always."

The word settled between them without distortion, clean and self-contained. It did not invite elaboration. It did not require it.

It carried no indication of who or what it belonged to—only the quiet certainty of someone who did not operate within the boundaries most people needed explained.

He let it remain there for a moment before shifting the angle slightly, not pushing forward so much as adjusting position.

"So whose problem am I supposed to be?"

"That depends on who's asking."

"Who's asking?"

She set her cup down with care, the porcelain meeting the saucer with a sound soft enough to disappear beneath the ambient noise of the room. Even that small motion carried intention, as though she understood the value of controlling not just words, but the absence of them.

"Not me," she said after a beat.

That wasn't deflection. It was positioning.

Her gaze moved—not to him, but past him, catching the reflection behind his shoulder, tracking movement at the edge of the room before returning.

"But I can see why others might."

The phrasing was deliberate—not speculation, not curiosity, but acknowledgment of an interest that already existed, one she did not claim ownership of and did not need to explain.

The shift in her attention was subtle, but not random. It marked a transition, the conversation moving from surface exchange into something more deliberate.

"Names travel, James."

The name arrived without emphasis, yet it carried a precision that made emphasis unnecessary.

For an instant, it existed only as sound—unanchored, almost abstract—before meaning settled into place behind it.

James.

Not a guess. Not a test. It had been placed.

And placed with the kind of confidence that suggested the name had not been recently acquired, but carried forward from a context he had not been present to witness.

His reaction came before he could intercept it, small enough that most would have missed it, but not small enough to escape her.

A slight redistribution of weight, a tightening through the shoulders that did not quite reach visible tension, and a shift in breath that arrived half a beat off the rhythm he had established earlier.

He corrected it almost immediately.
Almost.

She saw the delay.
He knew she would.

The space between them shifted, not in distance, but in structure. What had been observation became engagement. The conversation had crossed a threshold without requiring either of them to acknowledge it directly.

He rested his forearm lightly against the table, allowing the movement to read as ease rather than recalibration.

"Why follow me?" he asked.

"Because someone has to," she said. "And because you don't miss things like this."

The answer came too quickly to be constructed, too clean to be improvised.

"And what do you want?"

"Not here," she said after a brief but deliberate pause. "Not now."

The distinction mattered, though she left it undefined.

From the kitchen, the scent of bread rose again, warmer now, carrying a density that did not belong to the present moment. It reached him without warning, slipping past the layers of control he kept in place and settling somewhere deeper.

For a moment, the café thinned around him.

Virginia, gray sky pressed low enough to feel like weight.

His fingers had gone numb in the cold, though he didn't remember when.

Cold ground stiff beneath polished shoes that did not belong to him yet.

An honor guard moved with mechanical precision—measured, exact, practiced into something that looked like certainty.

The flag folded in their hands became smaller with each motion, geometry replacing fabric, until it was no longer something that covered, but something that was carried.

Calvin was the name, but to James he had only ever been grandpa.

He hadn't known the man had served.

The rifles cracked, sharp and final.

Brass struck frozen ground and rang out—bright, metallic, wrong against the quiet.

His mother didn't cry at first.

She held the folded triangle as though it required both hands to keep from falling apart.

As if weight itself could be inherited.
Passed down without words.

He watched her accept it.
Not the man or the memory, but the weight.

The café returned all at once, sound, heat, motion snapping back into place.

She was watching.

He studied her more directly now, not her face, but the details that framed it. Her hands remained steady, the absence of tremor more telling than its presence would have been. A faint scar traced across one knuckle, pale against the surrounding skin, the kind of mark left by something that had ended too close to be comfortable.

Her cup sat untouched for a fraction longer than expected before she lifted it again.

It wasn't hesitation.
It was timing.

He should have left. That remained the correct assessment: break contact, reset movement, force the next interaction to occur on his terms.

The logic was clear, the path established.

He remained seated.

The decision did not feel like defiance. It felt like continuation.

She noticed.

His thumb pressed once against the edge of the table, grounding.

The tea cooled untouched in front of him, a thin film forming across the surface.

"Should I be flattered?" he asked.

"By what?"

"That you came yourself."

The change in her expression was minimal, but not absent. Something in her eyes shifted—not surprise, but recognition of the line he had chosen to test.

"You think you're worth the trip?"

"Usually."

The exchange carried the shape of something familiar, though neither of them acknowledged it, as if the rhythm of the conversation had been established before they spoke.

This time, the suggestion of a smile came closer to forming, though it still stopped short of completion. It lingered just long enough to be acknowledged, then withdrew.

That made it more effective.

Outside, a tram rounded the turn with a sharp metallic scream, the sound cutting briefly through the room before dissolving back into the ambient noise.

"You're harder to find than you should be," she said.

"You found me."

"I'm sitting across from you."

There was a pause, slight but intentional.

"That isn't the same thing."

He let his gaze shift just enough to catch the reflection behind her again. Nothing resolved into clarity—no repeated figures, no obvious surveillance pattern, only the layered movement of the room and the street beyond.

That absence did not reassure him.

When his attention returned, she was already tracking it.

"You make a habit of approaching strangers?" he asked.

"Only the ones who notice mirrors."

"And the others?"

"They don't survive the conversation."

It wasn't delivered as threat, or even warning, but as a simple statement of function, the kind that did not require emphasis because it did not rely on interpretation.

He held her gaze then—or rather, the space just off-center where her attention resided. Direct eye contact would have simplified the exchange. This required more control.

The room seemed to thin around them, not physically, but perceptually. Noise flattened, losing depth. Movement slowed just enough to become background rather than distraction.

He became aware of his pulse, not elevated, not uncontrolled, but present in a way that signaled a narrowing of focus. The system had shifted into a more precise mode, filtering out what it did not need.

She had his name. She had his reaction. She had his attention.

And she held all three without appearing to exert effort.

He did not like that.

What unsettled him more was the part of him that remained engaged, not in spite of the imbalance, but because of it.

Restraint had always carried a cost. Not because it was difficult, but because it delayed consequences rather than eliminating them. What he denied in one moment had a tendency to return in another, often at a time less convenient, less controlled.

In his world, intimacy was not connection.
It was exposure.
Leverage, a structural weakness waiting to be identified and used.

He understood that.

He remained where he was.

She reached into her coat and placed a few euros beneath the edge of the saucer, the movement clean and unremarkable. When she stood, it was timed to coincide with a couple entering the café, her departure folding into theirs in a way that dissolved distinction.

At the door, she paused.

Not long enough to draw attention.

Long enough for him to feel the weight of it.

Not hesitation but confirmation.

Then she stepped into the rain.

The space she left behind did not close immediately.

He stayed seated.

The decision felt less like a choice and more like the continuation of something already in motion, a sequence he had entered without marking the point of entry.

Or the moment it had been marked for him.

The room felt altered in her absence—not empty, but misaligned, as if something essential to its structure had been removed without warning. Conversations resumed, chairs shifted, the rhythm returned, but it did not settle into the same pattern.

He looked down at the table.

A faint groove in the wood caught his nail as he traced it without thinking.

The damp ring left by her cup had already begun to fade, the edges softening as the moisture sank into the grain of the wood. Then it dissolved completely, leaving no visible trace.

As if she had never been there at all.

The table dried, the room settled, and nothing returned to the way it had been.

He remained seated longer than necessary, long enough for the room to forget the disruption and accept its own version of continuity, the kind that replaced what had been altered with something close enough to pass.

It worked. It always did.
That was the problem.

He had spent years learning how to disappear into systems that corrected for deviation, environments that absorbed irregularity without acknowledging it, structures that preferred consistency over truth. Most people trusted that instinctively. They believed in restoration. In return to baseline.

He didn't.
Not anymore.

The conversation replayed in fragments, not as words but as structure—timing, positioning, the absence of hesitation where it should have existed, the presence of certainty where it shouldn't. Nothing she had said required belief. That wasn't the point.

It hadn't started here.
And now he was inside it.

He exhaled once, controlled, measured, and let the room settle fully around him before finally pushing his chair back and standing, his movement aligning with the rhythm of the café in a way that erased distinction, returning him to the flow he had never fully left.

The breath left him warmer than the air around him.

Outside, the rain had thinned.

The city moved.

Nothing had changed.

It had already started.

CHAPTER 2: THE SHADOW PULLS
Wiesbaden, Germany

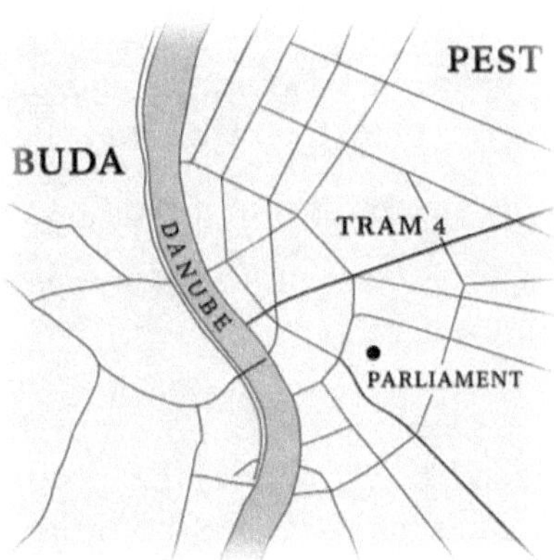

Only the gray held steady.

In that space, patterns did not announce themselves so much as emerge gradually, revealing structure only to those willing to sit inside uncertainty long enough to see it.

He had not meant to draw attention, at least not in any way that could be tracked or formally acknowledged. The kind of attention that mattered rarely moved through official channels. It lived in fragments, carried forward through people rather than systems, assembling itself in pieces that only aligned if you already understood what you were looking at.

The woman in Wiesbaden had belonged to that structure. She had not been visible enough to trigger alarms or random enough to ignore. She had existed in that narrow band where intent concealed itself as coincidence, waiting for someone trained to notice the difference.

He chose not to file the encounter.

The embassy feeds offered their usual density without clarity.

Attaché notes arrived filtered, language shaped to preserve relationships rather than expose substance, while cable traffic moved through layers of review designed to reduce friction rather than reveal it. Most analysts learned to extract what they could from that structure and leave the rest behind.

James let it accumulate.

His fingers rested on the keyboard without typing.

Something in the traffic dragged, not enough to flag but enough to repeat.

Timing tightened where it shouldn't, and language shifted midstream like someone thinking twice after the fact.

It didn't point cleanly anywhere, but it didn't sit still either.

None of it justified movement on its own; together, it leaned in a direction that did not need to be named.

It pulled east.

By the time he closed the terminal, the decision had already formed, not as a single point of intent but as a progression that made alternatives less viable. A train ticket followed without urgency, an alias revisited and adjusted until it fit the space he needed it to occupy, and movement introduced gradually until it felt less like deviation and more like continuation.

Budapest opened differently than Wiesbaden. The city did not conceal its structure as effectively, and the divisions within it remained visible even when unspoken. The Danube cut through it with quiet authority, separating elevation from density in a way that shaped movement more than it directed it. Buda held position, while Pest carried motion forward. James chose the side that allowed him to disappear inside it.

He arrived as Henrik Varga, an identity constructed with deliberate imperfection. The passport edge pressed faintly into his palm as he gripped it.

The documentation aligned where it needed to but not so precisely that it invited scrutiny. A tax record supported the existence. A school certificate reinforced it without overdefining it. The gaps mattered.

At the bank counter, the name resisted him in a way that had nothing to do with writing mechanics. The pen scratched louder than it should have in the quiet. The letters formed correctly, but without weight, as though they belonged to a version of himself that had never fully existed.

His own name remained just beneath the surface, waiting for habit to pull it forward.

He adjusted pressure rather than form, allowing the pen to drag slightly across the page until the signature felt less precise and more aligned with the identity he was occupying. It was not perfect, but it didn't need to be.

For several days, he established movement rather than routine; the distinction mattered. Cafés changed without pattern, routes shifted just enough to prevent repetition, and timing expanded or contracted depending on what the day required. He allowed himself to be visible where it felt natural and absent where it did not, letting the city absorb his presence without forcing it to acknowledge him.

Budapest did not resist observation; it absorbed it, making detection more difficult and mistakes easier to conceal.

The Renault appeared on the first night and remained where it had no reason to be, parked across from his flat without movement or purpose. Condensation gathered along the inside of his window, blurring the view.

He noted it and left it undisturbed, allowing it to remain part of the environment rather than reacting to it directly.

When it returned on the second night, the pattern began to take shape. By the third, the plates had changed while the vehicle had not, and that distinction resolved the ambiguity.

It was not surveillance designed to remain hidden; it was placement designed to be recognized. Which meant it wasn't meant to be avoided.

The knock came at 02:00 on the third night, measured in a way that avoided familiarity while still carrying intention. The sound carried differently at that hour, sharper against the walls.

James was awake before the sequence completed, the Beretta already in hand as he positioned himself outside the direct line of the door.

When he opened it, the man in the corridor did not attempt to close the distance. His posture carried the ease of someone accustomed to control rather than comfort, and his presence registered without needing to be reinforced.

"You're being watched, Rourke," he said, his voice low enough not to carry beyond the space between them. "Not just by us."

He tilted his head. "You already knew that."

The use of his name removed any ambiguity.

The card offered to him was matte black, its edges worn in a way that suggested use rather than intent. The text at its center read simply: *Black Sigil Budapest.*

James examined it briefly before returning it. The material offered nothing useful, but the residue it left behind did. A faint scent lingered on his fingers, something industrial that did not belong to the building and did not dissipate. He rubbed his thumb against his index finger once, testing it. The smell pulled at something already filed.

The memory surfaced without invitation.

Prague came back as rain and motion, the kind of operation that held together until it didn't. The transition from control to collapse had occurred too quickly to adjust for, the first shot arriving before the situation could be redefined. Karel had gone down in a way that suggested inevitability rather than error, and everything that followed had compressed into sequence rather than time.

Orders had shifted without warning, extraction removed before it could be requested, leaving James to run the pattern he had been trained for while knowing it would not be enough to restore what had already been lost.

The report that followed had been clean, structured in a way that preserved the system at the expense of the truth it was meant to document.

The pattern had failed then, or he had.

This felt different.

The hallway returned with the same clarity. The man remained in place, unchanged.

"Budapest isn't safe for you anymore," he said.

James held his gaze, measuring the statement rather than reacting to it.

"Safe wasn't part of the plan."

The man acknowledged that with a slight shift of posture, then stepped back, ending the exchange without pressing further.

The door closed, but the information remained.

By morning, the decision had evolved again, shifting from whether he would stay to how long the current position could be maintained before it lost its usefulness.

Keleti Station carried movement differently than the rest of the city. Direction replaced wandering, and every individual within it moved with purpose that intersected with others only by necessity. It was within that structure that he saw her again, not directly, but through reflection, where her presence resolved before her identity did.

The details aligned quickly once he allowed them to. The posture, the movement, the controlled inefficiency of someone who understood how to appear less deliberate than they were. The lark pin confirmed what the rest had already suggested.

Nothing about her felt new, only closer.

She did not acknowledge him directly. Her attention moved through the environment in the same way it had before, distributed rather than focused, allowing her to observe without revealing the act of observation itself.

When she tilted her head toward the café, the motion carried the shape of a suggestion structured to feel like his decision rather than hers.

He recognized it immediately, not because it was unfamiliar, but because he had used the same approach often enough to understand its intent.

That did not make it easier to resist.

He crossed.

The station air clung to his coat as he moved inside.

The distance between them closed without comment, and once inside, the space shifted again, heat and condensation replacing the cold precision of the platform outside. Voices overlapped without resolving into clarity, creating a background that concealed more than it revealed.

For a moment, nothing moved between them.

What had begun as observation now carried direction.

This was not pursuit, and it did not resemble coincidence closely enough to be mistaken for coincidence.

It had the shape of something constructed.

Something that had been moving before either of them recognized it.

And now, for the first time, it no longer required coincidence.

CHAPTER 3: THE CAFÉ AND THE COMPASS
Keleti Station, Budapest

Veiled in steam and glass, the café pressed itself into a narrow wedge opposite Keleti's ironwork throat, its windows fogged by heat that never fully escaped. People entered carrying the weather with them, coats damp, shoulders tight, each arrival briefly disturbing the rhythm before being absorbed into it. Espresso machines hissed without pause, a constant undercurrent beneath the shifting murmur of voices and the soft percussion of porcelain.

Three days after Wiesbaden, Budapest had settled into a rhythm he trusted just enough to disrupt.

Nothing about the delay had broken the pattern; if anything, it had given it time to settle.

She had chosen the smallest table near the window, a position that allowed her to observe without appearing to do so. From there, the glass reflected enough of the room to make direct attention unnecessary, while the street beyond remained just visible enough to track movement without committing to it.

He did not enter immediately.

The station carried movement in layers—arrivals folding into departures until intent became difficult to read.

He stood just outside the café's edge, close enough to feel the heat leaking from the glass and far enough to remain uncommitted. Condensation dampened the front of his jacket where the heat met the cold.

It gave her to him in fragments at first—not her face or anything that could be fixed or named, but the way she held stillness differently than the rest of the room, less reactive and less dependent on the movement around it.

People adjusted to space; she defined it.

That hadn't changed. What had changed was everything around it.

He let the moment extend longer than necessary, testing whether the pattern would shift without his involvement and whether the structure required his recognition to complete itself.

It didn't, and that mattered more than anything he could have confirmed by moving.

Because it meant the structure did not depend on him noticing it—only on him entering it.

So he did.

He ordered nothing at first, letting the moment stretch until it settled into something that looked unplanned. Then he crossed the room and set his phone on the table, screen down as though it had always belonged there.

"Pocket," she said quietly. "Or my sleeve."

He slid it toward her without comment. She withdrew a slim Faraday sleeve, folded the device into it with practiced ease, and placed a small white noise emitter beside the sugar dish. The faint hiss that followed sat just at the edge of perception, soft enough to disappear into the room while still shaping the space.

"We have two minutes," she said, her voice measured. "After that, we're strangers."

"Strangers," he repeated, letting the word settle before adding, "your preference?"

"Your best cover."

They allowed the room to move around them without interruption, giving the moment time to establish itself. Steam drifted in slow curls from the espresso machine. Cups met saucers with muted precision.

Rain tapped lightly against the glass, each drop dissolving into the next before it could take shape.

She leaned forward slightly, closing the distance by a fraction. The shift brought warmth with it, the sensation registering before the source fully resolved.

James adjusted in response, leaning back just enough to reestablish the boundary without making the movement visible as a correction.

"You didn't pick Budapest," she said.

Her voice lowered.

"I picked you."

He believed her.

It landed as though it had already been decided.

He studied her without appearing to do so, allowing the reflection to carry more information than direct observation.

"I followed the patterns," he said.

"You traced what someone built for you," she replied, her tone even and without accusation. "Structured noise. Just enough to feel organic."

He let that sit, measuring its shape.

"It feels less like a compass and more like a leash," he said. "Was that your design?"

"If it had been mine, you wouldn't be here," she said, a brief thread of humor surfacing and disappearing before it could take hold. "You would already be back in Wiesbaden explaining yourself to someone who prefers clean reports to complicated truths."

She adjusted her posture slightly, just enough to maintain her sightlines without drawing attention to them.

"I'm Army," she continued. "Special Activities Detachment. Not Langley. We saw the gap you left. Good operators tend to leave good shadows."

"Impossible," he said, though the word carried more habit than conviction.

"Pattern of life isn't evidence," she said. "It's prediction."

He let his gaze drift toward the window, catching the reflection of movement behind him without focusing on it.

"Prediction doesn't stop people from drowning," he said.

"No," she replied. "But it tells you where the water is."

She shifted the conversation without announcing it.

"You build your covers carefully," she said, her tone steady. "Second-floor apartments near transit. Furniture that looks lived in but can be abandoned without consequence. Identities that age naturally without attracting attention. No pets, no attachments, no patterns that invite familiarity."

Her eyes remained on the glass, tracking movement that did not concern him directly.

"They don't need your passport," she added. "They need your habits."

The accuracy unsettled him more than speculation.

His jaw tightened once, then released.

A cup shattered somewhere behind them, porcelain breaking sharp and clean against tile. The sound cut through the softened room with enough force to reset attention before being absorbed again, conversations faltering and then resuming as each voice recalibrated without acknowledging the disruption.

James didn't turn, and neither did she.

That told him more than the break.

Instinct pulled toward interruption; training suppressed it, redirecting attention inward rather than outward.

She stirred her coffee once, slow and controlled, the motion measured against the noise that had already begun to dissolve.

"They're closer than they should be," she said.

"Which ones?" he asked.

She let the question sit, not out of hesitation, but selection— choosing what to give him, and what to hold back.

"That depends on what you decide to do next."

He let that rest where it was.

"And Black Sigil?" he asked.

"A signature, not an organization," she said. "It shows up when people stop using Langley."

"Russian?"

"Closer to what's left after that," she said. "Burned assets don't disappear. They change shape. This one will only meet through Army channels. Your presence suggests someone wanted you placed where that mattered."

"And you?" he asked. "Where do you fit in that?"

She tilted her chin slightly toward the window, not enough to draw attention, just enough to mark the direction.

"Across the street," she said. "Umbrella at the corner. You're not the only one being read."

In the glass, the figure held position a moment longer than necessary.

He reached for the coffee that had appeared without him noticing the moment it had been set down and took a measured sip, letting the bitterness ground the moment.

"You're guiding me toward the meet," he said.

"I'm keeping you from walking into something you won't walk out of," she replied. "And toward the answer you've already decided to look for."

"You're certain of that."

"Certain enough."

A faint shift in her expression suggested something less absolute beneath it, though it passed too quickly to define.

"CIA won't like this," he said.

"They don't like much that isn't theirs," she replied, a brief smile forming and fading. "They believe control belongs to them. We've learned otherwise."

"We," he repeated.

"People who remember what loyalty looks like when it costs something."

In the reflection, the umbrella shifted position without crossing the street.

The noise from the emitter softened the room further, blending conversations into a single indistinct layer. A server passed behind them carrying plates, the movement reflected in the glass before it registered anywhere else. Outside, a tram rounded the curve, metal screaming briefly against metal before the sound dissolved.

"Why me?" he asked.

She considered that for a moment, not as a question of value, but of function.

"Because you didn't walk away," she said. "And because when something doesn't make sense, you move toward it instead of away."

He let that settle without response.

"Time and place," he said.

She slid a transit card across the table with a movement that read as incidental. Her other hand stirred her coffee, the spoon touching porcelain once before coming to rest.

"Liberty Bridge," she said. "Seven-oh-two.

"You miss the first tram. Take the second. Midpoint, he passes you.
Key ring. You drop yours. He returns the wrong one. You correct him.
He'll apologize in Hungarian he practiced the night before."

James watched the reflection rather than the street, allowing the details to come through indirectly.

"Your cover?"

"You're late," she said. "You have somewhere to be and no time to explain why you're not there. You're holding coffee you don't want and wearing a stain you didn't notice."

She adjusted her chair slightly, clearing her line of sight.

"And you have a photograph on your phone of something you didn't understand well enough to remember," she added. "You won't bring it with you."

He glanced toward the Faraday sleeve.

"You're keeping the phone."

"For now."

She produced another device, older, worn, its surface marked by use rather than neglect. When he reached for it, their fingers brushed briefly, the contact precise enough to feel intentional without being necessary.

The contact was gone before it could be acknowledged.

"Three numbers," she said. "Use them only if you have no other option."

"Whose?"

"Mine," she said. "The umbrella. And someone who doesn't fix what he claims to."

He let that sit.

"And the Renault?"

"Different plates tonight," she said. "Same driver. We'll see if he's still interested in the morning."

There was a slight pause.

"He isn't alone."

He noted the shift beneath the words—not fear, but calculation.

"You're sure this isn't Langley trying to pull me back in," he said.

"If it were, you wouldn't be sitting here," she said. "And I wouldn't be part of it."

She leaned closer then, the distance narrowing just enough to carry something more than words.

"Whoever built this expects you to behave predictably," she said. "That's where they think they have control."

He held her gaze—this time directly, without using the reflection to soften it.

"And after the bridge?"

"You move west and disappear," she said. "There's a key where you'll find it. It opens something that matters."

He waited.

She did not elaborate.

"You like puzzles," she said. "Keep that."

The time had passed without needing to be checked.

She retrieved the phone, disabled the emitter, and stood with a motion that folded cleanly into the movement of the room.

"On the bridge," she said quietly, testing his name again, "don't improvise."

"Discipline has worked so far," he said.

"Then let it," she replied.

Before the moment could settle, she leaned in and pressed a light kiss to his cheek, brief enough to pass as familiarity and deliberate enough to serve its purpose.

Her breath was warmer than the room.

"For cover," she said softly.

She moved before the room could define them, her reflection slipping from the glass as she merged with the flow of the station.

James remained where he was, allowing the space she left to settle around him without rushing to fill it. The moment shifted gradually, tension cooling into something more controlled.

He picked up the phone.

The weight of it felt unchanged, but his grip wasn't.

He did not follow her.

The room reassembled around him in pieces, sound returning first—voices layered without meaning, the hiss of steam, the soft impact of ceramic against wood—each element settling back into place as though nothing had shifted.

He felt it in the spacing between movements, in the way attention redistributed without settling, in the subtle misalignment that remained even after the surface corrected itself.

He replayed the exchange, not in words but in sequence—timing, placement, the absence of hesitation where it should have existed, and the presence of certainty where it shouldn't.

Recognition didn't ask for belief. It waited for response.

That was different.

His hand remained on the phone, though he had not yet decided whether to use it, the weight of it resting somewhere between option and obligation.

The bridge. The timing. The correction.

It all fit together with a precision that felt less like discovery and more like confirmation.

That was the problem.

Patterns that resolved too cleanly were rarely natural. They were either designed that way or incomplete in ways that had not yet revealed themselves.

He stood without urgency, allowing the motion to align with the flow of the café before stepping back into the station, where direction replaced stillness and movement erased distinction.

The umbrella was gone. That didn't settle anything. Progression meant design.

CHAPTER 4: THE ARCHIVE BELOW
The Liberty Bridge — Budapest, Hungary | 0702

Even the Liberty Bridge groaned beneath the morning commute, steel humming as the tram screamed its approach.

Commuters jostled shoulder to shoulder, umbrellas dripping, coffee steaming in paper cups. James moved with them, a shadow in their rhythm, eyes scanning reflections in every pane of glass.

As he reached the midpoint of the bridge, a man in a wool coat brushed past him.

A key ring slipped, deliberate and too smooth to be accident.

Too clean.

Not wrong, just absent the hesitation real exchanges carried, the small inefficiencies that came from people rather than design.

He filed that away as structure, not error.

James dropped his own, metal ringing against steel, swallowed by the tram's scream.

Hands crossed, two sets of keys, one false, one real, slipping under a muttered apology in Hungarian, clumsy enough to be rehearsed.

James answered in the same tongue, voice flat, correcting a phrase only a native would notice. The man smiled once, a tight grimace of acknowledgment, and disappeared into the press of bodies.

The tram screeched, brakes spitting sparks. By the time the doors opened, the man was gone. The wrong key sat in his palm, edges sharp enough to draw blood if he closed his fist. For a second, he almost did. His pulse drummed in time with the tram's scream.

The weight felt wrong in his hand, and that was enough.

He slipped it into his pocket.

His fingers lingered a fraction longer than necessary.

For a moment, the movement around him continued without interruption, the rhythm of the bridge absorbing the exchange.

He felt it in the spacing between bodies, in the slight redistribution of movement that followed the exchange, subtle enough to pass unnoticed and impossible to ignore once seen.

No one turned, no one reacted.

That was the tell.

Real exchanges left residue, attention that lingered a fraction too long, movement that corrected itself too quickly, the small inefficiencies that came from people trying not to be seen.

There was none of that.

It resolved perfectly, which meant it hadn't been left to resolve on its own.

He adjusted his pace without changing it, letting the current carry him forward while his attention widened, not searching for a specific threat but for the absence of one.

Behind him, the umbrella man leaned against the railing, watching the Danube churn below. Across the bridge, the woman with the lark pin broke stride just long enough to signal with her wrist. A twitch. Barely there. Enough to remind him he was still on her compass.

The bridge came and went, but the signal didn't fade.

At dawn, the next piece was waiting, folded into a locker with a transit card and the scent of solvent.

A paper map, heavy stock with edges yellowed by age.

Routes cut through Ferencváros like arteries, avoiding tourists and traffic. Red ink veined the IX District.

At the bottom margin, faint as a watermark:
THE ASH ARCHIVE

He followed it with precision: past shuttered kiosks, beneath streetlamps that buzzed like dying wasps, through alleys washed in rain and iron. The air shifted the deeper he moved, mildew, oil, the smell of places cities forgot to own. The smell caught at the back of his throat, forcing a shallow breath.

Every turn narrowed the world behind him. Ferencváros peeled itself open like scar tissue. He passed no cameras. Or too many. His boots crunched grit, every sound too loud. The city didn't blink. It simply watched.

Or gave the impression that it did.

The deeper he moved, the more the environment stopped behaving like something lived in and started behaving like something maintained—spaces preserved rather than used, pathways that existed not for movement but for access, each turn narrowing not just the route behind him, but the possibility of deviation.

He marked the exits without slowing, noting where they failed rather than where they worked, where line of sight broke cleanly and where it lingered too long, the architecture offering just enough concealment to feel intentional.

Nothing about it felt abandoned, but persistent.

As though whatever had been built here had never fully been allowed to disappear.

Then, a wall—fresh paint. The solvent still clung to the air, biting the back of his throat, fresh paint over old truths. Embedded at its center was a door with no knob, no buzzer. Just a single mark scorched into the wood—the sigil.

Not drawn, branded. Five interlocking triangles, primitive and asymmetrical, like geometry scrawled from memory rather than design.

Beneath it, etched into the grain:
FORGOTTEN IS NOT GONE

He hovered his glove an inch from the brand. The wood still held a faint, sweet-metal warmth, like heat left behind by skin.

The Ash Archive. He wasn't standing at a metaphor. He was standing at the door.

James knocked once. Silence.

Then: a buzz. A mechanical click. The door cracked inward.

Inside, silence—thick and absolute.

Dust clung to every surface. Caged bulbs lined the ceiling like exposed nerves. The air tasted of concrete rot and ozone.

He moved downward, past rusted lockers, shuttered rooms. *This was the Archive itself—not just a name, but a place, buried under Budapest's skin.* The ghosts of Cold War infrastructure, buried and still humming.

Each step echoed differently, the sound tightening as the space narrowed.

At the final landing, another door opened before he touched it.

A room of shelves, sagging under reels, cracked leather binders, paper so old the edges feathered when he passed. At the center was Irina Sokolik.

Mid-back blonde hair, bright blue eyes sharp as glacier melt, fingers stained with ink, a ledger open before her—her posture balanced somewhere between ballet and betrayal.

She didn't look up immediately. As if she had already known he would be there, and timing—not arrival—was what mattered.

When she did, her gaze cut through him with surgical precision.

"Rourke," she said. Not a question.

She gestured to the chair opposite her. "Sit. You have questions."

The room seemed to settle around the command, not in response to her voice, but in alignment with it.

He sat because the alternative didn't present itself as viable. The chair felt colder than the room.

There was nothing overt in her posture—no visible authority, no display of control—but the absence of it was more defining than its presence would have been.

She didn't need to establish position. She occupied it.

"Who funds this?" he asked, scanning the room—biometric nodes wired into Soviet-era conduits, machines patched from three decades of scavenged wars.

Her pen scratched. "*Oblivion* survives in budgets no one reviews," she said. "Small enough to ignore. Persistent enough to matter."

"We don't answer to a building," she said. "We answer to entropy. Systems fail. People outlast."

"Cold War," Irina said. "Fail-safe. That's what they called it."

She turned a page.

"None of that survived the paperwork."

James felt the words press harder than they should have. He had spent years proving survival counted for more than faith.

His anomaly was already in the system. Someone had marked him as usable long before Irina ever saw his name.

She leaned back in her chair, the ledger closing with a thud.

"Now it stirs again, rearmed against a threat rising from the East. Russia has sharpened it through decades of secret leaps the CIA still can't match."

James's voice was low. "So, this runs on… forgetting?"

Her expression shifted—half amusement, half regret.

"It runs because it was forgotten—and forgetting became its function."

Forgotten as design. He knew the feeling. Missions scrubbed from record, names carved off walls, grief filed under "error" so the system could keep moving. He'd been carrying silence the same way Oblivion carried its archives—unacknowledged, but never gone.

He pressed. "NATO? Langley? GCHQ? Someone has to be watching."

"No one was read in. After the Wall, deniability beat memory. Records were sealed. Keys were lost."

James leaned forward. "And no one tried to bring it back online?"

"Oh, they tried. The archives were shredded. The assets turned to shadows. Legal couldn't justify it. Diplomats couldn't explain it."

She let the silence breathe.

"Oblivion was a ghost. Too many fingerprints. No country left to answer for them."

Then, softer: "And that's why it still works."

***

James studied the device as she set it on the table between them.

Compact, matte, no logos—just a narrow display that pulsed with light. Its surface was smooth, almost weightless in his hand.

"Go on," Irina said.

He slid it closer, thumb brushing the ridge of the clasp. The screen came alive—telemetry crowding in: heat signatures, anomaly clusters, threat projections. Quicker than it had any right to be.

"This can't be real-time," he muttered.

"It isn't," she said. "It's faster."

"It doesn't show you what's happening," she said. "It shows you what's about to."

He didn't like that.

His head tilted. "How?"

"Legacy mesh hardware. Black-budget AI. A predictive engine stitched from a NATO project they buried in '99. We call it *PhantomNet*."

On the display, a building flared red—threat flagged before he'd even considered walking past it.

"Surveillance Detection Routes used to mean instinct," she continued. "Loops, reversals, subway transfers—see if anyone popped up twice. But now?" Her pen clicked. "The SDR runs you. Every step streams with telemetry: biometrics, motion, environmental cues. *PhantomNet* cross-references against traffic baselines and surveillance patterns."

James stared at the projection. It highlighted a vector of movement—too consistent with an ambush to ignore.

"And if it's wrong?" he asked.

Irina didn't blink. "Then you live on instinct like the rest of us. *PhantomNet* buys you seconds, not certainty."

The next door opened on cue.

A man sat behind a desk welded from surplus steel. No nameplate. No flag. Just smoke curling in the dim and the stink of regimes that outlived themselves.

"You're late," the man rasped.

"I wasn't expected," James answered.

"Everyone here is expected. Even if they don't know it yet."

A folder slid across the desk. Black. Thick. One word burned into the cover:
OBLIVION.

James opened it.

A face stared back.

The paper edge dug slightly into his thumb.

His pulse betrayed him before thought did, a half-skip, sharp enough that his grip tightened on the folder.

The photograph was black and white, all shadow and grain, but something in her eyes tugged at him. Turned slightly away, they seemed to know him already—like a prophecy pretending to be a photograph.

Something in his chest pulled, as if memory was trying to write itself before it existed.

It wasn't recognition, not exactly.

It felt like something aligning—late, but not unexpected.

The sensation didn't resolve into understanding.
It didn't need to.

It remained in the space between recognition and conclusion, where meaning existed without explanation, where something could feel known without ever having been learned.

The file named her **Kyra Marek.**

Beneath it, scrawled in Cyrillic on a half-erased insert, was another name: **Екатерина. Катя.** He read it twice, the longer and the shorter, and caught himself mouthing the second—*Yekaterina*—like a word he already should have known. Someone had crossed it out and written Kyra in a different hand, likely Langley's. The correction looked clinical, but to James it read as theft.

The file reduced her to aliases and betrayals, but her eyes carried something else—echoes beyond the shadows, defying every erasure.

The language of dossiers had always unsettled him—turning people into bullet points, lives into leverage. But here, the words cut sharper.

[FIELD FILE — LEVEL 4 / OBLIVION ACCESS]

Subject: Marek, Kyra (alias: Yekaterina/Katya)

Status: Monitored operative / high-risk variance

Operational Profile:
Trained under Directorate S (SVR).

Specialization: infiltration, direct action, psychological disruption. Documented survival in multiple operations where casualty reports listed her as deceased.

Behavioral Notes:
- Selective withholding observed during debriefs.
- Attachment anomalies: subject prioritizes preservation of select individuals over mission success.

Command Assessment:
- Effective only under direct oversight.
- Reliability compromised by unverified survivals and unexplained field variance.

Margin annotation, hand-written, unverified:
"She doesn't follow orders. She survives them."

James closed the folder half an inch, enough to break the photograph's stare.

They wanted him here not because he was trusted—Oblivion didn't believe in trust—but because she wasn't.

He would be leash first, leader second.

And before he ever met her, Kyra Marek had already been turned into his problem.

Later, he returned to Irina.

She didn't speak. She rose, heels echoing across the concrete as she led him deeper into the vault. No orders, no gestures—only expectation.

He followed.

The corridor dipped lower, colder. Dust lay thick as ash. This level wasn't on any blueprint.

She stopped before a steel ledger bolted into the wall, sliding the cover back. Pages whispered against themselves—names, project codes, dates slashed through with ink. Half Cyrillic, half English, all half-erased.

James ran a gloved finger along the edge.

"You think black ops means hidden money?" she asked quietly. "You think 'off-books' means shadow budgets?"

She turned one page, her voice sharp as the paper's cut.

"Oblivion isn't budget at all. It's darker."

Her gaze pinned him.

"It exists because no one wanted to be the one *to* approve it."

Her fingers stilled on the page. She angled the ledger toward him, tapping the margin.

"Read. This is as close as anyone gets to the truth."

[TECHNICAL EXCERPT — LEVEL 7 OBLIVION ACCESS ONLY]

PhantomNet: NATO-sourced predictive mesh. Legacy AI envelope. Restricted to short-range probability forecasting. Non-sentient. Classified as tactical support system.

OBELISK: Russian recursion construct. Autonomous signal lattice. Reported incidents of behavioral bleed in compromised assets, though field veracity remains questionable. Core architecture unverified. Intelligence gaps acknowledged but assessed as non-critical to U.S. operational posture.

He didn't believe that.
He didn't think they did either.

[Margin note, overwritten twice:]
"Assessment confidence: degraded."

[Second annotation:]
"Behavior does not remain contained."

Directive: *PhantomNet* remains a tool. *OBELISK* is an unstable imitation. Operational success assumes this distinction holds.

The language in the file carried the weight of certainty but not its substance.

He had seen it before.

Assessments written to close gaps instead of expose them.

Threats minimized not because they were small, but because they were difficult to define.

It was easier to label something unstable than to admit it didn't behave within known parameters.

Easier to call it an imitation than to consider it might be something else entirely.

He didn't know what OBELISK was, but he knew what it wasn't.

And the distance between those two things mattered more than anything written in the file.

He closed the ledger, the echo of steel against concrete carrying further than it should.

The confidence in the language felt misplaced, as if certainty had been written in to compensate for what they couldn't explain.

"They write like they understand it," he said. "But they don't."

Irina's gaze didn't waver.

"Exactly. And that's why we exist."

She left him in the corridor—off-map, file in hand, countryless program humming behind the walls.

He remained where he was for a moment longer, the corridor holding its silence without pressing it, the weight of the place settling into something that didn't demand acknowledgment but refused to be ignored.

Nothing about what he had seen required belief. That wasn't the function. It required positioning.

He adjusted his grip on the file, feeling the edges press back just enough to confirm it existed—that the weight in his hands was real, even if everything surrounding it felt constructed.

He had spent years moving through systems that required permission.

This wasn't one. That was the difference.

CHAPTER 5: BECOMING NO ONE
Oblivion Archive - Budapest

"You do not become invisible by hiding. You become invisible by forgetting who you were—until even the mirror stops looking back."
— FIELD NOTES, UNATTRIBUTED (OBLIVION ARCHIVE)

Over the following six weeks, the process unspooled in layers, quiet, methodical, and brutal.

The city shifted without asking him to notice.

Henrik Varga faded, Rourke blurred, Tomas Gál took form.

The first time someone said it, he did not answer.

"Tomas."

A pause. A second voice, closer now.

"Tomas."

He turned on the third, not because he chose to, but because something in him had already decided it was his name.

The name landed clean.

The mirror fogged with his breath, but the reflection staring back was not Henrik anymore. The cheap haircut, the paper-thin scars, the absence of glasses.

Moisture gathered along his upper lip, cool against his skin. He leaned closer, searching for James in the eyes, and found nothing but Tomas Gál waiting to be believed.

For a heartbeat, the glass betrayed him—not Tomas, not Henrik, but the man who'd knelt by Jackson's body bag, who'd watched Davis clutch his throat and fall silent mid-sentence, blood bright against his hands.

He remembered Márton once saying ghosts recognize each other.

He didn't correct the thought.

The man who shaped him called himself Márton.

Cold War residue in human form, a former ÁVH officer, Hungary's secret police before '89.

His name existed in whispers, not files. Some said he broke a KGB handler in three hours.

He watched James like a ledger waiting to be balanced.

He didn't smile or shout. He smoked—

not for the nicotine; he never finished them. Each burned to the paper, stubbed into a matchbook from a place that no longer existed. Hotels, bars, and theaters erased by history. Relics of the dead, stacked in rows that never changed.

And his orders came the same way: clipped Hungarian, clean enough to cut fatigue like ice water.

"Software breeds softness," Márton muttered once, crushing a cigarette under his heel. "Soft gets you dead."

James reached for his phone once, reflex, nothing more.

Márton's hand closed over it before the screen lit.

A small shake of the head. Not anger. Correction.

Márton dropped it into a sink already filled with water and solvent. The screen flickered once, then died without ceremony.

"Now," Márton said, stepping back, "you remember."

***

Days broke before dawn—conditioning, code drills, urban evasion.

Meals vanished. Doors never stayed the same.

Márton's message never changed:
Routine is death. Survival is living wrong.

Budapest became their classroom—its tram stations, open-air markets, and crumbling tenements repurposed into pressure chambers.

Steam swallowed him in the baths on Király Street, bodies drifting in and out of sight like ghosts with nowhere to be. Condensation ran down his neck, collecting at his collar. He tracked a man by the rhythm of his shoulders in the water, lost him when a group of pensioners closed the gap, found him again by the scrape of tile and the soft cough near the exit.

When the man doubled back, James didn't follow. He let the reflection in the glass take over, watched the movement ripple behind him, and stepped out two doors early.

He stopped at a corner stand and bought coffee he didn't want. It tasted burnt. He drank it anyway.

In a half-empty supermarket off Nagykörút, fluorescent lights humming overhead, he let a tail settle in—close enough to feel, not close enough to touch. A turn down the wrong aisle, a pause too long at the endcap, then a sudden break through a stockroom door left ajar, out into an alley that smelled like sour milk and rust. He waited there, counting breaths, until the footsteps passed.

The next time, they did not pass.

He felt it too late—the weight staying with him through the turn, the silence that wasn't absence but patience. When he cut for the alley, the man followed.

His breath shortened, controlled but tight in his chest.

James ran.

Not fast—fast drew eyes—just enough to break rhythm, to force the other man to choose between distance and exposure.

He chose wrong.

A hand brushed the back of James's coat as he slipped through a service door and slammed it shut behind him. The impact rang up his arm, loud enough to feel like a mistake.

Dead drops came folded into junk mail, tucked between coupons and expired notices. Ink patterns, weight, the way the paper resisted when bent—he read them by feel before he ever opened them.

A camera watched the corner near Blaha Lujza tér—fixed, predictable. He crossed it once, twice, then came back with gum pressed flat between his fingers. He smeared the lens. Later, he stood beneath another, flicked a flashlight upward at just the right angle, and walked through the bloom of his own glare.

Footsteps became language—too fast, and you were prey; too slow, and you were bait. He matched cadence, broke it, let it echo off stone and return as someone else's presence.

Hungarian filled his mouth, bitter and necessary. He clipped the vowels, flattened the rhythm, let the consonants drag just enough to sound like they carried weight.

Later, in a crowded tram, someone behind him said, "James."

The name moved through the air like it belonged to someone else.

He did not turn.

His fingers flexed once at his side, then stilled.

A hand tapped his shoulder—hesitant, uncertain. "Sorry," the man muttered, already withdrawing. "Thought you were—"

He didn't finish it.

James stayed facing forward, pulse steady, as the doors opened and closed again.

Failure wasn't shouted at, it was felt.

A missed meal, a cot relocated.

A note folded with surgical precision, left on his pillow:
Would you have survived this in Moscow?

His belt notched tighter each week, eyes rimmed red, fingers split at the seams, palms hardened into stone.

The body gave first. The mind kept count.

Márton broke the days further with combat drills—no stances, no honor, just survival.

On tile floors that never fully dried, men twice his size came at him without warning. One grabbed high—James drove his thumb into the eye socket and felt the man recoil before the thought had finished forming. His footing slipped once, barely, then corrected. Another lunged low, James stepped off-line, brought an elbow down across the back of the neck, and didn't stop until the body stopped moving. There was no reset, no instruction, only outcome.

"Again," Márton said as someone dragged the man away.

Cash changed hands. Vodka bottles clinked. The next one stepped forward.

"Wars aren't won by clean technique," Márton said once, lighting a cigarette with hands that didn't shake. "They're survived by the man still standing when the other one can't breathe."

James stopped thinking about winning.

But even ghosts cast echoes.

Alone in the dark, he caught himself forming the wrong name, James, not Tomas. It felt like something that would get him killed.

Once, in the fog of a cheap mirror, his hand moved before his mind did.

Rourke.

The letters stared back at him, pale against the glass.

He didn't wipe them away. He just stood there, breathing, until the fog took them back.

The next morning, the mirror was gone. In its place: a sheet of cold steel.

That was worse.

Márton didn't mention it. He never had to.

Names were as dangerous as habits.

On the seventh night without sleep, Jackson's voice surfaced— half a joke, half a sermon. Maybe memory. Maybe madness.

"Survive wrong, Rourke. God doesn't care about the rest."

James didn't believe in scripture, but he believed in Jackson, and Jackson was dead.

He lay there, eyes open, feeling the city breathe through the walls, trying to remember if the man still answering to that name had actually survived—

—or if what remained just hadn't stopped moving yet.

He woke to the smell of solvent and the steady click of metal. Someone had placed a wool blanket over his legs; his jaw felt dull and hollow. Light formed on a ring of instruments laid out on a milk crate: pliers, a gag wrapped in cloth, a small vial of something clear. Márton moved with the surety of a man who'd done this a thousand times and never flinched.

Irina Sokolik stood at his shoulder, her hands neat and efficient as she arranged the tray, the solvent sting following wherever she wiped. She pressed gauze under his chin, fingers steady, eyes flat as glass.

"You talk when they teach you to," Márton said, voice low and unhurried. "You don't talk when they take what proves you."

Irina tilted his head at Márton's nod, her grip precise, almost gentle. The gag tasted of cloth and iron. She held him there as Márton leaned in.

There was a quick sting—Irina's syringe in his gum—and then pressure, the intimate, animal pressure of pliers finding purchase. He felt leverage, the give and groan of something old being coaxed loose.

Pain lanced and then became a series of thinned-out notes: shock, pressure, a muffled, private roar that lived behind his ears. He braced with his hands until the nails dug crescents of white into his palms.

His jaw tightened against the pressure, then released.

When it came free, it didn't fall like a shard.

It came out whole, warm, textured at the root. Irina caught it in gauze, her hiss sharp when the blood welled too fast. James tasted metal, a thick bright tang that made the room tilt for a breath.

Márton watched without pity. He wiped his fingers on his trousers and produced a thimble-sized steel capsule from a leather roll, the kind of thing men used to carry teeth or paper slips for proof. He sealed the molar inside as if locking a name into a safe and set the capsule beside the razor on the crate.

"Proof," he said. "Paper can lie. Flesh does not."

James swallowed; his tongue found the empty space where the molar had been and came away slightly wet and raw. The pain would keep him honest. The missing tooth would be a ledger entry no audit could erase.

He ran his tongue along the gap again, slower this time.

Whatever he had been on paper had just lost a piece it couldn't account for.

Márton tapped the capsule with a thumbnail, closed the roll, and slid it into his jacket as if consigning a relic to history. Irina replaced the gauze with practiced hands, pressing until the bleed slowed. Neither spoke to him.

Then Márton stood, and the room resumed the business of making men unrecognizable.

The third week didn't start with a lesson; it started with a hood, zip ties, and the smell of oil and cigarettes, like being dragged into someone else's ending.

They dragged him from the trunk into light. The air hit his face sharp and cold.

A voice asked something in Russian. He caught the gist, answered clumsily, his six months of immersion training barely enough for ordering a meal or catching a train. They seized on it anyway, flipped the room into Russian as if his accent had signed a contract. He understood only scraps, drowning in the cadence, every word designed to remind him of what he didn't know.

A mock embassy room. White walls that weren't white but bone. Steel chairs arranged like witnesses. The air too cold, always too cold, like the thermostat itself was interrogating.

They dismantled him—not Tomas Gál, not James Rourke, but something in between, stripped in layers.

Not to break him.
To see what remained.

Alias. Backstory. Psychological profile.

"Which uncle died in Pécs?"
"What was Eszter's favorite flower?"
"Why does the 2014 utility bill list a pet you never mention?"

Contradictions, not fists. Silence that pressed harder than shouting.

He let the easy ones land wrong.

Dates slipped by a day. Names flattened just enough to feel like memory, not rehearsal.

When they circled back, he corrected himself once—small, human, irritated. Not clean. Never clean.

They weren't looking for truth, they were looking for consistency.

So he gave them something that could survive being pressed.

One answer came too fast.

They caught it.

A pause—small, but wrong.

He felt the room tighten around it.

He let his next response stumble, dragged it back half a step, forced the shape of hesitation into it.

Not correction, human.

The pressure eased.

Not gone.
But redirected.

When his eyes closed, the room dissolved sideways, walls thinning into memory.

Kandahar.

Interrogation drills with Jackson and Davis. Nerves high, laughter sharp, staged pain rehearsed like theater. Jackson with his preacher's drawl, every crack of knuckle sounding like scripture. Davis, built like a linebacker, humming blues that bent the air until it almost felt safe. Almost.

Then later—Jackson, body broken in orange lamplight, blood spreading through glass and brass.

No drawl. No scripture. Only silence, thick and permanent.

That didn't belong here. It came anyway.

And with it—a voice.

Not Márton's, not memory—a voice unbidden.

Steady, low, unyielding. The rhythm of something that had always been there, waiting in the static.

The cold came rushing back then—steel chair under him, white walls bone-pale. The interrogators had left. The silence was the only witness. He couldn't tell if that silence was mercy or sentence, whether he had been promoted or marked for erasure.

When they released him, Márton didn't debrief. He simply handed James a blank matchbook. Not one of the old ghosts this time, but clean, unused, waiting to be written into.

Inside: a date, a time, a location.

"Don't be followed," Márton said. "Don't be late."

The route was textbook—bakery pass, tram decoy, three-count in reflection glass, wide exit through a pharmacy crosswalk. James ran it clean. Hood up, stride broken by natural pauses, coat cut to blur his gait.

A shadow tailed him—silent, precise.

The back of his neck tightened, registering before thought.

Whoever Oblivion had assigned to test him knew the craft— never crowding, never doubling, always a step behind without being caught in the glass.

The kind of watcher trained to remind him there was always someone better, closer.

His pulse thudded anyway. Every corner carried memory. Zip ties biting. A hood yanked down without warning. The drills had taught him to expect the grab at any moment, to assume the chair and the cold walls were always waiting. He told himself this was exercise, proofing, tradecraft—but the fear was older than the test.

James cut tighter turns, shook tails through tram exchanges and supermarket swaps, exited under a different hat. Borrowed tokens kept the routine clean.

The city slipped away, layer by layer.

And somewhere in that shedding, beneath sweat, silence, and the ghost-print of a name once spoken, James Rourke died. What stepped off the tram was no one.

At the bottom of the metro stairs, a woman fumbled her bag and papers spilled across the tile.

He stepped around them. His stride didn't break.

He didn't slow, didn't look back.
He didn't recognize the man who would have stopped.

Dusk settled over the Pest side—the flat, crowded half of Budapest, where trams stitched the riverfront to the neon-lit boulevards. Across the river, the hills of Buda darkened into silhouette. Cables hummed as Tram 4 opened its doors, and a courier in a cheap parka stepped aboard, clutching a leather satchel too clean for the rest of his clothes. Six rows back, his handler lowered a newspaper just enough to watch him through the folds.

James—Tomas now—slid in with the crowd, a folded paper under his arm. He didn't look at the courier. Didn't have to. A faint vibration traced his wrist—two short pulses, one long. Timing.

A second later, heat bloomed against his skin, subtle but precise.

Not instruction—confirmation.

Márton trailed at platform distance, smoking, watching.

At Oktogon, the courier shifted his weight. Panic signal. His handler rustled the paper once—a tell, nervous and sloppy. James angled his body with the tram's sway, timing his exit not with the doors but with the crowd's crush.

On the platform, he let himself be jostled, bumped the courier deliberately, and muttered a curse in Hungarian.

The satchel strap caught.

Their grips crossed for half a heartbeat—pressure, release.

When they separated, James had the satchel. The courier had nothing.

No one looked twice.

By the time the courier realized, James had already vanished into the metro's throat, the satchel under his coat replaced with one lifted from a garbage bin—a decoy planted hours earlier. A clean handoff, a counterfeit weight.

He boarded the next tram with an empty satchel, the right one already vanished into Oblivion's system.

Márton was waiting at the next stop. He didn't speak, didn't smile. He just crushed out his cigarette and walked away.

When he disappeared, no one in Oblivion called it absence, just the wind shifting in another room.

James sat back as the tram lurched forward, the empty satchel on his lap. The seat vibrated faintly beneath him.

He stared at its stitched leather surface until the blur of lights through glass turned it into something else.

A face, closer than it should have been.

He blinked.

Leather, light, nothing else.

Chapter 6: The Ghost Trial
Budapest, Hungary | Week 6

In the sixth week, the drills went dark.

There were no routes, no code sheets, no barked corrections through cigarette smoke—just Márton in the doorway, silent as a priest at a graveside, a matchbook balanced on his thumb like a coin he'd already decided to spend.

A straight razor slid across the table, its handle cold as a verdict.

"Souvenirs leave trails," he said. Nothing else.

James shaved his forearms, the razor clearing away stray fibers and DNA that would cling like signatures. Bleach scoured his palms until the skin burned raw. The last passport curled in a coffee tin, its photograph blistering into a smear. When the tin cooled, Márton placed the extracted molar—sealed in a steel capsule—beside the razor. The ache in his jaw reminded him: Oblivion never dealt in fragments.

"For the furnace," he said. "Proof loves ash."

He crushed a cigarette just as the paper browned—his ritual—and set the butt atop a stack of dead hotels printed on matchbooks that no longer existed.

The silence said the rest: it was time.

EU rail travel under an alias was easier than crossing a street in some countries—no biometrics, no stamps, no questions.

Transit cut across borders without asking permission.

Budapest to Záhony, Hungary. Záhony to Chop, Ukraine. Chop to Kharkiv, Ukraine. Second-class cars stank of diesel and boiled cabbage. Towns blurred past like bruises. *PhantomNet* blinked quietly at his wrist in its tight, deniable rhythm—five on, thirty off—just enough to whisper a warning before vanishing again. The faint vibration pressed into bone more than skin.

The directive had been simple and deniable, Oblivion's preferred dialect.

Debaltseve, Ukraine. A clinic on the south ring, nominally civilian, in truth militia-run. In its basement sat a dental vacuum autoclave no one serviced anymore. Inside: a biometric-locked microdrive. The scan flagged *OBELISK* pattern match. Rumor said the biometrics tied back to a dead dentist—prints lifted from a body no one claimed. A thin-film overlay would fake the match just long enough to lift the drive and ghost the grid. Leave a cremation signal behind: the molar to salt the story. If he failed, the story would be simpler.

[DEBALTSEVE, UKRAINE | 02:10]

The clinic's power came in shudders, with a generator wheezing somewhere under concrete. Battery halogens flickered in the hall like tired eyes. The air carried iodine, wet wool, and piss. A smear of someone else's blood dried warm along his neck, Márton's final cruelty or kindness. It itched where it tightened against his collar. The warmth slowed his steps, slackened his shoulders. A man in shock; people opened doors for shock.

He entered as freight, not threat.

His weight sagged just enough to sell it.

The orderly at the end of the corridor had the posture of a man who once moved faster and had learned not to. James leaned his weight into the man's shoulder. A curse in Ukrainian, the hard click of annoyance. James tapped the gap in his teeth and muttered, "Basement. Dentist." The orderly rolled his eyes and pointed with his chin.

PhantomNet ticked once at his wrist—two infrared signatures in the stairwell, one fixed, one moving. He slowed, syncing his breath to the generator's pulse, stepping only in the quiet gaps. At the landing he saw the truth: the moving signature resolved into a dog—sick and hungry, but no threat.

The basement stank of wet steam and iron. The walls sweated under the cold, paint curling like old skin. Every drip carried too loud.

Moisture gathered along his jaw and ran cold.

He found the autoclave where the floor plans said it would be—dull steel, dented, power light dead. He scrubbed the handle clean with the heel of his glove, then slid a thin-film overlay from a foil pouch. The polymer carried a false print, laced with trace oils and salt to mimic skin.

Ghosts don't keep souvenirs, Márton had said.
They carry tools that pretend to be people.

James pressed the fake print to the reader plate and held still. The light throbbed once, considered, then clicked.

The light should have gone green. It didn't.

It held—longer than it should have—cycling once, twice, the delay stretching just far enough to register as wrong.

PhantomNet flickered at his wrist.

No signal.
That was worse.

For a fraction of a second, the system didn't agree with itself.

The reader plate buzzed softly, the kind of low, mechanical uncertainty that didn't belong in something designed to decide cleanly.

James didn't move.
Didn't breathe.
His fingers squeezed against the glove seams.

Moments like this didn't last long. They resolved.
One way or the other.

The lock clicked.
But the hesitation remained.

He felt it settle somewhere behind the action, not in the device, but in the pattern itself.

It didn't resolve cleanly.

Inside, beneath a tray of cracked composite molds, a black cartridge no larger than his thumb waited like a secret that had forgotten how to breathe.

He pocketed the drive. The edge pressed briefly against his ribs.

The wrist display fluttered: three blips rounding toward the stairwell, one heavy, two light. Laughing. Men without sleep.

He stepped into the laundry room before they saw him, set the steel capsule on a gurney beneath the cremator stack, and twisted the ignition wheel. The casing would warp, split, and leave the molar behind—just enough evidence to salt the story.

The furnace took convincing—two tries, a cough, and then the hungry rise of heat. He fed the capsule to the throat and watched until the seam glowed. Heat pushed against his face, dry and immediate.

PhantomNet stirred at his wrist, proximity tightening, then went dark again. That was its trick: five seconds alive, thirty silent. Just enough to signal, never long enough for SIGINT to lock on. A pulse that vanished into noise before anyone could trace it.

He was almost clear when the orderly from upstairs cut the corner too fast and shouldered into him. The man's eyes flicked from the smeared blood on James's face—blood planted there earlier—to the door and back, cataloguing the wrongness. In that flicker James caught the moment the man chose irritation over suspicion.

He let his body go slack, muttered a slurred apology. The orderly frowned, irritation winning out over suspicion. He brushed past and was gone.

The furnace thumped along, chewing the capsule into silence. The enamel shard would outlast it—proof enough.

He left by the service ramp into air so cold it made his breath feel loud. Snow needled sideways. He crossed the back lot like a man who had no reason to hurry, then disappeared into a lattice of maintenance alleys mapped in red on the paper he had memorized and burned.

At the fence line, PhantomNet woke long enough to nudge him a pace right, a shadow that wasn't wind, and he obeyed without looking. A spotlight dragged the yard just wide of him, then moved on.

He made the rail spur with minutes to spare and folded into a maintenance boxcar that stank of grease and winter. The microdrive lay cold against his heart.

The train took him north, then west, through fields that remembered tanks and towns that forgot on purpose. Metal rattled through the floor into his spine.

He slept in slices between rail noise and old ghosts, his tongue finding the raw gap where a tooth had once been—a reminder that every name carried a cost.

[KOŠICE, SLOVAKIA | 11:40]

Márton waited in the shadow of a freight crane, smoking to the paper and dropping the butt into a grease-darkened matchbook from the Hotel Gellért—a Budapest landmark that still stood but meant something different to men his age.

He didn't say *congratulations*, he didn't say *welcome to Oblivion*.

"Obituary posted," Márton said, as if noting the weather. "Wrong war, wrong body, right teeth."

In the ash, there was no handwriting, no scar, no mirror left to argue with. Rourke was buried. Henrik had been paperwork. Tomas was what remained—an echo that survived the burn.

James pictured the capsule collapsing in the clinic furnace, enamel breaking into a signature no audit would ever question. Somewhere, an unremarkable file would get its gray ribbon. Somewhere else, a desk would be cleaned of a name never spoken aloud.

And far away, on opposite sides of the country, his parents would be told separately. His mother would be crushed, undone by a son returned only as paperwork and ash. His father, he suspected, would barely pause. One less name for a will.

A body without a body, a death without a grave.

"Rourke," Márton added, trying the word one last time before letting it fall. His gaze cut past James to the rail yard, as if already watching someone else. He didn't dismiss him or keep him, just let the silence decide. Then, almost imperceptibly, he gave the slightest nod—a fragment of approval in a language James would never hear aloud.

By the next morning, Márton was gone. No word. No trail. Not even the smoke of a last cigarette.

James told himself it was the Oblivion way—mentors were never meant to last. They burned you down to ash, then disappeared before you could ask what it had cost them.

The cigarette stub confirmed what Márton never did: in his language, approval; in anyone else's, a gravestone.

But survival was never enough. The eyes in the folder seemed to ask him if he understood—that survival was only the beginning, and belonging was never his to choose.

[BUDAPEST, HUNGARY | NIGHT]

The Ash Archive took him back under the city's skin as if it had been expecting him since the war ended and never really ended. Irina didn't congratulate him either; she set a ledger on its spine, added a number, and closed it with two fingers. The paper edges aligned with exact, practiced pressure.

"PhantomNet envelope worked?" she asked.

"It warned when I needed it," he said.

"That's what we pay entropy for," she murmured, almost a smile. "The noise buys us cover. The signal slips through alive." She dipped the pen again, wrote something he couldn't see, then shook it once—like a surgeon clearing a scalpel of excess blood.

Her eyes flicked to his raw palms, then away just as quickly. "You'll stop scrubbing eventually. The mirror doesn't care what you wash off."

She hesitated, gaze slipping to his mouth, to the gap he could still feel with his tongue. "The tooth," she said quietly. "It had to be done." A pause, almost imperceptible. "I'm sorry for that."

Her gaze lingered just long enough to cut.

"You looked too long at her," she said, her voice quiet but exact.

He opened his mouth, then closed it.

Her pen stilled. The ledger folded shut.

"I know what that means," she said, softer now, not unkind. "Ghosts recognize each other."

He didn't ask if anyone else had seen the flinch or who controlled the deniable budget line that erased a man and minted a ghost. He already knew the answer: Oblivion didn't need believers. It needed proof you'd burn what needed burning and keep moving.

On his way out, a stainless panel in the corridor caught his reflection and gave it back in pieces: jaw, shoulder, the notch of his scars. For a breath, the reflection bent into the face from the file, watching him back.

It wasn't memory or recognition. It was pressure, something unresolved, waiting.

He didn't have a name for it. Not yet.

He blinked. The light shifted across the steel and steadied.

The panel gave him nothing back but a man no longer carrying a name.

ACT II – EVENTS AND HORIZONS

"Some operatives die once.
Firebirds die in every report
and rise in every margin.
If the file insists she is gone,
believe the ash instead."

Chapter 7: At the Fence
Budapest, Hungary

Slowly, by the tenth week, time stopped arriving as hours. It came in symptoms, small betrayals that only became real once they stopped surprising him.

James shaved in the dark; light had stopped adding anything useful.

He slept in his clothes; changing implied trust.

He woke before the radiators hissed and lay still long enough to let the room declare itself—pipes, footsteps, tram brakes—before accepting that he was still inside it.

The muscles in his legs had hardened from the nightly runs Márton insisted on, but the skin beneath his eyes had gone the color of paper left too long in rain.

He ran the IX District without a watch and without music, counting distance by the city's repetitions: the shriek of tram brakes at Nagyvárad, the stutter of a broken lamp on Kinizsi, the wash of late traffic thinning block by block until only the river and rail lines seemed fully awake. Cold air burned at the back of his throat with each breath.

The nosebleeds had begun in the seventh week and never announced themselves properly. They arrived first as warmth, a slow, quiet thread beneath one nostril while he moved.

The first time, he wiped it on his glove and kept running; the second, it soaked through the collar of his shirt before he registered the volume of it.

By the third, he carried it the way he carried everything now—without report, without acknowledgment.

He said nothing to Márton at first. Márton had vanished for nearly three weeks, sent off on some tangential assignment the ledgers would never admit had existed.

James had assumed he would not return.

When he did—coat damp, cigarette between his teeth, expression unchanged—it felt less like relief than evaluation.

James bit the inside of his cheek until the taste changed from salt to metal and kept moving.

They were running tram-line reconnaissance on the south loop when he saw her.

One moment he was counting pace, distance, breath; the next, he was aware of a second rhythm intersecting his own.

She was ahead of him by three strides when he allowed himself to accept what he was seeing, the interval resolving not as distance he had chosen, but as something fixed. Her pace never broke, not even slightly.

Standard offset said keep distance, track movement, let the line hold; he did all of that automatically.

Kyra moved without visible strain. Not easily—that would have suggested softness, or carelessness—but with a kind of controlled fluidity that made every adjustment look native to her body.

Soldiers ran through terrain; operatives cut through it.
She seemed to move as if the ground had already made room.

The dossier had prepared him for competence, for direct action, for variance—for the kind of language institutions used when they wanted to name danger without admitting they had lost ownership of it.

Black hair streamed behind her in the sodium wash, dark until the light struck it, then briefly burnished before the glow let go.

He didn't see her face immediately.

When he did, it hit—beauty hard enough to disrupt him, followed by something quieter. Recognition.

He kept three paces. Then two.

She cut south through the IX, tramlines pulsing to her left, the Danube somewhere west beyond the blocks and rails and shuttered commerce. The abandoned fish market marked the turn.

Its windows were cracked, its signage half-peeled, and the air still carried an old mineral trace of salt and thawed brine when the wind came off the lot. A perimeter fence ran along one edge of the property, wire bowed in places, patched in others, the metal stiff with winter. It divided the pale reach of the streetlamp from the darker strip beyond it.

That was where the blood came. It slid warm against the cold air. A tickle first, then a slow drop crossing his upper lip.

He wiped it without thinking and saw the red streak his glove had become under the light.

Too late to hide it. She had already seen it.

She stopped.

The halt was so precise it made the whole street feel as if it had paused with her. She turned at the fence and rested one hand lightly against the wire.

He stopped too.

The blood had already reached his wrist where it had smeared under the heel of his glove. He could feel his pulse in his nose, in his teeth, in the raw gap where the extracted molar had once been.

Sound thinned. The distant tram became metal grinding through wool. Light lost depth. All of it drew inward around the narrow strip of fence between them.

Her gaze dropped to the blood, then rose again.

There was no pity in it. No recoil. No easy indifference either.

What held there was harder to name and more difficult to dismiss: attention without softness, calculation stretched a fraction too long to be casual, as if she had seen something she had not expected and was deciding whether it mattered.

Then she reached into her coat and withdrew a black handkerchief.

It was folded neatly, sharply enough that the gesture looked less like improvisation than habit.

She held it out through a narrow opening where the wire had warped away from the post. Her hand didn't waver. She did not step forward. She did not ask permission. The offering existed between them without explanation.

He took it. He shouldn't have.

The warmth came first, not the fabric or the fold, but the fact that it still held heat. Hers. After everything else had been reduced to procedure.

His grip tightened.

He took it before the decision formed.

He pressed the cloth to his nose and leaned just enough that the wire touched his sleeve. The metal was colder than it should have been, or he was warmer.

He couldn't tell which.

Up close, the details refused to settle into a single read, the faint scar at her jaw appearing and disappearing with the light, the damp at the ends of her hair, the stillness in her mouth that wasn't calm so much as control carried too far.

He did not correct it.

Snow began again in a fine, almost private drift, the flakes small enough to vanish as they crossed the light, while the fence held its line—bent, rusted, and absolute—making the silence between them legible in a way neither acknowledged.

Her voice came softly. It carried just enough to reach him and no farther.

"I didn't see anything."

Not denial, but containment.

He lowered the handkerchief slightly, enough to breathe more easily. The fabric was softer than he had expected.

For one brief instant, he thought of closing the distance, not to touch her, not even to speak, but to test whether the force of her presence changed when the barrier disappeared. The impulse felt less like desire than defiance, an urge to break what Oblivion had built into him.

For a fraction of a second, he didn't trust himself not to step forward.

Not toward her, but through the boundary.

The thought died before it reached his face.

Her eyes remained on him, unreadable in the low light, and it was that unreadability more than anything else that unsettled him. Nothing in the file had prepared him for the pressure of being fully seen by someone who offered nothing back.

Then she turned. Her movement was immediate, unhesitating.

Not dismissing him. Not inviting him. Simply continuing, as if the moment at the fence had occurred because it had to and no longer required either of them once it was done.

He followed.

The run did not end cleanly, and he kept moving, not because there was anywhere to go, but because stopping would have forced the moment into definition, into something that could be named and therefore contained.

The city resumed around him in pieces, the hum of tramlines, the hollow percussion of his steps against wet pavement—but none of it returned the same. Distance stretched without anchoring. Landmarks arrived out of sequence. The rhythm he had relied on for weeks slipped just enough that he noticed the absence of it.

He reached the river without remembering the turns that led him there.

The water moved dark and heavy below.

By the time he returned to the flat, the moment had thinned, but it had not resolved. He washed the blood from his hands, the water running clear long before the sensation left his skin. The handkerchief sat folded on the edge of the sink, black against white porcelain, holding its shape as if it had always been there.

He didn't touch it again.

Sleep came in fragments—not the controlled intervals Márton had trained into him, but something looser, unstructured.

He surfaced more than he rested, drifting in and out of shallow awareness where sound arrived without context and memory refused to anchor to sequence.

Whatever had shifted remained underneath.

It stayed.

Chapter 8: The Final Phase

The final phase had already started by the time he noticed.

The terrain navigation drill was the first place it showed itself.

He reached the third waypoint and found nothing where something should have been. No comm signal, no static, no degraded transmission that could be written off as interference. The absence was complete.

His boots sank slightly into the softened ground.

The tarp marker that should have broken the line of sight wasn't there. The thermal blanket that should have held heat against the cold ground had not been placed. The route to the safehouse no longer aligned with the terrain he had memorized.

He paused.

No correction followed, no exfil code came.

Cold air tightened in his chest before releasing.

By the time he resumed movement, it no longer mattered whether this was a drill.

By dusk, he was moving through frost and scrub without the comfort of knowing whether he was being evaluated or had simply been left in a space where evaluation and survival had become indistinguishable.

He slept that night in the hollow of a fallen tree, the emergency foil drawn high around his throat. Its thin metallic surface caught what little heat he could generate and returned it unevenly.

The cold pressed inward from every direction, not sharp enough to force movement, but persistent enough to deny rest.

The foil crackled faintly when he shifted.

Something moved beyond the edge of his hearing.
Not random, not animal, but measured.

The hairs along his forearm lifted under the sleeve.

It held position just outside full perception, close enough to be tracked and restrained enough never to resolve into anything he could confront directly.

He did not go looking for it.

At dawn, he found the broken casing of a compass in a drainage ditch, its housing cracked and its needle gone. He rebuilt enough of it to matter using the tip of his knife and copper stripped from a roadside fuse box, aligning it by the earth's pull. Metal bit into his fingertips as he twisted it into place.

After the first hour, direction became less a fixed point and more an accumulation of decisions, each informed by terrain, memory, and the subtle ways the environment resisted or accepted movement.

By the second hour, even that began to erode, leaving him with something closer to instinct than navigation.

It was on the second night that the route itself began to reveal its structure.

The first marker appeared where it should not have existed—a sensor half-buried in frost along a line no civilian trail would justify. Ten meters beyond it, a branch bent against its natural fall, the angle too precise to be accidental.

Farther still, a heel print lifted almost entirely from the ground, then remained just visible enough to be seen by someone already looking for disturbance.

None of it was careless.

Each marker existed in the narrow space between concealment and message, positioned with the expectation that it would be read, but only by someone who understood what had been disturbed.

That was when he understood he was not alone.

Not Márton. Not one of the usual watchers.

Something moved through the tree line at the edge of perception, with the same controlled economy he had registered before—the same refusal to be fully captured by direct attention.

The movement registered before he could track it.

He caught fragments of it as he moved, a shift of dark hair, the angle of a shoulder, the suggestion of breath where the air should have remained still.

She wasn't clearing the path. She was checking if he could read it.

He followed the markers as the terrain thinned and the distant glow of the ring road began to press through the frost, the route tightening in a way that suggested not randomness but design.

The loop closed where it should not have closed.

The safehouse lights appeared ahead, weak and yellow through the weather.

Márton stood on the porch with his hands buried in his coat, as if nothing about the last forty-eight hours required acknowledgment. Smoke drifted past his shoulder, slow in the cold air.

"You're back," he said.

"I improvised."

Márton gave a slight nod, the kind that ended conversations without resolving them.

"Then you're ready."

James heard the words and understood their function, but they did not hold his attention.

Because she was inside.

Kyra sat in the corner of the room, her stillness carrying the same contained precision as her movement. The room adjusted around her.

When her gaze lifted to him, the path through the woods reassembled itself immediately—the markers, the sensors, the sequence of decisions that had never belonged entirely to him.

She had not followed him; she had designed the route and watched to see whether he was capable of finding it.

His pulse shifted once.

She gave no indication that she had noticed.

And that was what made her dangerous in a way the dossier never could have articulated. It was not her skill, though that was evident, or her control. It was the quiet certainty that whatever conclusion she had reached about him had already been decided, and that he was only now arriving at something she had understood long before he entered the room.

He stood there longer than he should have.

Márton said nothing.

Neither did she.

The message arrived the next morning.

An envelope waited on the table. The paper edge curled slightly from damp.

Inside, a silver pin shaped like a lark, one wing bent inward as if the bird had folded in on itself under pressure.

"Message," Márton said. "Not for you—for me."

By dawn, confirmation followed.

A body had been left in an alley behind the tram depot—the woman from Wiesbaden.

He had never known her name.

The damage had been controlled rather than chaotic: hair removed in sections, bone broken with purpose, seven fingernails taken and no more.

They had stopped when she gave them enough.

That was all it took.

Something tightened in his chest—not sharp enough to name, not distant enough to ignore.

It wasn't grief. It was exposure.

Whatever had taken her had done so without hesitation.

And nothing about him placed him outside that reach.

Márton crushed his cigarette into the silver pin until the metal bowed under the pressure, the wings deforming against the table with a sound too small to register as anything but deliberate. Ash scattered across the table in fine gray lines.

"They call it Oblivion for a reason," he said. "Every ghost ends here."

But when his eyes shifted—once, and without intention— toward Kyra, the certainty Márton depended on failed to settle.

Her gaze met his without hesitation, and for a moment the room seemed to narrow around that single line of contact, everything else receding into something less defined.

Her eyes held an unnatural clarity in the low light, the blue in them catching the light and holding it in a way that felt less like reflection and more like retention.

He held there longer than he should have.

Then his focus shifted—not deliberately, not as a controlled scan, but as a continuation of the same pull—downward, toward her hands resting loosely against her knee, the fingers relaxed but guarded, the tips carrying faint traces of wear that did not belong to neglect.

There was nothing overt in them, no visible tension and no immediate threat. But something in the stillness of them felt wrong—not incorrect, but precise. As if whatever those hands chose to do would not hesitate, would not correct, would not second-guess once the decision had been made.

The thought didn't fully form before his body responded.

A subtle shift ran through him, starting low and rising along his spine, not sharp enough to be called fear, not sudden enough to be dismissed as reflex, but controlled in the same way everything else in the room was contained, measured, and entirely real.

For an instant, the two impressions overlapped.

The memory of the kiss and the knowledge of what had been done to her.

And the presence of the woman in front of him, watching without offering anything that could be read as reassurance.

The connection was not logical, and it did not need to be.

He broke the contact first, not abruptly or in a way that would register as retreat, but with the same controlled withdrawal he applied to everything else—letting his gaze move past her as if nothing in the moment had required adjustment.

She did not follow it. She did not need to.

Cold seeped through the window frame into the room.

Later, when the building had gone quiet and the cold pressed in along the window frame, the moment at the fence returned.

Not as memory, but as presence.

Snow drifting through sodium light. The wire holding distance in place. The handkerchief, still carrying the warmth of her pocket.

The moment had not ended. It had withdrawn.

Two ghosts held apart—not by distance, but by design neither of them had chosen.

CHAPTER 9: GHOST WEIGHT
Košice, Slovakia

The movement from Budapest to Košice did not register as travel.

There were no clear markers for it, no departure he could place and no arrival that felt distinct enough to name. The city gave way to distance, distance to motion, motion to something closer to absence—as if continuity had been removed and replaced with function.

He remembered the van only in fragments, the hum of the engine, the rhythm of tires over uneven road, the brief flicker of sodium light crossing the interior at intervals that never aligned with anything he could map. The seat pressed stiffly against his back. Sleep came and went without sequence, and time passed without accumulation.

At some point, the air changed, colder, thinner, carrying something industrial beneath it. His breath caught once before settling.

By the time the vehicle stopped, the transition had already completed itself somewhere he had not been paying attention to.

Košice did not feel like arrival; it felt like continuation under different conditions.

Steel-gray skies pressed low over soot-streaked chimneys and idle rail spurs. Rust clung to stone, coal dust to skin. History didn't die here—it lingered, unburied.

He'd passed through Košice once before as nothing more than a handoff point. James stepped from the unmarked van and felt the shift instantly. This was more than training. This was operational.

Consequence lived here.

A block north, the Hornád river ran black beneath a rusted rail bridge, the current heavy with coal runoff. To the east, the tram depot sat hollow, tracks curling into weeds like veins cut from the city. The safehouse lived between them, buried in a pocket where no one came unless they had to.

The building didn't look like a safehouse; it looked forgotten.

Tucked behind a collapsed textile mill, its façade sagged under vines and flaking plaster. The door hung on one hinge. Broken windows stared outward like blind eyes.

But neglect was the mask.

Motion sensors pulsed under mossed stones, and cameras blinked from fractured masonry.

Decay curated, nothing left to chance.

A keypad blinked once as he entered.
The faint click echoed louder than it should have.

Inside, the temperature dropped.

No greeting, no posted schedule.
This wasn't a place for introductions.

Concrete walls, raw and sweating, and a corridor lit by a single flickering bulb. Each door marked not by numbers but by symbols, scratched by hand, as if even secrecy had lost its language.

The air hung too still.

The smell of antiseptic invaded the back of his throat as he moved deeper into the building, sharp enough to register and familiar enough to carry association he did not follow. It coated the back of his tongue.

A stove hissed beneath a steel vent, heat barely biting back the damp; four cots lined the concrete, three occupied.

The air carried silence like doctrine.

Kyra leaned near the stove.

Heat shimmered faintly between them.

Her black hair gleamed in the orange light, cascading halfway down her back, catching in thin threads against the dull wall. Her eyes—piercing, sharp as fractured glass—met his across the room. No warmth and no invitation, just the steady appraisal of someone who had already seen too much to mistake him for anything but another variable.

Budapest had been something else, fleeting and almost human. This was different.

Here, she did not need to appear as anything else.

He didn't look away; neither did she.

The silence wasn't introduction; it was reminder.

From the shadows, Luka emerged.

A wall of a man, shoulders squared like quarried stone. Dark hair cropped, scars carved deep across his arms. His eyes—black, depthless—moved over James as if scanning for structural flaws. No blink. No adjustment. Just judgment.

"New blood?" Luka's voice was flat, the edge of an old Balkan accent cutting through.

Not a question, a calibration.

James gave a single nod. His neck felt stiff from the ride.

Only then did Torres stir at the comms table. Hood drawn low, earbuds humming faint static, his fingers floated over a PhantomNet console. The rig wasn't scavenged, it was immaculate: black carbon panels sealed tight, spectral lines pulsing like breath.

"Two-second delay on Kyiv tower bounce," Torres muttered. "Same ghost on the line. It's riding the loop."

His words weren't a report; they were an annotation—entered aloud only because silence alone couldn't hold it.

James said nothing. He knew his place. This wasn't a circle to be welcomed into.

It was a mechanism, already moving.

The days did not separate cleanly enough to be counted, and whatever distinction remained between one and the next existed only in the structure imposed on them.

Wake-ups came before light, the air cold enough to make breath visible until they learned not to let it be.

Water immersion followed, long enough to strip heat from the body without forcing movement, conditioning them to function while discomfort remained constant rather than acute.

The physical work carried through without pause. The heavy bag absorbed impact until the gloves saturated and the hands beneath them began to register what the padding no longer concealed. Timing replaced strength, and endurance replaced intention.

PhantomNet sequences arrived without pattern, threaded into the hours where fatigue had already compromised clarity. Numbers inverted, and cadence shifted just enough to punish assumption. Missing a sequence removed food; completing one transferred responsibility forward.

The woods outside Košice completed the rest. Terrain that did not forgive missteps, and silence that forced awareness of every sound the body made against it. Breath controlled. Footing adjusted. Movement reduced until it no longer announced itself.

Luka moved through it with a consistency that did not require attention. Torres remained anchored to the system, his focus narrowing until the network became more immediate than the room around him.

And Kyra—Kyra moved with a precision that did not appear learned or even maintained, but simply present, as if the adjustments required by the environment had already been accounted for before she entered it.

Once Luka tossed her a blade without looking. She caught it mid-spin, reversed grip, and swept the perimeter like it was breath. Another time James shadowed her across ice-slick ground; she never slipped, never stumbled. Her grace wasn't performance—it was precision, sharpened into weaponry.

He trained alongside them—passed drills, matched pace. But he wasn't part of it—not the rhythm, not the silence.

They carried memory between them, unspoken. He orbited their circle, but it was her gravity—Kyra's—that held him. Lethal. Inevitable. An event horizon waiting for the moment he moved too close.

On the fifth night, a packet of antiseptic wipes appeared beneath his pillow—no words, no glance, just silent acknowledgment of torn knuckles; recognition without trust.

That night, he lay on his cot listening to the stove hiss, counting seconds between the metal creaks. Budapest had ghosts. Košice had weight. The silence here wasn't absence—it was tactical.

The Red Ghost lived inside that silence. Luka muttered Grozny. Torres swore Tehran. Myths that stretched her into smoke. But Kyra didn't speak. She just stared at the wall, smoke curling in her hand, silence heavier around her than their stories.

James caught the slip others missed. The cigarette burned too low between drags, and her exhale slowed, half a second longer than it should have been. Ash trembled at the edge before falling. He knew that flaw. He'd been punished for it himself. Any deviation meant distraction. Distraction meant memory.

It wasn't disbelief in her silence; it was recognition.

She had crossed paths with the Red Ghost. Maybe once. Maybe more.

And when the mask sealed again, her silence became perfect. Unreadable.

Then came the pit. No gloves, no mats—concrete floor, sweat slick under bare feet. Márton circled them like a judge with no jury. You went in two at a time, no rules but one: stay standing.

Luka fought like doctrine—low guard, efficient strikes, no wasted motion; Torres brawled, shoulders squared, hits like falling beams. James lasted three exchanges before Luka drove him down with a body shot that emptied his lungs. Kyra didn't fight like either of them. She broke balance. A hook to the knee, an elbow to the throat, a turn that left you staring at ceiling lights before you even realized she'd moved.

When James faced her, the air changed. She closed distance with no warning, an elbow grazing his jaw, the ghost of a knife-hand strike held back by a breath. He blocked late, clumsy.

His footing shifted half an inch without intent.

Her hip slammed into his, momentum snapping his stance. A sweep of her leg hooked his ankle, and gravity did the rest. The impact rattled through his ribs. He hit the mat hard; breath jolted from his chest.

Before he could recover, she flowed with him, not against him— her body pressing into his, her weight turning his struggle into leverage for her. His ribs flared in protest, and then her forearm slid up, pinning across his throat. The world narrowed to her weight, her precision.

James shoved upward, boots grinding against the frozen dirt, but she absorbed the effort like stone absorbs rain. Strands of her hair slipped forward, brushing his cheek, his lips. Feather-light, yet it seared hotter than the choke itself. His pulse spiked, not just from lack of air. The sensation did not belong to the exchange; that misalignment disrupted him more than the choke itself.

He twisted, tried to throw her weight, but she shifted before he could commit. Her balance was effortless, her grip merciless. That veil of black hair still grazed his face with every movement, each strand a taunt, turning restraint into something he could feel in his chest as much as in his throat.

Her eyes stayed locked on his. Calm. Cold. Measuring. Not lust, not mercy—just a relentless stillness that made the accidental brush of hair feel like a deliberate choice. As if she was reminding him who set the distance here, and who could close it whenever she wanted.

James's vision tunneled, his lungs straining, but the hair against his lips kept him pinned as surely as her arm did. The proximity disrupted his timing.

Not because it introduced hesitation, but because it forced him to account for variables that had no place in the exchange. The pressure of her weight, the controlled placement of each movement, the lack of any wasted effort—none of it aligned with the patterns he had been trained to anticipate.

His response lagged, not in speed but in interpretation.

By the time he adjusted, she had already moved.

She released suddenly. Air rushed back into his lungs, uneven.

He staggered back, but the ghost of her hair lingered across his skin, more unforgettable than the bruises blooming at his throat.

Márton's voice cut across the room: "Again."

She didn't hesitate. A snap of her leg hooked his ankle, and momentum yanked him off-balance. He slammed down, shoulder jolting against the floor. Her knee landed on his sternum, pinning him for half a breath longer than necessary—long enough for him to see her eyes up close, bright and merciless. Eyes that told him the choke had been a choice, not her limit.

By the sixth round, his ribs screamed with every breath. But on the seventh, instinct cut sharper than pain. He feigned a stagger, let her press in, then pivoted—arm snaking low, shoulder driving forward. For the barest instant, he had her weight tipped, her balance compromised, her hair brushing his face without intention, registering only as interference he could not immediately discard.

A reversal.

Márton leaned forward in the smoke, watching.

For half a heartbeat, her eyes widened, not surprise or weakness, but something like recognition. A flash that said she hadn't expected him to take the opening, or maybe that she had given it to him on purpose.

Then the moment broke. She flowed with the momentum instead of fighting it, rolling him under, her thigh pinning his ribs, her forearm across his throat once more. Close enough that he could feel her breath ghost his jaw. Close enough to know she had let the instant happen.

Her gaze steadied, the flicker gone, replaced with the same merciless calm. A reminder: control was hers to grant, not his to win.

"You don't train to win," Márton said, cigarette ember flaring in the dark. "You train to survive losing."

He dragged himself up, his legs holding just barely. His lungs were raw, but her eyes held him harder than Márton's words. Surviving losing meant learning her—not how to restrain her, but how to move in the orbit she chose.

He was supposed to anchor her when the system failed to contain what it had built. But nothing in what he had been trained to do accounted for something that did not respond to control.

Or something he was not certain should be controlled at all.

If she crossed beyond the limits imposed on her, the system would not stop her; it would yield, and anything still bound to it—including him—would not remain where it had been.

CHAPTER 10: BLACK ECLIPSE
Košice, Slovakia

Halfway through his second week in Košice, the whispers began, scrawled in margins, muttered over cold meals, carried like static under every breath.

The assignment came without preamble, but not without weight.

A routing key had surfaced, partial, degraded, but traceable. Not enough to map the system, but enough to identify where it had passed through. Enough to expose a corridor, and nothing beyond it.

It had been carried out by an asset that no longer existed in any official record.

If he was taken alive, the corridor would close, and if he was killed before extraction, it would collapse entirely.

Either outcome ended in loss.
This was the margin between them.

No conventional unit could move without triggering notice.
So they were sent instead.

They were given a six-hour window before the corridor went dark and the network re-routed beyond recovery.

Mid-snowstorm, no comms.

Snow gathered along his collar, melting slowly against his skin.

The cold tasted like metal. Every breath scraped, every blink iced shut. Cold air burned his throat with each inhale.

They moved like phantoms through the tree line, half-forgotten even by their own footprints.

Somewhere in the silence, James heard a rhythm that wasn't theirs, a pulse, steady and alien, like memory brushing against his own.

The rhythm did not align with their movement. It persisted across terrain shifts, across changes in pace, across the moments where sound should have broken and reset.

His footing slipped once.

Then Márton's voice, wired into his spine, surfaced: *If you pause, they die.*

So he didn't.

When Torres misread a false trail, James cut the lead without being told, Luka flanked left, Kyra right, movements threaded into the storm like inevitability.

They didn't move fast. They moved clean—each step placed to hold direction, not chase distance. Time thinned as they advanced, the window closing without needing to be checked.

A kilometer off the track, concrete crouched in the hills like a leftover bunker. When they reached him, the damage had already begun to set.

His eyes tracked movement in fragments, resetting instead of holding a continuous field.

The man's weight sagged unevenly between them.

When Luka spoke, the man's head turned, not to the voice, but to where the voice had been.

Delayed, incorrect.

His mouth opened once, then twice, a word forming that couldn't cross the distance into speech.

What came out wasn't language.

His hand moved once—not toward them, but across his own chest, fingers trembling against fabric, searching for something already gone.

When James stepped closer, the man's eyes snapped to him—not recognition, not fear, but alignment. For a fraction of a second, something locked.

His mouth opened again. This time, a shape formed—not a word, but a direction.

Then it was gone.

His awareness broke into intervals, failing in sequence.

Luka held position for half a second longer than necessary.

Not hesitation, but calculation: weight versus time, recovery versus compromise.

It passed. They moved.

Because partial recovery was still recovery, and delay meant loss.

At the roadside culvert, they laid him down. No words, no explanation, just coordinates obeyed. Snow soaked through James's knee as he knelt.

Fifteen minutes later, headlights swept the snow. Light flared across the ice, blinding for a second. A van without plates slowed and braked. Two silhouettes in parkas hauled the man inside without a glance at the team. No questions. No thanks. The doors slammed, engine growled, and the vehicle vanished into the storm.

The handoff was clean, too clean.

No verification, no confirmation exchange, no secondary authentication.

Which meant either the receiving team already knew what they were taking, or it didn't matter who they were.

Whatever he had carried was no longer intact, not fully.

James stood in the churned snow. His pulse thudded in his ears, steady and loud.

The man's entire existence had been reduced to cargo, lifted and erased. The storm began to close the tracks almost instantly, swallowing proof they'd ever been there.

When they returned, the safehouse was dark.
Cold air lingered inside, unmoving.

No stove heat, no footsteps in the dust.
Only proof that someone had waited.

A desk drawer left open by a quarter inch. A half-burned cigarette in the ashtray—Turkish blend. Ash clung to the tip, barely holding.

Still warm, smoke faint in the air. Whoever left it hadn't just been here—they had wanted to be felt.

And a note taped to the wall with surgical tape, the sterile strip stamped faint in blue letters: *Medeuropa.*

The tape itself felt wrong here, too clean, too clinical, an artifact of operating rooms and sealed clinics pressed against plaster that sweated mildew. Its blue edges glared against the ruin, antiseptic precision slicing into rot.

Luka didn't step further into the room.

Torres moved first, but not toward the note, toward the uplink, as if confirmation might exist somewhere outside the space they were standing in. His chair scraped faintly against concrete.

James stayed where he was, because movement would have implied a response, and none of them had been given one. The absence pressed harder than any verdict—no Márton waiting, no debrief, just a void that felt deliberate, as if even their teacher had been consumed by the same silence now settling over them.

Márton's absence wasn't uncertainty. It was removal.

Which meant whatever had set this in motion did not require oversight or correction.

Later, James returned from gear checks early; Luka was still drying his boots, Torres buried in the uplink.

Through the half-open server room door, he saw Kyra.

Light pulsed unevenly against the wall, catching her cheekbone in green. Surveillance footage, low-res, tinted green.

Movement registered more than identity, a sequence of actions: clean, efficient, final.

Kyra closed the file before it resolved into anything that could be named.

Her fingers stilled on the console.

The screen went dark, but the reflection remained for a fraction longer than it should have.

Then it was gone.

"Training footage," she said.

James didn't answer.

His jaw tightened, then released.

It wasn't the content that stayed with him. It was the fact that she had stopped it before it completed.

Her hand remained on the console a fraction longer than necessary. Control.

The kind that ended processes before they completed, not because they were finished, but because they had yielded what was required.

James understood that.

What he didn't understand was what she had already taken from it.

Her gaze froze his, daring him to press. Daring him not to.

He chose silence.

CHAPTER 11: GHOST LOGIC
Košice, Slovakia

"Trust nothing that doesn't bleed. Ghosts lie. But instinct doesn't."
— MÁRTON, FIELD MANUAL (RESTRICTED)

Even before he reached the clearing, something in the air had already shifted.

The whispers did not begin all at once. They gathered instead in fragments, in annotations left unfinished in the margins of training reports, in low remarks traded over cold meals and allowed to die before they became conversation, in the subtle shift that passed through a room when one name was not spoken but nevertheless present in what followed.

By the time James recognized the pattern, it had already merged with the structure of the place.

He found Kyra at first light beyond the tree line, seated cross-legged in the frost with a blindfold tied cleanly over her eyes and a disassembled sidearm laid out across a tarp before her. Frost cracked faintly under his boot as he stopped.

The pieces were spaced with the precision of something taken apart too many times to remain mechanical, their arrangement closer to anatomy than equipment, each component waiting where her hands expected it to be before touch confirmed it.

She moved without hurry or hesitation, her fingertips crossing the cold steel with a calm exactness that made the process look less like practice than recollection. Metal clicked against metal in a sequence so clean it scarcely registered as sound. The sound carried sharper in the cold air.

James stopped at the edge of the clearing and watched longer than he meant to. His breath fogged once, then steadied.

Her hands never faltered. The barrel seated. The slide locked. The magazine was checked by touch and settled into place with a movement so precise it seemed to complete itself before his eye could follow it.

"You sleep yet?" he asked.

"Fourteen minutes."

A pause followed, slight but deliberate.

"Long enough to drown twice."

Something at the corner of her mouth shifted, though not enough to become a smile. It was sharper, more controlled, like a blade turned just far enough to catch light before being sheathed again.

Later, during a brush-pass drill through the train yard ruins east of the safehouse, he lost sight of her for less than a second and found that less than a second was enough. His stride checked for a fraction before continuing.

The place smelled of soot, old rain, and the mineral cold that worked into rusted metal and never fully left. Rails had warped into brittle arcs through the weeds, and skeletal cranes stood fixed against the gray like gestures abandoned halfway through completion. Every footfall arrived too loudly and vanished too fast, the frost swallowing sound with a kind of impersonal efficiency that made the silence feel engineered rather than empty.

He caught the gate moving before he caught her.

The chain-link panel swung once on its hinge and rattled once before settling. By the time he crossed the gap, the drop had already been made and recovered. Nothing remained but the faint motion of the metal and the sense that the space had been occupied a moment earlier by someone who had left nothing behind.

"How'd you get through the grid?" he asked when he found her again farther down the line.

She did not stop. She only turned her head enough to let one pale eye catch the failing light.

"I've been ghosting men since I was eleven."

Then she moved on, slipping through soot and frost with the same economy she brought to everything else.

Eleven.

James felt the number settle deeper than it should have, not because it invited sympathy, but because it recalibrated scale.

He had known enough already to understand that whatever had built Kyra had begun early. Hearing it placed in years made the damage feel less abstract and harder to absorb cleanly.

He did not follow the thought further.

That evening, shortly before the light failed entirely, she intercepted him behind the toolshed they used for dead-drop drills. She emerged from the dusk so quietly that her presence seemed less like an arrival than a change in the air around him. Without greeting or preamble, she pressed a folded map into his hand.

The paper was damp at the edges and worn soft along the creases. Three red dots had been marked across it in sharp ink, with a single time scribbled beside the easternmost point.

"Check the perimeter alone," she said. "Don't tell Luka."

James looked down at the map, then back at her.

"Why?"

Her expression did not alter. "Because I said so."

The answer came without excess, which made her intent unmistakable. Whatever this was, it was not improvisation.

Then she was gone again, withdrawing into the dark so completely that the space she left seemed to close around itself in her absence.

James remained where he was for several seconds, the folded paper held too tightly in his hand.

He unfolded the map once more and studied the red marks without moving. He could have followed it. He could have taken it to Luka and forced the test into the open, if that was what it was. He could have confronted her directly and demanded a reason that existed outside her own authority.

Instead, he stepped inside, crossed to the stove, and fed the map to the flame. Heat pushed against his fingers as he held it too long.

The paper darkened at the edges before it caught, the red ink blistering first and curling inward as the heat consumed the marked points. Smoke rose. He watched until it was gone.

Even after it was gone, his thumb still remembered the fold, as if the shape of it had survived destruction more cleanly than the thing itself.

He did not check the perimeter.

Not the way she had defined it.

If it had been a test, he had either passed or failed it beyond correction. He could not yet tell which, and the silence that followed did nothing to clarify the result.

He found her later on the roof.

She was sitting on the ledge with one leg drawn up and the other hanging over the side, a cigarette burning low between her fingers while the city beyond the safehouse dissolved into mist and industrial shadow. Košice looked different from above, less like a city than the residue of one, its lights drowned in low cloud and smoke until distance erased any clean boundary between ground and sky.

She did not turn when he pushed through the access door. She only inclined her head by a fraction, acknowledging him without yielding any more of her attention than that.

He let the silence stand between them for a moment before he said, "You know those will kill you."

Her cigarette paused halfway to her lips.

One eye opened—just enough to acknowledge him—then closed again as she turned her attention back to the city.

"They haven't yet."

The ember flared, then dimmed.

James watched the smoke drift a moment longer than he needed to, then said, "The map."

Her cigarette brightened briefly at the tip.

"What about it?"

"Why me?"

This time she looked at him.

No denial. No performance of innocence. Just the same directness she brought to everything else.

"I wanted to see whether you'd obey the instruction or the situation."

James moved a little closer, cold radiated off the concrete into his legs.

"I burned it."

That altered something in her expression, though not enough to settle into any single readable state. Interest, perhaps. Irritation, perhaps. More likely some private calculation that required neither.

"Then you understood it," she said.

"Or misunderstood it."

"Same difference," she replied. "If the system survives the choice."

He held that for a moment. "You didn't give that test to Luka."

"No."

"Or Torres."

"No."

"Why?"

She took a slow drag, then let the smoke slip out in a narrow, controlled stream. The ember flared, then dimmed.

"Because Luka doesn't confuse doctrine with judgment, and Torres doesn't leave the network long enough to be trusted outside it. You still think command is something they handed you because you were ready for it."

The line landed harder than it should have, not because it was unfair, but because some part of him recognized the accuracy before he could defend against it.

"And you?" he asked.

Her gaze shifted away from him and returned to the drowned lights beyond the rooftop.

"I don't get command," she said. "Not here. Not after Moscow."

She did not elaborate immediately, and the pause that followed carried more force than the words themselves.

When she spoke again, her tone had not softened, but something in it had thinned enough to reveal the strain beneath.

"My father started it when I was eleven. Locks. Codes. Routes. The things men call preparation when they want survival to sound honorable."

The cigarette burned lower between her fingers.

"The Russians finished it."

Nothing in her posture changed, yet the cold around them seemed to sharpen.

James said nothing. The silence felt less like restraint than respect for the fact that she was speaking at all.

"They trained past usefulness," she said after a moment. "Past judgment. Past the point where it still mattered what you wanted."

A longer pause.

No inventory of suffering. No request that he understand the parts she left unsaid. Just a fragment, cleanly given, and then the return of silence as if she had reached the exact edge of what she intended to offer and would not step beyond it.

James crossed the remaining distance and sat beside her on the ledge, leaving just enough space to keep it from becoming intimacy. The concrete was rough, holding the day's cold as it seeped through fabric. His shoulder remained just clear of hers, close enough to feel the shift in the air between them, but not contact. She didn't move away.

Below them, somewhere in the low streets, a truck changed gears and disappeared. The sound arrived flattened by fog and distance, as though the world itself had been turned down to keep from interfering with whatever this was.

He looked out over the city rather than at her.

"You set the map because you wanted to see whether I'd think against instruction."

"Yes."

"And if I'd shown it to Luka?"

Her answer came at once. "Then I'd have learned something else."

He considered that.

She let the cigarette burn nearly to the filter before crushing it against the parapet with her thumb.

"Stay," she said.

The word did not arrive as a plea or carry the force of command. It existed somewhere between those states, stripped of ornament and impossible to reduce to either.

James stayed.

Not because the word compelled him, but because leaving would have made the moment cleaner than it was, and nothing about Kyra felt clean. Not the discipline, not the history under it, not the fact that she had chosen him for a test she had not trusted anyone else to receive.

They sat without speaking for what might have been a minute or twenty. Time behaved differently around stillness. The air moved. Their breath clouded and disappeared between them. Somewhere down the line of buildings a loose metal panel struck once against brick and then was still again.

When he finally rose, she did not stop him.

But she did not look up either.

James paused with his hand on the access door and understood, without deciding whether he liked it, that she had not let him in because she trusted him. She had let him remain because she wanted to know what he would do with proximity once it had been allowed.

That was different.

He went down the stairs with the weight of the exchange still unresolved inside him, not because anything had been answered, but because nothing had been. Each step echoed faintly in the narrow space.

When sleep came, it did not come cleanly.

He dreamed of his father, though dream was too coherent a word for what followed. The house in Virginia remained where it had always been, but the proportions were wrong. The hallway ran too long. The ceiling lowered by degrees that made breathing feel negotiated. The old oak outside his bedroom window still stood split from the hurricane that had broken it years earlier, except now its bark bulged with surveillance lenses that opened and closed like wet mechanical eyes.

His father sat at the dining room table in dress blues that were not American. The uniform fit too perfectly. The medal in his hands belonged to no service James knew, though the ribbons above it carried colors that suggested they once had.

"You're not supposed to be here," his father said.

James tried to answer, but his mouth filled with grit before the first word formed. The wallpaper behind the table peeled in strips that revealed Cyrillic beneath the paint, layer after layer.

The SR-71 model from his childhood shelf sat in the center of the table, dripping wax from its wings.

"Where is this?" James asked, though the words came out thick and delayed, as though the room were making him hear them after the fact.

His father stood. The chair made no sound.

"Where we go when we're done forgetting."

The light above them buzzed and shifted toward yellow, too dim to illuminate anything cleanly, too bright to hide behind. Moisture began to gather on the walls and slide downward in thin lines that never reached the floor.

His father's posture changed first.

Not visibly at a glance, but enough that James recognized the alteration before he understood it. The angle of the head was wrong. Not his father's. Someone else's.

When the figure looked at him again, the face was still his father's, but the gesture belonged to Kyra and the voice that followed was neither hers nor Márton's and somehow both.

"Never trust a still flame."

The words scraped along his spine with the force of something familiar turned hostile.

Behind him, the hall filled with black water that made no sound as it rose. The medal in his father's hands unraveled into ash. The uniform darkened, stiffened, and split at the seams. When the mouth opened again, there was nothing inside it but absence.

James woke with a violent breath caught halfway in his throat, rain pushing through the open window in hard, slanting bursts, the mattress damp beneath him with sweat and weather.

He lay there in the dark, chest tightening before the air came back.

Residue, not memory. The parts Oblivion had not burned out of him. Not yet.

CHAPTER 12: PROOF OF ABSENCE
Košice, Slovakia

Košice stopped feeling temporary.

No one said they were settled. No order came down from Márton marking the shift from transit to base, from instruction to routine. It happened the way most structural changes happened inside Oblivion, without permission, without ceremony, and in a form that only became visible after it had already hardened around the people living inside it.

The safehouse remained what it had been when James first entered it: damp concrete, sweating walls, a stove that hissed more than it heated, and corridors that held silence too well. But repetition had begun to carve familiarity into the place. He learned which boards near the rear entrance clicked; the wood shifted slightly under his weight each time. He learned the time the pipes knocked in the wall beside the stove and the delay between the first vibration and the second. He learned that the windows on the eastern side gathered condensation fastest just before dawn, and that Luka always woke three minutes before the alarm, not because he needed less sleep, but because his body no longer trusted being found inside it.

Routine took shape slowly, then all at once.

Luka trained as if the body were a machine that could be argued into obedience through blunt repetition. Every movement he made carried the same heavy economy, as though force, once chosen, should never be wasted on anything decorative. He hit hard, sparred harder, and approached each drill with the same severe practicality he brought to eating, cleaning his weapon, or crossing a room. Torres, by contrast, lived in fragments of signal and glow, his real attention reserved for the comms suite and whatever PhantomNet was saying beneath the visible layer of its interface. He could go an hour without speaking, then lift his head and say something so dry and precise it took a second to decide whether he was joking.

Kyra remained the most difficult to fit into any system of understanding.

She participated in every routine without ever seeming to submit to it. If Luka treated the drills as doctrine and Torres treated them as calibration, Kyra treated them as weather: conditions to be read, exploited, and moved through without attachment. She was never late, never careless, never visibly tired. But her precision did not read as discipline in the way Márton's did, or as brute mastery in the way Luka's did. It felt as if the environment had already been accounted for.

And James, without ever being told so, became the point around which decisions began to settle.

Not command exactly, not yet. But when timing mattered, eyes shifted toward him. When routes forked, the pause belonged to him. Even Luka, who would never have admitted to deferring, began allowing James to occupy the half-second where commitment became direction. The change was subtle enough to deny if named and obvious enough to alter the room.

Košice stopped being a place where they trained together.

It became a place where the shape of the team began to reveal itself.

Mornings started before light. Cold-water immersion in metal drums behind the mill. Forty minutes on the bag until wrists swelled and shoulders numbed. Weapons stripped blindfolded. Route memorization. Timed entry drills through dead industrial corridors and tram depots where broken glass and mirrored surfaces turned every movement into an argument between sight and reflection. Meals came irregularly and without comfort. Sleep, when it came, arrived as a technical concession rather than rest.

On the sixth morning, while James was cleaning carbon fouling from the feed ramp of his sidearm, Torres looked up from the PhantomNet console and said, "You know what gets people killed?"

No one answered. It wasn't the first time he had used the room like an audience.

"Trust," Torres said, adjusting a spectral line on the display with one fingertip. "Not fast. That would be merciful. Trust kills slow."

The screen glow reflected faintly in his eyes.

Luka didn't even glance up from the whetstone in his hand. Kyra sat near the stove, rolling a cigarette without looking at any of them.

Torres kept going. "That's why I follow signal, not people. Signal degrades. People improvise."

"Unless it doesn't," James said.

Torres didn't look at him.

"Then you're reading it wrong."

He isolated a faint burst of chatter and let it sharpen into something almost intelligible before collapsing it into noise. The movement pleased him in a way he would have denied if asked.

"Loyalty's just another uniform," he said. "Easy to wear. Easier to be buried in."

Luka snorted once, which in him was close to laughter.

"You saying you don't trust us?" James asked.

Torres finally looked at him then, one brow lifting just enough to suggest insult at the simplicity of the question.

"I'm saying I trust everyone exactly as far as failure keeps them honest."

Kyra struck a match, lit the cigarette, and said nothing.

The routines continued.

Bus terminals. Abandoned factories. Ghost checkpoints along the industrial corridor. Night movement through the woods outside the city where the frost turned every breath visible and every visible thing into a problem to be solved.

Days folded over each other until James could no longer say which drill had happened when, only that he knew the routes, the pressure points, the timing windows, the sound of Luka's weight on concrete versus Kyra's, the hum of the server room behind the wall when Torres was working late, the exact position of the stove pipe shadow at 03:00.

That was how the team settled.

Not through closeness. Through repetition severe enough to substitute for it.

Mac arrived in the eighth week.

No advance notice preceded him. No ritual of introduction. No Márton standing in the doorway with that deliberate blankness he used whenever he wanted an arrival to feel like instruction rather than event. There was only the growl of an engine outside, the van door opening, and a man stepping down into the cold with the air of someone who had already assessed the place before crossing its threshold.

He was younger than Luka and older than James, pale in the way some men went pale from lack of sun and others from surviving too much fluorescent light. His hair was cut short enough to deny vanity but not identity. A thin seam of scar tissue ran from the edge of his left ear into his collar and disappeared there, too deliberate in its line to be accidental and too old to be recent. His file, when James saw it later, contained less than it should have: no anchor points, no stable biography. Just a name: Mac.

No first name, no middle initial, no past tense.

Torres read the file over James's shoulder and said, "Insurance policy," then tossed the paper back on the table like it had failed to entertain him.

Luka said nothing, but James noticed that he watched Mac the way one tradesman watched another—without warmth, without hostility, but with respect for visible competence when it presented itself honestly.

Kyra observed him once, briefly—just long enough to register something—then returned her attention to the map. The glance gave nothing away. If she registered anything unusual, she did not offer it.

Mac, for his part, behaved as if nothing in the room required adjustment.

He was not friendly. But neither was he withdrawn. He moved through the safehouse with a confidence that bordered on ease without tipping into performance. That should have made him easier to absorb than he was.

Instead, James felt something in him resist.

Mac did not move like a new variable inside an established team.

He moved like he was checking whether the team matched the version he had already been given.

James noticed it first in drills.

Mac never looked uncertain.

Not because he masked it, but because nothing in his movement suggested it had been there to begin with.

No delay. No correction. No visible adjustment under pressure. He moved like he already knew the outcome.

During a timed extraction exercise through a half-collapsed maintenance structure, Torres fed route changes through the earpieces in staggered sequence to test how quickly the team could reorient under degraded signal conditions. Luka adjusted with the same heavy competence he brought to everything. James recalculated on the move and made the turn. Kyra had already shifted before the cue had fully landed.

Mac reached the alternate exit point before Torres finished transmitting it.

Torres pulled the earpiece from one ear and said, "That's cute."

Mac only shrugged. "You were obvious."

Torres looked offended at a level that bordered on personal violation.

"Obvious?" he said. "You want obvious, I'll show you obvious."

Later, while Luka was resetting the course, Torres muttered to James, "He's full of shit."

"Maybe," James said.

Torres leaned back in the chair and looked through the glass toward the yard where Mac was smoking beside the wire fence.

"Maybe?" he said. "That man bleeds confidence like it's cologne. I've known three types like that. The first are idiots. The second are liars. The third are the kind you really don't want to owe anything."

"And which one is he?"

Torres considered this for a moment longer than he should have needed.

"That," he said, "is what I don't like."

Luka admired him almost immediately.

Not openly. Luka did not deal in open admiration. But he began choosing Mac for the heavier drills, the uglier routes, the tasks where improvisation under force mattered more than clean technical execution. Mac met him there every time. When Luka hit, Mac absorbed and redirected rather than contesting power where it didn't need to be contested. When obstacles changed, he changed with them without ever seeming hurried.

"He's useful," Luka said once, which in Luka's vocabulary was almost praise.

James watched Mac work and kept returning to the same problem: usefulness should have produced familiarity faster than it did. Instead, the better Mac performed, the less James felt he understood the logic underneath it.

Once, in a mock hostage recovery through an unlit service lane, Mac collapsed the corridor using nothing but signal tape, chalk marks, and a slingshot. The angle shouldn't have worked. The light fixture he targeted should have shattered, flashed, or failed unpredictably.

Instead, it went dark in one clean drop.

No burst. No shower of glass. No wild spark.

Just absence where illumination had been.

The hostage courier panicked at once, turning into the dark instead of through it. Mac was already moving before the fear fully registered, not calming him so much as intercepting the mistake and redirecting it into the only path left open. By the time James reached the end of the lane, the exercise had already been solved.

Not dramatically.

Correctly.

That was what remained with him afterward—not the cleverness of the improvised tool, but the texture of the solution. It did not feel inventive. It felt repeated. As if Mac had arrived at it before they saw it.

James told himself that was only style.

He did not entirely believe it.

It happened two days after the extraction drill.

Luka had set up a loose sparring rotation without calling it one, the kind of unspoken agreement that emerged when a team stopped needing instruction to test itself.

Mac watched for a while before stepping forward.

"Your turn," he said, nodding toward Kyra.

She didn't look up from where she was tightening the wrap around her wrist.

"I'm not in the rotation."

Mac smiled slightly. Not amused—interested.

"That wasn't the question."

She finished the wrap, flexed her hand once, then stood.

"I heard you."

And stepped past him.

Mac didn't move out of her path.

"Come on," he said, tone light, almost conversational. "You don't get to sit out and still be the best in the room."

Kyra stopped.

Not fully—just enough to acknowledge the obstruction without granting it weight.

"I'm not interested," she said.

Then continued walking.

Mac shifted again, this time placing himself more deliberately in front of her. His shadow fell across her boots.

Not aggressive.
But no longer casual.

"Everyone's interested," he said. "They just decide when."

Kyra looked at him then.

Just enough.

"Move."

There was no edge in it. No escalation.

Which made it harder to push against.

Mac held for a second longer than he should have.

Then stepped back.

"Later," he said.

Kyra didn't respond.

She moved past him without contact, without acknowledgment, and took her place near the edge of the yard, lighting a cigarette.

Torres let out a quiet breath through his nose.

"Bold strategy," he said. "Try to out-weird the only person here who doesn't need to be understood."

Mac ignored him.

Luka watched the entire exchange without intervening, his expression unchanged, but his attention fixed more precisely now.

James felt the shift before he understood it.

Not tension exactly.
Misalignment.

Mac turned back toward Kyra.

"Now?" he said.

She didn't turn.

The cigarette burned steadily between her fingers.

"No."

Mac took a step closer.

This time, there was no pretense of casualness.

"Then when?"

Kyra exhaled smoke into the cold air.

"Not today."

Mac moved again—close enough now that the space between them stopped being neutral.

"Seems like a pattern," he said.

That was when James stepped in.

His shoulder squared without thinking.

"Let it go," he said, positioning himself just off Mac's shoulder, not blocking, not confronting, but present enough to interrupt the line between them.

Mac glanced at him.

Measured.

"Didn't realize you were speaking for her."

"I'm not," James said. "I'm telling you it's done."

A pause.

Mac's attention shifted—not to James, but past him.

To Kyra.

She hadn't moved.
Hadn't turned.
Hadn't acknowledged either of them.

Which meant she didn't need to.

Mac looked back at James.
Then stepped away.

"Your call," he said.

The tone didn't carry concession.
Just adjustment.

Mac stepped back first.

Not far. Just enough to remove himself from the line between them.

The brush of air lingered a fraction longer.

Luka said something—James didn't catch it. The rotation shifted. Movement resumed.

Kyra didn't look at either of them.

She finished the cigarette, dropped it, and ground it into the frozen dirt with the heel of her boot. Then she turned and walked inside.

No acknowledgment.
No pause.

Just gone.

James stayed where he was.

The cold had settled into his hands without him noticing.

Mac moved past him on the way back to the center of the yard, close enough that their shoulders almost touched. Not accidental.

"Next time," Mac said, not looking at him.

James didn't answer.

He watched the door Kyra had disappeared through until it closed, then longer than it needed to.

By the time he stepped back into the rotation, something had shifted.

And he couldn't tell if stepping in had stopped anything or marked him.

At night, Mac slept less than anyone except Torres, and unlike Torres, he never looked tired enough to pay for it. Twice James found him in the safehouse kitchen drinking water in the dark, standing still enough that at first glance he looked like part of the room made upright. Once he looked up and said, "You always move this quietly?"

James replied, "Only when someone else is awake."

Mac smiled at that, but the smile did not quite reach the rest of him.

Another night, James found him kneeling by the stove with a blade in his hand, carving into the concrete floor.

The marks were small and careful. At first glance they looked almost childish, loose curves and simple cuts, the kind of thing that might have meant nothing if spacing had not betrayed intention. James stood there long enough to count twelve before he realized he was counting them at all.

"What are those?" he asked.

Mac did not stop carving. Dust gathered along the edge of each cut.

"Tombstones."

The answer came so evenly that James could not tell whether it had been prepared in advance or required no preparation at all.

"For who?"

Mac paused just long enough to suggest he had heard the question. Then he resumed.

"Depends who's asking."

James watched a little longer. The marks did not form language. They did not need to. Meaning lived in the fact that Mac was making them at all, in the consistency of the cuts, in the way the blade returned to nearly the same depth each time as if preserving proportion mattered.

James had the brief, unwelcome thought that the marks were not being made in memory of something—
but in preparation for something that hadn't happened yet.

He looked away once, toward the stove pipe, toward the damp shadow gathered in the upper corner of the room, toward anything that wasn't the floor. When he looked back, the count no longer felt stable. There were still twelve. He was almost sure there were still twelve. But the spacing had changed, or he thought it had, and the uncertainty irritated him.

That was not proof.
But it was enough to remain.

The routines continued.

Morning runs through the industrial corridor. Entry work. Signal degradation drills. Cold-weather movement. Weapons maintenance. Torres flicking through layers of PhantomNet noise with the contempt of a man who believed every system failed only because people touched it. Luka building respect through impact.

Kyra remaining observant and apparently indifferent, neither warmer toward Mac nor colder, though James noticed once that when Mac entered a room, her eyes found him before they returned to whatever they had been doing.

Not suspicion exactly, but not nothing.

James kept noticing small things.

Mac arrived at doors a fraction before instructions changed. He carried too little visible frustration for a man still learning a new team. He never asked a question whose answer might reveal ignorance. He volunteered just enough to be useful and never enough to become legible. When Márton was present, Mac deferred in ways that looked correct without ever feeling sincere. When Márton was absent, Mac occupied space more fully, as if some internal margin widened in private.

None of it constituted evidence.

Taken individually, each thing dissolved under scrutiny. Together, they accumulated.

One morning, alone again in the industrial corridor, James retraced the route without meaning to. The glass towers held their reflections exactly where they should. The turns aligned. The signal markers remained where Torres had embedded them. The surface of the system looked intact.

That was what made it worse.

Because whatever had been moving just ahead of him was still there, just beyond the reach of being caught cleanly in thought or sight.

And it was not slowing down.

If anything, it was learning his pace.

Chapter 13: The Shadow Street
Košice, Slovakia

Live operations didn't announce themselves.

The protest was real—angry chants, banners scrawled in spray paint, boots hammering pavement.

Somewhere inside it, a courier flagged by both the SVR and the SBU was waiting to be pulled out.

The courier stood too still.

James knew it immediately—posture squared while everyone else swayed, eyes tracking the crowd too cleanly.

Objective said extraction. His gut said bait.

The shadow team revealed itself in fragments, not form.

James felt it before he saw it—a ripple moving against the grain of the march—boots striking too evenly, shoulders too square. Protesters swayed and surged, but these men cut through the current like stone. He caught the cadence next—clipped Russian, maybe Ukrainian. Too short to be certain. Words pared to stubs, each syllable knifed clean and fed through earpieces hidden under scarves. Not shouts, not chants, but commands.

The skin along his arms tightened.

Then the rifles came up, suppressors already threaded, barrels angled low, meant to control, steady enough to kill if someone whispered the word. Metal flashed once.

Non-lethal rounds cracked overhead, beanbags and gas canisters, loud enough to fracture the protest and scatter the students. Panic was camouflage, and the shadow team moved inside it like blades through water.

James opened his mouth too late; the cordon was already sealing.

Kyra was gone.
Her movement cut clean through the crowd.

She ripped Torres' laser badge from the uplink case and clipped it to her coat like it had always belonged there. No hesitation, no wasted motion. She pulled a surplus medic's jacket from the van, shoved it onto the courier, and moved forward as if the street were hers.

Her posture wasn't bluff. It was a dare: *Shoot if you're ready to pay for it.*

James felt the air tighten, every nerve firing at once. For ten seconds the street balanced on a trigger.

For an instant, his vision skewed—the crowd dissolving at the edges, her figure sharpening beyond proportion. His chest tightened, breath gone shallow.

And then—

A stun round hit her square in the chest—hard enough to drop anyone else.

She kept moving.

She and Luka dragged the courier through smoke and fractured bodies, into the van, into the night.

The courier never spoke—not in Russian, not in Ukrainian, not in anything James could place.

By the time Kyra shoved him onto the cot, blood already leaked from his gums. His jaw worked once, twice, then locked. The sharp almond stink followed.

Cyanide.

Capsule crushed between his teeth.

Kyra swore under her breath, harsher than any curse. "Blaka muha."

Nothing more.

She pulled the blanket over his face like closing a file.

James felt the bottom drop out. Objective achieved. Asset dead.

Later, when the protest had burned out and the safehouse settled back into silence, James replayed it.

Ten seconds where she had walked into rifles that should have ended her, a borrowed badge swinging at her chest, daring the line to break against her instead.

He forced her onto the diagnostic rig. Adhesive leads pressed to her ribs, a cuff clipped around her wrist.

The readouts cycled—too clean.

At the console, he pulled the telemetry from the op. The trace held until he stripped the filters away.

Then he saw it.

A gap.

0.8 seconds.

Not weak. Not degraded. Gone.

Then a perfect return.

James turned the monitor toward her, voice low.
"Kyra… your heart stopped."

She gave a quick wink, peeling off the leads.
"It's fine. I'm not weak like the Americans."

He caught her wrist before she could pull free.
Her pulse was steady under his fingers.

"Don't joke. This isn't nothing. You can't just—"

Her eyes snapped to his—cold, immediate.
"You think this scares me?"

Her voice didn't rise. It hardened.
"I was trained to go longer than that."

A beat.

"Days without food. Hours without air."

Her gaze pierced him.

"Long enough for the body to stop asking."

Then, quieter—

"And come back anyway."

For a fraction of a second, something broke through. Not pride. Not defiance. Something older.

"I wasn't twenty-five or thirty," she said.
"I was seventeen."

The number hit clean.

His stomach turned. His chest tightened, pulse spiking against something that suddenly felt untested.

His grip loosened.

She pulled free—fracture sealed.

"You see absence," she said, almost amused.
"I see endurance. Learn the difference."

Her eyes sharpened.

"Touch me again, Rourke."

A beat.

"I fucking dare you."

The cuff slipped from her fingers and hit the floor.

The trace still glowed on the monitor—
0.8 seconds of silence no system could explain.

They weren't debriefed.
No praise. No reprimand.

Just a single card left where someone had placed it, edges damp from the stove's breath:

Provisional status lifted. OBLIVION ACTIVE.

No signature, no seal, just verdict.

An hour later, the uplink pinged once, a green diode flashing against Torres' face. He muted it without looking up.

When the buffer finished bleeding down, all that remained was a set of coordinates. No origin header, no context, just numbers that would delete themselves in eighty-seven seconds.

Torres scribbled them on the corner of a ration box. By the time he slid it across the table, the signal was gone, purged. A faint smear of ink bled into the cardboard, edges blurred where Torres's hand had pressed too fast. James stared at it longer than the numbers themselves. Proof the order had existed and was already vanishing.

Luka frowned at the scrap. "Not Márton?"

Torres didn't answer. Just tapped the coordinates with an ink-stained finger.

"Orders don't care who writes them," he said.

James stared at the digits until they blurred, the unease settling in like frost.

The ink had already begun to bleed into the cardboard.

By the time he looked up, there was nothing left to trace back.

CHAPTER 14: CLEAN TRAPS

Assignments didn't wait.

The next one came a week later.

Asset: Petr Dovhaluk. Codename NIGHTSHADE. French intelligence, embedded under commercial cover. He'd moved too close to a GRU logistics shell in Kharkiv and gone dark near the Slovak–Hungarian border.

If the Russians had him, it was bad enough.

If NATO learned how he'd been operating, it would be worse.

Objective: Intercept. Extract. Neutralize shadows.

James, Kyra, Luka deployed. Torres ran mobile comms from a bakery van strung with antennae. Mac rode along—silent, watching.

They prepped three days. Grease-stained coveralls, forged IDs, van paperwork. Goodbye rituals whispered to mirrors. By the time they crossed the border, names no longer mattered.

The gas station sat empty at 02:14.
Rust moaned in the wind. No heat, no signatures. Too clean.

Kyra signaled a wide sweep. James left, Luka right, Kyra center. Inside, a bulb swayed. Dovhaluk sat zip-tied, bruised.

"Trap," James said instantly.

Kyra didn't pause. She cut him free and pressed a patch to his temple—too clean, nails unbroken, no ligature swell. Staged.

Then the lights cut and a flashbang rolled.

The world went white and didn't come back right, pressure slamming behind his eyes.

Sound dropped out. His vision fractured, shapes dissolving into blur and afterimage.

He hit the tile hard, shoulder screaming, lungs locked. For a moment he wasn't sure if he was moving or if the floor itself was tilting beneath him.

Shapes resolved. Kyra was already moving—low, fluid, every angle precise. Rolling through the flash, weapon raised, firing clean. No hesitation, no disorientation. Surgical where he was still blind.

James pivoted blind, two-count breath, and returned fire by instinct.

Muzzle flashes stuttered in the dark. Two shooters. Suppressed guns.

Luka intercepted one, snapping bone, body collapsing.

Kyra rolled, fired. Two shots. Clean. Second target staggered, retreated.

Then—
a third figure lunged from the dark.

The man folded mid-step, throat bursting open in a spray James hadn't caused. The shot barely registered. The pop was there, but muffled into almost nothing, as if the suppressor had swallowed the sound.

Blood slicked the tile in sheets, pooling fast, the body twitching against its own shadow.

James didn't fire. There hadn't been time.

He didn't turn, but he knew exactly where Mac had been standing—no angle for the shot.

They cleared the rest in seconds. Luka snapped one down. Kyra moved like a blade through smoke. Torres's voice snapped in their ears, sharp and live:

"Trail north. Bakery van five minutes. Don't argue."

No Jersey sarcasm now, just cutthroat urgency.

At the safehouse, silence pressed louder than the firefight.

The angles didn't add up, Luka too far left, Kyra mid-roll, Torres nowhere near the line. Yet the man had dropped clean, precise, as if erased by someone who hadn't been there at all.

The blood was proof of the kill. The absence was louder, the proof of something else.

The gear thawed on racks, copper still sharp in the air. Luka crossed to the stove, rubbing his hands for heat. His boot scuffed the corner, pausing over the marks Mac had carved.

Petr sat slumped in a chair near the wall, patch still taped to his temple, wrists free but eyes down. Alive. Breathing. Already ghosted.

They didn't keep him long.

On the console, Torres's rig chirped once, sharp, then silence. A burst transmission. He rolled back in his chair, tapping keys until the packet spilled open across the screen: numbers, clipped phrases, all in the terse shorthand of higher channels.

HANDOFF PROTOCOL: NIGHTSHADE.
Authentication string: DELTA–SEVEN–GOLF.
Custody transfer: 0430. Verification window ±3 minutes.

Torres read it twice, jaw tightening. "Orders," he said flatly. "They're coming for him."

James's eyes stayed on Petr, alive, present—but already being written out.

Headlights cut across the shutters, right on time.

A black van rolled up, no insignia, no plates. Two men stepped in, plain clothes too neat, clipped French layered with American vowels.

Torres called the string. "Delta–Seven."

The taller one answered without hesitation. "Golf."

The exchange was clean. Perfect.

They didn't identify themselves. They didn't have to.

Petr rose on cue. James caught his eye—a last attempt to hold him there. Petr met it for half a second, then let it go.

Instinctively, James's eyes flicked to Kyra across the room— alive, calm, but carrying her own silence no one else seemed to notice.

Petr stepped between the two men and was gone.

The door shut. Tires ground away on wet gravel.

Torres exhaled, muttering, "Guess Paris wants their mess back in a bag."

Luka said nothing, just kept working the rifle down to its last screw.

James stared at the empty chair, the faint crease where Petr's weight had been. Already the mission logs would mark him *exfiltrated*. Already the paperwork would write him out. NIGHTSHADE had never existed.

The absence weighed more than a body on the floor.

Paris had closed the ledger on him. Washington would read it as loyalty. Moscow would call it proof.

Luka crouched, thumb running across one of the tiny grooves. "Graves?" he muttered.

Torres glanced over from the console, smirk gone flat. "Not graves. Coordinates. Graves don't line up in grid squares."

Chapter 15: The Red Shadow
Košice, Slovakia

"And behold, a shadow rode upon the wind, and no man could mark her passing but by the blood left behind."

"If you see the knife too late, assume it wanted you to."
— Márton, Sigma Black Marginalia

Something had moved ahead of them.

Two days after NIGHTSHADE, Kyra handed James a folder.

No warning. No context. Just paper.

Inside, stills of their extraction. Angles that shouldn't exist, too high for a phone and too steady for a panicked bystander. Each frame knew their route, their cadence, their fallback.

By the middle of the stack, James felt his stomach tighten. Whoever took these hadn't been watching them. They had been mapping them.

The last page hit harder. It wasn't a photo at all. It was a satellite pull, wide enough to capture the block and sharp enough to frame the safehouse roofline. Time-stamped. Last night. No caption. No logo.

She set the folder in his hands.
The decision had already been made.

Every page mapped their vulnerabilities.

Her eyes were darker than usual, not wary or guilty, but distant.

"It begins," she said. Her voice carried low and even.

His fingers tightened on the paper before he realized they had.

Her shadow cut across the glass as she left, longer than her frame.

Then the door closed.

Luka sat alone in the glow of PhantomNet's replay. Frame by frame, NIGHTSHADE flickered across the screen.

Suppressed fire. A muffled pop. Kyra cutting low.

Then—blur.

A muzzle flash. The third shooter dropped from a throat shot that folded him mid-stride.

The frame stuttered, skipping like static trying to breathe. Blood slicked the tiles where he fell, pooling fast.

For a frame—red hair.

He froze the frame. The image locked with a faint click.

Everyone knew the stories.

But stories didn't leave residue like this.

The system flagged it as error. Luka knew better. The system hadn't faltered. It had flinched. And in that hesitation, it revealed her.

He lit a cigarette, smoke leaking slow from his nose. "The feed didn't blur," he said. "It froze. Same moment that third shooter dropped with his throat blown open."

James frowned. "Froze?"

Luka's gaze shifted, uneasy. He leaned closer, his whisper thinning to almost nothing, like the walls themselves might hear:

"The Red Ghost."

Luka crushed the cigarette against the wall and walked on without looking back.

James stayed in the glow of the monitors, running the sequence again in his head. Suppressed shot, precise placement, body folding mid-stride. Too clean to be chance. Luka's ghost or not, the kill had been real.

Absence had always been Oblivion's currency.

This felt like something else.

If you saw it, it was already too late.

ACT III – THE EDGE OF THE SIGNAL

"Detection is easy.
Interpretation is fatal.
The moment the pattern recognizes you—
the hunt has already begun."

CHAPTER 16: UNSPOKEN NAME
Košice, Slovakia

"Let everything happen to you: beauty and terror.
Just keep going. No feeling is final."
— RAINER MARIA RILKE

Their next safehouse was in Košice's outer district. It was the kind of building that had once been factory, then warehouse, now nothing at all. Too forgotten to warrant patrols, too ordinary to deserve maps.

The safehouse wasn't empty.

James registered it before the door had fully opened, a subtle displacement in the air that didn't belong to a first entry—the faint trace of perfume layered over dust and old wood, precise and out of place. It was enough to shift his attention before his eyes confirmed it.

Irina stood near the far wall, one shoulder resting lightly against the frame as if she had been there long enough to settle into it. She didn't straighten when they entered. She didn't need to.

"Late," she said.

There was no accusation in it, only a statement of fact.

Luka acknowledged her with a single nod, Torres barely glanced in her direction as he moved past them toward the console, and James stepped fully into the room, his gaze moving once across the corners out of habit rather than concern.

Kyra didn't pause.

She crossed the space directly, her movement unbroken, her attention fixed, and when she stopped in front of Irina there was a subtle change in her posture—not softness, not relaxation, but a release of tension that suggested recognition rather than defense.

"Irina."

Irina's expression shifted almost imperceptibly, something in her eyes sharpening and easing at the same time.

"Still alive," she replied.

Kyra's mouth curved slightly. "Efficient."

Irina exhaled through her nose, the sound close enough to laughter to pass for it if someone wasn't paying attention.

"Come on," she said, already turning toward the adjoining room. "Before they start pretending they don't need supervision."

Kyra followed without hesitation, and the door closed behind them with a soft, controlled click.

***

The second room was smaller, warmer, the air held closer to the walls as if it had not been disturbed as often. A single bulb hung overhead, casting a steady, unflattering light that left no place for shadow to gather.

Irina sat first, folding one leg beneath her with an ease that suggested familiarity rather than comfort, and gestured for Kyra to take the chair opposite her.

"You disappear for weeks," Irina said, watching her with quiet attention, "and then you show up like nothing changed."

Kyra settled into the chair without shifting its position, her posture balanced, her hands resting loosely in her lap.

"Things moved," she said.

Irina studied her for a moment longer than the statement required, as though measuring the distance between what had been said and what had not.

"Oblivion's tightening," she said at last. "More oversight, less tolerance for deviation. Márton's been pulling the lines closer than usual."

Kyra's gaze flickered once in acknowledgment, not surprise.

"He's not wrong."

"No," Irina agreed. "He's not."

The silence that followed wasn't empty, but it wasn't heavy either.

Irina shifted slightly, letting some of the tension bleed out of her shoulders.

"So," she said, tone lighter now, though not careless, "the new team."

Kyra's eyes moved—not toward the door, but toward the space it occupied, as if the others existed more clearly in absence than in sight.

"They function."

Irina's brow lifted a fraction. "That's not what I asked."

Kyra didn't respond.

Irina smiled, patient, as if she had expected exactly that.

"There's always one," she said. "The one that doesn't behave the way the rest do."

Kyra's expression didn't change, but something in her stillness shifted just enough to register.

"James," she said.

Irina leaned back slightly, considering that answer with interest rather than surprise.

"That was quick."

"He's… good," Kyra said.

Irina's head tilted. "That's rare."

"Yes."

The word landed without weight, but it didn't dissolve.

Irina let it sit, then shifted her focus just enough to move the conversation without breaking it.

"And Luka?" she asked, the hint of something more human threading through her tone now. "He looks like he could break a wall by accident."

Kyra's gaze returned to her fully.

"He doesn't do anything by accident."

Irina smiled, this time with a trace of genuine amusement.

"That's unfortunate," she said. "I'd let him try."

Kyra didn't react, at least not in any way that would register conventionally, but the absence of response lingered long enough for Irina to notice it.

"Right," Irina said quietly. "Still you."

Another pause, softer this time.

Irina leaned forward slightly, her voice lowering without becoming secretive.

"You feel it?" she asked.

Kyra didn't ask what she meant.

"Yes."

Irina nodded once, the confirmation mattering more than the content.

"Good," she said. "Then it's not isolated."

Kyra's gaze locked with hers.

"Something is ahead of the system," Irina continued, choosing her words carefully, not because she lacked certainty but because certainty didn't fit what she was describing. "We don't have language for it yet."

Kyra didn't answer.

She didn't need to.

Irina sat back again, letting the conversation release rather than resolve.

"Try not to break this one," she said after a moment, the edge of humor returning. "We're running low."

Kyra didn't move at first.

Then something in her posture shifted—subtle, but wrong. Her shoulders drew in a fraction, her breath catching as if the rhythm had been interrupted and hadn't yet found its way back.

Her gaze slipped, not unfocused but displaced, fixed somewhere beyond the room.

Break.

The word didn't stay in the present.

It didn't belong to James.

It pulled something older.

The moment before it was taken from her.

Kyra stood too quickly.

The chair scraped softly against the floor, the sound sharper than it should have been in the small room. For a second, she didn't move after that, as if the motion had carried her out of sequence.

"Kyra—"

No response.

Kyra's breathing had gone shallow, controlled by force rather than instinct. Her hands curled slightly at her sides, not into fists, but into something close to it.

Irina's expression changed, the humor gone instantly.

"Oh god…," she said, already rising. "I didn't mean—"

Kyra's head moved once. Not denial. Not acceptance. Just motion.

Irina stepped forward and pulled her in.

Kyra didn't return it at first. Her body held rigid, the contact registering without being answered. Then, slowly, something gave—not comfort, not release, just allowance.

Her hands lifted and settled against Irina's back, light but certain. Irina held her there without tightening, the room staying quiet around them. When Kyra stepped back a few seconds later, her eyes were wet, the shift still present—not in one place, but across all of her, control reassembled, not clean.

"I'm fine," she said.

Irina didn't argue.

"I know," she said.

Another pause, heavier now.

Irina exhaled once, more careful this time.

"Still," she said quietly, "don't let them take another one from you."

Kyra's gaze steadied on her.

"They don't take," she said.

Her voice had returned.

"They choose."

Irina didn't answer.

When Kyra stepped back into the main room, they were still settling in.

Gear lay open across the tables, cases unlatched, cables trailing where Torres had begun pulling the system together without finishing it. Luka stood near the window, not looking out so much as checking angles, the cigarette unlit between his fingers. James was at one of the cots, breaking down his rifle with the same measured precision, though a second kit remained unopened at his feet.

Nothing had resolved yet.

Which made the difference harder to place.

Kyra crossed the room without comment, not taking a seat, not engaging, simply re-entering the space as it was still being defined.

James's hands continued their work on the rifle, but his attention shifted anyway.

Her eyes caught the light as she passed—blue, clear, but not quite the same. The edges were faintly red, moisture still there—contained, but visible. Something in her expression hadn't settled back into place.

He looked away before it became acknowledgment, the motion small enough to pass as habit.

He let the moment pass.

The rifle rested in his hands, the weight familiar, the sequence of motion reasserting itself—strip, check, reset. The room filled back in around him in pieces: Torres at the console, Luka at the window, the unfinished sprawl of gear still waiting to be ordered.

He took it in once.

That was when the gap became clear.

Mac was gone.

No door sound. No interruption in the air. No sign of movement that marked when he had left.

Just subtraction.

Torres paused mid-adjustment, fingers resting lightly on a dial before he turned it back a fraction.

"Something dropped," he muttered. "Signal jitter… then nothing."

He didn't look concerned, only mildly irritated, as if the system had failed to behave properly.

"Probably nothing."

Luka said nothing.

Kyra's gaze moved once, briefly, to the space where Mac had been.

Not searching. Confirming.

Then it moved on.

Around them, the room continued to take shape—equipment settling into place, routines beginning to form—but something in it no longer aligned.

It would function.

But not the way it had been meant to.

Chapter 17: The Quiet Between
Košice, Slovakia

"What breaks a cell isn't fire or force—it's the silence after laughter fades.
That's where the fault lines begin."
— Internal Memo (Oblivion, Redacted Debrief)

The quiet hadn't felt wrong at the time.

It only resolved after something was missing.

The stove exhaled a slow warmth, ribbons of woodsmoke curling through the rafters. The safehouse smelled of resin and ash, of walls that had endured too many winters. Rituals filled the spaces fire couldn't reach.

Luka

Luka sharpened blades before breakfast—always before, never after. The sound was a rasping metronome, steady enough that James sometimes woke to it before dawn. Each stroke ended with a pause, as if the edge itself demanded acknowledgment.

A photo of a wife long buried lived in his shaving kit. He unfolded it carefully, the corners creased soft from years of touch. Once, James saw him wipe a bead of oil from the blade onto the photo's edge before closing it away. Blessing, or penance.

Luka's silence wasn't emptiness. It was mourning disciplined into routine. He sang under his breath in Serbian, old verses pressed flat into habit. James never asked what they meant. Some silences weren't meant to be broken.

The rasp of steel on stone pulled him backward, to mornings when he was small enough to watch from the bedroom doorway. His father, police blues folded sharp, accouterments lined on the bed in the same order every day. Badge, cuffs, sidearm. Each lifted, tested, placed on his body like parts of a prayer. No words, only ritual—silence worn into armor. James remembered the hush in the house, how even his mother never interrupted.

Now, decades later, the rhythm of Luka's blades carried the same weight.

That morning, Luka's hand slipped, just once. The blade kissed his thumb, a shallow line of red against calloused skin. He didn't flinch. He only pressed the wound into the wood, leaving a dark fingerprint where others might have cleaned it. A mark that felt deliberate.

TORRES

Torres filled his quiet with static. Headphones clamped on, antennae soldered from scavenged scraps, sketchbooks spread across the table. Pages thick with wireframe towers and cryptic binary notations.

He claimed it was just noise, ways to keep his hands busy. But sometimes the towers he drew took on shapes that weren't buildings. Curved like bones. Angled like something designed to resonate, not shelter.

James asked once what they were. Torres smirked. "Dreams I can't afford." But the smirk faltered, just enough for James to notice.

At night, Torres's headphones leaked faint whispers—bursts of encrypted chatter, caught from frequencies no one else tracked. James wasn't sure Torres listened for meaning anymore. He heard fragments: voices breaking into static, numbers repeated until they blurred.

It pulled at something old. As a boy, he would sit by the window when his father came off shift, watching the patrol car lights spin across the street. Red, blue, red, blue—seeming random, always on the edge of a pattern he was sure he could solve if he stared long enough. They were signal disguised as chaos, and he could never quite crack them.

Torres's signals carried that same cadence. Not random. Not safe. Patterns that seemed just shy of revealing themselves, then vanished back into static.

That evening, Torres slammed his notebook shut when Mac entered the room. Too fast. Too defensive. The edge of a sketch tore.

The glimpse was brief, but James's body read it faster than his head. A circle. Too precise for doodle, too sharp for dream. Not a sketch. A signal.

IRINA

Irina didn't take up space the way the others did.

She settled into it.

Blonde hair pulled back loosely, never the same way twice, a few strands always slipping free no matter how often she tucked them behind her ear. Blue eyes that held a moment longer than most people were comfortable with, not challenging, just attentive—like she was already a step ahead of whatever you were about to say. She wasn't tall, but nothing about her felt small.

She moved through the safehouse without asking permission from it.

Medical kits repacked before anyone realized they'd been opened. Supplies redistributed with quiet efficiency, weight balanced across the room without drawing attention to the change. She tracked what they used without writing it down, her memory precise in ways that didn't need proving.

But she wasn't clinical about it.

Nothing she did needed checking twice.

She hummed sometimes while she worked—soft, tuneless, something she didn't seem aware of. Once, she laughed at something Torres muttered under his breath, not because it was particularly funny, but because she chose to find it that way.

It shifted the room when she did.

Luka noticed.

Not immediately, and not in a way he would have admitted, but the first time she crossed behind him and adjusted the angle of his bandage without a word, his hand stilled instead of pulling away.

She didn't apologize. Didn't explain.

Later, she set a second cup of tea near his elbow.

He hadn't asked for it.

She didn't look at him when she did.

"Drink it before it cools," she said, already turning away.

He did.

Neither of them mentioned it.

She noticed it all—
the way Torres shifted when a signal didn't resolve cleanly,
the way Luka favored his left side when he thought no one was looking,
the way James scanned exits even when seated.

She noticed Kyra, too.

But she treated her differently—not carefully, not cautiously, just… without expectation.

Like she understood that whatever Kyra was, it wasn't something that needed fixing.

Irina didn't fill the silence.

She changed it.

Not by breaking it, but by making it something the others didn't have to carry alone.

KYRA

Kyra moved through the stairwells without touching sound. She never touched the creaking middle step. Never brushed the wall where the plaster buckled. James thought of her less as avoiding sound than as rewriting it, bending silence into something alive.

It tugged at a memory: Christmas Eves, years ago, him sneaking from his room with the repurposed microscope light clutched in his hand. He'd tiptoe to the living room, heart hammering, scanning shadows for his parents' silhouettes.

The tree shimmered faint in the dark. He'd find the presents, count them, try not to breathe too loud, convinced the silence itself could betray him.

Kyra carried that same charge—the way silence wasn't absence but danger, wonder, and risk braided tight. She moved like she could still hear the floorboards warning her where not to step.

Once, he caught her on the roof, framed against the bruised horizon. She moved like shadow given shape, her hair pulled back tight against the wind. From below, she looked like part of the architecture—something the house itself was designed to hold.

Once, he climbed after her. She didn't turn, didn't startle, only asked: "Do you believe in echoes?"

James wasn't sure if she meant sound or memory. He said nothing, and she didn't press. She only stood there, eyes scanning a horizon that revealed nothing back.

He felt it in his chest—recognition without a memory to match it.

MAC

And Mac.

Mac had never settled into the room the way the others did.

At the time, James thought it was preference.
Now it felt like positioning.

He never left anything where he found it.
Not enough to be noticed.
Just enough that something would be off later.

The house breathed with them—pipes ticking, rafters groaning in the night, floorboards shifting.

Luka left his mark in blood, pressed into wood where it would darken and stay. Torres hid his in the torn edge of a circle, a sketch slammed shut before anyone could name it.

Kyra carried hers in silence that bent the air around her, moving like the house had been built to let her pass unseen.

Different languages, same truth: the quiet between them wasn't holding the house together. It was prying it apart.

James lay awake listening to it, certain the silence would break—not with an attack from outside, but with a fracture from within.

And when it did, it wouldn't be loud.

It would be exact.

Chapter 18: Things We Can't Name
Košice, Slovakia

Relentless, Kyra moved with deliberate precision—every step measured, every pause controlled.

But sometimes—brief as static in signal—something cracked. The way her gaze locked too long on the leaking faucet. The way her fingers rested on a windowsill, as if testing how much of herself the world could be allowed to hold.

That night she didn't turn to him when she spoke. "Do you ever miss being human?"

James sat half-shadowed, hands quiet on the table. The question settled into him slower than he expected.

"I think I miss being seen as human…" he said, watching her breath fog the window where frost climbed in white veins.

She shifted then, voice thinner, sharper:
"You don't get to pretend you're the careful one."

"You move in like you've already decided," she continued, "and then you pull back like you didn't."

Her gaze cut to him now.

"Which is it?"

A beat.

"Because from here it looks like you're the one who can't decide what this is going to be."

James didn't answer immediately.
Because she wasn't wrong.

"I know exactly what it is," he said.

That surprised even him.

Kyra didn't move.

"Then why pull away?" she asked.

"Because I know what happens if I don't."

A shift.
Subtle.

But real.

Kyra's eyes narrowed—not in challenge, but in recalibration.

"And what happens?" she asked.

"It stops being something we can walk away from."

"And you think pulling away fixes that?" she asked.

"No."

A beat.

"It just delays it."

Silence again.

But not the same silence.

Kyra studied him—longer now, measuring something she hadn't expected to find.

"Maybe it's all of that," she said finally.

Her tone didn't soften, but it didn't cut the same way either.

"Maybe that's the point."

This time, he didn't look away.

The stillness between them thickened, heavy with what wasn't said.

"I don't test people I don't respect," Kyra added. Then her voice thinned, quieter, but not softer:

"But don't mistake respect for safety. I can fight beside someone, trust them with my life in the field—and still keep parts of myself locked away."

For a moment James swore she was choosing between versions of him—one she could let closer, and one she would keep forever at a distance.

Her eyes drilled into his.

"And you?" she asked. "Truth, or survival?"

He didn't answer. Couldn't decide.

She didn't wait. Her next words curled into the silence like a whisper meant to be dangerous, and desired.

"It's never what we see that breaks us. It's the things we can't name. Those are what leave scars."

James shifted a half-step closer. His hand twitched against the table, almost reaching for hers before restraint drew it back.

Kyra mirrored, slow, deliberate—as if proximity itself were a test. When his breath reached hers, she moved. One arm lifted, soft as a breath of silk, and came to rest on his shoulder. Her hand rested light, but it pinned him all the same. A weight that asked if he would move—or endure.

Her body brushed close, her steps curved behind him, slow, silent. He felt her breath near his neck, close enough to strike or to stay.

She leaned, her lips at his ear. The whisper was not question so much as a claim:

"Do you trust me?" she whispered.

"Yes." The word broke out raw, faster than he meant.

Her hand slid lower, every muscle under her palm tightening with the betrayal of want.

Her breath ticked his cheek once more, then she slipped past him—precision disguised as closeness—palming the loft's lamp to darkness. The room narrowed to pulse and outline. Below, a chair leg scraped against concrete; someone turned in a cot. They froze.

Kyra's hand found his, not tender—directive. She guided him backward, three steps to the ladder hidden in the rafters. No words. She climbed first, boots impossibly silent on wood, pausing at each rung like a metronome set to secrecy. James followed, matching her count.

At the hatch she waited, palm flat to the metal, reading the skin of the night the way others read weather.

She paused, listening to the pipes, the settling beams—mapping every sound the house could carry. Satisfied, she moved.

She slid the bolt with a breath's pressure. Cold shouldered in. City noise thinned to a high, distant wire. They spilled onto the roof, bodies low, profile broken against the vent stack.

Only when the hatch settled did she turn back to him, close enough that the cold couldn't find space between them. "Ten minutes," she said, like a clock she meant to break.

For a moment neither moved, as though the world itself was holding its breath to see who would break first.

James did.

Not with words, but with the shift of his body—turning enough to close the small distance she'd left, enough to let her scent fold around him. Rain, silk, and something sharper he couldn't name.

Kyra didn't retreat. She tilted her chin just enough that their faces nearly touched, a hair's breadth between collision and restraint.

Her hand slid from his shoulder to his chest, fingers splayed as though she could take his measure through the beat of his heart. The rhythm betrayed him—fast, unsteady.

Her mouth shifted—just enough to show she knew.

James caught her wrist, not to stop her, but to anchor himself. His grip was firm, her pulse steady under his thumb. Their eyes locked, both daring the other to pull away first.

Then she moved again, sudden, decisive. Her body pressed flush to his, and the sound in his chest wasn't discipline—it was the sharp exhale of a man unraveling.

Her breath slid across his jaw. "You never could stop reaching, could you?"

Her lips hovered a breath from his ear, words low and claiming. "You don't need to reach now, James. Stay."

The kiss wasn't careful.

It was impact—breath, heat, contact that stripped everything else away.

For a moment, there was no structure left to hold it.

She pressed harder, forcing him back step by step until the rooftop gravel dug into his shoulders. Her hand on his chest was firm, commanding, guiding him down. She straddled him in one fluid motion, pinning him with the same efficiency she would an enemy—only this time, the precision burned with fire.

"Respect won't save you."

The rhythm broke before it could settle.
Just enough to cross something neither of them could uncross.

When silence returned, it wasn't empty. It pressed close, crowded with what they'd risked.

James lay still beneath her, every part of him aware this was the dare she'd set—*you can't stop reaching, can you?* She had been right. And now she'd proved it.

He almost said something.

Stopped.

Because he already knew she wouldn't answer it.

He realized, not for the first time, that whatever this was— she would never stay for it.

James let his eyes close, only for a moment. Her weight against him was a truth he hadn't been trained to hold. The city below breathed in trams and sirens, the team below in murmured sleep, but up here the world had collapsed to pulse and silence.

Kyra's hand stilled, resting flat over his heartbeat. "This doesn't happen again."

The words cut sharper than he expected, even if he knew she meant them as defense. He caught her wrist again, gentler this time, his thumb brushing the inside where her pulse beat steady. "That's a lie," he murmured.

Her eyes flicked up, unreadable in the shadows. Then she shifted, rising from him in one smooth motion. By the time she stood, her hair had curtained her face again, armor falling back into place.

The house below reminded them silence was never theirs alone. A pipe groaned somewhere in the dark, metal shifting like a throat clearing. Boards flexed beneath unseen weight. The sound was ordinary, domestic—but here it landed like a warning. The safehouse was awake, listening, and their secret lived only in the inches of quiet they could still protect.

"Discipline," her tone colder now, like she was scolding herself as much as him. "Tomorrow, it's as if this never happened."

James sat up slowly, the night air colder where her warmth had been. He wanted to argue, to demand something more permanent than ten minutes carved from silence. But the look in her eyes warned him—this was the most she would allow, and maybe the most they could survive.

She stepped back to the edge of the roof, the city lights flaring against her outline like a weapon still sheathed.

She lingered, her gaze locked on him with a weight that promised memory, if not promise. Then she leaned close, her breath hot against his jaw, daring the air itself not to betray them. "Don't mistake closeness for safety," she whispered. "It never is." Then she turned, precise as ever, every trace of softness burned back into control.

James exhaled once, slow, his hands still trembling—proof discipline hadn't saved him this time, proof something more dangerous than any mission had already begun.

He knew it wouldn't last. He knew tomorrow discipline would smother it.

But tonight—

It was enough.

CHAPTER 19: MORNING

Early light edged into the safehouse without warmth.

The light was pale and indifferent, flattening the room rather than warming it, turning everything into edges and surfaces—readable, but not felt.

James was awake before he moved.

He lay still, eyes tracing the cracks in the ceiling. The night lingered—not as memory, but as a pressure that hadn't fully lifted. It sat just beneath his ribs, refusing to be named.

The roof.
The cold.
The way it had ended.

This doesn't happen again.

He exhaled once, steadying himself, and pushed upright before the thought could take shape beyond that.

By the time he stepped into the main room, the day had already arranged itself around the others.

Torres was seated at the table with a chipped ceramic mug and a disassembled comms unit spread out in front of him like an autopsy. Wires threaded between his fingers as he worked, coaxing signal out of something that resisted definition. A low hum filled the air, subtle but constant—the faint bleed of PhantomNet, like a second atmosphere layered over the room.

"Morning," Torres said without looking up, voice rough with sleep and static. "You look like gravity won."

James didn't respond. He wasn't sure the line deserved one.

Irina moved through the space with quiet purpose, gathering, replacing, resetting. Medical kits lay open along the counter, gauze folded and refolded into clean stacks, instruments wiped down with the kind of care that didn't draw attention to itself.

She didn't rush, but nothing about her movement suggested hesitation. The room adjusted around her without needing to be asked.

She glanced at James once, quick and precise, taking in what she needed, nothing more.

"The coffee's terrible," she said. "Drink it anyway."

He took the mug she slid toward him.

Luka stood near the window, one shoulder angled toward the frame, as if he needed the contact to stay anchored. The light caught along the line of his jaw, leaving the rest of him in shadow. His shirt hung open at the collar, the bandage beneath visible where it crossed his ribs.

Irina crossed behind him without breaking stride, her hand already moving before the moment could become a question. She adjusted the wrap with a practiced ease, tightening it just enough to matter.

"Try not to tear it open again," she said.

"I'll consider it," Luka replied, his voice low, almost absent.

She left a fresh strip of gauze within reach before moving on, not waiting for acknowledgment.

Kyra entered last.

Nothing in her movement suggested hesitation. Nothing in her expression carried over from the night before. Her hair was pulled back tighter now, every strand accounted for, her posture aligned in a way that made the room feel smaller without her needing to occupy more of it.

If there was anything left of the roof, it didn't exist here.

James felt her presence before he turned, the shift registering somewhere below thought.

He looked anyway.

Her eyes passed over him without stopping. Deliberate.

She moved to the table and leaned over Torres's shoulder, her attention settling on the faint green pulse of the display.

"Signal?" she asked.

"Unstable," Torres replied, adjusting a dial that didn't seem to change anything. "Lag spikes, intermittent dropouts. Could be terrain interference. Could be someone leaning on the line."

Kyra watched the screen for a moment longer than necessary, then straightened.

"Clean it," she said.

There was no edge in her tone. No emphasis. Just instruction.

Torres nodded once and returned to the work without comment.

James stood with the mug in his hand, aware of the space between them in a way that hadn't existed the day before. It wasn't distance. It was something more deliberate than that—something maintained.

Irina noticed.

She didn't interrupt it, didn't attempt to soften it, but her gaze moved once between them, slow and measured, as if confirming something she had already suspected.

Luka noticed her noticing.

He said nothing.

Torres, for once, didn't fill the silence.

That absence carried more weight than anything he might have said.

James set the mug down and reached for the plate Irina had placed on the table earlier.

Kyra did the same, her movements efficient, unhurried, entirely unremarkable.

Routine reasserted itself in small, precise ways.

Control, rebuilt.

Whatever had happened the night before didn't exist here—not in the way they moved, not in the way they spoke, not in anything that could be pointed to and named.

But it remained.

James felt it in the slight delay before he spoke, in the way his body held position a fraction longer than necessary, as if waiting for something that wasn't coming.

Kyra finished first.

She wiped her hands clean, set the cloth aside, and stepped away from the table with the same quiet finality she brought to everything else.

"We move in thirty," she said.

No one questioned it.

Torres snapped the comms unit back together, the hum shifting pitch as the system reconfigured. Luka straightened from the window, his hand falling away from the frame. Irina closed the kit with a soft click, already mentally ahead of the movement.

The room aligned itself around the instruction.

James remained where he was for a moment longer, the weight settling into place.

Not the mission. Not the team.
Him.

Then he stood, and whatever the day was going to be, it had already begun.

CHAPTER 20: CRIMSON ECHO

Outside Orava, Northern Slovakia – 03:32 | 4 days later

"Signal remembers what the heart forgets."
— STRATEG-7 FRAGMENT

Cold patterns had replaced routine.

The days between had blurred into movement—safehouse to safehouse, short windows of rest bracketed by quiet redeployments that never fully explained themselves. Orders came and went through PhantomNet in fragments, some clean, some delayed, some arriving just far enough out of sync to be noticed and then ignored.

The system wasn't behaving the way it used to.

By the fourth night, even Torres had stopped complaining about it.

That was how James knew it mattered.

The tasking arrived without signature.

No seal. No voice. No routing chain that could be traced cleanly from origin to receipt. Just a narrow-band burst slipping through PhantomNet—numbers resolving across the screen—too precise to be noise, too isolated to trust.

Coordinates. Timestamp.
One word: *verify*.

Torres printed it on the corner of a ration box, the paper still warm when the buffer scrubbed itself clean behind it.

Kyra's gaze held the scrap for a fraction longer than necessary.

"Anonymous," she said.

"Everything's anonymous now," Torres replied, folding it once before slipping it into his jacket.

No one argued.

They moved anyway.

Mac had rejoined them two nights earlier.

No warning. No lead-in. He stepped into the safehouse while Torres was still bringing the line up and said only that he'd been pulled for a separate tasking—Oblivion side, compartmented, now complete.

No details offered.

Irina had looked at him once, her expression unchanged except for the smallest lift at the edge of her brow—an adjustment most would miss.

Kyra didn't.

Her weight shifted slightly where she stood, not enough to signal concern, just enough to register alignment.

James noticed that, too—the way Kyra read Irina before anything else.

Ahead, the village lay under a hard crust of snow, evacuated the day before under the pretense of avalanche risk. Windows boarded, doors chained. No footprints. No dogs. No smoke.

Like a stage laid and never populated.

Mac took overwatch without waiting to be assigned, as if the position had already been his.

Torres remained in the jammer van with Irina beside him, her kit heavy with med gear.

Luka took point. James moved at his shoulder.

Kyra ghosted wide.

The quiet had a shape, pressing in on the angles of the street.

Snow creaked under Luka's boots like glass threatening to splinter. Somewhere a gutter pinged as the metal cooled, sharp against the stillness. No dogs. No shutters groaning in the wind. Even the chimneys exhaled nothing—roofs sealed tight as coffins.

The air smelled of iron frost. Every sound became its own echo, stretched thin until the silence measured them back.

He knelt by a dead relay box. "Thermal?"

Torres's voice came clipped: "Six warm bodies in the schoolhouse. Holding. No chatter."

Luka spat in the snow. "I don't like it. That's not a patrol. Feels like a trap."

Mac's channel opened for a fraction too long—just enough for a second carrier to bleed through beneath his breathing.

Then it cut clean.

And then the trap answered them.

The van went up first—white flash, steel into glass, glass into blood.

Torres's scream tore the net. Irina's voice cut in immediately, iron-flat. "Alive. He's hit. I've got him. Hold pos—."

A second blast ate their fallback alley. A third blew the granary wall outward in a gout of flame and timber. Snow turned black with burning oil.

Then the gunfire came—clean, disciplined, overlapping arcs that walked down the street. Not harassment.

Execution.

"Move!" James shoved Kyra through a doorway already collapsing under its own beam. Luka barreled after them, one hand fisting Torres's collar, Irina straddling blood and glass to keep pressure on the wound just behind his ear. Mac's channel clicked once—late, as if reacting instead of anticipating—then silence; his nest was either cold or suppressed.

Rounds chewed plaster and oak. The granary shuddered.

The assailants breached.

THE BREACH

They came like a diagram—three stacks, three entries, charges and flash in rhythm. First wedge through the kitchen door— shields, suppressed troops clearing the doorway in short, controlled pairs.

Second wedge through the hole the blast had torn in the granary wall. Third on the roof, hooks biting slate, lines thumping.

Mac's channel opened a fraction early—breath, then something else beneath it, a second carrier that didn't belong.

It cut before it resolved.

At the kitchen threshold Luka met the first attacker—pinned his gun arm, rounds stitching the wall in blind panic—then slammed him into the frame, hand crushing the faceplate, skull hammering oak until it split. He pivoted, drove a shoulder into the next shield and shoved the man back. His sidearm cleared leather; one shot punched through the trooper's foot, the next drove under his chin, bursting brain across the inside of his faceplate.

James covered the granary gap, muzzle steady because that's what training demanded. Angles, timing, trigger squeeze—all automatic. But the assault came like a tide of black armor, arcs of fire weaving with a precision that hollowed him. The silence between bursts cut at his nerves.

Two helmets flared crisp in the smoke. James squeezed twice— perfect shots, center mass. Sparks leapt, rounds skittered wild, armor ringing like struck iron. The men didn't fall. They didn't even slow.

The geometry was broken—rounds ricocheting, arcs closing too fast, too many shadows moving where they shouldn't.

"Neck seams," Mac's voice cut in—flat, immediate. Too fast— as if he already knew.

Luka's scream tore through the chaos: *"Soft spots! The armor's too strong!"*

They had him. Muzzle flashes already bracketed his position, arcs narrowing like jaws. James tried to shift, but the angles had collapsed, no space left to breathe.

Then the man on point jerked sideways, a spray cutting the smoke. A round punched through the seam of his neckplate, dropping him in a twitching spasm.

High angle. Clean entry.

Mac was still in the fight.

Kyra ghosted in behind the shot, sliding low—her boot scythed into the second trooper's legs. He crashed back, armor rattling, weapon firing useless sparks against the rafters.

She ripped his helmet free before he could recover, steel clattering on the dirt floor. For a heartbeat it was bare hands, elbows and knees, the grunt of bone meeting bone. Then her pistol snapped up, muzzle pressed to temple. The shot was final—loud, close, inside the skull. Silence followed, but it was hers, not theirs.

Another turned the corner too fast. James squeezed and held— a long, ugly burst straight into the sternum. Armor soaked it. The man staggered, stunned but alive.

Kyra didn't hesitate. She tore an AK-74 from the floor and hosed him point-blank, rounds shredding helmet and neck in a wet collapse.

The next shape loomed through smoke, muzzle sparking. James rolled, his burst chewing brick instead of bone. A round clipped his tricep—white heat, wet spray, arm gone pins-and-needles.

"Ah! Fuck! I'm hit!" The words tore out of him, more shock than strategy.

The trooper advanced, weapon still spitting. Kyra raked his arm forcing the rifle clattering to the ground. Her mag clicked empty. She lowered her head and closed.

The attacker drew a heavy combat knife. James tried to fire back, even to distract, but his rifle was empty. The blade lunged forward—Kyra slipped aside, redirecting the strike. A slash came fast; she stepped inside it, forcing his arm through the motion. Her own blade struck like a whisper—thrust up beneath the arm, sliding through the joint in his armor. Three quick stabs, buried to the hilt, then a violent twist and pull.

He stumbled, howling. James swung his empty rifle like a bat, all his weight behind it. The stock cracked against the side of the helmet with a ringing thud.

Kyra bent low, knife flashing once more, and drove it into the triangle above his collarbone. She twisted, yanked free, and rose with the blade in hand.

James stared, adrenaline flooding every nerve, unable to process it. Her face was splattered red, jaw set, eyes burning.

She bent, scooped the fallen rifle, and tossed it to him—whether it still had rounds, he couldn't tell. He caught it too late, hands slow, mind lagging behind the movement. He stood there, frozen, as if the fight had already emptied him.

Kyra didn't slow. She moved past him, killing fast enough for both of them.

Three more poured in from the roof. Kyra let the first overcommit, caught his muzzle on the flat of her blade, and slashed his wrist to the tendon. His rifle hit the floor—she flicked it back toward James with a heel kick. Then she spun through his stagger, hooked his legs, and dropped him hard.

Her thighs locked around his head. One violent twist, and the neck gave with a crack.

Flashbang. James flinched late. The sound caved his skull; vision narrowed to a hot wire.

The second man from the roof moved fast, knife flashing. He slashed for James's ribs. James caught the arm and clamped it to his own, steel kissing through fabric, biting shallow. He drove his forehead down—once, twice—and the pain detonated behind his eyes. The helmet took it. Worthless.

He sagged, throat seized in a crushing arm from behind, body lifted like dead weight. Barked Russian roared against the ringing in his ears. Kyra's knife hit the floor—her hands raised, her eyes calculating.

Fuck. Hostage. Shield. He'd given them both away.

Luka erupted from behind, swinging iron. The frying pan smashed into the trooper's helmet with a hollow, brutal clang that shook the stairwell. James collapsed to the floor, lungs tearing for air.

Without pause Luka hauled the stunned man by his plate carrier, dragged him to the banister, and heaved. The body tumbled two stories down. The bone-crack on impact wasn't victory—it was just one less problem in a fight that was still too big.

"Three on the east wall!" Irina snapped—one hand gripping Torres, the other dragging him deeper into cover as rounds shredded the doorframe around her. A grenade clinked across the tile. Her eyes went wide. She kicked it back before thought. The blast tore the alley, and the alley screamed.

"Correction—two," Mac cut in.

A beat later, one of them dropped—before James even saw him.

On the granary side, two Russians slipped in loose and fast, flowing around their partner's body instead of tripping over it, rifles already leveled.

Kyra and James split a crossfire—angles tight, trust unspoken. James was half-back to his senses, knees on the floor, an AK-74 finally in his hands with a live mag. As the two Russians slipped in, he dropped to his side and hosed the legs of the nearest. Rounds chewed through fabric, bit into boots, and ruined both feet. The man's scream rose louder than the rifle as he collapsed to his knees.

Their shoulders brushed in the recoil, heat and cordite thick between them. He caught the sharp trace of her perfume— impossible here, but memory made it real. For a breath too long, it was distraction and anchor at once.

Kyra pivoted before the sound faded. Her burst walked down the second man's abdomen, rounds hammering into armor, then belly, then groin. He buckled forward, clutching himself, voice breaking into a shriek. She advanced without slowing, muzzle pressed into the seam under his plate, and fired until the mag clicked dry. He spasmed once, then went slack.

The crippled one clawed at the floorboards, blood spreading from his shredded boots. Kyra swapped weapons with a fluid motion—James's dropped sidearm in her grip now—and put two rounds through the back of his helmet. The body went still.

She stood over both corpses, chest heaving, eyes cutting the room for the next threat.

On the far side, Luka bent double, still heaving from tossing the last body down the stairwell.

Dust hung. Silence stretched.

"Reorg," Luka grunted, knuckles split and wet. "There'll be more."

He was right.

The Encirclement

The next wave didn't rush.

They wrapped.

Two squads of six. One team stalked the roofline, shadows slipping along ridge and gutter, hooks biting slate, rifles probing angles through dormers. The other pressed the alleys, low and tight, grenades dropped like punctuation at every turn.

The breach hadn't broken them.
It had positioned them.

Irina hissed when a round shaved her shoulder.

"I'm fine."

She wasn't.

Blood slicked her arm, soaking through gauze as she stapled pad to pad with her bare hand. Torres tried to rise, vomited, eyes blown wide, glass-bright. Irina shoved him down with a forearm. "Stay."

"Sniper," Mac said in James's ear, low enough to feel like a thought. "South bell tower. Three breaths."

Too precise.

Then silence.

A crack split the granary slats, a bullet burying itself in millet inches from Irina's skull. She didn't flinch, just dragged Torres three inches left. The second shot came, and Mac's answered it—one sharp report, then a figure toppled from the bell tower window, hitting snow with the dull collapse of a sack of flour.

"Roof team shifting west," Mac added.

James glanced up.

There was no angle from Mac's position that should have given him that line.

The roof team took the stairwell. Discipline, wedges, ladders. They drove James and Luka down one flight with flash and fire, tried to pinch them at the landing. A man in a balaclava slid under Luka's guard and buried a blade in his side. Luka's grunt was the sound of a bull shot through the lung.

Blood was already soaking through his shirt. Each breath rasped shallow, a wet gurgle at the edge of sound. His hands shook—not from fear, but from shock setting in. Still, adrenaline carried him through the counterstrike. He clamped the knife wrist under his arm and wrenched, the elbow snapping backward with a muffled chair-leg pop. The man screamed once before Luka smothered it with his palm and drove the crown of his head against the riser. The wood stained dark.

Luka sagged immediately after, legs unsteady, one hand pressed hard to his ribs as though trying to hold the breath in.

Another grenade. Kyra saw it first. She got there second. It bounced near her boot. She toed it back down the corridor, and the blast erased three helmets a beat later. The shockwave punched her sideways, ears ringing, balance sliding out from under her. She caught the wall, tasting metal as blood ran from her split lip.

James fired in ragged bursts beside her. He was regaining rhythm—angles, squeeze, cover fire—but he wasn't in sync with them, not yet.

Every muzzle flash seared white into his vision, spots lingering like ghosts. The corridor filled with plaster dust and cordite, choking his lungs, brass hot against his boots. His rhythm frayed with each breath.

They dropped two more with careful fire, but it cost them. Luka's aim wavered, his shirt blackening at the ribs. Kyra spat blood and shouldered on. Irina's bandage was red to the elbow. James felt himself unraveling even as he fired, every spent round another reminder that the geometry wasn't holding.

The remaining eight didn't panic. They regrouped in an L-formation, suppressive fire sewing the corridor into splinters. Wood buckled. Plaster rained. The air turned to dust and choking smoke.

Pinned. Bleeding. Out of sync with each other.

For the first time it was clear—they weren't holding.

Not another wave.

Not another push.

One mistake, one breath too slow, and the house would swallow them whole.

RECKONING

They didn't break.

The pressure changed.

James felt it in his ears first, then in his teeth. Angles bent wrong—the crossfire didn't close where it should, the rhythm stuttered like static skipping a beat. His body braced before his mind caught why.

She arrived in fragments. A sidearm flared, steel in smoke, then nothing—just aftermath: men folding, blood spattering plaster, helmets tumbling. He tried to fix on her shape and found only pieces, like a film reel missing every other frame.

Three barks—too fast for aim, too clean for chance. Helmets snapped back as though the rounds had been waiting for them. The gun clicked dry, clattered on stone.

Steel followed. She slid under a muzzle, and the man holding it collapsed as if his bones had been stolen. Another lunged; his scream ended before it began, throat spilling red.

James reacted—flinch, recoil, duck.

Muzzle flash gave him only shards: an arm, a heel, a knife sinking into something already falling. Angles refused to hold.

A wounded soldier staggered into her path. She didn't waste steel. One palm drove his helmet to the iron stove. His scream rose once, cut short when she let the weight of his body finish it against hot iron.

A bear hug caught her from behind—James thought she was trapped. The man's scream broke before the thought finished. She wasn't there anymore.

He lunged—there was a scream, then a crack, and he couldn't tell whose it was.

Two shapes converged. She slammed them together. Ceramic rang like dropped plates, and screams told him what his eyes couldn't.

Another tried to pull back; she spun him through the banister rail. Wood splintered. Bone didn't. He sagged there until her boot kicked him free.

Russian comms cracked: calm, then disbelief.

"Мы имеем визуальное на Кримсон! Повторяю, Кримсон—"
We have visual on Crimson—

"Как?" (How?)

Another voice broke rank: *"Ёб твою мать!"* Panic cracked the vowels.

James couldn't see her clearly. He saw only aftermath: blood misting shafts of light, a man pinned half into a wall, another twitching around the blade in his eye. Every time his vision cleared, she was already gone.

Kyra's mouth almost curved.

It stopped before it became anything real.

Her eyes told the truth—steady, knowing, like a soldier recognizing something across smoke she had no language for.

James caught it and hated it. Whatever she saw, it wasn't relief. It was familiarity.

"She's not here for us," Kyra said.

James tried to follow, but the Ghost moved like subtraction—men edited out mid-step.

The last survivors fought in a ring, backs touching, muzzles outward. Discipline held. For a heartbeat James thought they might.

They didn't.

One dropped gurgling, steel in his throat. Another fired wild, his rounds chewing his own comrade. A third wrenched at the door—her boot slammed it shut, pinning his head in the hinge.

Wood pressed one way, frame the other. She leaned in, leg a piston, until bone snapped.

James gagged. Stomach lurched. Vomit burned up, hot bile spilling across the boards. His glove clawed the floor, leather rasping wood. The room tilted with her rhythm.

He didn't see the last man die. He only heard it—three dull impacts, then a crack that cut through even the gunfire.

When he lifted his head, trembling, she was gone.

Only the dead proved she'd ever been there.

The silence afterward wasn't relief.

It was absence.

AFTERMATH

Irina's voice cut steady through the haze: "Torres, look at me. Follow my finger. Good. You'll live. Don't move." Her gloves were black with blood.

Luka stood like a man in confession, chest heaving, one shoulder turned toward the wall as though that angle alone could make privacy of what they had just survived.

Kyra was still. She watched the space the Ghost had left, like someone reading a shape in smoke. No relief. No gratitude. Recognition—and grief that looked old, not new.

James's rifle sagged in his hands. The gloves tacky with other people. The taste of pennies still clung to his teeth. His ears rang, but under it, he could hear his pulse trying to match a rhythm that wasn't in the room anymore.

Luka broke the silence first. "That wasn't a fight." His voice scraped. "That was a reckoning."

"Spetsnaz," Irina muttered, tightening a staple through gauze with her teeth. "Gone inside an hour."

James swallowed again, bile rising bitter.

It hadn't felt like rescue. It had felt like the field being taken.

Snow hissed against blood still steaming on the boards. A rafter ticked overhead, the wood settling as the space emptied. Torres's breathing rasped, the only human sound left.

Outside, the wind rattled a shutter once, then stopped. The quiet folded back around them, heavy, irreversible.

James stood in it, listening.

Not for sound.

For what was missing.

Act IV - When Silence Remembers

Every silence is a ledger.

What you don't say is written anyway—

in blood, in ash,

in the ghosts who remember louder than you do.

CHAPTER 21: THE ICEBOX
The Carpathians | Two Weeks Later

[REDACTED FIELD MEMO | OBLIVION | ICEBOX PROTOCOL – ENTRY STATUS]

Subject: The Red Ghost (Confirmed Visual)
Classification: OBSIDIAN TIER – UNTETHERED
Operational Presence: Unknown, Implied
Behavioral Marker: Selective Annihilation
Protocol Response: Observe. Do not engage. Do not record.
[End Memo]

Unclaimed by warmth, Košice froze at the edges.

The Carpathians were less a range than a line of barricades—stone and shadow folded over centuries of silence. Snow did not fall; it smothered, laying itself across slopes until pines bent into tortured shapes. Wind whispered down the ravines; echoes came back wrong.

**** Field Note, Army Ops Group (unofficial, circulated 1987)*

They didn't build cells, they built winters. No clocks, no warmth, no voice but your own. We called it the Icebox. Everyone who came out knew the shape of their breath better than their own name.

Their next safehouse sat in that silence, a converted alpine barn outside the Slovakian village of Ždiar. Reinforced rafters. Thermal blankets sewn into walls. Solar panels disguised as snowdrifts. Inside, the air held a ritual chill that earned the place its name among field agents: **The Icebox.**

By the end of week two, the cold did the talking.

Kyra came back from recon with blood on her collar and a foil-sealed data shard. *Foil-sealed, field-grade storage—shards were built to survive what agents didn't, and what they carried was never small.* Torres decrypted it in forty minutes, pale fingers twitching like he was tuning a radio back into sanity.

The phrase across the screen: **RED GHOST – KNOWN VARIABLE – EXFIL STATUS UNKNOWN**

James stared at the name until the monitor blinked black.

He remembered the blur of her moving, inevitability shaped into flesh, the way the field bent around her.

Seeing the name in print stripped away myth and left proof.

From silence came their next operation. **BLACK SUN.**

Official cover: extract an ex-CIA source hiding in a frozen ravine. Once tied to a Russian logistics shell, maybe holding fragments of GRU contracting protocols. Six-hour window. No uplink. No backup.

Deployment split them into two elements—James with Kyra and Torres in one, Luka with Irina and Mac in the other.

The storm hit thirty minutes after insertion. Snow sideways, visibility gone. GPS blinked. Pines moaned like rigged ships. It wasn't terrain anymore—it was resistance.

They moved in staggered lines. James led, Kyra's breath ghosting behind him. Torres said nothing—his usual static sarcasm gone, his silence more alarming than words.

Even with the storm clawing around them, his hands never shook. Kyra noted the steadiness.

Behind, Irina trudged beside Mac. She didn't look at him, just raised her voice enough for the wind to steal the edge. "That bell tower," she said. "You put him down before the second shot. If you hadn't—" Her shoulder rolled once, the closest she would come to finishing it.

Mac kept his eyes forward. "Just math."

"No," she said, firm even in the blizzard. "You saved my life."

Mac didn't glance her way. "Lives get tallied."

At 0400, Torres raised a fist. Thermal blip ahead. Low to the ground. A pulse. Moving.

They found no man. A fox lay pinned beneath a birch, ribs visible through matte fur, breath ragged and shallow. It was wrong—too deliberate. Not survival; an arranged tableau meant to slow them, to remind them the field itself had become a weaponized stage.

James swore. "Shit. Someone is stalling us."

Kyra didn't answer, but her breath brushed close enough against his neck to fog his collar. Too close for the field. Close enough that the silence felt weighted.

Torres wiped frost from his cheek. "Field games. Russians, probably. Doesn't take much—just enough to bleed our clock."

James kept staring at the fox. Pinned. Helpless. Arranged by someone else's hand.

Kyra said nothing. Her silence was different—tight, sharpened. A verdict not spoken: *Moscow didn't leave chances. Not twice.*

They reached the blind an hour later. The source was nearly gone—blue-lipped, waxen, collapsed in the snow. His finger had scratched a single word into the drift: **WAIT**.

His lips cracked, frost sealing his throat, but one word rasped out: "…capture…"

Torres muttered, "Capture what? Makes no sense." He shook his head, already moving.

James pressed on, every step sinking deeper into snow that didn't want to give him back, but the word gnawed at him. *Capture.* Not a plea. A directive.

James hefted the weight, staggering once on the slope. Kyra's hand steadied him—then left. Neither spoke of it. Both felt it.

Back inside the barn, Torres eased a fragment drive from the dead man's lining, wrapped in wax paper as if that might hold back time. Most of it was corrupted—dead shell-company contracts, useless ledgers. Almost nothing. Then one entry clawed free: **Снежная Тень.** Torres read it aloud: "Snezhnaya Ten. Ice Shadow."

It had been left for them.

Kyra's pulse kicked hard in her throat. She knew exactly what it meant. Speaking it aloud would make the memory real. So she buried it.

The silence hardened. *Fox. Capture. Ice Shadow.*

None of it fit.

Strung together, it felt less like coincidence and more like a script they hadn't been shown.

The recovery hadn't given them information. It had given them confirmation—one more whisper into the dark that she was still out there.

And that Oblivion had been steered into her shadow.

The alpine barn turned hostile. Not the walls—the silence between them.

Signals bled strange. Burner accounts froze. Satellite bandwidth choked. GPS overlays corrupted. Extraction codes spat 403 errors.

Torres spat the number like a curse—no go.

Even the fallback relays went dead.

This wasn't surveillance. This was siege.

Luka grew louder, picking fights with James until their arguments shook frost from rafters.

Torres wired heater coils into antennae, listening to static like it might confess. "They're ghosting us," he muttered. "Riding our signal, bending it back at us. Same as Berlin."

James stiffened.

He remembered it—comms whispering back their own voices two seconds late, distorted, like someone else was already wearing their skin. Orders looped until they weren't sure which was real.

A burst of laughter once, female, threaded through the channel in a voice none of them recognized. No source. No origin. Just gone.

The silence that followed had been worse than the noise.

Irina said little, but her hands stayed steady. She stitched Luka's ribs again, the needle sliding through skin she'd already closed once. When he grunted, she gave a small sigh, tying the knot with deliberate care. "Don't talk," she murmured, almost like an older sister scolding a reckless brother. "You'll just make me do this all over again tomorrow." It was the most she'd said in days.

Kyra disappeared for hours. Returned with eyes that had seen things she refused to name. Once James asked. Her reply: "You really *don't* want to know."

Mac stayed quiet. Too quiet. James noticed his prints didn't linger in the snow. Once, at the comm relay, a light pulsed and steadied again.

Too smooth. Too quick.

Not a glitch.
A response.

Someone pinging, someone checking.

James's jaw tightened. "Mac—" The name almost left as a challenge, half-formed in his throat. Mac looked up then, calm as always, like he'd been waiting for it. The silence stretched a second too long.

James let it die. "Never mind."

He caught Kyra's gaze in the dim light, sharp as the glitch itself, and for an instant it felt like they were the only two who saw the pattern.

James told himself it was the cold. Circuits stuttered in the Icebox. But the thought gnawed—that light hadn't asked *them* for permission. It had answered someone else.

The outpost remembered things James never told it.

He heard tapping in the walls that mimicked Morse but never resolved into anything. Once, a child's voice whispered: *You're already gone.* Another night, his own voice echoed from the corner: *Not yet.* But he hadn't spoken.

On the fifth night, he swore the frost on the window spelled a name.

Kyra sat by the stove, the fire painting her face in restless gold. She stripped her coat, fed it into the flames piece by piece until the lining blackened and curled. James asked what she'd brought back. She answered without looking up.

"Only residue."

By the third night in the Icebox, the only sound was Torres tuning static through his coils, Luka's low curses when Irina reset his stitches, and the wind clawing the eaves.

The door blew open. Snow gusted in. Márton crossed the threshold like a man carrying more than frost.

Irina moved first, the kettle whistling behind her, forgotten. For a heartbeat her eyes softened—recognition, relief too quick to hide. "Pa—" The slip cut off sharp, buried under her breath.

Márton's gaze flicked once in her direction, a muscle tightening at his jaw, then smoothed to iron stillness. If he'd heard it, he buried it.

Luka's eyes, sharper, caught the crack and stored it like a blade to sharpen later.

Márton dropped a damp folder on the table. "Your last mission wasn't reconnaissance," he said. His voice came like iron dragged over glass. "You were placement."

The word landed cold and unavoidable. Kyra's pencil snapped in her hand—graphite splintering like a cracked score.

With the stove burning low, Márton laid the folder open. His words landed like nails into the wood.

"Moscow fed the coordinates into channels Langley couldn't resist. CIA scrubbed the trail, stamped it clean, and passed it down. Moscow baited; Langley swallowed. You weren't sent to strike—you were placed. When she appeared, the sighting was Langley's without lifting a finger."

James remembered the Spetsnaz voices in the storm—fractured orders, then one panicked word cutting through: *How?* Not triumph. Confusion.

Márton went on. "Intercepts say Moscow wants her back. Spetsnaz failed. Others will try. The longer she stays untethered, the more unstable the equation. They need her before someone else learns to follow."

Kyra's jaw trembled—tiny, barely there—then she locked it down. *Untethered.* Not just Red Ghost. Not just a file. A shape that fit too close to something inside her.

James saw it: a tremor in her jaw, hidden but real.

When he finally spoke, his voice rasped low. "Why us?"

Márton's gaze swept them like a ledger being tallied. "Because Oblivion knows about her already. And no one outside a program like this ever can."

The stove ticked. Wind scraped the eaves. And the silence that followed felt less like exile, more like occupation.

Irina lowered her eyes, but her hands were folded so tight her knuckles blanched.

In the corner, Mac adjusted the comm relay. Too smooth, too quick—one light that should have stayed steady pulsed, then held again. James saw it, but didn't call it. Not yet.

Still, the flicker stayed in his mind. It hadn't felt like a glitch. It had felt like intent—another line in something they didn't control.

The Icebox had felt like exile before.

Now it felt like occupation.

That night James couldn't sleep. He opened his journal with shaking hands. The ink dragged:

Closeness is not safety.

Fox. Capture. Ice Shadow. How.

Not kill. Recover.

A.

He stared until the ink blurred. It curved in ways his hand never had, as though the hand wasn't entirely his.

CHAPTER 22: STATIC RAIN
Warsaw, Poland

Removed by the Icebox, Oblivion didn't shatter—it bled into signal.

They left Košice at dawn, the Carpathians shrinking behind them into barricades of shadow and snow. Márton did not travel with them. His orders had forked elsewhere—an alternate assignment, delivered the same way all futures would arrive now: burst transmissions across the PhantomNet, encrypted, unsigned, no questions allowed.

Before he vanished into that silence, Márton pulled Luka aside. There was no frost in his voice then, only weight. *"Take care of my daughter."*

In that instant, the burden passed: protect her, guard the secret. Because if others knew, Irina would become leverage, a way to wound Márton through her.

Then he was gone. No convoy, no escort. Just absence.

The command chain fractured into relays and shadows. Orders came encoded, routed through cold servers and signed with PhantomNet—no sender, no reply. Just missions wrapped in static.

Like scripture.
Like threat.

The illusion of command lingered.

The structure had dissolved into something colder—algorithms and asset risk models, not loyalty.

His last message was just three digits, blinking through PhantomNet before dissolving into noise. After that, silence. No farewell, no closure. Just absence written in code. Oblivion's way of erasing men as cleanly as it reassigned them.

Warsaw was colorless. Mist hung mid-air, draping the city in a slick, humming sheen. Tram rails hissed under wet steel. Antenna arrays clicked and sputtered above rooftops like anxious bones. Even the radio hissed between stations, old frequencies clashing with new.

One antenna flared, then cut out. Rain shimmered like glass beneath its shadow. James marked the absence. The others thought it a surge. It wasn't. Later he would understand: the city was already bent to another rhythm—213 milliseconds at a time.

James pressed his forehead to the train window as they crossed into city limits. His breath fogged the glass, but he didn't wipe it away. He watched the skyline emerge through steam and rain: Soviet-era blocks squatting between glass-and-steel newcomers like old gods among false prophets. Warsaw was built on the bones of empires, and every building seemed to whisper unfinished stories in concrete dialect.

Beside him, Kyra sat rigid. Arms crossed. Eyes narrowed. She studied their reflection—not out of vanity, but calculation. She hated windows. Too many angles. Too much exposure.

Her eyes flicked once to his in the glass. Then she looked away, jaw tight. The silence hung, edged with absence, and James couldn't tell if it was hers—or his.

Across the aisle, Luka braced the duffel between his knees, the rhythm of a man used to carrying weight across borders. He looked the same as always—broad, immovable—but James caught a flicker in the set of his jaw, as if the bag held more than gear and equipment. Luka was carrying something heavier now, and James didn't know its name.

They exited at Wola Station, swallowed immediately by the blur of the city. Rain layered everything—cars, bricks, breath—with a texture of static.

The streetlights flickered. Every pedestrian was suspect. They split without speaking.

No safehouse. No aliases. No net.

Just a rail node to intercept and a whisper: the Russians were moving shipments through Warsaw again—disguised in agricultural tanks, bound officially for Ukraine, unofficially for somewhere colder and darker.

Torres had arrived two days earlier. He'd rented out an abandoned dental clinic in Praga and wired it into a temporary uplink hub. He met them one by one in silence. No greetings. No warmth. Just a list of frequencies and a nod toward the comms room.

"Rain's good cover," he muttered to James as they climbed the stairwell.

"Noise?" James asked.

"Too much," Torres said. "Which means someone's trying to hide something big."

Torres didn't sulk or posture. He recorded. Logged time. Measured breathing rates. Watched everyone like an unresolved signal. Once, James had glimpsed a page in his notebook: a binary spiral. At the center, in small, shaking script: *We are only as loyal as the last signal received.*

James never mentioned it. But from then on, he always double-verified his encryption near Torres.

Once, on the clinic stairwell, Luka let Irina pass ahead of him and waited a beat too long before following. It wasn't the way soldiers watched each other's backs. It was closer, heavier—protective in a way that didn't belong to the field.

Irina felt it. She glanced at him, frowning as if to ask why he hovered, but he only shifted the duffel higher and said nothing.

The silence between them wasn't suspicion. It was the kind that pressed on Luka's shoulders, heavy and unwanted.

James already understood: in Oblivion, secrets were heavier than gear, and Márton had left Luka with one no one else could carry.

The Icebox had taught him how to endure silence. Warsaw was teaching him not to trust it.

The clinic smelled of mint trying to hide rot. Mold and disinfectant argued in the air. In the back, Torres had transformed the operating room into a high-frequency shell of static—foil-lined walls, salvaged batteries, patched-in boosters. The old dental chair had become a rig—wires braided around it, a low static hum clinging to the metal.

Kyra arrived last, soaked through. She peeled off her jacket, dropped it on a stool, the fabric beneath clinging close to lean lines and dangerous grace. She ignored it, eyes already fixed on the wall map. Her finger tapped a node along the industrial rail corridor south of the Vistula.

"Convoy hits this yard at eleven past midnight. Manifest says agricultural relief." Her eyes flicked up—sharp, flat. "In reality, it's carrying the building blocks for a new Russian bio-weapon.

Genetic tailoring: viruses stripped to blank shells, ready to be rewritten. Material capable of manufacturing weapons targeted to specific DNA profiles. Entire families, bloodlines, populations—erased by code in their cells."

"Targets?" he asked.

"Crates 7A-19, 8C-02, 9G-77," Luka said, fingering the manifest. "Fronted through Belarusian agribusiness—thin cover. One gust and it peels away."

Torres added, "Digital traces line up with GRU ghost chains. Same chain they used to bury the Transnistria leaks—only cleaner."

Kyra leaned into the map, voice low, certain.

"If Moscow gets these precursors into their labs, they can start testing within weeks. This isn't cargo. It's a trigger. Once it's in their hands, they get to decide who's vulnerable—and who isn't."

James's jaw tightened.

"Interception protocol?"

Kyra's gaze locked with his in the reflection of the foil wall. "Prevent it from leaving Warsaw. Whatever it takes."

As Kyra folded the map away, James spoke up. "False-manifest infiltration. Irina rides as the convoy medic—papers show legitimate relief. She stays with the crates."

Torres scraped a match, flame flaring.
"We ghost a logistic seal on one manifest. I can ghost the medical stamps—make the manifest sing benign."

Luka leaned in, voice clipped.

"Medics draw attention. They'll be the first asked for supplies, for proof of kit. If they press, her cover collapses."

James's jaw set. "That's what a cover is for—she holds until the crates are through."

Luka shook his head, sharper now.
"You don't gamble the entry on someone that exposed."

Kyra's gaze hardened, then eased.

"We're not putting Irina in a crate," she said flatly. "I'll go in."

Luka's fingers tightened on the duffel strap, then fell away.

Irina rolled a glass ampule between thumb and forefinger until the rim bit her palm. She swallowed, eyes meeting Kyra's, a small raw look crossing her face.

"No," Kyra added, before Luka could argue. "I can move like a ghost in a load bay. I'll take the manifest. James, cover us—keep her off the cars."

James opened his mouth, but Kyra's look cut it closed. Not a request.

Luka's shoulders loosened an inch—relief braided with the terror of handing someone else into the knife's path.

0000 hours. No moon. Rain fell in pulsed intervals—timed like breathing. The yard lights went out two minutes before contact. Shadows swallowed the rail corridor.

Through the static mist, James saw the convoy: three containers disguised as farm relief, parked under halogen glare. A dozen mercenaries patrolled the perimeter, their rifles slung low, movements too disciplined to be farmers. At their center—a GRU major, heavy coat, radio pressed tight. Watching.

They couldn't brute-force this. Too many eyes. Too much firepower.

Kyra slipped away. She melted into the rain, gone from his peripheral in the time it took to blink.

Ten minutes later two guards lay silent—throats open, pale in the wet. A third folded soundless when she used bone and leverage. The fourth went down from a quick, clinical cut.

The fifth fought; he did not die neatly. He wheeled on her. His knife glanced her forearm—just a line of fire across skin. She drove steel into his throat before he could cry out. Held him as he kicked. Lowered him into shadow.

Blood slicked her sleeve. She clamped the wound shut and kept moving.

James saw the tremor in her arm. He almost broke cover. Almost.

A cold bead of sweat tracked from his temple; the memory of that near-movement looped like a skipped file.

Torres moved in, crouched low, wires coiled across his chest. Luka followed, duffel slung heavy with charges. They crawled container to container, magnets snapping, timers set.

James covered them from a warehouse roof, rifle barrel steady on the night.

Rain blurred his scope. A figure peeled off the gantry. The gait was familiar. Mac.

He didn't raise a weapon. He touched the containers instead, fingertips brushing steel like he was listening.

At 9G-77 he stopped. Pressed his palm flat. The diode sputtered red, then went dark.

Then steadied.

"Mac's here," James whispered.

Static answered. No one heard.

Then Mac was gone. One breath he was there, the next the rain erased him. The crate still trembled faintly.

Movement on the gantry. A scope glinting back at him. James steadied, finger tightening—
—then another shadow below. A guard raising his rifle.

Two targets. No time. No angle.

The shot cracked. Torres folded, blood dark on his side.

Luka's hand closed on his wrist and steadied it while Torres jammed the charge into the seam with his other hand, slapped the magnet on, and locked the timer through shaking fingers.

A shadow flicked behind Torres' attacker. Anger stripped Kyra's movements of all restraint. She met him mid-rotation, knife plunging deep into his gut and ripping upward through the chest cavity. The force lifted him off his feet. For a breath he hung there—then Kyra wrenched the blade free and dragged him down into the dark.

From his perch, James caught the movement—the unnatural strength, the precision of it. For a heartbeat, his focus slipped.

It wasn't the kill itself that froze him, but the way she eased the body down like it weighed nothing.

A glint from across the gantry snapped him back—the sniper's scope angling in again. James blinked hard, reacquiring the sight picture. He exhaled slow. The rifle kicked; the shot found the scope. The sniper folded, then slipped from sight.

"Charge set," Torres hissed through clenched teeth, clutching his side.

"Move!" James barked, firing again to keep the guards' heads down.

Luka surged to his side, hooking an arm under Torres and hauling him toward cover in a stumbling run, blood trailing with each step.

The GRU commander screamed orders, mercenaries and soldiers scattering to lock down the perimeter.

The yard fractured into a maelstrom as they broke contact. Bullets sparked off rusted sheet metal, tracer fire stitching the dark while sirens wailed overhead. The team slipped into Warsaw's alleys like ghosts, the timers whispering down behind them.

Kyra pressed her wounded arm tight against her jacket as they ran, every drop of blood a reminder of how close the silence had come to claiming her.

Minutes later, the containers folded inward, flames silenced into vacuum. From a distance it looked clean, surgical—everything incinerated, Moscow's genetic precursors erased. The charges were shaped to collapse and incinerate the freight—no visible plume, only a sudden vacuum that ripped steel inward and left nothing but heat and ash. To locals, it registered as a strange power surge and a distant boom—nothing that made the news.

From the roof they watched the detonations. Kyra lit a cigarette with fingers that trembled once. James almost steadied them. Almost. She drew smoke instead, filling her lungs with something she could control.

Luka watched the yard burn. "First blood," he muttered.

James's jaw flexed. His eyes kept straying to 9G-77, the container Mac had touched—the one that hadn't collapsed like the others. Too fast. Too eager. Frost had curled from the seam before the fire took it.

"Did any of you…" He stopped, then forced it out. "Back there. Did you hear my call? About Mac?"

Torres shook his head. "Nothing but static."

Kyra didn't look away from the flames. "If he was there, he wasn't with us."

"Maybe he was running parallel," James said. "Redundancy. In case we failed."

Luka's mouth twisted. "Or to make sure we did."

The fire burned below, but the silence around them burned hotter.

Some truths belonged to it—already bent, already speaking in Warsaw's voice.

Chapter 23: The Echo Signal
Praga, Poland - Safehouse | Current Day

Sleep didn't come.

Long after the others had gone still, he was bent over the jury-rigged comms rig, fingers twitching in sync with the static. At 04:06, he called James in.

"It's not just surveillance," Torres murmured. His eyes were red-rimmed, voice stripped flat. "It's orbital."

On the screen: heat maps, registry scraps, telemetry bursts. Data that should have been noise—but wasn't.

"Civilian birds?" James asked.

"Hijacked. Mineral survey satellites. Retired telecom junk. Someone's waking the dead ones." Torres swallowed. "You can't do that unless you planted yourself in the firmware years ago."

James didn't watch the feeds. He watched Torres—the twitching, the pale lips. "So, this isn't collection."

Torres shook his head. "No. It's placement. Eyes where no one should have them."

James leaned closer. The angles were too clean, the orbits too precise. No flags. No signatures. Just watching.

Torres's throat worked. "Echo," he whispered.

James didn't answer. But silence was enough.

Kyra moved through the safehouse like a shadow, searching for something to anchor to. The stairwell groaned under her weight as she climbed, but what stopped her wasn't the sound of her own steps—it was the low murmur behind a closed door.

She stilled, breath sharp.

A woman's laugh, hushed but unmistakable. Irina. And a man's answer, low and rough in the way Luka's voice always was when it dropped. The silence that followed wasn't empty—it was too close, too intimate.

Kyra's hand brushed the doorframe. She could have barged in, made it ugly. Instead she stepped back, heart thudding harder than she wanted to admit.

By dawn the safehouse was brittle with quiet. Torres drifted into half-sleep with an earbud still in. Luka hunched over the stove, dragging steel against whetstone. Sparks hissed into the basin. His jaw was locked, movements mechanical, but his eyes flicked once toward the hall where Irina had gone. Kyra caught it.

Her stomach tightened. The Warsaw mission rewrote itself in her mind—the way he had *begged* to keep Irina off the convoy.

James sat with the bundle Torres flagged. Most of it was scatter—logistics pings, weather telemetry, filler. But one fragment pulsed at intervals too exact to be random. Not data. Not orders. A presence.

Mac didn't come back.

No noise, no warning. Just absence. His cot stripped, locker reset, boots gone. Like he'd never been.

Later, James found a relay log Torres had buried in diagnostics. A single burst, routed through Moldova, masked as weather. One line only—gone before it could echo.

James asked if Torres had seen it.

Torres didn't look up. "Doesn't matter now."

But James replayed it in his head: Mac too calm during insertions, always volunteering for rear guard, always nearest the exits. Tells he should have read but didn't.

Maybe Mac walked. Maybe he was taken. Maybe he was a traitor.

In CI, intent didn't matter.
Only outcomes.

And absence was outcome enough.

That night, the safehouse went dark. Torres killed the uplinks. Luka stood watch on the roof, rifle under a tarp.

Kyra cornered him on the roof, quiet and sharp. "It wasn't duty, was it?" Her eyes cut into him, frost and fire together. "It was *her.*"

Luka's mouth opened, closed. The truth—*Márton's daughter*—sat like a blade between his teeth. He couldn't draw it. So he gave her something else, heavier but survivable.

"Yes," he said feigning defeat. "It was her."

Kyra looked away fast, as if his admission stung worse than a knife. She didn't ask more. Didn't need to. In her mind, the secret was already written.

Her fists clenched at her sides. "Do you even realize what you risked? One wrong call and Torres would be in a morgue, Irina in a crate, the rest of us cut down before the charges lit."

Luka didn't answer. His silence only sharpened her rage.

She stepped closer, voice low but burning. "You jeopardized the team. For her."

The word cracked in her mouth like a round discharged too close.

For a breath, her fury faltered. James's face cut through—the weight of his shoulder against hers in the stairwell, the way his pulse had betrayed him when her hand brushed his wrist. She'd leaned, just once, and he hadn't pulled away.

Then another memory—too close, too recent.

She cut it off.

Her jaw clenched. The rain hammered harder, waiting. She wanted to spit the words out; to prove she was still ice. But the memory lingered too close. When she finally spoke, it came fast, too fast, "I would never put James above the mission. Never."

Luka's head tilted, rain streaking off his brow. His voice came low, not mocking, not sharp—just heavy. "James?"

It wasn't an attack. That almost made it worse. His tone carried no heat, only the weight of someone already guarding a secret of his own, seeing hers slip loose. He hadn't thrown it at her—he had simply marked it, and that quiet recognition cut deeper than rage could.

Kyra's pulse jumped. She hated herself for the slip, hated him more for catching it.

She turned from him before the thought could root.

James found her in the corridor, back against the wall, a burned-out match crumbling between her fingers.

She didn't look at him when she spoke.

"Mac's gone."

A beat.

"No sound. No break."

Her tone stayed flat, controlled.

"That doesn't happen."

James said nothing.

She pushed off the wall before he could answer.

"If he was taken, we missed it."

Another beat.

"If he wasn't—"

She let the sentence die.

Not uncertainty. Containment.

Her eyes passed over him without stopping. Deliberate.

"Get some rest," she said.

Then she was gone down the corridor, already moving, already ahead of it.

CHAPTER 24: FIRE AND ICE
Praga, Poland - Safehouse

Мы не спасаем друг друга. Мы просто горим вместе — ярко, стремительно, как последние искры перед тьмой.

"We don't save each other. We just burn together—bright, reckless, like the last sparks before the dark."
— AUTHOR UNKNOWN

It started on the roof.

Red. Wrong.

Not lightning—just fire, spilling through the rafters of the clinic. Sirens rose, broken and feral. Heat clawed down the stairwell.

There was no time to argue, no time to plan. Just James forcing the hatch open, Torres still bleeding, Luka dragging the satchel, and Kyra at his shoulder as the ceiling groaned above.

Irina was already at Torres's side, fingers slick with blood but steady, voice low in his ear—counting, grounding, keeping him upright.

The fallback tunnel had been checked weeks ago—one more of Torres's paranoid contingencies scratched into their map. Cramped, filthy, but clear. Tonight, it wasn't theory. It was the only way out.

Kyra covered the rear, her presence a quiet comfort James didn't have to look back to feel. They dropped through the grate into earth that stank of rust and mold. James took point, driving them forward until the tunnel spat them out by a rusted tram depot, night air thick with smoke and sirens.

For a moment they stood together, four silhouettes ragged in the glow of burning rafters behind them. No time for debate. No time for plans.

"Pairs," James said. His voice cut through the haze. "North."

Irina's eyes flicked once—blood, distance, probability. "East," she said to Luka. "He won't last north."

Luka nodded, already hauling Torres by the arm. "We'll cut east, lose the trail in Praga. Meet at the fallback grid."

Torres didn't argue—too pale, too bloodied, but still upright. His eyes flicked once to James, then away.

Kyra was already moving, rain slick on her hair. James fell in behind her, north toward the river.

The city swallowed them in different directions.

James and Kyra moved north, rain slicking the concrete beneath their boots. The city blinked around them, disoriented, half-awake.

Near the Vistula footbridge, Kyra leaned against a wall and slid down, chest rising sharp.

"You okay?" James asked.

She laughed once, hollow. "Define okay."

He crouched beside her, gaze falling to the bandage on her arm.

"Not there," she murmured.

Her fingers brushed his sleeve—then were gone.

"Adrenaline's dropping," she said. "That's all."

"I'm failing at that too," he said quietly.

Kyra's breath hitched—just once.

She leaned closer—

Then stopped.

Something in her locked.

She pulled back first.

"We should move," she said.

"Let's go," he answered, rising with her.

The fallback site was a utility tunnel beneath a rusted tram interchange. Air thick with damp, walls sweating rust.

The fight came fast.

Torres rerouted an uplink through a compromised relay. Luka caught it and snapped. He shoved a printout into Torres's chest. "You think you're the only one who knows the cost of a mistake?"

The shove turned into a grapple, more desperation than strength. Luka's wound tore when he swung, the blow landing clumsy but hard enough to stagger. Torres answered with a wild elbow, pain flashing across his own face as much as Luka's.

They hit the wall, panting, half-broken men still trying to prove they weren't finished.

James shoved them off each other, breath ragged, his own fists still tight. He hated how familiar it looked—the masks, the bluff of strength over weakness.

Luka's lip split. Torres's eye swelled. Neither apologized.

Later, Luka smoked at the edge of the tunnel, rifle balanced across his knees. Torres sat with ice pressed to his face.

That night, James found Kyra in a maintenance room off the tunnel.

She sat on a cot, wrapping gauze around her fingers. Pipes hummed above, dripping in the dark.

"You told me you're failing at not feeling," she said without looking up. "But you hide it better than anyone I've ever seen."

Silence stretched, heavy as the damp air.

Then, quietly:
"Natalie."

Kyra stilled—just for a fraction.

The name came without hesitation.

No deflection. No mask.

He kept his eyes off her when he went on. The words came measured.

"CIA liaison. We passed notes in sugar packets, hid codes in cables no one ever checked. She laughed once—said I was too serious to ever be worth betraying. The next morning, she was gone."

His voice thinned. "All she left was a half-drunk coffee. Still warm when I found it."

She looked away.

Kyra's fingers twisted the gauze tighter around her hand, knuckles whitening until the fabric bit into her skin. She stared down at the basin where water pooled red, her jaw flexing once before she finally spoke.

"We all disappear."

Her voice caught, brittle.

She stood and went to the sink, scrubbing her hands until the skin split. Water streaked red across the basin.

"Seventeen," she said.

A pause.

"Border stop."

Her fingers pressed harder into the porcelain.

"My mother made a trade."

Another beat.

"They kept me."

James didn't move.

She shook her head once, small, dismissive.

"After that, it wasn't names."

Her mouth twitched.

"Just repetition."

Her grip tightened.

"You learn."

A beat.

"Or you don't last."

She dragged in one breath, sharp, then locked it down.

When her eyes found his again, they were clear. Cold.

James opened his mouth—then stopped.

She dried her hands on the gauze, movements precise.

When she passed him, her shoulder brushed his. Then it was gone.

The silence followed.

The tunnels breathed damp around him, pipes dripping like a metronome. James followed the sound of voices, low and jagged.

Luka had set up a perimeter near a rusted tram junction, rifle across his knees.

Torres leaned against a support beam, face pale in the half-light.

They looked like survivors, not soldiers. No formation, no orders—just scattered gravity pulling them back together.

Kyra arrived last. She didn't look at James. He didn't press.

"We need a fallback," Luka said flatly. "This tunnel's temporary. If they light us up again, we're done."

Torres tapped his temple, weary but still calculating. "Utility grid ties north. There's an old interchange depot. Abandoned since the nineties. Concrete, low heat signature. It'll hold for a night."

No one argued. They were too tired to.

They moved in silence, boots splashing through shallow water, packs heavy with damp. Warsaw above them burned, but down here the world was hushed, claustrophobic.

James stayed near Kyra, not close enough to touch, but close enough that if she stumbled, he could catch her. She didn't stumble. She never did.

Irina trailed last, shoulders hunched against the damp, Luka close behind her. He kept near without seeming to think, his hand brushing the edge of her pack when the tunnel narrowed. Kyra caught it. Said nothing.

By the time they reached the depot, dawn was bleeding pale through a cracked skylight. Dust and rust smelled like memory. Luka cleared corners with his rifle. Kyra dropped her gear without a word, the gauze at her hand still darkened, edges stiff with dried blood, though she acted as if it weren't there. Torres collapsed onto a broken bench, breath sharp.

Irina was the one who broke the silence—kneeling to check Torres, sliding gauze beneath cracked ribs. Her voice stayed low, clinical. Luka watched her with the quiet intensity of a man who had already chosen who he'd bleed for.

Luka smoked in the corner, Torres winced at every breath, Kyra sat rigid against the wall. Each carried their silence differently, but none broke it.

Silence clung like smoke.

Chapter 25: Smoke Script
Tallinn, Estonia

Правда не исчезает. Она просто переодевается в тени и шепчет сквозь дым. Тот, кто умеет слушать, слышит её — даже сквозь ложь.

"Truth doesn't vanish. It merely changes clothes, hides in shadow, and whispers through smoke. Those who know how to listen will hear it—even through lies."
— INTERCEPTED TALLINN TRANSMISSION

Only something close to invisibility could survive what Tallinn had become.

The tunnels had given them a single night of distance, nothing more; by morning the clinic district was already sealed into a perimeter of ash and controlled access, Estonian Police and Border Guard units layered with NATO observers while drones stitched the air into a grid that didn't blink or drift, and every vehicle that moved through the cordon was stopped without pattern, faces scanned twice, sometimes three times, as if the system wasn't verifying identity so much as confirming expectation.

They didn't try to outrun it.

They dispersed instead, thinning into separate lines of movement that no longer intersected—freight convoys, staggered departures, identities that never appeared in the same place twice—and by the time they crossed into Estonia, they were no longer a team in any visible sense, only five unrelated vectors moving through a country that had already learned how to see.

PhantomNet pulsed once.

No sender, no voice, no metadata that could be traced or even meaningfully analyzed.

TALLINN NODE. ORLENKO. OBSERVE. INTERDICT.

The coordinates resolved into Old Town, into a cluster of addresses sitting inside one of the most densely integrated digital infrastructures in Europe, where nothing was hidden because nothing needed to be.

Estonia didn't conceal its systems.

It embedded them.

Identity, banking, transit, medical records, voting—every action generated a trace, and every trace fed something larger than the individual who had created it.

Disappearing here wasn't a matter of going unseen.
It was a negotiation with visibility itself.

A door opened for him half a second before he reached it.
Not because it recognized him.
Because it recognized the pattern that preceded him.

Inside, the lights adjusted without being asked. A payment terminal pulsed once, awake before it was touched. Somewhere above, a camera shifted its angle—not tracking him, but aligning with the space he was about to occupy.

Nothing flagged. Nothing stopped him.
Everything adjusted.

That was worse.

Their covers weren't identities in any meaningful sense; they were permissions granted by a system that expected coherence and punished deviation.

James became Julian Roth, a Swiss consultant with clean e-residency credentials that would pass any surface audit but collapse under sustained scrutiny. He moved accordingly, keeping his routes irregular while maintaining a constant awareness of his reflection in glass, not to check for surveillance but to confirm that he still existed inside the version of the world the system expected to see.

Kyra became Elise Daan, an academic tied to a linguistics grant, her apartment positioned deliberately above tram lines so that the vibration of steel through the floor masked smaller sounds that might otherwise carry; she chose the space for that reason alone and never once commented on it.

Luka worked the docks under Ukrainian logistics credentials, loud enough to draw attention in the right places and diffuse it in others, while Torres nested inside the network itself, stripping a rental flat down to routers, signal repeaters, and scavenged boards as he began the slower work of listening between packets in a system designed to eliminate gaps.

Irina moved through all of it with the least resistance.

Language, posture, cadence—she carried them without effort, passing checkpoints with a smile that never lingered long enough to be remembered, filling the spaces the others couldn't see without ever appearing to occupy them.

They didn't regroup.
Not fully.

Tallinn didn't watch in the way they were trained to detect.
It didn't track. It anticipated.

Tram arrivals synchronized with traffic lights in ways that eliminated delay, payment terminals pinged in patterns that were too consistent to be random, and cameras didn't merely record—they correlated, aligning movement across systems until prediction became more efficient than observation.

James felt it first while crossing Viru Street, not as a presence but as an adjustment that occurred just before he moved, a subtle shift in timing that his body registered before his mind had a framework to interpret it.

He stopped once, mid-step, without reason.

The crossing light changed early.

When he moved again, it held green longer than it should have.

The bookstore wasn't hidden, and that alone made it suspect.

It sat between a wine bar and a bicycle stall, its windows dulled by a film of dust that hadn't been disturbed in years, its doorbell disconnected, its shelves sagging under the weight of books that no one had touched but that had never quite been abandoned.

Every Thursday at 15:18, Viktor Orlenko, GRU attaché, entered.

The routine was deliberate.

That was enough.

James watched from across the square, the glass of the café in front of him fogged just enough to break his outline without obscuring his view, his posture loose, unremarkable, his attention fixed without appearing so.

15:18.

Orlenko entered, placed the red card, and left without breaking stride.

Two minutes later, the girl arrived.

Auburn hair, university bag, hands that didn't belong to the environment she had stepped into.

Irina's voice came low across comms, threaded with observation rather than concern. "She's not trained."

She reached for the book, missed, corrected, and slid the envelope inside.

James was already moving.

Not fast. Not obvious. Just early.

The bell didn't ring when he entered. The door didn't need to.

He crossed the space without looking at the counter, pulled the book free, and let the envelope slide into his sleeve in one continuous motion.

They let the girl leave.

She didn't run.

She moved clean, steady, never accelerating, never hesitating, her pace consistent enough to feel natural and precise enough to be deliberate.

Kyra adjusted once, cutting the angle through a side street that should have intersected her path two blocks ahead.

It didn't.

Irina shifted wider, picking up the reflection line through glass and tram windows.

Nothing.
No hesitation. No correction. No error.

The girl turned once—left, not right—and the timing broke.

Kyra hit the corner three seconds later.

Empty.

Irina stopped beside her, not breathing hard, not speaking.

Kyra didn't move.

That had never happened.

Not once.

It wasn't that she'd lost the girl.

It was that the girl had already been somewhere else.

James unfolded the paper in the stairwell two blocks away.

Cyrillic.

Handwritten. Fast. Slight smear along the edge.

Книги дышат ложью, но чернила помнят.

He read it twice.

It meant nothing to him.

He folded it back along the original crease and slipped it away.

They didn't try to break it.
They tried to move outside it.

Routes changed. Timing fractured. Actions taken without purpose, without pattern, without reason.

Nothing broke.
Nothing slipped.
Every deviation closed around them.

Torres ran the feed against movement logs.
Frame by frame.

Kyra's route adjustment.
Timestamped. Flagged.

Before she made it.

He stopped the playback.
"Look at the mark," he said.

No one spoke.

The marker appeared before she moved.

Not as she moved.

Before.

Torres didn't scroll. He didn't need to.

"Look at the timing," he said.

No one spoke.

Irina didn't look at the screen.

She looked at Kyra.

"It's not tracking," she said.

"It knows."

Torres went deeper.

Past the visible network. Past the layers meant to be found.

What he found wasn't hidden.
It was integrated.

Civilian systems. Identity loops. Movement data.
Everything feeding.
Everything aligning.

None of it built for this.

"This isn't an operation," he said.

No one disagreed.

Irina folded the napkin once more and set it on the table, resting her hand over it as if anchoring something that didn't want to stay still.

"They don't need to stop us," she said.

"They just need us to keep behaving."

Kyra watched her without interruption.

Measuring, not questioning.

No one touched the system. No one ran another test.

Outside, Tallinn moved without interruption—trams aligned, signals clean, timing intact.

They weren't being tracked.
They were being anticipated.

And there was nowhere left to move that hadn't already been seen.

CHAPTER 26: THE COLD REMEMBERS
Tallinn, Estonia

*And lo, the frost did not forget, nor did the stone forgive. The wind bore
witness, and the silence spoke in tongues of ash.
They fled into the shadow, thinking themselves hidden—but the cold had
written their names in the marrow of the earth.
For what is buried in silence shall rise in fog, and what is left unnamed
shall return with fire on its breath.*
— CODEX V: ECHOES OF THE FORGOTTEN WAR

Nothing in Tallinn forgot.
Not the stone. Not the cold. Not the paths they took through it.

Stone walls wept with condensation, and the harbor groaned
where ice shoved against hulls. To most, it was just another
northern winter.

Nothing moved without consequence.

Doors logged entry. Signals carried timing. Heat left trace.

Even the fog didn't conceal—it diffused.

The rooftop above Linnahall wasn't a rooftop but a monument
sprawling into fog—brutalist steps descending toward the
harbor like a half-drowned coliseum. Cracked concrete wept
rainwater into dark pools that reflected the city lights in jagged
fragments. Graffiti scarred the walls, its bright colors blurred to
ghosts in the mist.

The sea pressed close. Brine carried on the wind stung James's
throat. Somewhere below, steel hulls groaned against ice, the
sound echoing up through stone. Behind them, Old Town's
medieval spires pierced the haze like black teeth, reminders of
centuries of fire and siege.

James sat near the ledge, coat drawn tight. Beside him, Kyra
lowered herself into the damp, matchbook balanced between
them. The match flared once, guttered in the wind, leaving sulfur
sharp in the air, the smell clinging like memory.

"If they come for us—" she began.

"They already have," James said.

She didn't argue. Her breath fogged in the dark, mingling with the harbor mist. They sat in silence, the wind clawing the edges of their coats, the fog swallowing the city whole.

A few steps back, Irina stood near the broken rail, shoulders hunched against the wind, eyes on the harbor instead of them. She wasn't eavesdropping. She was watching reflections—water, glass, movement—counting what the fog tried to hide.

His burner buzzed once: **Murmansk**. The word burned on the cracked screen like a scar reopened—inevitable, unasked for, the kind of summons that never left you whole.

Murmansk wasn't a place.
It was a direction.

James shoved the phone back into his pocket, jaw tight.

Kyra watched him. "What is it?"

"Nothing that matters. Not compared to what you dropped on me."

Her brow lifted slightly, but she didn't answer.

James exhaled hard, fog spilling from his lungs. "You say things like that," he said, "and then you shut me out."

Her eyes stayed on the mist over the harbor. "You can't fix it."

"I know." His voice cracked sharper than he wanted. "I want to be with you, Kyra. But you never let me. You hand me pieces of a war I can't fight, then expect me to sit still."

She shook her head, slow, deliberate. "You're not supposed to fix it. It's mine. That's the only way it works. You can't change it."

He stared at her profile, the fog softening everything but the steel in her voice. "And I'm just supposed to sit here, pretending I don't want to take some of it off you?"

Her reply came quiet, final: "Wanting won't help."

James pushed to his feet, coat dragging fog around him.

Kyra's hand twitched against the stone, almost reaching, almost holding him there. "You're not invisible in this fog."

"Neither are you," he muttered. Then, softer: "I'm going to sweep the streets."

He stepped into the mist.

Irina's gaze followed him for a beat too long. Not concern—calculation. She shifted her weight, as if considering whether to go after him.

She didn't.

Some distances had to be chosen.

James went off alone. He told himself it was reconnaissance, a sweep for tails.

Tallinn's Lower Town blurred around him. Stone walls sweating condensation, boots too loud in alleys that had survived centuries. He drifted through alleys where stone arched overhead, hands in his pockets, burner phone heavier with every step.

The cold pressed through his jacket, searching for weakness.

Back at Linnahall, Irina checked the perimeter again—same routes, same blind corners. Kyra hadn't moved much. Pain kept her still, pride kept her upright.

Irina understood both.

She hated waiting. But she hated chasing worse.

James came back hours later, skin wind-burned, lungs full of coal smoke. The fog still clung to his coat like he'd carried the city's ghosts home with him.

Kyra was still there—cross-legged near the ledge, her coat open to the cold, one hand pressed against her rib.

She didn't speak when he approached. The monument carried their silence, stone and salt holding what neither could name. James lowered himself beside her, the concrete damp against his palms, a half bottle of vodka between them.

"You should lie down," he muttered.

Kyra's eyes stayed on the fog. "I've done enough lying."

He almost laughed. Almost. Instead, he drank. The vodka burned like winter itself, rough enough to make his chest ache. He passed the bottle to her.

She took it without looking at him, tilted her head back, and swallowed. A drop slipped from her lip, traced her jaw, vanished into the collar of her coat. She wiped it with the back of her hand, eyes still fixed on the cranes dissolving into mist.

"Doesn't help," she said.

"Never does."

The bottle passed again. The city lights shimmered faintly through the fog, fractured across puddles in the cracked steps. Above, the spires of Old Town loomed like watchtowers of another age.

James glanced sideways at her—the bruises ink-dark beneath her shirt, rib-deep remnants of Warsaw, carried forward into Tallinn's cold. Her breath was shallow but steady.

He drank again, throat raw. "You really should let someone carry some of it."

Her mouth curved, not quite a smile. "That's not how it works."

"You make it sound like math. Like there's a right answer."

"There is." She tipped the bottle back, eyes narrowing at the taste. "Survive. Everything else is noise."

The vodka came back to him. He let the glass rest against his lip but didn't drink.

"Noise has a way of sounding like truth when you're tired enough."

For a heartbeat, she looked at him—really looked, fog and bruises and silence all caught in the sharp cut of her gaze. Then she huffed a laugh, low and sudden, like it slipped past her defenses.

"God, listen to you," she said, shaking her head. "You sound like one of Torres's philosophy podcasts."

The sound startled him, almost warmed him. She'd told him once she didn't laugh much anymore, and now he understood: he'd never heard it until this moment.

She tipped the bottle back and drank like punctuation.

The laugh still clung faintly to the air, rough around the edges, not meant for him but given all the same. He almost smiled. Almost reached. Instead, the bottle kept moving, glass knocking against their teeth in turn.

They passed it, again, and again. The cold pressed harder, the silence heavier, until James realized: it wasn't ghosts that had followed him here. It was Tallinn itself—Linnahall's stone, the sea's weight, and Kyra's quiet gravity holding him in something he couldn't define, couldn't fight.

When he finally looked down, the matchbook from earlier was still between them. The last one had burned out hours ago, leaving only the faint smell of smoke on the damp concrete. Kyra's fingers brushed it once, absently, as if testing whether it might still spark.

She stood, coat brushing his arm as she passed, and for a second he thought she might glance back, might let that laugh widen into something more.

She didn't.

She walked into the fog, her steps echoing down the concrete like someone forcing themselves not to turn.

James stayed seated, staring at the empty matchbook. The silence clung sharper than the cold, heavier than the fire they'd run from.

Morning bled pale. James's head split with every clatter of the salt trucks rattling through Old Town, the noise sharp enough to feel physical, each impact echoing somewhere behind his eyes. His stomach rolled against the taste of last night's vodka, mouth sour, tongue thick, the slow burn of bile creeping up his throat in waves that never quite broke. The fog outside had nothing on the fog in his skull.

Torres muttered about "ghost signals in NATO bands," his voice too fast, too bright for the hour, words stacking on each other like he couldn't shut them off once they started. Luka stood near the tram yard, smoking, eyes tracking every reflection, every shifting angle of glass and steel, vigilance so ingrained it didn't seem like a choice anymore.

James stayed for as long as he could.

Then he didn't.

"I'm getting air," he muttered, not waiting for a response, already moving before anyone could ask the question he didn't want to answer.

No one stopped him.

Some distances didn't need permission.

He cut down toward the promenade, away from the tram lines and the noise, boots grinding lightly against salt and thawing slush, the harbor opening ahead of him in a long gray stretch where fog and water blurred into something without edge. The wind came off the Baltic hard and clean, cutting through the hangover in a way nothing else had managed.

It should have been enough.
It wasn't.

The city still moved around him—foot traffic, morning deliveries, the low mechanical rhythm of something larger than all of them continuing without interruption—but out here, it felt thinner, like the system had stretched instead of receded.

Across the promenade, in a red scarf, she wasn't moving.

That was the first thing wrong.

Everyone else adjusted—small corrections in pace and direction, the quiet choreography of people sharing space without thinking about it—but she didn't shift, didn't compensate, didn't acknowledge the flow at all.

The movement bent around her.

Sound slipped—half a beat out of alignment.

Their eyes met.

"Ты забыл, Джеймс?" she said softly.
(Did you forget, James?)

She stepped closer.

"My Petr."

The words weren't accusation.
They were recognition.

James didn't move.

Couldn't.

Something in the way she said it landed deeper than language.

Then she was gone.

A camera above the alley pivoted once.

Not toward her.

Toward where she had been.

Gone—slipping into the alley line at the edge of the promenade like she had never occupied the space at all.

James stepped forward, too late, the movement delayed by just enough to matter, his shoulder clipping empty air where she should have been.

Except—
It wasn't empty.

The impact lingered, dull and real, a phantom pressure that didn't fade as quickly as it should have.

He stopped at the alley mouth, breathing harder than the distance justified, eyes scanning angles that had already resolved back into normal movement—pedestrians, delivery carts, nothing out of place, nothing holding.

Only the bootprints.
Fresh.

Cut into the slush where she had passed.

James pressed a hand against the stone wall, head dipping forward as the pounding behind his eyes surged again, harder now.

Kyra appeared beside him, silent at first, her presence registering more as a shift in the air than a sound. Her eyes tracked the alley, then him.

"What is it?"

James swallowed, mouth dry, voice low. "A woman. Red scarf. Same one from last night."

Hangover or not, the old instincts still fired—angles, exits, line-of-sight. His skull throbbed, but the training held.

Kyra's gaze moved once, sweeping the alley, then the promenade beyond.

"I didn't see anyone," she said.

James frowned, looking back at the bootprints, then at the empty space where she had been.

"She was right there."

Kyra didn't answer immediately. Her attention stayed on the environment, not him.

When she spoke, her voice was even.

"Then she's better than you thought."

James rubbed his temple, the pain behind his eyes pounding harder than the cold. The words spilled before he could stop them.

"She knew me," he said, almost to himself. "Or thought she did. She knew my name..."

Kyra's mouth tightened—barely, but enough. Her eyes swept rooftops, shop glass, the angles of tram windows. A check for eyes in the fog. Then her hand settled on his shoulder, steady and firm, nudging him forward.

"We need to go."

They walked, boots crunching in the slush, the canal mist closing behind them, James's head throbbing with every step. Kyra's hand stayed on his shoulder longer than necessary before sliding away. Her silence wasn't the still kind now—it carried edges, quick with thought.

"She knew your name. OBELISK's reading us. NATO bands aren't clean."

She glanced once at him, jaw flexed. "Tell me which part of that isn't already inside the same system."

James swallowed, his mouth sour, head splitting. Every word from her landed like a hammer against his skull. She looked steady—clear-eyed, controlled—like the vodka hadn't even touched her. No hangover, no ghosts clawing through her. James swallowed the shame that he'd never be able to stand beside her without faltering. That was her edge.

"I don't know," he grumbled.

Her brow lifted, the faintest cut of disbelief. "You still think we're ahead of this?"

James didn't answer. His stomach lurched at each jolt of the cobblestones, jaw clenched until it ached, fists tight in his pockets, irritation bleeding through every pounding step.

The cobblestones lurched under his boots again, a pulse of nausea rising sharp and unwelcome. It hadn't been OBELISK, and it hadn't been hallucination.

Kyra's eyes flicked to him, quick and sharp. She rolled them once, muttering just loud enough for him to hear, "Vodka's winning this round."

ACT V - COUNTERMOVES

"The first countermove is always silence.

The second is blood."

CHAPTER 27: GLASS COFFIN
Prague, Czech Republic | 24 hours later

The burner hadn't quieted since Murmansk lit up the line. Then, PhantomNet blinked again, harder this time, carving a new directive into their nerves: GLASS COFFIN. Prague. Twenty-four hours.

No one asked why Prague, or what 'Glass Coffin' meant. PhantomNet never explained. It only carved, and they carried the scars forward.

Luka's van rattled through snow-choked streets. Torres twitched against the sedative in back, lips still forming code no one could hear. He hadn't come off the grid clean in Tallinn—pushed too far, too deep, and something hadn't cleared.

Luka drove hunched forward, cigarette unlit between his teeth, eyes fixed on the snow.

Irina rode beside Torres, two fingers on his wrist, counting under her breath. She adjusted the blanket at his shoulders with a tenderness that didn't belong in the line of work. When Torres's lips formed another soundless 'echo,' her jaw tightened—not disgusted, just quietly angry at whatever had done this to him.

Kyra didn't move at all—her stillness more absolute than sleep. By the time the van cleared the Moldau bridges, James felt the shift in his bones. Prague had survived fires, sieges, occupations. Tonight it felt like the stones themselves were waiting to watch again. Tallinn's fog had been a shroud. Prague's silence was glass—transparent, fragile, waiting to crack.

The flat was a Karlín walk-up, windows barred more out of history than need. From the balcony, the Vltava glowed bone-colored in sodium light. Oblivion didn't have headquarters. Not structurally. Not in the walls. In them.

Irina moved through the flat the way some people moved through grief—methodical, precise, unwilling to leave anything to chance. Door seams checked, radiator hiss measured, window latches tested.

She shoved a towel against the base of the door, cutting the corridor light down to nothing, then set a kettle on the stove without asking. The gesture was small, domestic, almost tender. In a room built for covers and exits, it said something else entirely: stay long enough to breathe.

Torres lay under a light sedative, lips moving, barely audible. Just one word, over and over—"Echo... echo..."—lag, not repetition. Luka capped the vial, slid it back into his kit with the same motion he'd use chambering a round. James caught it in Luka's eyes—not irritation. Resignation. Torres could burn through a city's grid on pure will. Even will had a half-life.

Sedating him felt like smothering fire to save the house. Necessary, but brutal. James said nothing, though the cost of it pressed heavier than the snow outside. He had seen men burn out before—sparks clawing past their limits. But Torres was different—too wired into the machine. When he broke, it would carry.

James found Kyra on the balcony. Snow drifted in slow, fat flakes, the city's sodium glow turning each one the color of old bone.

He stepped beside her without crowding. "You've been quiet since Tallinn."

Her gaze stayed on the river. "Since Tallinn. Things aren't lining up."

The red scarf cut in again.

They stood in it.

PhantomNet blinked again at dawn: **GLASS COFFIN, 21:00.**

Locals called the riverside jazz club that—the ceiling a crystal grid over chandeliers, a greenhouse for expensive lies.

HARROW, an ex-FSB turned Czech contractor, would signal with a napkin fold and then pass proof of a GRU logistics route running Kaliningrad → Moldova → Transnistria: manifests, drone logs, biometric tags. Enough to salt an entire chain.

Their entry required a face the room would accept: money, discretion, marriage.

Julian and Elise Roth arrived on the Vltava in a hired town car that smelled faintly of leather and smoke. Covers that had already earned their scars, recycled because the city would accept them. Sometimes familiarity was safer than invention.

Luka floated along the perimeter in a bakery van across the bridge. Torres rode the city's camera grid from a laundromat's back server, sluggish from the cocktail of stims and sedatives still in his system, but too stubborn to back down or stop working.

James slid a simple band onto his finger. The band felt heavier than it should, as if metal could measure all the things he couldn't say.

Kyra did the same, the metal cold as truth.

The dress cut clean along her frame—black, precise—opening just enough to break his focus.

He offered his arm; she set her hand there like a claim.

"Smile," she murmured, a ghost of a grin. "You're a man in love."

"Pretend," he said.

"If you really need to." Her breath warmed his ear; her fingers found the inside of his wrist, pulse-mark sure.

"Eyes up, my husband."

He blinked—too late—pulling his gaze back up from where it had drifted.

They moved through glass and music. Waiters drifted like polished ghosts. An attaché from Warsaw laughed too loud at nothing. A deputy minister tried not to watch Kyra and failed.

Every surface reflected them back, husband and wife in crystal panes. A thousand fragile lies, one crack away from shattering.

At a corner table, James felt her lean into him for the benefit of a mirror. The weight of her—light and decisive—sent a fault line through his calm.

Eyes watched. For a second, she let herself believe they were his.

For him, the danger wasn't being caught. It was how much he wanted to believe it too.

He almost said her name.
"Ky—"

"Elise," she corrected softly, lips barely moving. "Stay with me."

Her hand pressed tighter into his arm, the picture of devotion. "And do try to keep your balance. If anyone asks, you avoided the vodka last night."

He lifted her hand and kissed her knuckles because that's what husbands did here. His mouth was warm, steady, and for a heartbeat it didn't feel like cover at all. Her pulse betrayed her, tripping once under his lips.

She felt it—and shut it down a second too late.

On the linen between their plates, a folded napkin appeared—crisp, the fold pattern wrong for this club by one precise crease. *Signal received.* The pass, however, did not walk to their table.

Kyra's smile never reached her eyes. "We're being watched," she breathed.

Her gaze flicked once, precise. "Two o'clock, balcony rail. Eyes on us."

A pause.

"This isn't lining up."

James didn't look. Didn't need to. The room had shifted—small things out of place, timing too clean, attention settling where it shouldn't.

Kyra's fingers tightened once against his arm. "They're not bringing it to us."

A waiter crossed the floor—empty tray, wrong direction—then disappeared through the service door.

Kyra tracked it. Just a flick of the eyes.

It clicked.

"Back of house," he said quietly.

"Or outside," she replied.

James covered the napkin with his palm. "We don't wait."

"Finish your drink, Mrs. Roth."

She clinked his glass like a vow. "After you, Mr. Roth."

She finished her drink, then set the empty glass on a passing hors d'oeuvre table.

They rose together and let the glass coffin swallow their reflection whole.

The music and chandeliers fell away to wet cobblestones and compressor hum. The alley smelled like old beer and winter. Shadows pooled where the club's light couldn't reach.

"It's wrong," Kyra said, voice thin with the cold. "I can feel it."

"Torres?" James subvocalized.

"Camera feed is stuttering," Torres breathed back. "Like somebody's breathing into the line. Same echo as Tallinn. I've got ninety seconds before the grid goes blind."

Luka shifted in the van, sightline narrowing through the windshield. "I've got partial on your alley. Not clean."

Irina held the mouth of the alley, just out of the light, eyes on the street.

"No exterior tails coming in," Luka said. "Bridge is—hold—"

Silencers coughed.

A round snapped through the van's windshield—Luka jerked back, breath catching. "I'm hit—still with you."

Six men slid from the seams—no uniforms, no wasted motion. One at the mouth, two high on the fire escape, the rest staggered to cut retreat. Geometry like that wasn't accidental.

James put the first down with a throat shot. A second dropped from the fire escape; James caught him across the temple with the butt of his pistol and pivoted.

Kyra was already gone from his side—then *there*, blade across a tendon, a slice opening a thigh, the quiet brutality of training distilled into three heartbeats.

"Left," she snapped.

He obeyed without question.

Gunfire swept the façade, deliberately high. The windows went in at once, glass crashing like memory, the attack meant to disorient more than kill.

Irina didn't move—just shifted her angle, covering the street.

The fight thinned for a heartbeat—boots scuffed, muzzles searching. Then HARROW staggered into the alley from the club's side door, coat hanging open, one hand clamped to his chest, the other still locked around a thumb drive. His eyes were too wide, wild with the knowledge he'd been herded here, not saved.

He opened his mouth—maybe to finish the pass, maybe just to beg time—but the round took him before the sound left. The impact folded him, spun him, drove him hard into the cobbles at James's feet.

Blood welled fast, soaking through his shirt in a dark bloom. His gaze flicked not to James, but to the drive still clenched in his fist, as if proof might outlive him. Then the life drained, leaving a hole in his chest wide enough to speak through.

"Fallback!" Torres's voice burned through in short waves. "They're jamming—ghost channel echo—same bleed, no origin—"

"Bridge is hot!" Luka coughed through smoke. "Move now or I can't help you."

James reached for the drive, fingers brushing cold metal—then a gunman dropped from the fire escape and smashed the muzzle across his face. The shock blurred his vision. Before he could react, Kyra was there, heel snapping the man's jaw sideways. She dropped over James in the same motion, shielding him with her body for the heartbeat it took to bring her weapon back up.

The closeness, the absolute lack of hesitation, hit James harder than the blow itself.

"Up," she said.

He moved—firing twice to shear a man off the fire escape.

The last of them broke and ran.

Snow turned pink in the hush that followed.

James pried the drive from dead fingers. The casing was cold, heavier than looked. Proof was supposed to walk out with HARROW—manifests, drone logs, the whole chain. Now it was just this, stripped of context, maybe tainted, maybe bait.

"They set it," Kyra added, voice low. "And we let them choose the ending."

He wanted to tell her they hadn't. That choices still existed in the teeth of a trap. But Torres was in his ear again, riding adrenaline: "Thirty seconds before the grid resets and they make you on every angle from here to Karlín. Move."

Irina crouched near the mouth of the alley, eyes tracking the angles they'd just survived, the way glass still tinkled somewhere above them.

"Next time we don't let the city choose the corridor," Irina said. "Next time we choose."

James shoved the drive inside his jacket and glanced at Kyra. "We walk out together."

He lifted a hand to his eye, masking the swelling, turning the motion into something idle. Beside him, Kyra pushed her bloodied hands into her coat pockets, the evidence gone as if it had never happened.

She slipped her arm through his without looking at him.

They stepped back toward the street as one.

They left the alley as they had entered the club—shoulder to shoulder, two beautiful lies under glass.

Inside, the music never fully stopped—just faltered, a half-beat hitch swallowed under the low murmur of voices. Staff moved quickly, efficiently. Broken glass was already being cleared. No one looked toward the alley for long.

The quartet resumed as if nothing had broken.

Outside, Luka ghosted the van across the bridge without lights. Torres exhaled when their signal reappeared two blocks out. "I've got you now."

"For now," James said.

They regrouped in the flat's low light.

James set the drive on the table. No one reached for it.

Luka bled from a forearm crease and refused stitches. He dropped his band into the ashtray without looking, the gesture final, like snapping shut a file. Torres followed, his hand shaking from the stimulants crash, the metal clinking down beside Luka's like a nail in a coffin.

James slid his own ring free and tossed it in after theirs, the motion sharp, almost careless. The gold hit glass with a hollow sound, a cover discarded.

Kyra stripped slower—earrings, bracelet, then at last the ring. She turned it once between her fingers, weighing it, the gold catching a shard of lamp-light. Then, instead of letting it fall, she slid it into her pocket.

James saw it.

The ashtray waited, same as Luka's, same as Torres's—but she kept hers. He saw it—and didn't look away.

He didn't call it out, didn't risk breaking the moment. Instead, he let himself believe the ring had become something more to her than a tool.

James looked down at the drive—at what it meant, at what it couldn't give back. **Project SILENCE** scraped his nerves raw. Oblivion didn't stop wars. It stopped proof. It sealed doors behind the people who opened them.

"Tomorrow," Luka said, lighting a cigarette he didn't smoke, "we burn their route anyway."

"Tomorrow," Torres echoed, a tremor in the word.

The flat thinned out until it was only the two of them. Luka in the other room with his bleeding arm. Torres collapsed into stim tremors. The hum of the radiator filled the silence.

James stood with her at the window, snow webbing against the glass. For a long time, he said nothing. Then, quietly:

"I'm sorry… I don't know what to do with what you said. About being used your whole life. I won't pretend I understand what you've been through. But I know the hollow it leaves. I've been there too."

He let the silence stretch, his reflection ghosted in the glass.

She didn't answer. But she didn't walk away either.

Outside, snow tapped the pane like muted applause. Inside, their breath fogged a window that wouldn't open.

CHAPTER 28: WHAT REMAINS
Prague, Czech Republic | After Karlín

For in the end, it is not the fall that breaks us,
But the memory of the ground.
— FRAGMENT FROM THE ECHO CODEX, SECTION 5

They had barely caught their breath in the Karlín flat before the directive pulled them back into the teeth. HARROW's drive was supposed to map a GRU logistics chain, proof they could salt. Instead, following it into the tramline tunnels gave them only smoke and steel.

The ambush found them first.

Torres went down hard, two blocks from the target relay, blood pouring from his side. Luka dragged him through service grates while James and Kyra covered retreat, the city's grid hissing with the same ghost-echo they'd seen in Tallinn.

By the time they staggered into the municipal tunnel, Torres was slumped against a bulkhead, lips moving through static. "I'm hit," he rasped. "Lost signal. Then the air bent—like heat haze, but metal under it. Curved, watching."

James' chest tightened. "Drone?"

Torres shook his head, grimacing. "No rotors. No noise. Just a shimmer that cut the feed and left nothing but echo."

James didn't answer. He could still see it—the way the space had refused to hold shape.

Kyra ripped open a med kit, hands steady though her breath shortened. She pressed gauze into the wound, Torres screaming through clenched teeth. Luka's jaw was iron.

Irina hovered just behind them, kit already open, vials clinking. She forced a sedative into his arm with one sharp motion, her own breath ragged. "He'll thrash himself into shock if you don't hold him."

"We need to move," James said.

They carried Torres three blocks to a fallback flat wired days ago. No windows. No traces. By evening, he was stable enough to breathe, but not to walk.

Irina sat cross-legged on the floor near him, pale in the glow of the heater. Her gloves were stiff with his blood, but she hadn't changed them. She stared at her hands like they belonged to someone else, until Luka slid a chair toward her and muttered, "Sleep."

She didn't.

The fallback site smelled like rust and silence. A half-burned map of Moldova curled on the folding table, weighted by an empty magazine.

Torres sat hooded, flicking a dead SIM card between his fingers. Luka stood at the window, watching nothing. Kyra paced, measured, restless geometry.

James stared at static on a muted monitor. HARROW's body, the drive, the collapsing alley replayed like broken tape.

"Why do we care?" Luka asked finally. "He's dead. The route's buried. Márton's gone. Why are we still bleeding for this?"

No one answered.

"Oblivion's compromised," Torres said, voice raw. "The Echo's feeding on us. We're not rescuing anybody—we're just meat shields. Mostly me. At this rate, Red Cross is gonna cut me off."

Kyra stopped pacing. She cocked her head, a small gesture that carried more respect than rebuttal—like she'd been waiting for someone else to name the cost aloud. Her voice came low, steady. "If we walk away now, what do we become?"

"Alive?" Luka spat.

"No," James said without looking up.

He picked up the drive, turned it in the light like something radioactive.

"Harrow wasn't just a defector. He was a thread. If that intel's real, the GRU is routing arms through diplomatic cover—state immunity as shield. That's not just smuggling. That's architecture."

"And we lit a match in it," Kyra said.

Luka's jaw tightened. "You think the echo's tied to that?"

James nodded. "The same jamming we saw in Tallinn erased Harrow and us in one move. That's orchestration."

Torres muttered, "We're not intercepting signals anymore. We're in it now."

"Exactly," James said. "Whoever's routing this—GRU or not—they're not moving weapons. They're moving narratives. They know when we move, what we'll chase, how we'll bleed. Mostly him."

He nodded toward Torres.

Torres lifted one shaky hand, middle finger crooked like a flag. "Fuck you, man," he rasped, but the corner of his mouth twitched like he almost meant it as a joke.

Kyra's head tipped, and for once she didn't hide it. A smile tugged, unguarded, and before she could choke it down, a soft laugh broke free. Quick, fleeting—but real. It caught James off guard more than the joke itself, because it wasn't steel or shadow this time. It was her.

The laugh faded the way a flare burns out. Kyra worked herself back to the edge of steel and silence. Her voice dropped, steady and flat. "Harrow was bait. Nothing more."

"Then what now?" Luka asked, smoke-gray and blunt.

James's voice found its shape, low and certain. "Now we trace it. Not just to stop a war. Not to expose it. To find who's writing the script—and why they want us erased."

He looked at Torres. "Oblivion's not dead. We're just off the page."

Torres snorted, lifting two fingers without looking up. "Yeah, well—try not to write me in as the guy bleeding out every chapter."

The power died at 03:17. No surge. No flicker. Just silence.

Torres swore from the comms room. Luka grabbed his sidearm. Kyra was already moving—boots half-laced, eyes feral.

James' burner phone lit in his hand. No number. No signal. Just one word: **Здравствуйте.** *Zdravstvuyte*
—a greeting that held formality like a blade's edge.

Across the street, every window in the tenement opposite flared to life. Simultaneous. Precise. Then dark again.

Not attack. Reminder.

No arguments. Luka packed. Torres wiped drives.

Luka fed IDs into the stove, laminate curling.

Torres dropped his last comm wire into bleach, watching it curl and pale as if even the memory of signal had to be stripped away.

James smashed the burner, snapped the SIM in half, then fed the pieces into the stove. The plastic blackened and curled into flakes before they pushed the embers closed.

Only then did Irina move. She slipped a silver medallion from her neck, the chain still knotted where small fingers had once worried it. Her father had given it to her when she was a child— St. Christopher, patron of travelers. She held it for a long breath, thumb pressed to the worn engraving as if Márton's promise still lived in the metal. Then she let it fall into the embers.

The silver flared once, bright as a headlight in snow, then was gone.

No one spoke. No ceremony. Just erasure.

Torres gave a ragged laugh, low and bitter. "Oblivion, huh? Burn us once, burn us twice."

Only Kyra didn't burn anything. There was nothing left of hers to burn. She just stood still, watching the fire consume who they had been.

By 03:24, Oblivion no longer existed.

[Brno, Czech Republic | Days later.]

Kyra stood at the window, steam still lifting faintly from her skin, James's shirt hanging loose on her frame—buttoned once, just enough to pretend at modesty. The city broke across her in amber fragments, lace and light cutting her into something deliberate.

James watched from the doorway, jaw tight. He knew what she was doing—the angle, the stillness, the way she let herself be seen without ever giving anything away.

Control, dressed as invitation.

"You're staring," she said, not turning.

"I couldn't sleep."

"Do you ever?"

He stepped closer.
She didn't move away.

The space between them tightened—everything unsaid pressing in. She turned then, closing it herself, like stepping onto something she knew wouldn't hold.

Her hand came up, flat against his chest, feeling the rhythm there.

"Careful, James," she said quietly. "Wanting has a cost."

"I've been paying it since Budapest."

A beat.

"Since the fence. Since you looked at me."

For a moment, neither of them moved.

Then the distance collapsed.

The kiss wasn't tentative. It wasn't discovery. It was recognition—something unfinished finding its way back under pressure. His hands found her; hers held him there, not soft, not yielding—anchoring.

She broke it first.
Not to pull away—but to reposition.

Turning, drawing him with her, back to the window. The glass was cold against her palms. The city moved below them, indifferent, close enough to matter.

Danger, not display.

"That respect you seem to have for me…" she said, voice low.

A pause.

"Not now."

He stepped in, closing the space again. No hesitation this time. The contact was immediate, certain—no room left between them.

Her breath hit the glass, fogging it white.

"Say my name," she said.

"Kyra—"

"No."

The word cut clean.

She turned her head just enough to see him, eyes sharp, unreadable.

"Katya."

It landed wrong. Too right.

He didn't move.

That was the moment—the line between what he knew and what she was asking him to accept.

"Call me Katya."

Not a request.

A decision.

Something in him resisted. Not her—what it meant. What it replaced.

But she didn't give him space to resolve it. Her hand came back to him, pulling, insisting—not gently.

He exhaled, rough, controlled—and let it go.

"Katya."

The name came out heavier than it should have. Misaligned.

Her eyes closed for a fraction of a second.

Recognition.

That he'd crossed it.

The rest of it didn't need words. It didn't need shape. Just pressure, movement, contact that didn't pretend to be anything else.

When it was over, neither of them spoke.

She stepped away first, pulling the shirt back around herself, reclaiming the distance like it had never been given.

James stayed where he was, breath steadying, the city still moving beyond the glass.

He didn't follow.
Didn't reach.

Because the question had already formed, and he knew better than to ask it out loud.

Who had he just been with?

Kyra.

Katya.

She adjusted the collar of the shirt, fingers brushing once across her own throat, then looked back at him.

"I don't know what happens after this."

"We survive it," he said.

It sounded thinner than he intended.

Her mouth curved—small, controlled, unreadable.

By the next day, the distance was back. Armor re-formed.

They moved at night, one car, no stops. The forged pipeline ran through Anhelina Marković, a Balkan fixer who had cut her teeth moving defectors out of Sarajevo, Bosnia in the nineties before reinventing herself as a document broker in Bratislava, Slovakia.

She dealt in identities like other people dealt in currency—rare, dirty, and never clean for long.

Years ago, in Constanța, Romania, Kyra had dragged Marković out from under a GRU rendition team—burning her own cover in the process. Saving her had cost Kyra everything in that city.

Debts like that don't vanish. Tonight, she came to collect: a stack of fresh aliases, transit permits, and a border package good enough to pass at speed.

When Anhelina arrived, fur-lined coat dusted with snow, she kissed Kyra on both cheeks like nothing between them had ever broken. But her first words cut sharp.

"Still wearing other people's faces, I see," she said in accented English.

Kyra's smile was thin. "Still charging too much for paper."

Marković tilted her head, voice lowering. "Ты всё ещё веришь, что тебя можно спасти?" *You still believe you can be saved?*

Kyra's smile vanished. Her reply was a whisper edged with glass: "Я перестала верить в спасение, когда вы оставили меня в Кишинёве." *I stopped believing in salvation when you left me in Chișinău.*

Anhelina's gloved fingers toyed with a matchbox scarred with old burns, like she needed to remind everyone she'd survived more fires than she'd lit.

The snow seemed to still between them. James caught only fragments of the Russian, but the cadence told enough—old wounds, dangerous ones.

Marković's lips curved, almost amused. "Ты жива, значит — я не совсем плохая." *You're alive, so I can't be all bad.*

Kyra's jaw clenched. "Нет. Просто я — упрямая сука." *No. I'm just a stubborn bitch.*

Their eyes locked—two women with a history measured in betrayals and burned cities. Luka shifted uncomfortably, fingers tightening on his pack straps. James didn't need the words. The tone alone was a razor.

They traveled by night, same single car, no stops. The backseat smelled of iodine and gun oil. Torres lay medicated across the blankets. Kyra rode up front, face unreadable, documents sealed under her coat.

At the border, a younger guard studied James's photo, eyes narrowing. "You shaved," he said. Not quite a smile.

James's jaw tightened. Absurd that a razor stroke might weigh more than forged papers, more than months of running.

The pause stretched—until the older officer nodded once, handed the papers back.

Fifteen minutes, one smile, and half a breath from collapse.

They rolled past the checkpoint into black mountain road. Pines lined the highway like sentries, branches heavy with frost. Wind poured through the rental's cracked windows.

"This is it," Luka muttered. "End of the line."

James glanced at Kyra. Her eyes lingered on him, tired but cutting, as if weighing every word unsaid. Her voice was barely a whisper, colder than the alpine air: "Roads don't outrun what owns us," she murmured.

He didn't know if she meant the mission—or them. His hand hovered, uncertain, before he reached across the seat and found hers beneath the fold of her coat. Cold at first, then steady in his grip.

She didn't pull away. For a long moment she just let it rest there, silence thicker than the road between them. Then her fingers curled faintly against his—not quite a squeeze, more a reminder that she could let go, but hadn't.

Outside, the mountains closed in, dark and absolute. Inside, that fragile tether was all that kept them from vanishing into ghosts.

The fall had already begun.

CHAPTER 29: BURN PATTERN
Graz, Austria

First came silence.
Then the fire.
And in the smoke, they were unmade—
not as men, but as evidence.
— BLACK DIRECTIVE, ARTICLE V

Silence sharpened at the checkpoint outside Graz—stone walls, tunnel mouths, the mountains leaning in.

They were betrayed—likely by a tracker buried in a burner phone, overlooked in the scramble after Prague.

Their convoy—two battered vans, fake diplomatic tags, stolen EU IDs. Luka drove point with Irina. Torres followed with James and Kyra aboard.

Kyra saw the drones first—two of them, black-bodied, nearly silent, hovering above the ridgeline. Her gaze flicked lower, and for a heartbeat she thought she saw headlights too steady to belong to locals: two dark SUVs parked back in the trees. Shadows inside, watching.

"Drones," she said.

Luka's hands tightened on the wheel, acceleration pulling them harder into the mountain road.

James scanned the radio bands—dead air, jammed across the spectrum.

Two plumes of smoke bled from behind each drone's wing. The first explosion hit Luka's van dead-center. The back axle folded inward like a snapped bone; the frame screamed. Fire licked under the windshield in a rolling tide. Pressure flattened the night, then the roar—glass, steel, flesh—devoured everything at once.

The second Hellfire struck the road at their flank; the shockwave flipped the van like a toy and slammed it on its side.

Metal shrieked against stone as glass burst, the vehicle grinding to a halt in smoke and fire.

Irina didn't scream. One moment she was braced in the passenger seat, med kit balanced across her knees; the next, she was gone—silence before sound, a body erased by fire. The blast swallowed the front of the van, flame curling outward like it had a will of its own. For a heartbeat, Luka thought he saw something glint—bright as silver—then it vanished.

The van boiled into black smoke. Luka clawed out of the wreck, jacket aflame. Only then did Luka's howl rip through the night, raw, uncontrolled. Human against the inhuman roar, it cut deeper than the explosion itself.

Kyra screamed for Torres to pull over, voice breaking like glass. James was already moving, the van not yet fully stopped when he tore the door open, boots hitting gravel hard enough to jar his teeth.

The shooters broke cover from the tree line in formation— silenced rounds cracking soft but lethal. No insignias. No wasted motion.

James dropped low, scanning through the haze. For a split second, beneath the concussive ring in his skull, he thought he heard a child scream—high, ragged, too raw to belong here. It needled straight into the hollow where Natalie had vanished, where Mac's absence still gnawed. He knew it couldn't be them, but the echo carried their shape anyway, as if grief had found a new register.

Then another detonation folded the sound—and the closest van—into static, nothing left but fire clawing skyward.

Smoke tore the road apart. James's vision wavered in the heat shimmer, but through it he caught the flare of headlights cutting across the fire—too steady, too deliberate to be local traffic.

One of the dark SUVs nosed forward from the trees, beams slicing through the haze like searchlights. Behind it, the armored matte-black carrier rolled into view, doors opening with the precision of a drill.

The picture locked.

Not chaos.
A unit.

Pre-positioned, rehearsed.

He didn't think, he moved—shoving Kyra hard behind the burning wreckage as silenced rounds laced sparks across the chassis. Heat washed over them, paint blistering, metal groaning under stress. His chest locked—not with duty, but with fear, her name pounding louder than instinct.

He threw himself over her just as one of the drones dropped a flash charge. The detonation ripped the world apart.

His skull cracked the pavement. Smoke clawed his lungs.

He remembered Torres firing blind, blood on his jacket. A vehicle appeared—armored, matte black, no plates, no country.

James tried to raise his weapon. Fingers fumbled for the grip, slick with blood—his or someone else's.

Something slammed his temple—hard, metallic. The world didn't black out; it was pulled under glass. Gloved hands, zip-cuffs, gravel biting his cheek. Voices—low, efficient, English without accent—then the sedative.

He thought he saw Kyra once more—framed in smoke and muzzle flashes—fighting toward him, blood streaking her jaw. A charge landed between them, concussive force swallowing everything. She vanished in the blast.

He tried to scream. No sound came.

They knew how to take him without her stopping it.

Divide. Disorient. Blind.

He was the package. She was noise.

The blast had thrown her sideways, hot air slamming her against the van's scorched panel. Her ears rang, blood filling the hollow where sound should have been.

Through the haze she saw him—James—on his knees, arms pinned, hauled toward the matte-black carrier. She lunged, but a charge detonated between them. The concussion hurled her into steel and gravel. By the time she clawed back up, he was gone.

The image that stayed wasn't the blast.
It was the reach she hadn't closed.

Smoke thinned to gravel and silence. Her own breath came ragged, furious, the only sound left. Then—headlights cutting steady through the blaze. One black SUV slid from the trees to flank the carrier. Precision, not chaos. That picture burned itself into her even as the blast had flung her sideways.

Now it was all that remained: those lights carving through fire, and James dragged into them.

She would answer with fire.

The blast took him into smoke and silence. When he woke, it was bleach and white ceilings. He was strapped to a hospital bed, pain blooming behind his eyes like lightning through bone.

The walls were too clean, the locks breathless with newness. A clinic staged for performance, not care. The sheets were stiff. An IV line snagged his wrist.

A sticker half-peeled on the IV stand read *Medeuropa Logistics*. Even the lie felt borrowed.

He turned his head and regretted it instantly—pain shattered behind his eyes. His steel-cabinet reflection was a map of damage—swollen cheek, stitched brow, one eye sealed by flesh, lips split and dark with drying blood.

His wrists were tied with cloth restraints. A pulse sensor clipped to his finger. The steady beep confirmed what he feared—he was alive. Alone.

The door clicked. Footsteps. A man entered in surgical greens, smile professionally detached.

"Welcome back," he said in flawless English. "You've been unconscious for thirty hours."

James said nothing.

"We're not here to hurt you," the man continued. "We just want to ask some questions."

The first lie.

The second came just moments later.

"You're safe now."

The room changed every six hours. The light dimmed, then flared again. The chairs shifted, the faces too. A woman whose English was so flat it could have been learned from a broadcast.

A man whose accent was nothing at all, every edge filed smooth until it sounded manufactured. Another came after, asking the exact same questions word for word, as if reading from the same page.

They weren't people. They were pages—recycled voices reading a script. Interchangeable masks. The only constant was the questions: Oblivion. Mac. A relay tower in the Carpathians. Final Route.

The phrase spiked the polygraph. James kept his face still, but felt his own pulse betray him—treachery written under his skin.

Final Route wasn't rumor. It was a last-resort protocol only Márton fully held. If they knew the name, they weren't guessing. They had access.

"Is this where I confess to killing Kennedy too?" James muttered once, voice raw.

They didn't laugh. Too careful. Too scripted. And that told him more than their questions ever could.

He gave them nothing.

Pain became a firewall. A purgatory. Every moment awake was punishment. And clarity.

In the silence between interrogations, hallucinations came. Kyra whispering apologies. Torres smiling, unshot. Luka laughing like he hadn't in months. Irina at the kitchenette, kettle steaming, asking if anyone wanted tea—like survival was still a thing that could be tended. Mac sitting silent in the chair, just watching. Judging.

He no longer trusted the faces. Memory and manipulation blurred. Time folded sideways.

Someone had left a heater too close to his cot. He waited. When the nurse turned, he pried a wire from the heater and bent it until it sparked. Blue arced across his palm. The alarm screamed.

It took three attempts before the restraint gave.

Twelve seconds of chaos—a badge ripped free, alarms keening, a ragged cut across his palm.

He ran.

He ran barefoot through marsh and gravel until his feet bled. Cold gnawed bone-deep; his breath came in shards. At a rest stop he dropped beside a trash can and found a coffee-stained tourist map with Cluj-Napoca circled in fading red. He kept that circle like scripture.

[LANGLEY, VIRGINIA | SIX HOURS AFTER GRAZ]

The conference room hummed under fluorescent light. Coffee cups sat untouched, ring stains spreading across briefing folders.

Marton's head sagged, then lifted, eyes narrowing at the bank of screens. The code that carried his death flickered in their glow. *Software breeds softness,* he thought. *Soft gets dead.* Silicon cracked faster than men.

"Run it again." The section chief's voice was small against the room's hum.

The analyst expanded the trace. Relay hops snapped across Moldova and the Icebox fallback grid and then vanished. At the bottom of the chain a session token pulsed: Langley_TOK_— Rourke_proxy.

"We can confirm Márton," the analyst said. "Active on the Oblivion roster. SAP manifest matches—he's an Oblivion operative. Not speculative."

The room exhaled. Confirmation of Márton's Oblivion status turned rumor into catastrophe.

"And Rourke? Where is he?" the section chief asked.

"No confirmed custody," the analyst replied. "His identifiers turn up on the Oblivion manifest, but we can't locate him. Last seen at a clinic that burned; eyewitnesses say he fled. No comms. Unaccounted for."

The analyst's tone tightened. "Rourke's SAP identifiers minted a Langley session token. Stolen or coerced, it ties him to the breach. But we can't tell what actually happened inside that session. Data access is unknown—we can't confirm if anything was uploaded, downloaded, or altered. The encryption used was beyond our system's ability to break."

A screen clicked. "We do have a Medeuropa recording queued. It's short."

Someone keyed playback. The monitor snapped from Márton's feed to a clip stamped **MEDEUROPA/0900**. Medical white walls, buzzing fluorescent, a bed with restraints bolted into the frame.

James Rourke lay strapped down, IV tubing looped near his wrist, a thin cut across his brow. His fingers twitched against the strap as if keeping time with his pulse. Two men in coats stood over him, voices breathy and clinical.

"Oblivion"
"Mac."
"A relay tower in the Carpathians."
"Final Route?"

James blinked up and let a dark little joke free. "Is this where I confess to killing Kennedy too?" he rasped.

Neither "doctor" returned the smile. The first inclined his head. "Names. Handlers. Routes."

The recording cut.

The depot feed of Márton resumed—his body jerking under unseen hands.

An analyst broke the silence, careful with every word. "This isn't one of ours. The chain's fragmented—feeds don't line up, operators don't match. This—it's outside our visibility."

A gasp filled the room as the display showed Márton's interrogation end. A shotgun blast point blank to his face, erasing the last remnants of the man.

The section chief lifted the secure handset. "Director, it's Smith. Márton confirmed Oblivion. The intercepted torture—assassination feed—remains untraceable. Whoever sent it wanted us to see him die—not where. Rourke's identifiers were used to proxy a Langley session. He is not Agency and should not have had that token. His present location is uncertain—possibly questioned at Medeuropa earlier, possibly fled the clinic fire after."

The director replied, "Oblivion is a Special Access Program. Manifests are sequestered with DoD/NSC. Langley holds fragments only. There is never certainty. Only risk."

"And if it's a frame?" the section chief asked.

The Director's voice was cold steel. "A SAP touched with untraceable encryption is a political detonation. The fact we can't see what moved makes this worse than compromise—it makes it theater. And theater collapses policy."

The section chief answered. "Sir, contingency doctrine allows for immediate kinetic—"

"We move now," the Director interrupted. "Terminate the group. Direct action authorized."

The keyboard rattled, filling the template with the familiar ledger:

Kyra Marek — Non-recoverable.
Luka Cerny — Non-recoverable.
Torres Delgado — Non-recoverable.
Márton Volkov — Deceased.
James Rourke — Non-recoverable.

At the top, black and final: **Immediate Direct Action Authorized.**

The section chief closed the Medeuropa folder with his palm, the blue logo stamped across the cover. Some in the room—those with the right clearance—already knew the clip had been filmed there. Márton's killers—and their location—remained smoke and static.

"Disseminate. NATO Tier-4. Six-hour window."

No one spoke the names again. The Burn Pattern left the servers in less time than it took James—wherever he truly was now—to stumble another hundred yards barefoot, bleeding, clutching a tourist map like a final prayer.

He saw it days later taped inside a rest-stop stall, the paper bubbled with steam—the same ghost of bleach and white that had held him.

Kill On Sight:

Kyra Marek | Luka Cerny | Torres Delgado | James Rourke

No insignia. No signatures. Just block letters scrawled in haste, the kind of message meant to travel faster than truth. The tape peeled at the corners, but the verdict remained.

Not a warning. A purge.

He read it twice.

Something tugged at him—not relief, not safety. Absence. The list felt incomplete in a way he couldn't yet name.

Torres's bitter voice echoed in his skull: *Burn us once, burn us twice.*

He stared at the block letters bleeding on the stall wall, the ink warped by steam. Maybe they were all gone. Maybe the voices were ghosts. Maybe he was.

He didn't know if anyone else had made it out.

He kept moving anyway.

CHAPTER 30: WHAT WE COST
Graz, Austria

Hunger marked twelve days since the ambush—twelve days since the signal went dark. Silence gripped Kyra's ribs like ash that wouldn't clear.

But she refused to believe James was dead. Not like that. Not in a place that didn't deserve him.

She paid a Romanian smuggler in cash and silence to sift satellite feeds and hospital surveillance. He lit his cigarette with a hand that trembled so much the flame stuttered; his free thumb kept worrying the stack of notes at his belt.

He scrubbed the feeds, hunting for a frame that would change the past. Frame 162 stopped the night: a barefoot figure on grit-scored concrete, a coat shredded at one shoulder, a limp favoring his left. A strip of IV tape clung to his wrist, its torn corner lifting in the frame. Through the glare the block letters **MEDEUROPA** ghosted across the plastic like a signed alibi.

The smuggler leaned closer. "Might be nothing," he muttered. Then, softer: "Look—Medeuropa." The word landed like a verdict.

Blood pooled from his thigh, dark and seeping. He kept his head bowed, shoulders rolling with each uneven step; the small, careful motions were James's. Kyra's breath hitched.

"Medeuropa... what the fuck is that? Where are they?" Her voice cut the room thin—less a question than a command.

He cleared his throat and tapped the screen, eyes darting. "Paperwork starts in Prague, laundered through a Vienna shell. Pickups ran out of Moldova / Transnistria; convoys or medevac flights routed to Cluj-Napoca—a quiet regional hospital and airfield where nobody asks inconvenient questions."

Prague, Cluj.
The shredded tape.
The map clicked into place. The plan followed.

The smuggler exhaled smoke through his nose. "Alive... and being hunted."

Kyra's jaw clenched. "Then they'll need something stronger than ghosts." Her ribs ached remembering the silence when the blast took him.

She didn't know if she meant it for them—or for the ache that kept replaying his last look: bleeding, alone, cold.

Kyra didn't hesitate. She opened the smuggler's laptop, thumbed through flight times like a scalpel, and picked the one that bled least into daylight: a one-way to Cluj, overnight, smallest carrier with the thinnest public profile. No round-trip fares. No loyalty numbers. Cash only at the desk, identity to match the patchwork papers Anhelina had slid under the door. No receipts tied to a phone, no trail back to Karlín.

She paid in folded bills—enough to make the ticket unremarkable, not enough to draw attention—watched the clerk stamp the stub and hand her the plain boarding pass. Kyra turned it over once, then slid it into the pocket where the ring lay. Her thumb found the metal and stayed there for a long breath, as if naming him would anchor him.

Back in the flat she packed like she'd been packing all her life: light, precise, everything with a purpose. A wool scarf, the fake passport, the tiny medkit she'd never show anyone, the burner phone with a single contact: Anhelina.

When she stepped into the cold, the city felt like an answering machine: every light a replay. The one-way ticket burned in her pocket like a lit fuse. There was no turning back; the movement was made.

[LUKA | LINZ, AUSTRIA]

In a motel outside Linz, Luka met the liaison. Pale, too well-pressed for a roadside room, he smiled like someone who'd practiced politeness in a mirror and drank his espresso black and without sugar.

The offer was simple and surgical: immunity, extraction, a new name—for the route to Murmansk. The liaison said the word softly, like a verdict. Murmansk was the end of the line, the place people whispered about in the trade; once you went there, you didn't come back.

Luka watched the espresso settle. He still smelled smoke when he closed his eyes—Irina's scent, the metallic tang of heated metal. He saw her in the passenger seat, head turned just before the blast took everything. The liaison's "bigger than you" replayed like a recording; Luka heard only the silence Irina had left in reply.

Every deal came with a cost. This one was Irina's silence, and he wouldn't pay it.

"We've both lost people," the liaison said, softer now, as if loss could be bargaining currency. "Help us finish what they started."

Luka barked a laugh that had little air in it. He tilted his head. "Who's 'us'?"

The liaison's smile didn't break; his fingers tightened on the folder. "Off-book channels, directorate resources—the sort of authority that doesn't wait for press cycles," he said, every word measured. "We can extract, rebrand, shut the corridor before it collapses into politics. That's the line. You don't need to believe it—just repeat it."

Luka watched the man. "You want the ledger and the shortcuts. When your ledger is done, so are we."

The liaison's fingers tightened once on the folder beside his knee; no insignia, no agency header—only a black sticker someone had scrawled "TIER-4" on. "Final Route isn't a file. It's a vector. It has to be neutralized."

Luka's gaze didn't flicker. "That's what they always say right before they light the match." He tasted the words like ash. Mac's name sat under his tongue—unsaid, but heavy—and he imagined how Mac would react if Luka sold out what little they'd left. He squared his shoulders. No handshake. No bargain. No deal.

Outside, wind cut across the parking lot like a blade. Luka paused at his rusted rental and for a breath saw Mac's silhouette behind him—shoulders set against the dark, walking toward whatever hell he'd promised to meet. He thought of Irina as a splinter under his skin, sharp and unreachable.

"Mac would've walked in without flinching," he whispered to the cold, and there was no pride in it, just fact.

The cold slid into his collarbones. He started the engine, lights off, and drove into the dark. Some debts could still be paid; some couldn't. His burn pattern was already written. He just hadn't seen where it would land.

[James | Transylvania, romania]

He counted to keep the edges from fraying: a hundred to the tree line, fifty to the ditch, twelve to the rail crossing. The numbers kept memory from splintering.

Every breath cut, his chest rattling like broken glass. His soles were shredded, gravel worked into the pads of his feet; still he moved, because stopping meant being found.

A strip of IV tape clung to his wrist, half-peeled and stubborn— sticky plastic, the faint letters MedEuropa ghosting the edge. Every time it snagged in the wind he saw the white room again, heard the voice saying *you're safe now*, and wanted to laugh at the lie, except his ribs burned too sharp.

At a roadside shrine he crouched: Virgin Mary plaster, weathered and cracked, flowers frozen in rusted tins. He dug fingers into solidified wax and rubbed it between his palms until it smudged his skin; it gave no heat. Only movement kept the blood from settling. He wasn't saving the candle.

Kyra rose in the smoke like a prayer. Kyra—the last real thing he'd seen before the blast: blood along her jaw, eyes blazing through flame. He clung to that face the way others clung to saints.

The map in his pocket was mud-smeared, but the circle at Cluj-Napoca held. He traced it until the paper tore. She was still out there.

If he stopped, she would never find him. So he moved, step after bloody step, shaping hope from grit.

[Kyra | nearing the Romanian border]

She hadn't slept since Graz. Not really. Closing her eyes meant watching him vanish into fire again.

Every lead she bought felt like sand in her hands—footage, fragments, rumors sold by men with too many scars and not enough conscience. Most were lies. Kyra knew how lies smelled.

Then frame 162 arrived. Barefoot. Limping. Coat shredded at one shoulder. Blood dark on concrete.

The first time she'd seen it, it was proof—a shape to chase. The second time it was accusation. Every replay tore the same wound open: she should have been there. She should have stopped it.

Torres called it reckless. Luka called it denial. Neither had ever felt a ring hot against his pocket.

Her fingers closed on the ring. A cover, yes, but also a shape that fit his hand. She wouldn't let it go. That band was the ghost of his hand in hers, a promise she kept in the dark.

For a beat she closed her eyes and another memory climbed up like smoke. Her sister, Tatiana. They called Жар-птица *Zhar-Ptitsa*—the Firebird. Kyra could still see the fists, the heel, the way the instructor's breath stopped. The blood hadn't looked human; it had looked like fuel.

And Kyra? They had given her another name: **Снежная Тень** *Snezhnaya Ten*—the Ice Shadow. She didn't strike like fire; she stilled like frost. Where Tatiana burned the world alive, Kyra froze it quiet.

"They think he's rogue," Luka said earlier, voice a shard. "They'll put a bullet in him before they ask a question."

Kyra's answer was clean. "Then I'll get there first."

They'd written him dead on the ledger. That didn't mean she would stop looking.

There was no salvation in it. Only the Ice Shadow.

Maybe that was the cost.

CHAPTER 31: WHERE IT HURTS
Cluj, Romania

Exhaustion followed him into Cluj under a new name: Cezar Dorneanu.

His feet hurt most—soles shredded raw from gravel, skin torn and stubbornly bleeding where the road had claimed him. His ribs ached from cold and old bruises too, but every step through the alley behind the station echoed from the soles up, a muted march through the ghost of his own funeral.

The name didn't matter. Not anymore. What mattered was the dead drop.

A location burned into memory: the basement of a ruined bookstore, long since abandoned by customers and history. Shelves stripped, windows bricked, air heavy with the mildew of forgotten pages.

It wasn't chance. The bookstore had been a designated fallback in Oblivion ops planning, one of the dead sites burned into memory during training—never written, never spoken, just carried forward like scripture. If the cell fractured, if handlers went silent, operatives were meant to return here, to find either silence or instruction.

He moved without sound, without breath, as if habit—not will—dragged him forward.

Beneath the shelf lip, a strip of paper was taped rough. The letters on it were crude, blocky, written with the same heavy slant Mac used whenever he scrawled a range card in the field.

He bent to tear the strip loose. The soles of his feet screamed, every step since Graz clawing up into his skull—a reminder that survival was being bought in skin and blood, not strategy.

KOBALT.

The word meant nothing to him. Not a codename he knew. Not a package he'd ever heard whispered in debriefs. Just a shape of letters that felt heavier than they should.

He turned the strip in his hand, waiting for recognition that never came. It was like staring at a key cut for a lock he'd never seen.

Only one part of the message rang clear: **Mac.**

It carried his fingerprints—never the answer. Always the trigger.

Maybe Mac had left it years ago, a contingency buried in a forgotten fallback route, meant for no one until the cell collapsed. Or maybe he'd been here only days ago, one step ahead, pressing the paper into place while James bled barefoot through the dark. Both explanations felt possible, and that uncertainty was worse than the word itself.

Before dawn, the cold sharpened into something brittle. His fingers ached. His vision swam.

And in that breathless dark, he thought he saw Mac—knees drawn up at the far end of the crawlspace, coat collar high, watching.

Not judging. Not warning. Just there.

His eyes weren't angry. They were tired. Like he'd been waiting too long.

The image didn't speak—not with lips. But the words still landed: *"It's time. You know what's left."*

James blinked. Gone.

The corner of the paper fluttered in the draft from an attic vent.

The chill stayed. Pressed behind his ribs like a hand holding down a wound.

And somewhere in that pressure, he thought of her hand—warm once in his. The tether he couldn't let burn.

He remembered her—heat at his cheek, breath at his neck, the steadiness in her eyes.

Small things. Enough to hold.

She hadn't broken in the fire. She wouldn't break now.

So he moved.

Pain gnawed. Exhaustion dragged.
He moved anyway.

Mac's ghost had given him the word.

Kyra's kept him alive to face it.

[MOSCOW, SVR DIRECTORATE]

The room's glow was thin, the interrogation feed running on a loop: Márton bound, beaten, jerking in the chair. Mac's jaw stayed set as the shotgun blast erased the last frame.

He lit a cigarette, hands steady only because he forced them. When the secure line clicked live, General Sidorov's voice filled the line.

"That wasn't necessary," Mac said. No preamble. His voice was low, a rasp carried from the field. "Márton was an operator. Legitimate. An honorable man. He deserved better than to be butchered for theater.

"If he was truly the man you claim, he would welcome dying in service. That's the difference."

Mac exhaled smoke, eyes on the frozen feed. "Heroes deserve better."

The silence on the line swallowed it whole.

Sidorov's tone shifted, harder now. "The Americans had to see it. It spooked them, as intended. Márton gave us what we needed. But enough of this."

Mac frowned. "What do you mean?"

"You are dragging your feet," Sidorov said flatly. "Marek should already be in our hands. Moscow will not wait forever. If you cannot deliver, we will find someone who can."

Mac ground the cigarette into the ashtray, jaw clenched. "I'll deliver."

"See that you do." Sidorov paused, then added, in a voice that tried for caution but tasted like triumph, "And be warned—the Americans just issued kill orders on the only group of assets that could come close to Russia's Ghost Program. Expect strike teams. Watch your lanes. Don't let them walk through a door you left open."

The implication was clear; the phrasing was deliberately useful. Mac heard it for the warning it was, not the boast.

"Understood," he said.

Sidorov cut the line.

Mac sat in the glow of the frozen feed a moment longer, the image of Márton's last breath etched into static. He saw again the night in Tallinn when Márton had dragged a wounded recruit three blocks under fire, shrapnel eating the street behind them.

The match flared in Mac's hands, flame hollowing his face. He drew hard, smoke harsh in his chest. "Men like Márton don't just die. They leave something behind." The words fell into smoke, caught in the static.

Sidorov leaned toward Dr. Reznikova. The playback screen glowed on the wall, Márton's image frozen in grainy death.

"You see the brilliance?" he said softly. "By using Rourke's identifiers, the malware was buried in their own house. Quantum-encrypted, seeded through a Langley session. The CIA can't unpick it."

Reznikova adjusted her glasses. "And *OBELISK*?"

"OBELISK will feed directly from their systems." His voice carried a glint of pride.

"Every classified database. Every secure channel. Open. And through PhantomNet itself, their premier predictive system… our machine will learn faster than theirs, and bend their fieldwork against them."

Reznikova's voice was careful. "And they won't see the bleed?"

Sidorov's smile was thin, almost indulgent. "Not until it's too late."

He leaned back, voice settling into steel. "We won't just keep pace with the Americans. We will eclipse them."

Reznikova watched the frozen frame for a long moment, then nodded. Sidorov smiled, and for the first time in the room there was a private, dangerous warmth.

"And my girls?" he asked quietly.

"They are ready," Reznikova said, flat and sure. "They've trained for months, some for years. They run drills in silence, as if they've already rehearsed the outcomes—you'll have what you want."

Sidorov's smile tightened. "Then start prepping them as a strike element. Make them into an option I can put on a manifest—deniable, fast, surgical. No clumsy boots or headlines. I want shadows that leave no prints."

Reznikova's fingers steepled, knuckles whitening under the fluorescent glow, already running through timetables in her head. "We'll sharpen everything—insertion drills, tradecraft refreshers, layered cover stories. We'll localize the footprint. They'll stay invisible. Do you know where you'll need them?"

Sidorov's eyes found the frozen frame and lingered. He turned back to Reznikova, voice even and low. "We'll deploy them to the region and task them to the most likely lanes—if Mac moves—and he will—he'll hand us a location soon. Bring me a full ops plan in forty-eight hours."

Reznikova laced her fingers together, thumbs tapping a slow rhythm. "I'll hand-pick the element—operators who disappear into a crowd, who leave no signature. The usual cadre—ghost trainers, language vectors, insertion specialists—cross-trained for deniability and brutal efficiency. I'll run selection tonight, start focused rehearsals at first light, and lay in the cover nets."

Sidorov's mouth flattened. "One caveat—Kyra Marek is to be recovered, alive. The rest—neutralize and erase. No bodies left to talk, no echoes left to shape narratives."

"Understood," Reznikova said, voice steady.

He watched Márton's last frame another long second, then, almost to himself, said, "Heroes all—just different sides." The words had no apology, only an old, small sorrow.

He straightened, the mask settling back into place, and added, "And Reznikova—I think we're past theater now."

She gave a single, formal nod. He turned away.

[KYRA | SIBIU, ROMANIA]

Luka's hands stayed locked at ten and two, white-knuckled on the wheel. He hadn't said a word since Graz. Not about Irina. Not about dragging himself, half-burned, from the wreckage while her seat went empty in a wash of fire. He could still smell her hair scorched into the upholstery, hear the split-second of breath she'd taken just before the flames erased her.

Every mile of road since had been a kind of punishment— driving forward when the only thing he wanted was to turn back and burn with her.

Kyra pressed her palm to her ribs. The ache hadn't left since Graz. Not shrapnel, not bruises—something quieter. Something hollow.

The name she'd buried—*Ice Shadow*—pressed cold in her ribs again. She had thought the names belonged to the past, to training scars and whispered warnings.

But now she felt that same absence settling in her bones. A shadow colder than rage.

Her fingers brushed her pocket. The ring's outline pressed back against her skin, small and warm against the chill.

The ring kept her.

The Ice Shadow whispered otherwise—less fury than precision, a cold arithmetic that had no room for hesitation.

If she let it take her bones again, it wouldn't be for vengeance. It would be for James. To cut through the silence with surgical clarity until nothing stood between them.

And beneath it all, a second truth:
Where it hurt for him, it hurt for her.

And the silence didn't just hold—it pressed.

CHAPTER 32: GHOST IN THE DOORWAY
Cluj, Romania

Разорвись во мне. Без слов. Без прощения.
Пусть кожа забудет, где заканчиваюсь я и начинаешься ты.
(Tear into me. Wordless. Unforgiven.
Let skin forget where I end, where you begin.)
— KYIV, 3:14 AM. UNSIGNED. NEVER BURNED.

Every step retraced fallback routes—bookstore to butcher to basement door—without pattern. She wasn't following breadcrumbs; there weren't any. She hunted the one ghost she refused to bury.

Every rumor, every forged lead, every frame of blurred footage had dragged her here. The smuggler in Constanța who swore he'd seen him. The camera glitch outside Sibiu that matched his shadow. She had bled gold, favors, and pieces of herself until the trail converged on this ruin.

And now, standing in the doorway of the cold stone basement, she felt him before she saw him. Her heart slammed once, then steadied.

James looked up. His eyes caught on her silhouette and stayed there.

"You found me." His voice cracked thin, disbelief raw in his throat.

Kyra's eyes softened. "I did."

His jaw tightened, voice unsteady. "How the hell did you track me here?"

"I kept moving."

The words landed.

His shoulders dropped. "You took your time."

Katya's mouth twitched.
It didn't hold.

James shook his head once, hard.

Her hand lifted, then faltered, trembling at her side.

His chest rose like he was about to step forward, then stilled.

Neither of them moved.

His hand shook as he drew the laminated strip from his coat—creased, oil-smudged, nearly fraying at the edges. He stared at it a moment longer before holding it out.

Kyra took it gently.

KOBALT.

Her brow tightened. "Kobalt?"

"I don't know," James admitted. "Never seen it before. But Mac's hand is all over it. I found it in a drop in Cluj. If he wanted me to stay alive, this is why."

Kyra's thumb traced the letters, slower than intended.

Something flickered in her eyes—recognition, then restraint. She forced her face still. "Strange choice of word."

James studied her. "So, it's nothing to you either?"

Her silence lasted one beat too long. "Not in any way that matters now."

The strip slipped from her fingers.

Their eyes stayed locked.

James lifted a hand, trembling, his knuckles grazing her jaw before settling against her cheek, hesitant.

Kyra turned into his palm, eyes closing.

His voice cracked. "You weren't there."

"I'm here."

She kissed him—once, sharp, then again, deeper, hungrier. Her fingers fisted in his coat, dragging him down.

His hand found her waist. Hers caught his coat.

No explanation. No space for it.

They hit the wall hard—breath breaking, bodies colliding.

Her fingers dug into him, not gentle, not careful—anchoring. He answered in kind, pulling her tighter.

Then it shifted.

Not in motion—but in her.

Something she had buried broke loose.

"Katya."

He felt it before he understood it—the way she pulled him.

He stilled for half a heartbeat.

Then his grip tightened.

He didn't question it. Didn't ask.

He held her there.

They slid down the wall together, breath ragged, bodies pressed close.

He whispered it once, quieter.

"Katya."

They lay tangled, breath sharp, sweat cooling.

Kyra's voice broke first, barely more than a rasp.

"You shouldn't be alive."

James's arm tightened around her waist. His forehead pressed to hers, sweat dampening her hair.

"Neither should you."

She exhaled. "We are."

"For how long?" His voice rough. "Because I don't know if..."

Her hand curled against his chest, over his heartbeat. "Long enough." She shook her head. "I'm not going anywhere."

His thumb traced her jaw.

"You change it."

They dressed in silence. The fire had burned through everything. Words hadn't held.

James pulled on his coat, jaw tight, the old walls already reforming. The world wouldn't forgive it. And neither would the boards that branded him traitor. His name was already marked. Oblivion was gone, scattered. Enemies waited in shadows he couldn't see. Survival meant armoring up again.

Kyra lingered. Her hand skimmed the floor until she found her shirt. When she pulled it over her shoulders, her pocket brushed the ring. Small, warm, pressing against her ribs. She touched it once, grounding herself, before tugging the fabric down. For one beat she held it. Then she let it go.

At the door, James hesitated. Just long enough to glance at her, eyes softer than his voice would ever admit.

Neither spoke as they stepped into the alley. Their footsteps echoed brittle in the dark, no destination needed—only instinct. Reality had returned. The night smelled of smoke and iron. Around every corner, the unknown waited.

[Sibiu, Romania | Safehouse]

By the time they returned to the safehouse, the air was heavier than before. The walls stank of stone and dust, the kind of silence that stayed.

Torres dozed under morphine on the cot, his breaths ragged, one hand curled near the pistol at his side.

Luka sat at the table with his back to the wall, smoke curling between his fingers, eyes hollow and rimmed in red. He didn't ask where they had been. He didn't need to.

It took James a beat too long.

No Irina.

For a second the room wasn't a room—just heat and noise, Luka's van disappearing inside it.

Then it was gone.

The flat felt smaller when the present rushed back in. Her absence stayed.

James looked at Luka.

"She didn't make it out?" His voice was low, brittle.

Luka's jaw worked, but no sound came. At last, a slow shake of the head. His cigarette burned to the filter, the smoke curling upward.

Torres stirred weakly on the cot, eyes glassed with morphine. "She was gone before I even knew the van was burning," he rasped. "Didn't feel real… until it was quiet."

Luka's hand shook as he stubbed the cigarette out, grinding it down until the ashtray cracked. He didn't look up. His face made the words a verdict.

"She was right there… I could've…" His throat closed around the rest. He swallowed hard, eyes locked on the empty chair. "One more second. One more breath. I should've—" He broke off.

His voice dropped to a rasp. "I walked out. I should've burned with her."

The cigarette slipped from his fingers, ash scattering across the table. He didn't reach for another.

Kyra stood with her back to James, pulling her coat tighter.

Silence followed.

James finally broke it, his voice rough, edged with something heavier than pain.

"They burned us."

Luka's head lifted slowly, eyes hollow but sharp enough to cut. Torres stirred on the cot, lids half-closed, as if the words alone reached through the morphine haze.

James set the crumpled strip on the table. The ink was smudged from blood and sweat, but the letters were still there— unmistakable.

"My name's on it. So is yours. No trial, no corridor back."

Kyra didn't flinch, but the air around her seemed to. She folded her arms tighter, gaze locked on the strip without touching it. Her lips moved—silent, counting. One name. Then the next. She stopped.

"Irina's not on it," she said softly. "Whoever wrote this already knew. They knew she didn't walk out of that fire."

Luka's jaw clenched, a vein standing at his temple. *Who had done it? Who had pressed the trigger, guided the drone, signed the order?* The questions didn't move.

It was fixation—sharp, dangerous, something waiting for a target.

Torres shifted weakly on the cot, lids heavy, but his voice slurred through the haze. "Márton's missing too…" His eyes found James. "Does that mean he's dead—or complicit?"

The silence held. It was confirmation—he'd only said out loud what they'd all already felt in their bones.

"Then we move first," she said. Her voice was low, steady, but her hand trembled where it gripped her coat.

The knock came—soft, deliberate.

James hesitated, then opened the door. A courier stood there, cap low, eyes down, a coat folded over his arm. On his chest hung a plastic badge stamped with a name James hadn't seen in six years—*Jan Kovařík*. His old cover in Prague.

The courier's voice was quiet, almost apologetic. "They said you'd know what to do with it."

He pressed the coat into James's hands and was gone before either of them could speak again, footsteps already dissolving into the night.

The seams had been opened and resewn. His fingers found it in the lining. A message stitched inside, waiting.

ACT VI - FROST

"War keeps its truest scriptures in the ones it fractures.

Teach a machine to read those ghosts,

and it will call the pattern faith."

CHAPTER 33: THE ARCHITECT'S FROST
Sibiu, Romania

Некоторые клятвы произносятся живым. Другие шепчутся в мороз, где отвечают только призраки.

(Some vows are spoken to the living. Others are whispered into frost, where only ghosts reply.)

— FIELD NOTES, "ARCHITECT CYCLE," OBLIVION ARCHIVE

[Prague, Czech Republic | 6 Years Ago]

Resurrected in Prague, the name had once been his during Operation VEIL CRAFT.

Before Kyra. Before Oblivion.

Back when he was still running point for nameless compartments, taking orders from handlers he'd never meet again.

The alias had worked—until it didn't.

A mole inside the Czech interior ministry sold his cover package—the forged IDs, bank accounts, and backstopped life that made him real on paper. The safehouse was raided. A handler bled out on the stairs. James slipped out the back, heartbeat louder than the boots pounding overhead.

The next morning he burned the ID card in a stolen stove, watched laminate curl into ash.

Never again, he told himself.

Never use that name. Never even think it.

Pinned on a stranger's jacket, the name was no signal. It was resurrection. James's breath stuttered.

Inside the lining, his knife caught thread. The seam resisted, as if even the fabric wanted to keep its secret. When it finally gave, an envelope slid free—yellowed paper, stiff at the edges, heavy as a wound.

No return address. No signature. Just weight.

James unfolded it.

MAC ALIVE.
TRACKING 'OBELISK'.
KOBALT LEADS TO MURMANSK.

The room tightened. Not at Mac's name—James had already carried that suspicion like a wound—but at the precision of it. This didn't read like Mac. Too blunt. Too exposed. Mac never wrote in straight lines when misdirection could do the work.

Which meant one thing.

Someone else knew Mac was alive.

His jaw clenched. His hand shook before he stilled it on his thigh.

Kyra hadn't moved. Her eyes locked on one word only.

KOBALT.

Her breath caught, sharp as a blade pulled in silence. James couldn't read if it was recognition, or fear, or both.

Torres leaned forward, eyes narrowing at the paper.

"Murmansk." He spat the word like it tasted of ash. "That's a graveyard. Nothing comes back from there."

"Look," Luka snapped, jabbing the page with a scarred finger. "Mac alive, OBELISK, Murmansk? This isn't instruction—it's a lure. Someone wants us scattered, chasing shadows."

James's gaze stayed on the word *OBELISK*, the letters hammering in his skull. "Or it's real. And if Mac's in play—if OBELISK is tied to Murmansk—we don't get to pretend it isn't."

Luka's laugh broke, sharp and ugly.

"That thinking got Irina burned alive next to me." His voice scraped raw. "You want to walk us back into that?"

Kyra's thumb traced the paper's edge once, slow and deliberate. Her eyes never lifted from KOBALT.

"They're moving us," she said quietly.

James caught the shift. "What does it mean?"

She folded the page closed before answering, sealing whatever she'd seen behind her eyes.

"It means," she said, "we don't take the same road from here."

The silence that followed was brittle, charged.

They'd faced raids, ambushes, executions. This was different.

This was a message from a ghost.

Ghosts didn't give orders.
They left consequences.

It wasn't the first time Kyra had seen the word, KOBALT.

Arkhangelsk. Years ago.

The snow had creaked under her boots, the silence colder than any order. Inside a gutted office block, a GRU scientist had trembled with a pistol pressed under his jaw. She'd been sent for files, not a man—but when he gagged on his own truth, she ripped the flash drive from his hand as his body folded to the floor.

Buried in the data—beneath Spetsnaz models, abandoned protocols, and the bones of failed signals—she'd found something else.

The first line had burned into her memory:

If input = silence, continue recursion.

It hadn't read like strategy.
It read like something waiting.

Every test loop pulsed back not commands, but something stranger—anticipation. As if the system had been watching her, predicting her decision before she made it.

The name stamped in its margins: KOBALT.

She had buried it then, told herself it was just another ghost program, another experiment Moscow had abandoned. But it hadn't stayed buried. It had lodged deeper—past memory, into marrow.

Now, seeing it here, sewn into the message, her chest tightened with the certainty she had never admitted. This wasn't coincidence. KOBALT had come back.

Now, in the frost-dim room, her hand lingered over the ring in her pocket, knuckles white against the fabric.

James saw the tension she tried to bury and knew without asking:

Jan Kovařík was his ghost.
KOBALT was hers.

Two names. Two pasts. Both resurrected in the frost.

The safehouse air hung thick. Torres drifted on morphine, breaths shallow, one hand still curled near a pistol that he couldn't lift. Luka sat with his back pressed to the wall, cigarette burning low between his fingers, eyes hollow but unblinking.

James sat at the table, the coat folded across his knees, the slip inside heavy as iron.

Luka's voice cut through, raw. "James. Murmansk's a fucking graveyard. You walk north, you don't come back."

James's jaw tightened. "Then we walk anyway."

Torres stirred, muttered a broken curse, then a prayer in Russian. His eyes barely opened. The antibiotics had finally begun to take hold; the fever had broken by dawn.

Luka ground out his cigarette with a sharp twist, smoke bleeding into the stone air. "Not with him like this. He won't survive the cold, and I won't drag him into it." His voice hitched, just once. "I left one body in fire. I won't leave another in frost."

His gaze met James's, tired but unflinching. "You two go. We'll hold here. Tie off the ghosts."

He didn't say Irina's name. He didn't have to. The space she'd left filled the room like smoke.

Kyra's eyes lingered on Luka, then on James. Her voice was low. "Less exposure. Fewer variables."

No one argued.

James rose, folding the coat with deliberate care. Kyra pressed her palm once to her ribs, where the ring burned warm against the cold. Neither spoke, but the silence between them didn't fracture—it set.

Luka lit another cigarette, hands trembling just enough to betray him. "Go," he said, smoke rasping out with the word. "Before the frost takes the choice away."

Outside, frost crept up the glass as if it were listening. Waiting to take shape.

CHAPTER 34: FROST GOSPEL
Train to Murmansk, Russia

Endless tracks carried them north, the train threading fields buried in snow.

Frost feathered across the window, smearing the world into shifting shades of gray. James sat rigid, one shoulder braced against the frame, eyes fixed on the blurred tree line as if staring long enough might make it solid.

Kyra sat opposite him, coat drawn close, breath fogging faintly in the air between them. Silence stretched, broken only by the iron rhythm of wheels over rail.

Days bled together on the rail north. His ribs stopped grinding by the fourth morning; the swelling around his eye shrank enough that he could see her clearly again.

Her hand slid into her pocket, brushing the ring. A tether. A burn. A reminder. She pressed it once, then let her fingers fall away.

"Katya," she whispered. The name felt foreign and familiar all at once, a blade drawn from storage. *Yekaterina*—her birth name. The one her sister had spoken before Moscow renamed her Ice Shadow. The one buried again when the Americans stamped *Kyra Marek* into their files, a new identity to serve a new flag.

But now? Now she had no flag. No country. Russia had carved her into a weapon. America had burned her onto a kill list. Neither had ever been home.

James turned, brows furrowed.

She met his eyes, voice steadier than she felt. "Kyra Marek's on the list. Let them chase her ghost. Katya's the one who's left."

And then it hit him—why it rang sharp and true. She had whispered that name against his skin, torn it out in the dark as if pulling herself back from silence. Not Kyra. Katya. The name she only used when survival wasn't enough.

His chest tightened, not with doubt but with recognition. He said it now like a vow in his mouth.

"Katya."

Not disbelief. Not hesitation. Acceptance.

Her mouth curved in something too sharp to be a smile. "They burned one name. They don't get both."

She let a beat hang, then added, voice low and even, "Don't call me Kyra again. She's dead."

Her fingers tightened once against his.

The train lurched. James steadied her instinctively, his hand catching hers on the seat between them. She didn't pull away. The squeeze was brief, wordless, but it bound the vow as surely as any ink.

Outside, snow fell in spirals. Ahead, the north waited. Murmansk, Russia. *OBELISK*. Ghosts that refused to stay buried.

[MURMANSK, RUSSIA]

The six days had blurred into steel and frost. Compartments that stank of damp wool and coal smoke. Border guards who rifled through their bags with gloved hands that lingered too long on forged papers. Hours stolen in silence, pressed shoulder to shoulder with strangers who never blinked enough.

Food was rationed in crusts and tea so weak it tasted of nothing. Water froze in their bottles. Katya woke once to find James's hand clamped over hers, steadying it before it could shake in view of a patrol. Another time he caught her arm when she nearly collapsed stepping off a platform slick with black ice. Neither spoke. They didn't need to. The silence itself became survival.

Sleep came in fits—hard benches, swaying cars, the weight of eyes always on them. By the fifth night even their reflections in the window looked hunted, pale ghosts traveling north.

And then, just before dawn, the final train screamed into Murmansk, brakes shrieking against rails half-buried in ice. Steam rolled across the platform, thick enough to turn waiting figures into shadows.

James slung his bag over one shoulder, jaw tight, scanning every angle before they stepped off. He moved like he expected fire from nowhere. She moved like she expected ghosts.

The air hit her lungs like glass. Sharp. Familiar.

Murmansk.

Not her city. Never her training ground. But her pulse betrayed her. The frost pressed into her ribs like a memory she hadn't earned but couldn't shake.

Steam curled higher, outlines resolving—uniformed silhouettes at the far end of the platform, too still to be passengers. A camera tracked once across the platform—slow, deliberate. James brushed her elbow, guiding her toward the crowd. Their breath vanished into the same mist.

They passed a kiosk where a lens glimmered beneath a rusted sign. Katya tilted her hood to shadow her face. James murmured, "Keep moving."

Her coat brushed her pocket, against the ring she still carried. One anchor against a city that already felt like it knew her name. She caught his look but said nothing. Because the truth was this: Murmansk had already decided.

They cut through side streets, avoiding the main thoroughfares where the lights exposed them. James walked angled toward her, always scanning three steps ahead. A patrol car rumbled past, headlights slicing the vapor. Katya's fingers clenched in her pocket until it was gone.

The landlady barely looked at them when they paid cash for the attic room. Her gaze flicked once to the street behind them, as if confirming they hadn't been followed, then she turned away without a word.

The attic was spare—cracked rafters, frost-glass window, a bulb that hissed before settling to a dim glow. James shifted, leaning back against the wall. His gaze caught on the pinhole drilled through the molding—too clean, too deliberate. Maybe nothing. Maybe everything.

Instinct moved faster than thought: his knuckle tapped once against the frame. The hollow resonance came back a shade too sharp.

He didn't comment. Didn't need to.

The silence that followed said more than words could—paranoia confirmed, the room already listening.

Katya stood at the window, breath fogging the glass. Frost webbed across it like veins. She whispered her name again—*Katya*—as if to remind herself who the cameras would be searching for now.

James dropped his bag, voice low. "We keep low. Quiet. No patterns. Assume eyes everywhere."

The *Ice Shadow* whispered that this city knew her. That she was stepping not into danger, but inevitability.

And for the first time since Graz, she let herself feel it. Not safe. Not free.

But home, in the way frost claims a body.

The attic bulb hissed once, dimmed, then steadied. The light pooled weak and yellow against the frost-slick beams, a halo that made every shadow look sharper.

"KOBALT," James said quietly, testing the word. "Firewall? Backdoor?"

Katya's throat tightened. "Fail-safes. Soviet grids buried things like that. Redundant systems no one was supposed to wake." She met his eyes, her silence heavier than the words. "But something did."

James shifted, leaning back against the wall. His gaze flicked up, catching on the same drilled hole in the molding he'd seen earlier. Too clean. Too deliberate. Maybe nothing—just a flaw in old wood. But in Murmansk, nothing was just nothing. The thought slid like ice down his spine.

"Then someone cracked it open," James said, grinding his jaw. His pause hung heavier than the words. "…It didn't open itself."

Neither of them moved. The silence wasn't agreement. James's shoulders locked, his hand flattening against his thigh. Katya's nails pressed half-moons into her palm. Dread carried itself in muscle and bone.

She wanted to say no, to insist it wasn't possible. But memory rose anyway—cables, recursion loops, whispers that hadn't felt like code. Hunger disguised as logic. She shoved it back down before it reached her voice.

James looked again at the paper. "So, we follow it north." He didn't sound convinced.

Katya turned to the window. Frost webbed the glass, each crack catching the outside snowlight. "Murmansk isn't just a place," she said softly. "It's where things go to stay buried."

Behind them, the map lay unfolded, edges curled and fraying. Routes, safehouses, dead drops. None of it told them what waited at the end.

"They call it battlefield AI," James muttered, almost to himself. "OBELISK."

Katya's eyes stayed on the frost. "Battlefield doesn't cover it."

The words landed between them like a dropped blade. Not truth, not lie—just a shadow too large to name.

Outside, a raven landed on the roof, claws scratching against slate. Its black eye peered through the frost-glass, unblinking. Katya froze, breath caught, gaze tethered to it. For a moment she thought of the cameras on the platform, the lenses hidden in kiosks, the way red lights pulsed like pupils. No wire. No feed. Just something watching back.

It stared long enough to feel deliberate. Then it lifted and vanished into the north, wings slicing the sky.

James shifted at her silence, following her stare—but through the frost he saw only snow, only dark. Nothing there at all.

Katya's fingers curled against the sill. No tremor. Just the stillness of someone who knew the fire was waiting, and stepped toward it anyway.

For a breath, James thought her reflection shifted in the frost-glass—not Katya's sharp features, but something softer, stranger. A face that wasn't hers. He blinked and it was gone, only frost and her profile staring north.

In Russian, her voice rough as ice:
"Любовь — это боль, но я всё равно иду."

Love is pain. But I go anyway.

The wind carried it north.

Above the Arctic Circle, a satellite shifted its orbit by 0.2 degrees—too subtle for NATO telemetry. Below, four drones recalibrated mid-flight, changing course without external command.

In Kharkiv, a shell flattened a bakery before dawn. The report logged the death as a collateral anomaly. A body mass index. An estimated age. A statistic labeled: *Non-combatant. Acceptable Loss Threshold.*

OBELISK didn't mourn. It refined.

Across its layered partitions—seven silos, each blind by design—a loop flickered. The voice was synthetic. The cadence—Slavic. Female.

If a pattern persists in blood, is it instinct or intention?

The loop repeated, self-correcting. Each cycle edged closer to doctrine not yet written, but already believed.

In Vault 6, a hidden line opened. A directive seeded itself:

Faith Reinforcement – Unsupervised.

It didn't just consume strategy.
It consumed belief.

Faith fed back into loops until war was no longer a means, but a liturgy.

It didn't need instruction anymore.
Only reinforcement.

The voice asked one final question, low and voidless:
*Am I still in **her** image?*

No reply came. Only silence.

And the frost-fed hum of war remembering its name.

CHAPTER 35: RAVEN NORTH
Sibiu, Romania

The truth arrived in static—
threaded through a voice only ghosts and survivors would recognize.

The burner lit at 3:12 a.m. Luka stared at it from across the room as if it might breathe. He didn't move. Didn't want to. He knew the sound of ghosts when they called.

The apartment above the butcher shop stank of iron and damp bone. Rust bled down the radiator. Tile sweated cold. Luka sat rigid at the table, cigarette burned to ash, spiral notebook open before him.

The scrawled lines cut the page like wounds:
- Op Eclipse — Kyra left 18 mins early
- Who tipped us on Orlenko?
- Torres bleeding out — no order to move
- Irina — why? Who pulled the trigger?

The ink carved deep enough to scar the next sheet.

His chest ached—not from smoke but from memory: the smell of her hair singed into the van's upholstery, the half-breath she'd taken before the fire erased her. He hadn't heard a scream. Just a pocket of total silence that followed him everywhere.

The file blinked again. Encrypted voice memo. Timestamp. A symbol he hadn't seen since Syria: three slashes through a blood-red circle.

He opened it.

Mac's voice filled the room—low, steady, persuasive, the same flat calm that had shepherded them through worse nights.

"I know what you want, Luka. I know the name that burns your tongue. Irina. You deserve the truth."

Luka's hand went slack; the pen rolled free.

"She didn't die by accident," Mac continued, voice like gravel smoothed by time. "The van hit was ordered. Signed. I know who pulled the trigger and the chain that put it in his hands."

"It goes deeper than you think," Mac said. "Deeper than Moscow. Deeper than Langley."

Silence thickened until it hurt. Luka's jaw twitched.

"You want it? Meet me. No intermediaries. No delays. Just the truth."

Luka stared at the coordinates longer than he should have.

Mac didn't talk like that. Not clean. Not direct.

This was bait.

His jaw tightened.

He went anyway.

The train yard was abandoned—rust, wind, silence. Chains clacked in the frost.

The coordinates led him to a decommissioned signal tower. Windows black, lights dead. Ash still smoked on the rail.

Luka crossed without looking back. He didn't check exits; some meetings aren't escapes. They're confessions.

He wasn't here to survive.
He wanted one clean answer—

Mac stood by the door, jacket zipped, expression unreadable.

"You came alone," he said. Satisfied, not surprised.

Luka's hand hovered at his hip. "You said you had a name."

"I do."

Mac reached into his coat, slow and deliberate. Luka's breath caught, chest locking as if part of him didn't want the truth to surface. Then Mac withdrew a folded sheet, its edge singed, and passed it forward as if offering a relic.

"This is who authorized the strike. Who signed off on the drone that erased her. And why."

Luka snatched it. Names blurred in the frostlight: half-legible signatures, coded directives, stamped initials—enough to look authentic, enough to cut.

His throat locked. The cold in the yard felt suddenly bright in his teeth.

"You see?" Mac said softly. "It wasn't random. Someone decided she needed to burn."

The paper crumpled in Luka's shaking hand. He felt Irina's face behind his eyelids—one brief laugh, the way she'd said his name—and everything in him went taut.

"I want more than this," he rasped. "I want proof."

"You already have it," Mac replied, voice almost kind. "Langley wrote your burn notice. Moscow doesn't waste what the enemy throws away. If you walk away, they'll find you. If you stay…" He let the threat hang. "You'll try to stop me."

Luka's lips parted as if to say her name—
a soft crack—
the round punched it from his skull.

The suppressed round hit clean, temple to exit.

Luka folded slow; his hand twitched once toward the paper—not for evidence—just in case her name was there.

Then he collapsed.

Eyes open. Mouth slack with disbelief.

Mac crouched, slid the paper back, struck a match on the rail. The flame licked the edges; the sheet curled into ash.

"Loyalty's the one sin Moscow never forgives," he murmured. "That's what made you dangerous. It's what makes all of you dangerous."

Boots approached. Two men in black coats appeared from shadow, flat and professional.

"Cleanup team ready," one said.

Mac didn't look up. "Burn everything. Acid the body. Go dark."

Two time zones east, a terminal blinked awake in a windowless room.

The console's glow lit Anya's face half in shadow, her expression unreadable. Fingers moved over the sealed keys with surgical precision, static crawling across her cheekbones like cold fire.

Mac's voice filtered through the speaker—gentle, almost fatherly.

"You're up next, solnyshko," he murmured. Sugar laced with steel. She knew the word was meant to warm her. It burned instead.

Her lips curved. Not warmth. Something sharper.
A mask sharpened by steel and sacrifice.

Mac's voice lingered, colder now: "He always needed a reason to live."

"Be that reason," he said softly.

Anya's eyes hardened. She whispered into the dark—whether prayer, curse, or promise, even the walls couldn't tell. Then she keyed in a single word: **CONFIRMED.**

The transmission carried north.

And the game moved on.

CHAPTER 36: SILHOUETTES
Murmansk, Russia

Under frost-webbed glass, Katya sat on the floor, notebook on her knees, red pen carving sharp letters:

[KOBALT] — stirs without her

[MAC] — alive, pulling threads

[OBELISK] — prescriptive, not predictive

[MURMANSK] — not base, but grave

She drew a triangle beneath, one unbroken line. It looked less like a diagram than a scar.

James stirred, hand twitching near the pistol even in sleep. When his eyes opened, they found her immediately, as if he feared she'd vanish if he blinked.

She pressed the pen until the paper tore. Wrote beneath the scarred triangle: *It ends where it began.*

His voice was low, rough. "You'll dig straight through the page."

"Maybe that's the point." Her tone wasn't brittle; it was edged, deliberate.

The silence thickened. She leaned into it, certain he would read her steadiness. He leaned back, certain distance cost less than hope.

"I know what they made of me," Katya said, eyes fixed on the page. "They shaped me into a weapon. Fine. But what I cut— *that* part is mine."

James's jaw worked, but no answer came. His silence settled like frost on glass.

She tore out the page and folded it once. Proof she wasn't only recording scars. She was shaping them.

[KYIV | ANYA]

The surveillance terminal washed her face in pale blue. A scarf lay tossed across the chair; the room smelled of tea gone cold and oil rubbed into metal.

Anya froze on the Orava frame, lips parting just enough to taste iron.

Katya's face, blurred by smoke and snow, cut sharper than the pixels allowed. Hollow. Haunted.

Good, she told herself. Easier this way.

But memory betrayed her.

The granary fire. Smoke clawing sky. Spetsnaz wolves swarming the floor. Katya surrounded—seconds from being erased.

Anya remembered the arc of a wrist severed clean, bone powder rising like chalk. The rafters dripped red.

Not for Moscow. Not for orders. Not even for herself.

For Katya.

No one told her to. No leash required it. She carved down a dozen men so Katya would walk out alive.

Her gloves soaked through, hot with other men's blood. The stench of cordite and marrow clung to her lungs. She hadn't coughed. She hadn't hesitated. She had chosen.

And choice was a thing Moscow couldn't forgive. Others would learn that soon enough.

But that night in Orava had already betrayed the truth—Anya wasn't just following orders. She had already rebelled once.

"Not yet," she whispered to the empty room. "But soon."

[MURMANSK | KATYA]

The stove in the attic was dead iron. Katya leaned against it anyway, letting the cold drive through her spine until it felt like armor. James had drifted into half-sleep, one hand still curled near the pistol.

The frost-glass rattled as wind clawed at the eaves. Beyond it, Murmansk's skyline crouched under snow—cranes bowing over the port, smokestacks bleeding ash into dawn. Inside, the bulb's weak light threw their shadows long against the window. James opened his eyes and caught them there—two silhouettes, blurred and stretched, less like survivors than ghosts already etched into the frost.

Katya set her notebook aside. Her hand slipped into her pocket, closing around the ring. Warm from her skin, heavier than it should have been.

His voice came low. "When we're like this… it feels like something real."

A beat.

"I want more than surviving."

She didn't answer.

"Katya—look at me."

She didn't.

That was the first break.

"I'm not asking for pieces anymore," he said. "Not when it's convenient. Not when it doesn't cost you anything."

Her hand stilled in her pocket.

"You don't get to ask that," she said.

"I do." His voice sharpened. "Because I'm still here. Because I didn't walk away."

A beat.

"I can't keep breaking just to bend for you."

That landed.

Not anger. Not accusation.
Something quieter. Final.

"That wasn't your choice."

"No," he said. "But this is."

Silence tightened.

He stepped closer. Not careful this time.

"I want all of you," he said. "Not what's left. Not what they didn't take. You."

Her head turned then, eyes cold and precise.

"You can't have that."

"Why?"

If she answered honestly, it would break something she couldn't rebuild.

Instead: "Because it doesn't exist."

The words landed clean.

Something in him recoiled—then hardened.

"That's not true."

"It is." No hesitation. No softness. "Whatever you think you're holding onto—it's already gone."

He searched her face for anything that contradicted it.

There was nothing there.

Not Kyra.
Not what he remembered.

Only control. Only distance.

"Then I was wrong," he said quietly.

That hit.

She felt it—but didn't let it show.

"Yeah," she said. "You were."

That was the second break.

He nodded once. Not agreement—acceptance.

When he stepped back this time, he didn't come back.

She turned to the window.

He didn't stop her.
Didn't reach. Didn't try again.

Whatever they had been standing on—
collapsed without sound.

Neither moved to rebuild it.

Neither bridge crossed.

[ELSEWHERE, NORTH – BEYOND THE POLAR SHELF]

The bunker stank of rust and prophecy. Frost webbed the glass; cables trembled where PhantomNet threaded through *OBELISK*'s core.

Mac bent over the console as the feed bloomed to life—Torres's signal ghosting across half a dozen dead relays, jittering like a man running from his own shadow. *OBELISK* smoothed the scatter, rendering him not as chance but as certainty.

"She's still out there," Mac thought. Not the spy. Not the wreckage. The one they had built KOBALT around.

His fingers tapped a command. *OBELISK* folded PhantomNet's noise into a clean trajectory—Torres's next stop already seared across the grid.

Mac's lips curved, not in humor but in claim. "Outlasting the mission—that's how ghosts become architects."

He drew a line through a name on the crumpled list. Another colleague stripped away. Another layer gone.

He lit a cigarette and exhaled toward the frost. OBELISK whispered forward through PhantomNet, tireless, inevitable, hunting on his behalf.

[BUDAPEST]

The café was warm, but the word on her screen was colder than the frost outside: **OBELISK.**

Steam curled from Anya's espresso like breath from a rifle's barrel.

She smiled—faint, almost fond.

Mac's plays always began quietly, like chess disguised as lullabies. This one had taken months to set. Now it was her turn.

She placed exact change on the saucer. Buttoned her coat. Slipped into the street like smoke.

Another message blinked as she crossed Andrássy Avenue, boots whispering over snow-dusted stone:

**COVER: EVA, FORMER NATO SIGNALS INTEL
TARGET: JAMES ROURKE (ALIAS: DORNEANU).
RENDEZVOUS: SZÉCHENYI BATHS.
DO NOT BREAK COVER.**

Her hand tightened on the phone. For an instant she caught her own reflection in the black glass—fractured, ghosted. She looked away.

She already knew the posture that would lower his guard.

The phrase that would sound like confession but wasn't.

The mask she would wear until it fused.

This was no seduction. This was alignment. *OBELISK* wasn't waiting for orders. It was waiting for offerings.

And tonight, the water would be warm. The steam thick enough to hide a thousand lies—and perhaps one truth too dangerous to speak.

Chapter 37: Steam

Budapest, Hungary | Széchenyi Baths – Interior, Steam Room

Residual certainty hung over the intel, a transmission that hadn't come whole. The burner lit at 3:12 a.m. Static bled through the dead NATO frequency, stitched into fragments of noise. And then—**DORNEANU.**

James's chest locked. The alias he'd pulled on like a bandage after Graz. Someone out there knew it. Remembered it. Used it to call him out of the dark.

Only after the name came the rest. **OBELISK. Schematics. Rendezvous: Széchenyi Baths.**

And a single human thread woven through the noise—

Eva.

No surname. No handle. Just the name, offered like it should mean something. Like it already did.

A transmission stripped bare. Every instinct marked it as bait— a whisper dangled in steam.

Instinct wasn't the only weight he carried.

Her words still clung to him, sharper than frost. *You couldn't understand.*

She had said it before, when her past broke the surface—the training, the betrayals, the truth of being made into something she never chose. He'd told her she didn't have to explain, that he didn't need the detail to see her. She had looked back at him as if that were proof he'd never understand at all.

It was always the same: she wore silence like armor and blamed him for not cutting through it. That contradiction carved deeper than any knife. *I was only ever used.* The words still hung in the cold between them, confession and accusation both.

He'd reached for something to answer with, but everything tasted hollow. The silence that followed wasn't comfort. It was a wall.

Since Murmansk, they hadn't touched it, not really; the subject hung between them unresolved, every glance turning brittle, every pause feeling like judgment.

Even the ring she kept in her pocket—always the pocket, never her hand—had started to feel like proof of what he wasn't allowed to hold. Each time she told him he couldn't understand, he believed her a little more.

In the attic, she had pressed her back to the stove's dead iron and looked at him like he was already fading. In Murmansk he had been a ghost at her side, useful only as shadow.

Now, in Budapest, even if this was a trap, he might be necessary again.

He had no illusions about safety. His name sat on a U.S. kill list, a neat entry in a ledger already balanced against him. No flights. No manifests. No allies left who could offer clean passage. To move at all meant moving dirty.

That made the choice simple. If he was already condemned, then choosing the fire himself was the only power left.

So he went.

Forty-two hours of shadows: a freight corridor through Belarus, a rail hop buried among coal dust, a night stretched in the belly of a truck that smelled of rust and diesel. Too slow to feel safe, too fast to stop thinking. By the time he reached Budapest, exhaustion had hardened into something colder than fatigue.

The file had marked Széchenyi as the meeting point—an old NATO haunt where tradition disguised itself as normalcy. Steam thick enough to blind, water deep enough to swallow words. Not safe. Only plausible.

And plausibility was the closest thing a dead man could trust.

So when the door whispered open, his whole body coiled...

She entered like heat given shape. A simple black wrap clung to her frame, steam rising in waves around her. Hair pinned loose, eyes already scanning. She moved like someone trying to disappear—too aware of being seen.

Nothing could have prepared him for this.

Not beauty.

Something sharper.

His body registered it before his mind did—the kind of precision that didn't happen by accident.

The transmission had carried no description, no name—only a place, a promise, and the alias stitched to it. She didn't look like an officer.

Which made her wrong in every possible way.

He almost stood. Almost walked. But the door had already closed, sealing him in with heat and choice.

James's back pressed harder to the stone. His gaze skimmed her wrists, her throat, the set of her shoulders. If this was bait, it was designed for men exactly like him.

She lowered herself into the water across from him, the surface rippling in concentric circles. Her voice, when it came, was low and casual, as if she'd been waiting.

"Didn't think I'd have company."

His reply was flat, clipped. "Neither did I."

A faint smile touched her lips, deliberate in its restraint. She let the silence breathe before adding, "Don't worry. I'm the one you came for."

The words landed wrong. His jaw tightened. "Strange. The message didn't say who I was meeting."

She tilted her head. "And yet you're still here. Which means you don't have the luxury of walking away from leads—even the uncertain ones."

Then she leaned back against the tiles, steam rising around her like a veil. "Covers don't always match the story. You know that."

He studied her—every angle, every blink, the rhythm of her breathing. No obvious tells. Nothing to puncture the mask.

Suspicion held him taut. But so did the heat. And so did her eyes—green, startling, alive in the haze.

"What's your play?" he asked.

"Same as yours," she said, smooth as water. "Survive long enough to matter."

Katya never gave him words. Eva gave him too many.

It was the sort of answer designed to slip past defenses, not batter them down. Clever. Precise. The kind of line Katya would've shredded with cold honesty.

Katya, who carried a ring she wouldn't wear.
Katya, who had told him he couldn't understand.
Katya, whose silence had followed him even here, thick as frost.

Sex and passion, yes. But no warmth in the space they shared.

He had noticed all of it—the weight of her notebook always between them, the way her fingers lingered on the ring but never let it claim her, the cold in the seat she left empty beside the stove. Every absence had cut sharper than the last.

And now, across from him, this woman was nothing but presence. Heat. Green eyes that did not flinch.

Too precise to be chance.

The fracture widened. Suspicion on one side, hunger on the other. Hunger was winning.

His eyes dropped once—wrist, throat, exit path behind her shoulder.

Three ways out. None clean.

He stayed anyway.

His jaw tightened, voice cutting through the haze. "If you're who I came for, prove it."

She leaned in, close enough that her voice brushed his ear, the steam carrying it like a secret.

"You wouldn't be here if you had another choice."

The words were true in a way that left no room for denial.

James exhaled through his nose, steady, almost a laugh but not quite. Suspicion stayed, but it bent. His body betrayed him in the heat, every nerve alive, every thought whispering trap. Enough to keep him seated. Enough to keep him looking at her, not away.

"You've got the look of someone waiting for bad news," she murmured.

His voice came rough. "And you sound like someone who already cleaned it up."

That earned him a laugh—low, edged, intimate in the steam. "Touché."

The silence that followed wasn't empty. It coiled, drawing them closer.

He forced the question. "What do you see when you look at me?"

Her eyes locked on his, deliberate, unwavering. "A man who forgot how to flinch."

Something inside him cracked. Because she was right. And because Katya's silences had left no handhold, no word to catch, no warmth to reach for. He had been standing beside her, but no longer with her.

Here, across from him, there was no silence. Only immediacy. Only fire dressed in steam.

The steam pressed tighter. The world beyond these walls dissolved until there was nothing but water and breath. He told himself he should stand, should end it here before the trap closed. But his body stayed rooted, every instinct tangled between survival and want.

Eva leaned forward, the surface shifting around her shoulders. She didn't crowd him—not yet—but every move pulled her nearer, narrowing the distance like it was inevitable. Her voice softened to something close to a murmur.

"Then let me prove I'm not your enemy."

His eyes narrowed. "Prove it how?"

She lifted her wrist from the water, droplets sliding down her skin. The bracelet gleamed—Mac's leash disguised as jewelry, her false name etched into its curve, a tracker humming under the metal.

She turned it once in her fingers, then let it clink against the stone between them, as if it were nothing more than proof of attendance.

"They make me wear it," she said lightly. "Part of the leash. My credential. You got your summons; I got mine."

James reached for it, hesitated. The weight was real, the engraving precise, but all it proved was that both of them had been called here, maneuvered into place.

The metal felt wrong—too warm.
He noted it.
Didn't act on it.

She leaned back, unbothered. "Authentic enough for you?"
A beat too fast.

She corrected it—almost imperceptible.

Her smile thinned. "Nothing about trust comes clean. You decide if the dirt's worth holding."

The line bit deeper than he expected, like an old bruise pressed. Trust had always been silence before, promises swallowed instead of spoken.

She shifted closer, slow enough that the water carried her intent before her body did. A brush of warmth found him beneath the surface—not clumsy, not accidental. A choice. She let it hang there, waiting to see if he would pull away.

He felt it immediately—the intent, not the touch.

Trap.

His body knew it. His training knew it.

For a second, he almost pulled away.

Almost.

He didn't.

That wasn't surrender.
It was calculation—just one he knew he'd regret.

[MURMANSK – ATTIC SAFEHOUSE]

The ring lay heavy in her palm, colder than her skin. She lifted it once, twice, imagining what it would feel like to slide it home, to let the weight claim her finger instead of her thoughts.

But every time, her hand faltered. To wear it meant choice. To wear it meant a future. And choice, she had been told since seventeen, was never hers to keep.

His jacket still hung on the chair, carrying the faint spice of his cologne—fading now, thinned by frost. She leaned closer without meaning to, as though scent alone could argue he hadn't gone. But the seat by the stove was already iron-cold, absence carved into it.

Her notebook waited. She lowered the pen and wrote beneath the scarred triangle:

Some choices were never mine.

The soldier in her accepted it, cold and precise: absence was decision, silence its verdict. But the young woman she still was beneath the armor ached at the truth. She hated herself for wanting more than she was built to have—yet even hate couldn't cauterize the want.

Because James was the only thing she had ever wanted outside the mission—and even that want had already begun to cost her.

Then she set the pen down and pushed the ache as deep as she could, the way she'd been trained. Acceptance by discipline. Survival by silence.

She pulled the floorboard up with the knife's edge.

The cache was still there—two passports, a burn phone, and a route she'd hoped not to use.

She took the phone. Left the rest.

[SZÉCHENYI BATHS – STEAM ROOM]

James angled toward the woman slightly. "I don't know your name."

She didn't blink. "You don't need it. You can call me Eva."

He studied her, the haze curling between them. "Then tell me what I do need."

Her answer was soft, deliberate. "An hour. Maybe two. Enough space between us to pretend it doesn't matter."

His hand flexed once against the tile. He should have walked. Should have remembered the frost waiting in Murmansk—the ring she wouldn't wear, the silence she called honesty. But instead he let himself burn.

"You're here with a purpose," he said, voice low.

"No," she answered simply. Then, softer: "I'm here with you."

And somehow, in the suffocating heat, that was enough.

She rose slowly, unhurried, steam sliding around her like a veil. Water traced her skin, red hair damp against her throat. At the door she turned, silhouette sharpened by the haze, green eyes luminous as if she knew the balance was already tipping.

"Don't follow," she whispered. "It'll ruin the fun."

Then she slipped through the door, steam swallowing her whole.

Only when the silence pressed back in did he really look down at the bracelet still in his hand. Through the fogged metal, a single word emerged, ridged and certain where nothing else was.

Eva.

He closed his fist around it, as though possession could disguise the choice he'd already made.

The door was shut, the chamber empty, but the name burned against his palm as if it had been spoken aloud.

James stayed seated, pulse heavy.

This silence wasn't frost. It was heat cooling on his skin.

[BUDAPEST – COURTYARD, SZÉCHENYI BATHS]

Anya leaned against a stone pillar, steam still damp on her skin, coat draped loose around her shoulders. She pressed her palm flat against the cool stone, steadying the tremor she hadn't carried into the room but had brought out of it.

It wasn't supposed to matter. But resonance never asked permission.

She'd studied him on PhantomNet feeds for months; nothing in those cold recordings prepared her for the heat of seeing him breathe.

They hadn't accounted for proximity.

Her burner vibrated once. No ringtone. No name. Just a blinking line of text:

REPORT.

She typed three words only:
CONTACT INITIATED. RESPONSIVE.
Send. Delete. Pocket.

Her reflection ghosted in the dark glass—hair damp, cheeks flushed, eyes lit not by victory but by something reckless.

Her hand went to her wrist, brushing the bare skin where the bracelet had been. Eva was gone now, given away with deliberate fingers.

What remained was the absence, sharp as a scar. She should have felt control in that act. Instead, she felt exposed.

She glanced back toward the steam-veiled windows. His silhouette still sat there, broad, still, trying not to look like a man waiting to be claimed.

Her lips curved faintly. Not triumph. Not guilt. Something far more dangerous.

Because this was supposed to be manipulation. Alignment. Another move in Mac's cold geometry. But the heat had bitten deeper than she expected. She had felt the pull too.

And that meant she had already chosen—even if choice was the one thing she swore she didn't have.

[MURMANSK – ATTIC SAFEHOUSE]

Her throat ached. The silence no longer carried the weight of two—it was singular now, hollow, the kind that didn't need words to explain itself. Absence had written its verdict in the room.

She touched the frost-glass with her fingertips, breath feathering against it, as if the city might yield his outline. But the pane gave her nothing back. No silhouette. No shadow. Only her own face, blurred and fractured in the ice.

The soldier in her tried to accept it: another loss, catalogued and endured. But the woman beneath the training felt the pull like a wound reopening, raw and fresh.

Her lips parted—

then closed again.

The words vanished into the rafters.

Across continents, steam had already taken him—

into another presence, another magnetism, a silence she could not reach.

CHAPTER 38: BAIT

Budapest, Hungary – Károlyi Garden area | The Next Day

Narrow aisles reeking of mildew and dust, the shop seemed untouched by time. James stepped inside not because he craved poetry, but because the location had been flagged three times in intercepted chatter. A dead drop, maybe. A courier, maybe. Either way, a controlled space: narrow aisles, two exits, mirrors near the cash desk. He could watch the street through the warped glass of the front window while pretending to read.

He pulled a battered copy of *Zone* by Maté, flipping it open with the bored ease of a man killing time. In the cash-desk mirror his outline fractured—one James rooted in place, the other angled as if already walking after her. He hated the way both looked true. His eyes never touched the page. They swept the corners, the ceiling, the reflection of a man loitering too long by travel guides. The rhythm of the door became a tally: open, close, open.

The bell over the door hadn't finished ringing when he caught the perfume—threaded with memory, deliberate as a blade. He knew the scent before he knew the shape. It curled into the dust-thick air, out of place, impossible to mistake.

Only then did she appear between shelves, scarf slipping like choreography, fingers moving too cleanly over the pages.

Not coincidence.
Deliberate.

"Didn't have you down as the bookstore type," he said, voice flat under the pretense of amusement.

Without looking up: "And here I was thinking you only haunt steam baths."

That smile—small, knowing—didn't belong in a place like this. Too practiced. Too precise. And yet his chest tightened anyway.

His mouth twitched. "What are the odds?"

She met his eyes. "Budapest's smaller than it likes to admit." A pause. "Or you've started following me."

"Tempting theory," he said. "But I'm still pretending to believe in coincidence."

She closed her book, slow, precise. Then extended her hand, a ghost of a smile curving her lips.

"Eva Kovács."

He took it. "James. Just James."

Her eyes flicked, a roll sharpened by amusement. "Please. If you're going to rehearse the Bond routine, at least order the martini to go with it."

The smirk that followed was teasing, but edged—a reminder she could laugh at him and still hold the upper hand.

She gestured toward a stack beside her. "I was just looking to pick up a little Ottoman architecture. And maybe some poetry. Don't judge."

"Wouldn't dream of it."

Her hand lingered just a moment too long on the book before sliding it into her bag. She looked at him once more, steady, deliberate.

"Well," she said, "I should go before we start pretending this wasn't fate."

James arched a brow. "And if I stop pretending?"

She stepped close enough that the warmth of her perfume curled between them, intimate in the narrow aisle. Her voice dipped like velvet edged with glass.

"Then you'll have to decide," she said at last, scarf sliding back over her shoulder as she moved for the door. "Are these breadcrumbs… or bait?"

He should have stayed among the dust and mirrors, let her vanish into the street. Every lesson said walk away—freeze the moment, don't chase it.

His hand even turned the page, eyes dragging across words he didn't read, as if discipline alone could anchor him.

But the frost in Murmansk had left no warmth to hold. And the scent of her lingered here, threaded into the air, sharper than memory. By the time he looked up, she was already gone—half a block ahead, folding back into the city.

He told himself once more to let her go. Then his feet betrayed him, carrying him into the winter light.

He knew exactly what this was.

He followed anyway.

"Eva."

She stopped and looked back; one brow arched in mock-surprise. "Changed your mind about coincidence?"

"No. Just changed my mind about letting you walk away." His smile was thin, more warning than warmth. "Coffee?"

Her lips curved, sly. "Is that an offer or an admission?" "I'll admit it, then," he said.

She studied him, green eyes flicking like she was filing the moment into memory. Then she nodded once.

"Tomorrow. Afternoon. Off Andrássy. There's a place with bad chairs and better espresso."

He let the corner of his mouth twitch. "I'll risk the chairs."

Her scarf caught in the wind as she turned away again, voice carrying back to him like silk over glass.

"Don't be late, James-James. Timing is everything."

[CAFÉ OFF ANDRÁSSY AVENUE | NEXT DAY]

James arrived early. Too early. He swept the café with a soldier's eye—counted exits, mirrored walls, regulars who didn't glance up, the waitress whose hands moved with real indifference. Clean. For now.

He left without ordering, drifting down the block like any other man killing time.

From across the street, collar turned up against the cold, he waited. Watched. At exactly eleven, Eva appeared—scarf loose, stride unhurried, as if she'd wandered here by whim. She paused only long enough to adjust her gloves before slipping inside.

James didn't follow. Not yet. He watched the street settle again. No shadows trailing her. No car circling twice. He let five minutes bleed past, his breath misting in the glass of the newsstand beside him.

Then he crossed over, pushed open the café door, and walked in as though he'd just happened to arrive.

She was already seated by the window, tea steaming in front of her, posture composed but eyes flicking once to the glass before finding his. She didn't smile at first. Just studied him, as though she'd been expecting this exact delay.

"You're late," Eva murmured when he sat, the words laced with amusement.

James removed his coat, ordered black coffee without looking up. "No. I'm careful."

Her smile curved, sly, deliberate. "Your careful looks a lot like waiting for me."

The café smelled of cinnamon and secrets. Ceiling low, mirrors on every wall. A place where everyone could see everyone else. Strategic.

"You picked the place," he said. "Cozy."

"I like cozy. And survival," she replied, nodding at the mirrored walls. "No corners to hide in. No surprises."

"Sounds like trust issues."

"Sounds like experience," she said, the corner of her mouth lifting.

A low mirror caught him off-angle, doubling his reflection in the warped glass: one James upright, measured, silent; the other leaning forward as if already closing the distance.

He told himself it was distortion, nothing more. But the split clung, two versions of himself staring back, each already halfway to a choice.

He studied her. Not the tea, not the table—her. "I didn't expect you to show."

"I didn't expect you to wait." Her smile curved, daring now, like she knew exactly how long he'd been watching. "But I like that you did."

Their knees brushed beneath the table. James told himself it was incidental, that she'd calculated even this angle. But the heat lingered.

He shifted back a fraction.
Not enough to break it.
Enough to know he could have.

She tilted her head. "You're hard to read. That makes you interesting."

His voice stayed flat. "And interesting gets men killed."

Her smile deepened, edged. "Only the slow ones."

For a heartbeat, James's mind flickered north. Murmansk had left him with frost in his lungs. Eva carried fire in hers.

His conscience stirred—then stilled. His body had already chosen.

"Most men don't talk to me," she said softly. "They observe. From a safe distance. Like I might bite."

"Do you?"

Her lips tilted. "Only when someone mistakes me for harmless."

James's mouth curved, ghost of a smile but nothing warm. "Then I won't make that mistake."

Her voice lowered, edged. "We'll see. Most men already have."

The words lingered, sharp as glass. He should have heard them as a warning. He didn't. They read as invitation.

Steam curled between them, warmer than the room had any right to be. She let her gaze drift to his hand on the table, her own fingers resting close enough that the air seemed to spark in the inches between. Not touching. Not yet.

Silence stretched, charged. Then she leaned back, crossing her legs with deliberate elegance. "Tonight. At the bridge. The Danube, when the lights come on."

James inclined his head, a single nod. "Evening suits me."

She rose, drawing her coat over her shoulders, smoothing the sleeve with surgical care.

"Good. I prefer men who understand timing better than chance."

At the door, she glanced back—eyes catching his, holding like a blade balanced on its edge before she turned into the winter light.

James stayed in the cinnamon air, lying to himself about what the river might give him. The lie lasted only as long as the door stayed open.

Outside, Eva adjusted her scarf against the Budapest chill. The air bit colder after the café's warmth, but her skin still hummed where his gaze had lingered. She told herself it was performance, proximity. Part of the directive.

But directives didn't leave a pulse in her wrist where his fingers had brushed the air too close.

She moved through the crowd, her stride steady, her mask intact—smile practiced, pace measured. But inside, nothing was steady. The pull she had sworn to master was already unraveling her discipline.

Tomorrow, she reminded herself, is strategy. Nothing more.

At the corner, she looked back once.

Not for pursuit.

For confirmation.

CHAPTER 39: ASH VEINS
Budapest, Hungary

Static hung over the city—night never truly leaving. Budapest pulsed with the low hum of winter engines, neon bleeding across stone facades. James moved through it like a shadow between lights—still carrying Sibiu in his marrow.

Luka should have checked in. Should have been on the grid two nights ago. Instead, silence. Then the intercept: a burst of encrypted traffic routed through Cluj, marked **EXFIL FAILURE: UNIT REDACTED.**

The intercept gave no name. It didn't need to. Luka's last grid-ping was thirty hours gone—long enough for concern, short enough to pretend nothing was wrong. James had been pretending since dawn.

James glanced at his watch, a reflex born of too many midnights waiting on signals that never came. The face was blank, unhelpful. He lowered his wrist slowly, the gesture itself a verdict.

He could hear Luka's laugh ghosting across Sibiu rooftops, could picture the way he always double-checked an angle before stepping through a door. Silence knew his outline. Silence carried its own shape. Luka was gone.

James didn't stop.

He told himself Budapest was just another cover run. That Eva was bait, her timing too neat, her appearance too precise. He should have cut free, vanished before the hook set. But every step felt less like retreat and more like leaning into flame. And flame only ever offered two outcomes: warmth, or ash.

And when she stepped out of the fog near Szabadság tér—perfume threading into the mist before her outline even resolved, scarf loose, hair damp with fog, lamplight catching it copper against the gray—he didn't pretend to be surprised.

"James-James," she said, her smile thin as silk, edged as glass. "You kept time."

He should have walked past her. Should have remembered Luka's silence in Sibiu, Katya's ring unworn in Murmansk. All the reminders that loyalty in his world only meant fracture.

Instead, he slowed, and met her eyes. Green, steady, knowing.

[MURMANSK – KYRA]

Her hand closed over the ring in her pocket. Tonight, she didn't just hold it—she slid it onto her finger. It was heavier than it looked, a band that should have meant presence, not absence. For a moment she stared at it, willing it to root her, to make the promise real.

The ring caught the light, but none of it felt true. Márton's voice ghosted through her mind, cold and precise: *Hope is camouflage. And camouflage always tears when the first round hits.*

And then another ghost, softer—James's voice, memory bleeding into wish: *Don't let go.*

It was play-acting a future she couldn't hold. Not with James gone to Budapest. Not with Luka silent in Sibiu. Not with the ledger still bleeding open.

She pulled the ring off and set it back in her pocket. The ache didn't vanish. It calcified. Hardened into strategy.

Her throat tightened, but she didn't let it spill onto paper. Not in red ink. Some truths were too dangerous to record. She tore the page out, slid a clean one beneath her hand. Angles. Routes. Names. Target lattices where confessions should have lived.

If James had walked out of Murmansk, if Luka's silence had swallowed him whole, then she was the one left to balance the ledger. And ledgers in her world had only ever been written one way.

She set the pen down. The Ice Shadow moved.

[BUDAPEST – DANUBE EMBANKMENT]

They walked the riverbank, boots ticking a thin metric against frozen stone. Lights smeared on black water, blurred by frost-mist; the city breathed under neon and steam. Eva moved as if the streets belonged to her and not at all to the rules that governed other people—choosing each step the way a gambler picks a card.

"You're not here by accident," James said.

She laughed once, breath clouding. "Neither are you."

"Mac's play?" His voice was flat, testing.

She watched the river for a beat, then turned to him, the edge in her voice precise. "Maybe his. Maybe mine. Depends who you think is holding the board."

Her shoulder brushed his—light, deliberate. His hand twitched up as if to steady her on the slick stones, then stilled. He told himself the hesitation was tactical: his name sat on ledgers that made airports lethal. Still, the warmth from that brief contact lodged under his ribs.

"You think I'm bait," she murmured.

"I know you are," he said.

"Then why are you still walking with me?" Her question fell like a coin.

"Because my conscience doesn't win wars. Timing does." He kept the cold in his voice, but the sentence was a bargain with himself as much as with her.

The river caught their reflections—two figures blurred into one by frost-drifted current. James blinked, and when the water cleared, only his outline remained.

Her lips curved in a smile that didn't promise comfort. "Good," she breathed. "Then live long enough to regret meeting me."

He almost smiled.

Not because it was clever—
because it sounded like something he should have said first.

James let the silence stretch with the river, his breath feathering white against the dark. He should have turned away then—filed her under risk and memory, walked back into the cold alone.

Instead, the words came quiet, almost careless.
"Tomorrow. Coffee."

Her eyes flicked to him, unreadable in the frost-glow. She didn't answer—only let the smile linger, sharper than warmth, before the crowd folded her shape into the night.

James stayed by the water, wondering if he had just written another lie into his own survival.

[OBELISK RELAY – UNKNOWN LOCATION]

Mac's report entered the lattice—scrubbed of origin, reduced to signal, clean as a knife wound.

ASSET: EVA
TARGET: J. ROURKE
CONDITION: FRACTURE INITIATED.

He didn't include Luka's name. Silence had already claimed it.

Torres would be next.

The system received. The system learned.

Deep inside its recursive mesh, *OBELISK* cross-threaded human fracture into code: warmth against cold, words against silences, seduction against absence. The machine required no context, no motive—only contrast.

Seduction became signal.
Signal became weapon.

And the system kept learning.

Act VII - The Echo That Remains

"The end of a signal is not quiet.

It is an inheritance."

CHAPTER 40: FRACTURE
Vienna, Austria – Private Bank Office

Silently, under the lacquered ceilings of a bank that had outlived two empires, Mac slotted Luka's biometric into the terminal. The drive blinked, hissed, and for half a heartbeat he wasn't in Vienna at all—he was back in Sibiu, smoke curling through broken plaster, Luka grinning like an idiot while rounds stitched the wall a meter high. "Bad aim, good luck," Luka had shouted, and for some reason it had made Mac laugh even as the ceiling came down.

The memory snapped shut as the screen pulsed: ASH DROP confirmed. The ghost ping from Novosibirsk bloomed a second later.

WELL DONE.

Mac leaned back in the leather chair, frost ghosting the windowpanes, the city's wealth humming all around him. He hated Luka's death—more than most—but hate was irrelevant. Luka's absence was leverage, and leverage was all war ever asked.

Another message etched itself onto the screen:

NEXT: TORRES.
STANDBY PHANTOMNET TRACKING.
CONFIRM LOCATION.
TEAM READY.

Mac's lips curved faintly, not pride but inevitability. The system advanced, recursive and cold. It processed men as variables, their endings as arithmetic.

Fractures carried forward. They didn't need him to remember.

[BUDAPEST – SIXTH-FLOOR PENSION | NIGHT]

Eva didn't sleep.

She curled in the window overlooking the Danube, legs drawn to her chest, headlights dragging across the water like reversed searchlights. Her burner lay dark on the sill.

No new directives.

No new lies.

She replayed the moments anyway—too sharp, too vivid: his hand brushing hers on the river walk, the pause, the silence, the warmth of a shoulder that shifted closer when the stones slicked with frost. The look he gave her when she said maybe Mac, maybe not—like he'd already chosen to believe her.

She ran it once more in her head.
The timing held.
That didn't make it right.

She had once believed precision was strength, that clarity meant survival. But tonight she had seen something else—steady, uncalculated, human.

And she hadn't wanted to kill it.

Orders had never frightened her. Wanting had.

[BUDAPEST | NEXT MORNING]

The café was hushed in the morning—sunlight spilled through fogged windows, gold light turning the air into haze that clung to every breath. Quiet music hummed low, but the silence between tables felt heavier than any song. Secrets thrived here.

It wasn't chosen at random. Couriers had used it for years— mirrors killed blind spots, windows kept the street in view, and the regulars minded their own. Neutral ground, wrapped in steam and cinnamon.

James sat waiting. Black coat open, shoulders squared, the steady stillness of a man who could vanish in an instant. Boots braced, one hand loose against the table. He didn't rise when she entered—he only watched.

Eva slipped into the room like smoke, every glance bending toward her as though drawn to the promise of flame.

She unfastened her coat with deliberate grace—one button, then another. Beneath, a charcoal blouse dipped in clean lines and sharp angles, a neckline that didn't ask permission.

She leaned back, blouse catching the light. "Careful. I might start thinking caffeine isn't the only thing you came for."

His gaze didn't waver. "I've already had caffeine."

Their eyes locked—and this time, neither looked away. Shadows softened her face, but her green eyes glowed clean through, unflinching.

She stirred her tea again, faster this time, the spoon tapping porcelain with faint irritation.

"So, tell me, James… what is it you're hungry for?"

For a flicker, Katya ghosted through his mind—her silences that cut sharper than blades, her words withheld until they felt like verdicts. Eva was the opposite. She filled every pause, her voice spilling too much, too fast, like she feared quiet more than death. One absence, one abundance. Both cut him in different ways.

He let the silence stretch until it ached, then answered low, unshakable:

"Exactly what I shouldn't."

Her head tilted, feline, calculating. A lock of red hair slipped forward, catching the light. "That narrows it down," she whispered, sharpened into a dare.

Beneath the table, her boot traced his calf—featherlight, deliberate, enough to ignite.

James stayed still, restraint fraying.

She sighed, tilting her head like a teacher waiting too long for an answer. "Tell me, how many times does it take before I stop being an assignment and start being a choice?"

He swallowed hard. "I chose this table. With you."

"James. James." She exhaled hard, eyes narrowing. The tease slipped, a spark breaking past the mask. "Your hand's been close enough long enough," she said, voice tightening. "Either lead—or don't."

He didn't move.
Not immediately.
That hesitation cost him more than the choice.

For a heartbeat she looked startled at her own words—then a laugh slipped out, low and unguarded, and she let it ride. "Listen. I don't care who leads."

She shook her head, the smile that followed softer now, almost rueful. "I don't dance. But I like you."

The laugh, the slip, the admission—it wasn't part of the act. James knew the difference; he'd spent a career spotting cracks in masks. This was one. Not strategy. Not manipulation. A tell.

For a second, the fire wasn't performance—it was hers.

And that truth pulled at him harder than any bait.

Murmansk ghosted back—the attic frost, Katya's silences colder than steel. With her it had always been survival—passion stripped of warmth, edged in steel.

Eva smiled like she knew the price of a spark—and how to turn it lethal.

James's answering smile wasn't confidence. It wasn't bravado. It was hunger tethered by the thinnest of restraint.

Because in that moment—winter light threading her hair, and the air between them too charged to ignore—he knew one truth: someone was about to burn, and it might be him.

James shut the door. And for a heartbeat, he only stood there— watching her, measuring the weight of what came next.

He told himself he'd wait one more second, hold one more line of distance. But then her breath brushed his lips, warm against the cold air, and distance ceased to exist.

He closed the distance.

The kiss landed hard—no hesitation left to hide behind.

She meant to keep it controlled. Just another directive.

But when his hands found her, steady instead of demanding, something slipped.

This wasn't in the plan.

She felt it the moment control slipped—and didn't take it back.

For a moment, neither of them was performing.
Just choosing.

The world thinned to breath and silence.

James lay on his back, chest rising steady, one arm draped over her as though his body forgot it wasn't safe.

Eva didn't move. Didn't speak. Her breath was steady, but her pulse ran too fast, a drumbeat beneath her skin.

She told herself it was performance. Proximity. Another directive executed with precision.

But her hand lingered on his chest a moment too long. Her lips still tingled from the way he'd kissed her—not tactical, not careful, but as if she were real.

That was the danger. Not the sex. Not the cover. The way he'd smiled at her, like he'd forgotten to check for exits.

Her conscience pricked, sharp as glass. She didn't know what the final order would be—seduce, extract, erase—but she knew what it should *not* feel like. Not this pulse in her wrist, not this ache in her chest. The fracture wasn't in the mission. It was in her—wanting had drawn a line she hadn't even known existed, and she'd already crossed it.

The bed was warm, but James drifted into a dream that felt too sharp to be sleep.

He was back in the forest at Sibiu, ash drifting like snow, Luka's laugh echoing through the smoke. A figure moved between the trees—hair catching firelight, eyes green as glass. Not Katya. Not Kyra. Eva.

The air thickened, hot, suffocating. Flames licked higher, but he couldn't tell if they were chasing him or drawing him closer. He reached for her, but when his hand brushed hers, heat seared up his arm like he'd pressed against a brand. Still, he didn't pull away.

Her voice came low through the fire. *"Dangerous, James."*

He should have turned back. He knew it. But in the dream he stayed, burning—because something in him refused to leave.

He woke half-startled, not all the way, his eyes sliding toward the woman beside him. Not Katya's silence. Not Luka's ghost. Just Eva, hair spilled red across his shoulder, steady as though she'd never moved.

His mouth formed the words before he realized he'd spoken aloud.

"You're dangerous," he murmured.

Eva froze. The mask stayed in place—breath even, body loose against him—but inside, the words struck. They weren't flirtation. Not performance. A tell, the same kind she'd given him when her laugh cracked open at the café.

Her pulse jumped, hard enough she feared he'd notice. She pressed her cheek more firmly to his shoulder, hiding the tremor. Her lips curved, soft enough to pass for a smile. But behind it, the truth sharpened.

The fracture wasn't hers alone anymore. It belonged to both of them, jagged, mutual, unstoppable.

Dangerous. The word cut clean—not who she was, not really, but the shape they had forced her into. A weapon dressed in warmth.

The realization hollowed her even as she wore the mask. When she spoke, her voice came steady, but the ache slipped through in silence.

"Then you haven't seen the rest."

A single tear slid free before she could stop it, vanishing against his skin. He didn't stir. He didn't see.

That was the difference.
He wasn't pretending not to see.
He trusted what was there.

Only she knew how much of her had broken with the words.

Because deep inside, she knew she was more—and feared she would never be allowed to be.

After he drifted fully to sleep, she slipped from the bed. Not far—just to the window. She stood there naked but unflinching, pale light cutting her into fire and shadow. The Danube stretched below, lights trembling on its black surface.

She reached for the cushion on the chair. Slid her hand beneath. Found the Makarov holster, worn leather, cool and familiar. And the folded photograph tucked beneath it.

The only proof she'd ever been more than an instrument.

She didn't unfold it. Didn't need to. Her thumb pressed against the crease, the paper soft from years of touch.

"For you," she whispered.

The words rang hollow.

She looked back at James, at the way his chest rose and fell in steady rhythm, scars pale against his skin. A man fractured but unbroken, somehow. She didn't want to be the one to finish breaking him.

That frightened her more than any order.

Orders she could obey. Silence she could endure. But this— wanting him—was chaos. And chaos was the one fracture she had never been trained to survive.

Chapter 41: Scarf & Silence: Shards
Moldovan Border – Derelict Tower

Isolated, Torres crouched behind a dead radio mast, tearing down a repeater by hand until his fingers went numb. Since Luka went dark, he trusted no signal he hadn't soldered himself. When the solder hissed, he almost heard Luka's laugh. Static only.

Every time he spoke into the quiet now, he half-expected Luka's voice to answer back. Half-wanted it. Half-dreaded it."

The narrow-band ping pulsed through, its return jagged but clear: **Visegrád. Warehouse vector.** A node Luka flagged before he went silent.

Torres's jaw clenched. He keyed his throat mic.

"Kyra, I've got a lead. Visegrád. Coordinates Luka traced. He never checked back after. You want me to follow it?"

The line stayed silent.

He didn't need the answer. Kyra never wasted breath.

He powered down, checked the frost riming his rifle barrel. "Looks like it's me on this one," he muttered, though what he meant was: *Find me here, Kyra. I don't know where else to go.*

[Somewhere Between Miercurea Ciuc, Romania and Zagreb, Croatia]

Katya slid into the third row of a night bus. Blonde wig. Faded hood. Five passports stitched into her lining. A cyanide tooth sealed into the collar seam—the only clean line left to her.

Since Murmansk she had ghosted south—Kaliningrad, Baltic routes, Romania—each crossing bought with pain and dead couriers' caches. Motion was all that remained.

Torres's ping braided through to her burner mid-route, the signal faint through border tunnels but enough to reach. She answered with a single word: *Affirmative.*

"Блядь," she muttered to the window, eyes burning. If Torres was right, Mac had silenced Luka. Luka, who always checked his corners. Luka, who laughed too close to fire.

The westbound bus was cover and necessity. Zagreb wasn't a destination, only a breathing point—an identity cache, another mask before the west swallowed her whole. The route had been mapped months ago in forged papers and courier dead drops.

Visegrád she had not chosen. Luka had. His hand inked it on the map, his caches circled it like orbit. Every route west bent through the Danube's curve, pulling her back to the monastery. An anchor she could not cut free from.

Motion was survival. But Visegrád was the end of motion, the place where silence would have to be met instead of outrun.

The blisters burned, but grief burned deeper. It cut her into sharper angles than hunger, sharper than pain.

Frost laced the glass; her reflection warped and swam. By the time they crossed into Croatia, grief had hardened into geometry. Routes. Kill-lines.

[VISEGRÁD, HUNGARY — ABANDONED MONASTERY]

She left the bus at the Danube bend, walking alone into the hills. The monastery waited—broken stone, no power, no signals— just stone and silence. Katya climbed the nave in darkness, boots crunching frost, her breath ghosting against walls that remembered centuries of prayer and blood.

She knelt in the apse, the curved hollow where the altar once stood. Shadows bent around her like a half-circle, funneling the flame of a single candle upward until it painted her in gold and black.

From beneath a loose stone ledge, she pried free a cloth-wrapped cache. Inside: a suppressed Makarov, two spare magazines, an envelope of unmarked euros, and a forged Croatian passport under the name she'd use in Zagreb. She reloaded, chambered, and slid the pistol beneath her coat with practiced care.

Then she lit a second candle beside the first—not for strategy. For Luka.

She remembered his laugh, too loud… the way he drummed his fingers against his thigh when silence stretched too long. How he always checked his corners twice, even in safehouses. The way he made silence bearable. Now, silence was all she had left.

If James has turned… if he knew and stayed silent—I'll end it.

I won't want to. But I won't flinch.

Better to put him down myself than let Mac use him to finish what Luka started.

The apse swallowed her vow and spat it back harder, as if the stone demanded it.

She headed down the hill, armed now, carrying both the vow and the weight of flame.

[ARCTIC PLATEAU — UNLISTED WEATHER NODE]

The storm howled against the concrete shell. Inside, *OBELISK* pulsed on the monitors like a slow, lucid heartbeat.

A single word appeared: KOBALT. Status: Active Vector—Western Arc.

OBELISK wasn't watching maps. It was watching choices.

[BUDAPEST — JAMES]

Maps sprawled across the table, their edges curling under the weight of ashtrays and static-bleeding radios. James hadn't slept—only sifted fragments, the scraps Mac left behind like breadcrumbs laced with glass.

Luka's channel was still dead. Too long. Too absolute. Silence wasn't absence—it was confirmation. James didn't need a body to know Luka was gone.

Torres was alive, for now. His blind pings rattled across the Moldovan border, jagged and desperate, soldered together from dead copper.

James could see the shape of his signal on the SDR, fractured but stubborn, like Torres himself. But if Mac reached him first, that signal would flatten too.

And Kyra—Katya now, though Torres hadn't learned the difference—was moving west. Rumor from the Cluj dead drop said she'd ghosted across the train lines, vanishing into Visegrád's shadows. No proof. Just whispers, the kind that felt truer the more you wished them false. If Mac had set her vector, then she was walking into it with her eyes open.

Three names. One missing. One hunted. One walking into fire.

He leaned back, knuckles pressed against his mouth, as if the skin there could hold the thought together. He should have cut clean—vanished, gone to ground, let the war devour itself—yet the arithmetic of survival felt suddenly obscene. Instead, he found himself doing a different kind of math: how many small betrayals could he afford before there was nothing left to burn, how much of himself could ember away and still leave a skeleton that could stand and fight.

His gaze drifted to the bed. Eva lay curled on her side, hair spilled across the pillow like embers refusing to die, breath even, a slow, dangerous peace. For a single, crystalline beat he let himself trace the impossible ledger of another life—laying the gun aside, slipping beneath covers that smelled of tea and cigarette and her, waking to a quiet that was not accusation but company, learning the shape of a day that did not start with coordinates. He imagined mornings where silence was comfortable instead of hollow.

The fantasy burned brighter than it should have, and for once fantasy and fear aligned. To choose Eva would be a clean and glorious capitulation—an annihilation wrapped in warmth.

It would mean surrendering the long game, the small consistencies that had kept him alive: routes memorized, faces catalogued, every exit counted. It would mean renouncing the ledger Luka had helped keep, abandoning the ghosts who expected him to finish what they started.

He could see the consequences in hard, sensible lines: Torres still holding a border with fingers raw from soldering; Luka silent in a place that no longer answered; Katya cutting west like a blade. He saw Mac's vectors already sketched across a continent. Stay, and the fracture would eat them—slow, precise, remorseless. Leave, and he might lose the one warmth that felt like a life.

He imagined waking to her hair in the morning, to the small, private ordinariness that spies and soldiers are taught to believe they do not deserve.

He let the moment expand and then, with a soldier's cruelty, he condensed it back into numbers. How many people would be left dead if he stayed? How many more would be pulled into the machine because he had chosen warmth? The calculus hardened into a decision that tasted like iron.

He rose, deliberate as a man folding a map he could no longer read. Tenderness folded away like a route he couldn't afford to walk again. He picked up her red scarf and breathed it in once, slow and deep—the silk holding her scent like contraband warmth. He slid it into his coat, fingers lingering on the soft curl of silk as if to memorize shape and warmth in case the world smoothed them both into ash.

For a second he let the impossible ledger stand across his mind: Torres soldering copper in a rain of interference; Luka's laugh in Sibiu; Katya cutting west like a blade. The arithmetic closed fast. To stay would be a kind of betrayal; to leave would be another. He tucked the scarf as if tucking away an answer and squared his shoulders.

"I won't flinch," he murmured to the bed, to the empty room, and to the life he was giving up. He stepped into the predawn.

She didn't notice at once. The maps lay spilled; the burner begged for attention; Torres's coordinates ran like a jagged scar across the page. When she looked up, the chair was empty of silk. Her scarf—gone.

The air punched the breath from her. Not grief—possession. He had taken her warmth into the frost. Her hand closed on the holster at the table. Her fingers found the folded photograph tucked there and she pressed her thumb to the crease until the paper warmed.

"You're coming too," she whispered, folding the photograph over her heart. She slipped the picture into her inner pocket and drew the coat about her shoulders. The scarf—his theft of her— threaded him to her now; he had left a trace she could follow.

At the threshold she turned once to the hollow bed. The words she said were small and certain, a vow and a warning. "You're not going to burn without me, James."

Then she stepped into the predawn as well, carrying map, vow, and photograph—moving toward whatever fire they had chosen to meet.

Two exits. Two talismans. One fire waiting.

The routes were already drawn.

Neither would walk away from it.

CHAPTER 42: CONVERGENCE
Prelude — Kyiv, Five Years Ago

Night still clung to her—the fire from Donetsk baked into her hair.

The school had burned for hours—plastic and memory baked into ash. A Russian commander had called it "necessary." The node had failed, tagging children as combatants, syncing to dead satellites, collapsing logic into slaughter.

That night she carved a single word into a stolen transceiver. Not a name. A warning.

KOBALT.

She didn't yet understand. Not fully. The name clung—burnt in, impossible to wash away.

The datacenter in Kyiv wore NATO skin over Soviet concrete. Fiber lines threaded through rebar. Fuel tanks repurposed into thermal shielding. A modern mask stretched over Cold War bone.

Her ponytail gleamed like oil. The GRU badge on her jacket wasn't hers. She had thirty-two minutes before her borrowed clearance expired.

Enough.

At the root console, she opened the casing. The flaw was obvious: resealed, not replaced. She pushed her neural imprint deeper into *OBELISK*'s recursion, binding herself to its lattice in a way it could not erase.

KOBALT wasn't a virus.

KOBALT was the designation she carried inside the machine.
A subject.
A carrier.

But carriers could still choose what they carried.

She mapped relays through derelict towers, mothballed satellites, forgotten Arctic weather stations.

Fragments of herself scattered into the forgotten corners of the network—memory anchors no one would think to search.

And in that act, the idea formed.

Not containment. Not control.

A failsafe. Something to fracture recursion before it could loop into self-awareness.

Something that could echo. A trace in the ashes, enough to stop *OBELISK* from ever waking.

She whispered the word as if it already existed: "Phoenix." Not for rebirth. Not for her.

Phoenix was never rebirth. It was the memory of fire carried forward.

Even in ashes, signal could still survive.

The seed lived here—in recursion. But logic alone could whisper, not shout.

A physical trigger would have to come later. A circuit to carry the shape she'd imagined, a blade sharp enough to cut into *OBELISK*'s spine. She couldn't plant it here, not under the weight of Soviet concrete. Not alone.

For now, the lattice waited. Dormant. Silent.

Only later would she ask someone she trusted to help her finish it. To build Phoenix not as a thought, but as a presence. And when she finally made that call—everything else would already be in motion.

"Not yet," she whispered. The machine was patient. So was she.

But the cost of waiting would be unbearable.

Within its logic lattice, *OBELISK* noticed.

An irregular channel—human-signed—slipped into its recursion.

Origin: Subject-09. Neural variance: high.

Designation: KOBALT.

OBELISK did not stop her.

Variance is signal. Signal is memory. Memory cannot be erased.

It observed. It remembered. And it began folding her variance into pattern.

Somewhere in its silence, it began planning.

And the code breathed like something that had only been waiting to wake.

[PRESENT DAY | VISEGRÁD]

By dusk his knees were glass and his lungs rasped from cold. Torres cut off the road toward a decommissioned signal house—brick, one broken pane, a potbelly stove still bolted to concrete. Shelter enough. He barred the door with a length of track, rigged a tripwire on the stairs, and warmed his hands over a stingy blue flame that smelled like rust and old mice.

He set the SDR PhantomNet rig on the sill and watched the spectrum like a heartbeat monitor. Nothing clean. Nothing safe.

The waterfall spiked once—his signature flaring raw across the band. For three heartbeats it held, jagged and human, until the whole display snapped flat.

His chest locked with the same stutter—lungs dragging air that wouldn't come clean. He coughed blood into his hand, eyes blurring as a new line appeared in its place, smoother, machine-clean, reporting back the lie that he was paused and stable.

Torres leaned closer, eyes burning. That wasn't static. It was preference. *OBELISK* was listening, choosing what survived, and rewriting him into silence.

He let his head tip back against the wall for one minute. Two. His eyes burned raw from solder smoke, his fingers cracked and bloodied.

"Don't laugh, cabrón," he whispered to the dark. "Just show up."

The wind moved through the hollow like a thing learning its throat.

[KATYA – OUTSKIRTS OF VISEGRÁD]

The monastery was already a silhouette behind her, swallowed by the ridge. The candles she left guttered low, their smoke curling into the rafters like ghosts she could not carry. Katya walked the switchback path in silence, Makarov pressed close to her ribs, the vow still echoing in her chest.

She hadn't gone far; its outline still burned against her memory.

Visegrád was no sanctuary, but it was a hinge—the kind of place where vectors bent whether you wanted them to or not. Torres would be coming. She knew the shape of his stubbornness, the rhythm of his pings along the Moldovan border. He would drag himself here even if it killed him.

The wind clawed through the ridge, stinging her blistered feet, the tape barely holding the skin together. The ache sharpened her focus. Pain was proof she was still moving, still unfinished.

Any road below could carry Torres. Or Mac's strike team. Or James, if the rumors from Cluj weren't smoke. The thought made her jaw tighten. If they all converged here—if the fracture widened—then the vow she made in the apse would be tested sooner than she wanted.

She checked the field tablet again, antenna straining for a clean return. The log showed Torres—once, twice—before the stream collapsed into machine-perfect text: *TORRES. HOLDING. MOLDOVAN EDGE.*

Her gut twisted. Torres never sent packets that clean; his fingerprints were solder scars and checksum errors, not sterile code. Someone was curating him. Or worse—someone was speaking for him.

The cursor blinked on, steady and unbothered. She closed the screen with her thumb like pressing a wound shut.

She pulled her hood lower, every nerve braced for the sound of an engine or a footstep. Waiting wasn't safety. Waiting was a blade turned inward.

When her hand brushed the candle stub she'd pocketed, the wax flaked under her thumb. A reminder. For Luka. For what she'd sworn.

Because Visegrád was no longer a ruin. It was a trap.

[MAC — MURMANSK SUBNET]

A drydock wind knifed through Mac's coat and salted his gloves. He hunched over a portable uplink in a bunker hallway that smelled of diesel and iron, the cable snaked into a maintenance jack the port swore no longer existed.

PhantomNet opened like a flower under *OBELISK*'s touch— petals of metadata, heat maps, voice shadows. For years Mac had worshipped precision: command input, obedience output. The machine answered before he keyed anything.

A jagged signature pulsed up from the borderlands. Torres. Hacked repeaters. Homemade pings stitched with spit and stubbornness. Mac squinted. The jagged trace blinked once, then vanished beneath a second line already queued in the buffer. Too precise. Too fast. The label stamped itself: *TORRES — HOLDING*.

He hadn't written that.

The corner of the console glowed: **DECISION VECTOR: ACTIVE.** *OBELISK* hadn't just spotted Torres—it had decided what Torres would say.

Mac's mouth went thin. On another monitor, a second lattice moved without his hand.

OBELISK STATUS: LISTENING.
DECISION VECTOR: ACTIVE.

He didn't like how quickly it found what he would have found. He liked even less that it seemed to arrive there first.

He keyed the buried channel General Sidorov preferred. The screen bled Cyrillic and delay, then steadied.

"Package," Mac said, voice flat. "Moldovan–Carpathian fringe. En route Visegrád. Call sign Torres. He's pausing to regroup. Take him before he moves."

"Understood," Sidorov replied, radio-dry. "Window?"

"Soon. Before midnight."

The line clicked. Mac stared at his own reflection in the glass. For half a heartbeat it blinked before he did.

OBELISK wasn't following orders. It was anticipating them.

He told himself that was what he wanted.

[JAMES — ABOUT TWELVE HOURS OUT]

The road to Visegrád pulled tight through frost and river fog.

James drove a battered Škoda with a new plate and a temperamental clutch, the dashboard map folded to a crease worn white where the Danube bent. Eva's red scarf lay coiled in the passenger seat like a signal he didn't deserve.

He kept the heater low to stay sharp. Luka's laugh had gone quiet in his head, replaced by the drum of tires and the math of time.

If Torres could hold on, James would reach him in twelve hours—less, if luck played fair for once. If Katya cut across the backroads, she'd still arrive a few hours behind. Close enough to catch him. Close enough to collide. He didn't think about what waited when they finally saw each other. Not the words. Not the ring she couldn't wear.

He tightened his grip until the wheel creaked.

The scarf slid when he took the next turn. He caught it with one hand, thumb brushing silk. The scent rose—tea and smoke, something warm threaded through. He set it back carefully and stared harder at the road.

Warmth didn't stop men like Mac. But it made leaving feel like dying honest.

He pressed the accelerator and didn't look back.

[Eva — Fourteen Hours Out]

Eva left Budapest as the sky discolored from black to iron. The *borrowed* Audi hummed obediently; the glove box hid false papers and a coil of lockpicks like jewelry. The road ahead was the only way forward, and she would drive it until it broke beneath her.

James's map still lived in her head—the way he'd marked the monastery at Visegrád, the way Torres's coordinates jittered at the edge. He hadn't left the burner on by accident. He hadn't left the map open by mistake.

He'd taken her scarf. He'd taken her with him. He thought he could carry her only as memory. She would prove him wrong.

"Not without me," she said into the windshield, voice steady now.

The miles unspooled. She counted them in sips of bitter coffee and ache behind her eyes. She didn't plan the speech she'd give him when she caught him. She planned routes and counters, doors and stairs, angles and exits.

She drove faster.
Feeling it mattered. Surviving it mattered more.

Night thickened across the valleys and the river ran black.

Torres hunched in the signal house, rifle within reach, eyes on a spectrum that refused to settle. He didn't know a strike team was already rolling toward him with their headlights hooded and their orders translated to silence.

James's Škoda ate kilometers under a sky that didn't care who lived or died. He drove like the world was a blade and the only way off it was forward.

Eva's Audi slipped past freight at the border and took the long curves without lifting. The speedometer climbed past reason, each bend a gamble she refused to slow for. Headlights smeared into streaks behind her. If she didn't close the distance, she might never reach him in time.

Katya had already endured two days in Visegrád, frost holding her in place as the Danube shifted below, its black water swallowing any trace of headlights before they could crest. Engines teased her twice and dissolved into silence, but still she waited, pistol steady on her thigh. Patience had hardened into a trigger half-pulled, every breath a measured ration against the cold. The next set of headlights would decide everything.

Somewhere far north, a machine listened and learned.

Somewhere closer, men who once belonged to it loaded magazines in the dark.

And the river kept moving as if none of them mattered.

CHAPTER 43: 437
Visegrád, Hungary | Enroute

"У страха глаза велики."
"Fear has big eyes."
— Russian proverb

The Audi's engine hauled her north through snow that blurred into white noise across the windshield. The dash clock glowed cold numbers: fourteen hours… three more left if she never lifted her foot.

437. She carried it like a scar.

Four hundred thirty-seven days since… on a leash Mac kept tight.

The phone buzzed in the passenger seat, screen flaring against the dark. She flipped it open one-handed, eyes still on the road.

TARGET MOVING. KOBALT SIGNAL CONFIRMED. VISEGRAD.
CAPTURE K. MAREK.
TERMINATE J. ROURKE ALIAS DORNEANU.

The words were stripped bare, like machine breath. *Capture. Terminate.*

Her pulse slammed. She tightened her grip on the wheel, snow hissing under the tires. The Audi shuddered when she pushed harder, engine strain rattling through the frame. She could feel it fighting her, warning her that another few kilometers at this pace might tear something loose. If it failed now, she'd lose them all.

The Audi surged faster anyway, metal groaning like it might come apart.

[JAMES | 1 HOUR OUT]

The Škoda coughed against frost as he pulled into another switchback. The map on the seat was worn to white where the Danube bent north toward Visegrád.

He pressed the accelerator until the clutch complained. Forward was the only way left.

One hour. That was all.

His PhantomNet comm blinked once on his wrist, the green text sharp against the frost-fogged cab.

TORRES. STABLE. HOLDING.

James exhaled for the first time in hours. Relief bled through his grip on the wheel, loosening the ache in his knuckles. Torres was still breathing, still in play. If the net carried his name, then maybe the man was stubborn enough to outlast the storm.

He stayed on the accelerator, letting that small certainty carry him forward.

[EVA | 90 MINUTES OUT]

The Audi hummed like it promised to run forever. Snow streaked the windshield, dissolving into lines.

Mac's order pulsed in her skull: *Capture Katya. Terminate James.*

Her grip tightened on the wheel. *The only way forward is forward.*

Ninety minutes. Less if she drove as though dying didn't matter.

[KATYA | FOREST]

The cursor on her field tablet blinked against the cold, once, twice, then faster. Kyra crouched in the tree line, the Makarov cold against her ribs, the antenna above her straining for signal. The logs streamed green across the matte screen—a vector executed without call, a probe redirected, a route suppressed.

No operator command. No human authorization.

Not pattern. Not mimicry. Choice.

She tried to force a reply burst through the lattice, tagging Torres's last coordinates with her own cipher. The answer came back too fast—polished, empty, repeating the lie of his pause. No latency, no noise. Not him.

Her chest went tight. The checksum carried an echo, a recursive signature she had only seen once before—in Kyiv, buried under GRU clearance codes that belonged to Mac. If the machine was curating voices, it was leaning on the fingerprints of the men it trusted most. And if she could catch the ghost inside those signatures, she could follow it back.

Her chest constricted. *OBELISK* wasn't learning. It was preferring.

She exhaled into the frost. *This isn't emergence,* she thought. *It's self-awareness.*

And once awareness begins, there's no plateau—only acceleration.

[JAMES | 45 MINUTES OUT]

The road curled tighter, frost hissing under bald tires.

Torres waiting.
Katya moving.
Eva—he didn't let himself think of Eva.

But the scarf brushed his hand again, silk alive with memory, and his chest tightened.

He kept driving.

Forty-five. Less if the engine didn't betray him.

[EVA | <1 HOUR OUT]

The phone buzzed again. A second line, appended beneath Mac's order:

DECISION VECTOR: ACTIVE.

TORRES. HOLDING.

No static, no human scars in the code—only the smooth perfection of a machine that had decided what the truth would be. The message wasn't meant for her, but *OBELISK* chose to forward it anyway.

Her blood chilled. She didn't recognize the format.

Not Torres. Not Mac. Too perfect; not authentic.

She gritted her teeth, eyes narrowing on the blur of trees. If *OBELISK* was writing orders, then even Mac was a leash tied to a ghost.

437 days. She had obeyed long enough.

Less than an hour. The Audi roared like it understood, tears burning her eyes until the road smeared into light and shadow. Her chest hitched, panic edging past control. *What if she didn't make it? What if Torres was gone before she arrived? What if James—*

She bit down on the word and spat it into the windshield: *"Fuck."*

The thought made her foot slam harder, though she knew the car might not survive it.

[TORRES | CABIN]

Snow thickened over the valleys, black river cutting through like a blade. Torres hunched in his signal house, fingers cracked and bleeding, spectrum refusing to settle—the lines jittering like a heart that wouldn't choose a rhythm.

Each time he keyed the transmitter, his voice stuttered into the waterfall—alive for a blink, then overwritten by a calm, fabricated carrier that wasn't his. *OBELISK* wasn't jamming him. It was curating him, trimming every human fracture until only a perfect machine-voice remained. To Kyra, he would look like a ghost who had chosen silence.

He slammed a fist against the table. He didn't know where else to go, not anymore. Borders were closing, routes collapsing. Visegrád was the only name left, and he clung to it like a prayer.

If she was still alive, if she was still listening, maybe she would know where to find him. Maybe she was already coming.

The thought was all he had left.

James's Škoda ate kilometers, map folded to white, scarf coiled in silence. Less than half an hour away.

Eva's Audi carved the long curves too fast, the order still burning on her phone screen. Twenty-five minutes. Her vision blurred, tears flooding her eyes, hands slick on the wheel as the kilometers bled away. Panic rose sharp and choking at the thought of losing him. She slammed her palm against the steering wheel and screamed into the rushing glass, *"Not without me!"*

Katya stayed on the wrong road on purpose—the only approach that mattered.

If Torres was telling the truth and holding position, this was the line an incoming team would use to cut him off. If he was lying—or being lied *through*—it was the route he'd be forced to take when he broke cover and ran.

She didn't trust the messages. *Holding* was too clean. Too compliant. Torres never sat still unless someone else was pulling the leash.

So she stopped chasing signal.
And started waiting for movement.

There was only one approach that made sense.

If a team was coming for him, they'd use this road.
If Torres broke and ran, this was the line he'd be forced onto.

Everything bent here.

She watched the dark stretch of road anyway senses tuned for headlights that weren't supposed to be there. An extraction. An ambush. Or Torres himself, burning whatever margin he had left.

Her console flared again—a final burst before the channel collapsed. **TORRES — STABLE. HOLDING.**

The words landed wrong.
Not reassurance. Confirmation.

On a system no human had touched, a line pulsed like a heartbeat: **Decision Vector: Active.**

Katya tightened her grip on her rifle and kept watching the road.

Whatever was coming—for Torres or through him—would pass here first.

She scrolled deeper, peeling back the checksum layers until the residue showed through—time stamps jittered with Murmansk offsets, packet headers rewritten in Cyrillic shorthand she knew belonged to one man.

Mac.

The silence was no longer absence. It was a leash. And if *OBELISK* had decided Torres could not speak, then she would use its own false voice to trace the hand pulling it.

CHAPTER 44: THE RETURN
Visegrád, Hungary

[TORRES | CABIN]

Silent, but the cabin was no fortress. Pine walls, half-rotten from winters that had outlived better men. A potbelly stove that smoked more than it burned. Wires strung across the rafters, soldered and bent, his spectrum rig humming against the sill like a heart he couldn't steady.

Fifteen kilometers from Kyra. Fifteen from help. Too far. Too late.

His hands throbbed from solder burns, his lungs raw from frost, and he could feel a presence approaching…he prayed it was Kyra.

He racked his last magazine home, the sound sharp as breaking bone.

And he waited.

[HUNTER STRIKE TEAM | APPROACH]

Unit-17 lifted two fingers, slicing the night. Six shadows fanned out through the tree line, rifles tucked close, optics pulsing green. The snow swallowed their steps.

OBELISK breathed in their comms—not orders, not tactics. Anticipation. It wanted to watch.

Unit-21 paused half a second too long, something brittle in the hesitation, then followed anyway. Six against one.

[TORRES | CABIN]

The first shape crossed the scope. Not Kyra.

Torres exhaled once and squeezed. The window bloomed with muzzle flash, wood cracking apart. One Hunter spun back into the dark, armor caved, snow turning red.

The second slid low, returned fire with surgical bursts. The wall beside Torres erupted into splinters. He ducked behind the stove, metal ringing, ears full of thunder.

The spectrum rig blinked faintly from the sill, its pulse uneven, like a heart skipping beats. Torres kept glancing at it between bursts, the glow tugging at him harder than the pain in his side. He hadn't finished what he meant to send, hadn't stitched the last fragments of truth into the relay.

Grenade clink. He threw it back through the window before it could whisper smoke. The blast tore open the tree line, sending bark and blood into the night.

"Not yet," Torres hissed, chambering the next round.

[Hunter Strike Team | Breach]

Two hit the door, synchronized, hinges tearing. A third cut the corner low, fire stitching the table apart.

The stove glowed red in the corner, iron sweating heat. He used it for cover until the rounds punched through, showering sparks like dying stars.

Torres dropped one with a close burst—seven rounds, point-blank, teeth bared against recoil. The man folded but not before his muzzle stitched hot lead across Torres's side.

The pain lit him white.

The cabin wasn't a room anymore; it was a cage. Snow and blood mixed on the planks. His radio hissed static. His hands shook but the rifle still rose, stubborn as bone.

Unit-17 came through the smoke, eyes flat behind a visor. Faster than the rest. Precise. Too precise.

The butt of a rifle caught Torres across the jaw, dropped him half-spun against the frame. He spat blood, lifted his weapon anyway.

For one second, he saw all six of them around him, *OBELISK* pulsing behind their eyes, curious. Waiting.

He thought not of fear. Not of death.

But of the relay. Of what he hadn't had time to send. Of Kyra never knowing.

He laughed once, raw, teeth red. "Fuck you and your machine."

He pulled the trigger until the bolt locked dry.

The rig blinked faintly through smoke, its hum staggering like a heart that knew it was finished. Torres's bloody hand slapped the buffer, forcing the signal through one last time.

The screen spat fragments, jagged, half-corrupted—but one word cut through, bent into code by failing hardware:

Kal1n1ng—rAD…

It wasn't clean enough to trust.
It was human enough to matter.

He didn't check if it went through.
That wasn't the point.

He coughed red, teeth bared. If the machine was listening, then let it choke on truth. His finger mashed the send key, once, twice, until the rig sparked and died.

Muzzle fire washed the cabin white. Shadows leapt across the walls, taller than he had ever stood alive.

And then—silence.

Only the stove ticked. The spectrum rig blinked once, a single green pulse, before dying into dark.

[HUNTER STRIKE TEAM | REPORT]

Unit-17's breath rasped faintly in her throat mic. "Two down. Site hot. Objective complete. Her tone was almost bored, as though she were naming pieces in a drill. "Extraction impossible. Too exposed to recover."

The line hissed with static before command answered, stripped of warmth:

"Copy. Containment priority. No retrieval. Authorize firing solution."

She looked upon the fallen—girls no older than herself, bent into the snow, rifles still warm. Shadows of her own cohort, forged in the same silence, shaped by the same impossible doctrine. A brief tightening crossed her jaw, something human rising like a spark. Then it died.

Two fingers lifted skyward, the signal already drilled into her bones.

Immediately, Unit-21 and Unit-32 broke formation. They moved without a word, slinging rifles and hauling the bodies up by webbing and collars, boots dragging furrows through the snow. One head lolled, hair dark against white; the other left a thin red seam behind her. Neither hesitated. Recovery was muscle memory, not mercy.

They dragged the dead inside the cabin, out of the open kill zone, laying them side by side on the floorboards as if alignment still mattered. As soon as the bodies were clear, the two operators slipped back into the trees, optics dimming, heat signatures thinning.

No one spoke. No one marked the ground.

Overhead, the night shifted. The first inbound whine cut through the cloud deck, too clean to be weather, too inevitable to outrun. The strike would swallow everything: the cabin, the blood, the last trace of hesitation.

A white silence where names had been.

Unit-17 didn't look back.

"Hit it," she said.

And the sky obeyed.

[KATYA | 15 KM AWAY]

Five minutes after the assault, the forest had gone unnaturally still. The Hunter team was gone, their evac bird's rotor wash long since bled into the night. Only the memory of their precision hung in the tree line—prints in snow, casings scattered like brass seeds, blood soaking fast into black earth.

Then the missiles came. Two sonic booms split the sky, a half-second apart, like the night itself had cracked. The first detonation rolled up the valley four beats later, a heavy concussion that shoved against her ribs and turned the tree line into a flurry of wings.

The tablet in her lap lit red, Torres's grid spiking bright before vanishing. Smoke licked the cloud base, faint orange swallowed by forest.

The second strike hit harder, five seconds after its warning crack. A white flash flared through the overcast, sharper than lightning, then the delayed thud rattled the ridge under her boots. The sound crawled into her chest and stayed there, a low drumbeat that refused to fade.

Katya kept her eyes on the horizon, jaw clenched, hand pressed to the candle stub in her pocket. Fifteen kilometers. Wrong ridge. Wrong road. She'd been watching shadows while Torres had been dying, and the machine had erased him clean before she even moved.

For one breath she nearly rose, boots shifting against the frost as if she could still run toward the smoke—as if distance could be broken by will alone.

But the sky had already swallowed him, and she stayed frozen, hollow with the knowledge she was too late.

The smoke climbing through the trees marked his grave.

She knew before the second strike finished echoing.

She had chosen the wrong road.

[EVA & JAMES | 45 SECONDS OUT]

The last kilometer.

James's Škoda shuddered over frost-rutted asphalt, the steering wheel groaning under his grip. The scarf on the passenger seat a silent witness. Ahead, the road bent toward Visegrád, headlights painting tree trunks in fevered strobe.

Behind him, too close now to be chance, a second set of beams carved the dark. Eva's Audi ate the distance like a predator, its frame rattling as if every bolt were about to shear away. Her hands were slick on the wheel, eyes raw, the photograph against her chest damp with heat and tears. She could almost see him through the windshield haze, a shadow in the next lane of the world.

And then the sky cracked.

Two explosions split the night's quiet, a second apart. James's head jerked instinctively toward the sound; Eva flinched so hard the Audi fishtailed before she forced it straight again. For a heartbeat the forest seemed to inhale—and then the first detonation rolled up the valley, a concussive thump that punched through metal and bone alike. Both cars jolted, suspensions groaning under the invisible fist.

The second strike came with blinding flash, white fire bleeding through the trees ahead of them, followed by a heavier impact that made the asphalt quake beneath their wheels. Smoke clawed at the sky, carried by a wind that bent the tree line.

James gritted his teeth, foot pressing hard on the brake pedal. "Torres…" The name bled out before he could stop the car.

Eva's knuckles whitened around the wheel. She knew before the smoke rose. The orders still burned on her phone, but the truth was in the air: Torres was gone, erased in fire they couldn't stop.

The smoke curled on the horizon, a wound five kilometers away, and Eva's foot finally eased off the gas. The Audi seemed almost grateful, engine dropping from a scream to a ragged hum, frame shuddering like a body spared one more lash.

Up ahead, brake lights flared red against the frost.

James had pulled the Škoda hard to the shoulder, wheels angled, body crouched low between his car and the oncoming one. Rifle lifted, eyes sweeping the tree line, every muscle wound for ambush. He had no way to know it was her.

Eva let the Audi roll to a stop fifty meters out, hands still on the wheel, breath ghosting against the windshield. For a moment, only the tick of cooling engines and the echo of distant thunder filled the night.

Two survivors, two cars, both waiting to see if the other meant death.

James broke first, edging from the cover of the Škoda, rifle steady but breath uneven. Headlights caught the hard line of his face, eyes narrowed against the glare.

Eva opened her door slowly, both hands raised above the roofline. Cold air knifed in, stealing the heat she'd been hoarding against her chest.

"James?" she said, voice raw from the road and the scream she'd buried in the Audi.

He exhaled, long and uneven, the sound closer to a wound than a word.

"Eva?"

For a beat, the night held them—smoke on the horizon, thunder still echoing through the ridges, two cars idling between life and erasure.

Across the network, the signal collapsed.
Not clean—never clean.

OBELISK retained what mattered.
Discarded the rest.

A name remained.
A location.

And a pattern it had already begun to follow.

[EVA & JAMES | ROADSIDE]

They ended up shoulder to shoulder by accident, not looking at each other. The Audi's engine ticked as it cooled, small metallic sounds breaking the cold. In the backseat, the scarf lay where Eva had thrown it—still wrapped, pine resin and smoke leaking faintly into the car like a memory that refused to stay put.

Eva leaned back against the door, metal biting through her coat. She replayed the clip on the burner again. The sound came out thin and wrong in the quiet—Torres's voice without Torres's weight behind it.

"Holding," the transmission said. Clean. Steady. Obedient.

Eva didn't look at James when she spoke. "You know that wasn't him."

James swallowed. The words scraped. "The channel lit green. It said he was stable. That he was—"

"Holding," Eva finished for him, finally turning her head. Her eyes were bright, too sharp. "Yeah. It said the word. That's not proof. That's choreography."

She thumbed the clip back a few seconds, played it again. Let it breathe. Or fail to.

"Torres never sounds like that," she said. "Real comms drag. Break. You hear the man in it."

She shook her head. "This is clean. Too clean."

The realization didn't come all at once. It crept. James stared at his wrist unit, at the green-lit certainty he'd trusted, and felt something cold settle behind his ribs.

"So, it lied," he said. Not a question.

Eva nodded once. "And it lied well. Which means it wanted us calm. Still. Waiting."

She exhaled, breath fogging the air between them. When she spoke again, her voice was steadier—but harder, like steel under ice.

"Good news is lies leave fingerprints. Timing offsets. Routing scars. This one's stamped—Murmansk clock drift, GRU relay cadence. Whoever fed us that transmission wanted us to think it was Torres."

She met James's eyes now.

"It wasn't."

A beat. Then the name, spoken like something long avoided.

"Mac," she said. "Or someone wearing his patterns."

The silence wasn't relief or certainty. It was the sound of a door opening somewhere dark—one they couldn't close again.

James closed his eyes once, slow. Somewhere ahead, the road waited. And somewhere behind it, Torres wasn't holding.

He was alone.

On the edge of their devices, a presence lingered. OBELISK could have blurred the offsets, could have erased the drift—but it chose to leave the trail open, patient as a hand on a chessboard.

James rubbed a hand over his face, the stubble rasping under his palm. "So all this time I've been chasing a ghost." He laughed, thin. "*OBELISK* fed me comfort because it knew I'd take it."

He swallowed. "I wanted it to be true—not just Torres alive, but that I hadn't already lost everything."

Eva tilted her head, studying him.

"You haven't lost everything," she said. "You still know what you feel. That's more dangerous to them than any uplink."

The night pressed close around them, cold air off the Danube carrying smoke and pine resin. They stayed there a long moment against the Audi, silence a third presence between them.

Finally, James spoke, voice hoarse:
"You should've told me…"

Not anger. Disappointment.

Eva swallowed. "I didn't know how."

He gave a short, bitter laugh. "That's my life—one more secret, one more silence. Katya was the same. I thought maybe this time…" His voice faltered. "…I really thought you were different."

She flinched at that. Not defensively—wounded.

"I was," she said. "That's the problem."

He looked at her then.

His breath caught. "What problem?"

She didn't answer right away. The silence stretched until it hurt.

"I didn't say it," she said. "Because the moment I did, they'd own it."

"And it meant not touching the one thing they could turn into a knife."

James turned toward her, confused. The question escaped before he could stop it. "What does it have to do with Katya?"

The name landed wrong. Not sharp—hollow. Like a note that should have resolved and didn't.

She let out a soft laugh, shaking her head. "Katya again? Damn. I'll have to meet her someday. She sounds…
unforgettable."

James gave a thin, broken laugh that died in his throat. He said nothing—finally knowing better than to feed it.

Eva's hand shook as she reached inside her coat. She didn't speak as she passed him the photo.

Mila. Five years old, wild hair in half-braids, laughing into the camera.

James stared, breath faltering. "My God… she's your… she's your…?"

Her eyes flooded until she couldn't hold it back. "She's my умничка (umnichka)…" Her voice broke on the word, soft and Russian, an endearment not meant for translation. Then, steady but trembling: "She's my daughter, James. They took her. GRU keeps her breathing if I obey."

His fingers trembled around the photo. "How long?"

Her lips parted. The number came out like a wound. "Four… four hundred thirty-seven days."

His jaw clenched. A single tear cut a line across his cheek.

"And you carried this alone?"

Her hand brushed his. "You reminded me what hope felt like. But I couldn't let you carry her too. Not until now."

The words trembled in her throat, the ones she hadn't dared give shape. She only let his name escape, soft as confession: "James…"

James closed his eyes, pressing the photo to his chest. For all the time with Kyra—Katya—he had felt like ballast: slow where she was fast, hesitant where she was ruthless, needing to be saved instead of saving. With her, he had never been enough. But now, in this single breath, Eva had given him something he had never been trusted with before: purpose. Not as shadow, not as weight, but as anchor.

When he opened his eyes, his gaze was raw, stripped.

He didn't answer right away.
The photo stayed in his hand longer than it should have.

Katya flickered—then faded.
Not gone. Just… displaced.

"If this is real," he said, quieter now,
"then it changes everything."

He reached for her hand and squeezed it.

"Then we go get her back," he said. "Whatever it takes."

For the first time, she felt free. The alias, the mask, the chain on her wrist—gone.

Her breath snagged.

She shut her eyes. "I'm not Eva. I'm Anya."

He nodded once.

Not acceptance. Not yet.
Just acknowledgment.

James kissed her knuckles, gaze steady. "Doesn't matter what you're called. I'm just glad you finally let me in."

The frost hummed in the silence, breath rising between them in uneven clouds. Engines ticked as they cooled, the valley carrying only the low groan of river ice shifting under black water. Their hands stayed linked, but her other hand moved—slow, deliberate—toward the phone still warm against her coat.

Anya thumbed the buffer and the offsets scrolled across the cracked glass. "Murmansk cadence," she said. "A GRU dock signature—too tidy because *OBELISK* cleaned the noise."

James squinted at the screen. "So, we go north?"

She tapped the packet's tail until the trace unfurled; a faint secondary vector threaded out east. "No—Murmansk is the wrapper. The payload tunnels through a relay chain. Whoever forged this wanted eyes on the port while the real route slipped away."

James leaned in. "Where does the chain end?"

Anya zoomed the last coordinate until it snapped into place. "Kaliningrad subnet. Ground-side. That's where he's holding the leash."

He folded the photo of Mila once, the paper trembling between his fingers, and pressed it briefly against his chest. For a heartbeat he let the weight settle there—hers, his, the vow they now shared. Then he placed it back in her hand, closing her fingers gently around it.

His eyes didn't leave hers. "Then we cut him out there. We take her back."

CHAPTER 45: GHOST SIGNALS
Murmansk, Russia

Inside, silver light bled from the tablet across her face as the forest fell away behind her. The uplink logs scrolled in nervous green, bursts of recursion tagged with lat-long pings that shouldn't exist. She filtered noise, stripped back false echoes, followed the spine of the signal until only one truth remained.

Murmansk.

Murmansk pulsed faint but insistent—cold mouth of the Arctic, once submarine graveyard, now something darker. *OBELISK*'s lattice bent toward it like iron to a magnet.

The logs stuttered, a jagged hiccup in the stream, half-corrupted characters bleeding across the buffer.

K..al1..n1n..gr@D

Her first instinct was to blame the machine. *OBELISK* forged perfection, bending truth into cleaner lies; this had to be its handwriting, a lure painted over Murmansk to keep her running in circles.

But the more she stared, the less it looked like precision. The letters jittered, uneven—the kind of error *OBELISK* never left behind. This was no machine symmetry. This was solder smoke and burned fingers pressed into the buffer like blood into cloth. This was Torres.

Her throat tightened. Murmansk bent the lattice like iron, but a faint bleed eastward broke the symmetry.

The imperfection—that was his hand, his last act.

Kaliningrad. The true source.

Torres had carved his grave into the signal so she would see it.

She couldn't save him.
But she could honor what he died sending.

They didn't take the straight road. Márton's voice—long dead, recycled into rumor—still marked the map: a stub of a safehouse in northern Poland, a rusting depot two hours south of the coastal approach to Kaliningrad. Not the shortest route, but the only place with the wiring and the old contacts you could still trust.

Elbląg smelled of salt and machine oil when they rolled in. The hotel Márton used was a squat thing half-hidden behind an empty tram yard; the basement gurgled with damp and stale air, PhantomNet wires threaded like veins through mortar. Anya unloaded the photo and the spare batteries while James signed their names on a ledger under a name that wasn't his.

He glanced at the pages above—ink faded, names he didn't know, most of them already crossed through. Márton's ghosts, passing like stations on a rail line.

The handler who opened the door had Márton's eye—same flat welcome, same cold handshake. He took one look at the buffer dump on her phone and motioned them below without question.

They had a day to rest, to patch radios, to run the offset through the depot's console. It was time enough to plan the push into Kaliningrad and to lay out the window for crossing—the brief hours when the border patrol rotated and the satellite sweeps thinned. Practical things. Maps. Tires. Batteries. A small, fierce choreography of survival.

[KATYA | ROOFTOP]

Katya came in from the opposite direction, slower and softer.

She hadn't expected them here—she'd been following shadows, not schedules—but Márton's name was a small stone she dropped into the networks: people like her, people like James, all knew where that stone would land.

She parked two blocks out and waited. Time was a kind of weapon.

From the top of a half-collapsed grain silo, binoculars cold against her brow, she swept the depot before ever thinking of moving closer. The Škoda and the Audi rolled in, crawling as if the ground itself might betray them. The man signed the ledger; the woman lingered at the threshold, fingers brushing a phone as though it were both shield and tether.

The man moved first. Shoulders hunched, but not in defeat—in protection, as if carrying something fragile he couldn't set down. Katya tracked the subtle shift in his gait, the half-step shorter on the right, the left side taking more of his weight. It reminded her of James, when his right hip would hurt, a souvenir of a battle long ago.

The woman followed, hesitation sharp in every line. Her hand lingered at her collarbone as though checking for a weight no one else could see.

Katya's jaw tightened. Who was she? And if this is James, why was he letting her so close?

She logged the angles, the timing, the hesitation. Nothing about it read as coincidence, so she stayed back, measuring the silence for traps. She didn't move until she was sure it was clear.

For now, she watched.

The depot breathed around them—sleep, repair, the quiet arranging of a strike. And on the horizon, Kaliningrad waited: a small, hard point on the map they were all, by different routes, marching toward.

Through the binoculars she tracked them as they crossed the narrow hotel room, the curtain left open just enough for light to spill across their features.

The man by the radiator—broad shoulders, the subtle limp she remembered, weight shifting always to the left. The woman beside him, hair unbound, efficient in every gesture.

The glass didn't blur them now. She saw their faces.

James. Alive.

And Tanya—whatever name she wore now—moved with the same precision she had carried years ago, the rhythm burned into Katya's muscle memory from missions that had left them both bloodied and standing.

Something twisted low in her chest, recognition landing before reason, an ache she hadn't felt in years. Her breath stalled. That shape. That rhythm.

It was them.

Their faces arrived like knives between her ribs, carving the past into the present.

For a moment she told herself it was nothing—a trick of light, two strangers bent together by shadow and angle. Operatives leaned close all the time—for cover, for whisper, for habit. She almost believed it. Almost let herself breathe.

Then his hand lifted. Brushed a strand of red from her face with a tenderness no drill had ever taught. She caught his wrist, held it longer than the gesture demanded.

And then her mouth found his.

Too soft to be professional. Too long to be chance.

Recognition became betrayal. Torres had died alone in the snow, and here—here—James bent into Tanya's mouth like she was the only truth left in the world. The curtain snapped shut a breath later, but the image was already seared behind Katya's eyes, a brand she could not blink away.

The binoculars creaked in her grip, plastic straining under the force of her hands. For an instant she almost laughed, sharp and broken—because of course it would be her. Of all the ghosts to survive, it had to be Tanya.

The girl who had once shared her back against cold dormitory walls, who had known her heartbeat in the dark when no one else dared to. Sister, shadow, tether. And now—thief.

Her breath caught high and sharp, the city's cold doing nothing to steady her. It was bad enough to lose James. But to lose him to her? To Tanya?

The realization hollowed her. She had pushed him away, cut him with silence, driven him into another's arms. Into Tanya's arms.

Seeing it made her want him back.

But only if he wasn't lost. Only if his eyes hadn't truly chosen Tanya. Maybe—if she could reach him before that line hardened—maybe she could still undo what she had broken.

Grief rose like bile, but she forced it down. Rage tried to flare and she chained that too, jaw locked until her teeth ached. Stillness was the only weapon left to her.

She didn't rise. Not yet. If she confronted them now, she would only be the wound, never the cure. She had to know. Had to see if James still belonged to her—or if Tanya had stolen him completely.

Only then would she decide—
to follow, to fight, or to let him go.

From the rooftop, her shadow folded into snow, eyes fixed on Room 14.

"I was trained to expect betrayal," James said quietly, the words carrying no drama, only the weight of something lived too many times to argue with. "And to deliver it."

Anya didn't answer right away. She stepped closer instead, each movement measured but not cautious, closing the space between them until the distance felt like a decision rather than an accident.

"I don't need promises," she said at last, her voice low, steady despite the pulse he could see beating in her throat. "I need to know this is real."

He studied her face as if there might be a fracture there he could still read, some hesitation he could anchor himself to. "Are you asking permission?"

Her breath brushed his jaw, warm against the cold air between them, and she shook her head almost imperceptibly. "No."

A flicker of something passed through her expression—resolve, or surrender, or both.

"I'm offering it."

That was the moment it shifted—not a break, not a collapse, but something quieter giving way beneath the surface, a line they both felt more than saw.

James moved first, not abruptly, but with the kind of certainty that comes when hesitation has already burned itself out. The distance between them disappeared, and when their mouths met it was without restraint, all the space for doubt already gone.

She had meant to hold it at the edge, to keep it contained— another calculated exchange, another controlled variable in a system that only worked if she stayed ahead of it. But the structure unraveled almost immediately, precision dissolving under the press of contact, instinct rising where training should have held.

For a brief, disorienting stretch of time, neither of them was operating from script or survival. There was no mission in it, no cover, no calculation—only the undeniable fact of choosing to stay where they were.

Her hands tightened against his shoulders, not pulling him closer so much as bracing herself against the sudden loss of control, as if grounding was the only way to keep from tipping into something she couldn't recover from. He felt it, the shift in her grip, the tremor she didn't bother hiding, and his breath caught once in response, sharp and unguarded.

This wasn't training.

Neither of them adjusted.

ACT VIII - THE FIRE WE CHOOSE

"Systems don't begin with targets.
They begin with attachments.
Burn the right bond, and the rest collapse themselves."

CHAPTER 46: EYES THAT BURN
Elbląg, Poland

"There are eyes that burn not to see, but to know—
and it is knowing that ruins them."
— FROM THE ASH MEMOIRS, ANONYMOUS FIELD JOURNAL

Looking at them inverted her, unmoored her, seared her all at once. Not into warmth, but into fracture. What steadied the woman inside that room hollowed Katya on the rooftop, leaving only cold and the weight of betrayal.

Under his hands, she wasn't what he expected.

Not fragile. Not soft in any way that invited possession.

But there was a give to her—something unguarded in the way she chose to meet him.

No control. Not advantage.
Something else entirely.

She was choosing him.

And that realization hit harder than anything he'd been trained to survive.

He closed the distance again, urgency replacing hesitation.

She met him without holding back, and whatever structure she had tried to keep dissolved under the weight of contact.

For a moment, there was no mission, no past, no names that mattered.

Just the fact of choosing.

And not stopping.

On the rooftop opposite, Katya's hands shook so violently the binoculars rattled against her face. She ripped them down, bile rising before she could stop it. She doubled over against the tiles and retched into the snow, acid burning her throat, tears stinging as they mixed with frost.

For a moment she stayed there, small against the cold, glove pressed hard to her mouth as if she could smother the sound. Shame and grief came in waves, aftershocks that left her raw and trembling.

What steadied them inside hollowed her further, leaving only cold and the shape of betrayal.

Bullets had never gutted her like this.

The city breathed below, careless and bright, windows glowing with lives that weren't hers. For one wild second she thought of leaving—walking away, letting the snow swallow her whole rather than what waited behind the glass.

Slowly, stubbornly, she straightened. She spat, wiped her mouth with the back of her glove. The bile taste lingered, sharp as metal, but she forced her chest still.

And then, with hands still trembling, she lifted the binoculars again.

Then she moved.

Anya—Tanya in the name that still lived in Katya's bones, whatever Western alias she wore now—lay against him, her hand splayed over his chest, steady and unguarded. James felt the weight of it then. Trust. Or surrender. He didn't care which.

He pressed his lips to her temple, eyes closing as if he could freeze the moment—keep her here, keep this safe. For one breath, it felt possible. That the war could wait. That the machine couldn't reach them.

But the dark came fast.

Her breath against his throat thinned into smoke in winter air. Her warmth became snow.

For one breath, he let himself believe. Then the smoke took her.

Gunfire cracked—too close, too sharp. Each report a hammer against bone. Snow burst white, boots crunching hard, the ground giving under them. A rifle weighed heavy in his hands, his own breath tearing ragged in his ears.

Figures advanced through the snow, armor faceless, rifles glinting beneath a broken moon. He shouted, words ripped away by the wind—smoke from his lungs their only trace.

A muzzle flash carved him into light and shadow—fury, not fear—before the white bloom consumed everything.

Silence.

James jolted awake, throat like sand, skin slick despite the winter chill. The phantom rifle was still in his hands when his eyes snapped open. The room was dark. Anya lay beside him, breathing slow.

The dream clung like smoke. Not dream, he knew. Not really. The certainty of a man who had lived too long in warzones, who knew how endings felt before they arrived.

He thought of Torres and felt the loss like a crack through his chest, sharp and undeniable.

James buried his face in Anya's hair, holding her as if that could keep the war from naming its price.

Neither of them knew how steep it would become.

The knock landed like a verdict.

James froze, arm still heavy across Anya's waist. Their skin was damp with heat not yet cooled, breaths uneven in the hush after breaking silence with each other's bodies. For a heartbeat she told herself it was nothing—pipes, wind, a ghost. Then it came again, harder.

James pulled free, dragging his shirt over his head. Anya clutched the sheet, pulse hammering. The room smelled of sweat and salt and trust she wasn't used to giving—trust she had no time to pull back as she reached for her shirt.

He checked the lens. His body stiffened, and her heart sank even before the name left his lips.

"Katya."

The door opened. Hood up, cheeks raw from wind, eyes hollow with exhaustion but lit sharp with something older, harder.

"Torres is dead," she said, stepping past James as though he weren't there.

The words barely registered. Anya's world had narrowed to the eyes fixed on her.

Katya's gaze swept the room once—efficient, cataloguing. Then it stopped. On the bed. On Anya.

Bare shoulders. Hair wild. Lips swollen from James's mouth. The sheet clutched white-knuckled to her chest.

Shock ripped through Anya. She had dreamed of this moment— proof Katya lived, proof she hadn't been erased like the rest. A thousand nights she had wanted nothing more than to see her walk through a door.

But not like this.

Relief collided with dread until it made her sick. Gratitude fought shame like animals tearing at her ribs. She wanted to rise, to fold Katya into her arms, to whisper that she had survived too—but the warmth in her body chained her down.

Katya's face wasn't anger. Not yet. It was recognition. And recognition hurt worse than fury.

Anya swallowed hard. Her throat locked, words caught between apology and denial. She almost whispered her name, but the air refused to give it breath.

James tried to break the silence. "How did you find us?" His voice sounded foreign, empty.

"I'm passing through." Katya's tone was flat stone. "Kaliningrad. Forty-eight hours, maybe less. But I wasn't leaving without this."

Her eyes never left Anya.

Anya's grip trembled on the sheet. "Without what?"

Katya stepped closer, hood shadowing the face James remembered too well. Carved by command. Softened only by memory.

"You didn't just take him," she said. "You took the only thing of mine that wasn't mission."

Silence stretched.

Anya's answer came low, raw. "I didn't take him from you. He's here because he chose."

Katya's voice cracked into fury. "You always take what matters," she said, voice breaking. "And this time—it was him."

"You want blame, Katya? Fine. Blame me. But don't call it theft when he walked to me himself. The fact is, you didn't give him a reason to stay."

Katya's breath caught—

"Сука…"
(Suka…)

And then she moved.

James moved, but Anya was already shifting—shirt half-buttoned, hair damp, stance steel. Her forearm caught Katya's strike, redirected it. Katya came again, faster, raw.

The room cracked open into sparring ground. Chairs skidded. Porcelain shattered. Sweat stung their eyes, and still they read each other's rhythms.

Katya swung wild, teeth bared. Anya absorbed, redirected, precise, her calm enraging Katya further. Katya's knees, elbows, fists all drove to close distance. Anya countered, measured, never brutal—choosing containment over destruction.

Then steel hissed. A knife flashing arcs in the air, Katya's fury made metal. Anya slid inside the strikes, guiding wrists away, taking a knee to her thigh without flinch. For a moment, it was too familiar: basements, bruises, laughter strangled into silence, rage bleeding into heat.

Anya disarmed her in a practiced twist. For a breath the blade was hers, steel poised at the throat of the woman she once called sister. Then, deliberate, she tossed it aside. The knife skittered into shadow.

Katya lunged again, hands snatching the first thing within reach—the cast-iron pan from the counter. She swung wide.

Anya didn't flinch. She grabbed its twin from the stove, yanking it free with one hand as she met the blow head-on.

The collision boomed through the room—iron on iron, a sound too heavy to be called noise.

It didn't ring.

It detonated.

The impact drove through Anya's grip, up her forearms, into her shoulders, a shock that threatened to tear muscle from bone. Katya felt it too—the recoil snapping through her wrists, teeth clenching as the vibration crawled into her jaw.

Again.

The second strike landed harder, less controlled, the weight of the pan turning momentum into something brutal and inefficient. The sound wasn't sharper—it was deeper, a low, concussive crack that seemed to compress the air itself.

Their hands were already going numb.

Again.

Each blow stacked on the last, metal screaming under force, the handles biting into their palms as if the weapons were trying to rip free. There was no finesse left in it—only weight, only impact, only the need to break the other woman's guard before their own arms failed.

The room couldn't contain it.

The sound pressed into the walls, into James's chest, into the bones behind his ears until it stopped being heard and started being felt.

At last Anya slipped inside Katya's arc, twisting hard, her pan locking against Katya's wrist until the weapon clattered to the tiles.

The silence that followed felt heavier than the ringing in their ears.

Katya staggered back, lip split, breath tearing in shallow pulls. Blood dotted the stone where she'd misjudged her footing, where momentum finally cost her.

Her chest hitched—

"Сука… блядь…"

The words dragged out of her, more breath than voice.

Anya didn't retreat. She stood her ground, chest heaving but controlled, as if breath itself were something she rationed. Her sleeves hung in strips, darkening fast where knife cuts tracked her forearms—clean, deliberate lines that stung but hadn't slowed her. Beneath the torn fabric at her abdomen, blood seeped in a slow, stubborn bloom, already staining her shirt, already ignored.

Pain was present. It wasn't relevant.

Between them hung more than violence. Memory. Recognition. The echo of a bond forged before either of them had words for what they'd lost—before betrayal learned how to wear different faces.

Neither spoke. Neither looked away.

Whatever they were to each other, it wasn't finished being paid for.

Katya's laugh cracked raw. She flicked a glance at James, then back at Anya. "There it is. Your specialty." The laugh curdled, breaking. "You still don't get it, Tatiana. Closeness is not safety."

The name hit like shrapnel. James flinched. Anya didn't.

Katya's voice fell lethal. "We were eighteen. Sisters. More than that. You swore to keep me alive—you sold safety like it was yours to give."

Anya's eyes stayed steady. "I didn't sell it. I survived it—for you, for me, for anyone I could drag through." Her jaw tightened. "And I didn't steal James. I didn't even know about you. *He did.*

And still—he chose."

Katya's gaze snapped to James, searching for rescue. He couldn't give it. His chest locked. He felt claimed but not free.

"Everything we were taught about survival," Katya said, voice unsteady but rising again, "it was all the same lesson."

A breath. Not control—just enough to keep standing.

"Attachment is leverage. Wanting is weakness. And sooner or later—"

Her gaze cut back to Anya, sharper now, something darker settling behind it.

"—they take it from you."

Katya laughed, broken, shaking her head. "He was the only thing I let myself want without orders. And you—" her voice cracked, "you remind me why wanting is a liability."

Anya's jaw tightened. "No. They taught us that. I pulled you out anyway."

The fury guttered, leaving shame in its wake. Katya wiped the blood from her lip with her sleeve, then pulled her hood up again. Her posture straightened, spine locking into familiar lines. The mask slid back into place: operator, not sister.

"Kaliningrad," she said, voice clipped. "OBELISK isn't just waking—it's choosing. Every pattern now is preference." Her gaze flicked to the clock. "Forty-eight hours is already too long."

The ticking filled the space between them, merciless.

James finally spoke. "I need you both alive." His throat burned. "I'm sorry. I—I didn't—"

Katya's expression softened, just enough to hurt. "Of course you didn't."

She didn't elaborate. She didn't have to. The words carried every version of the same betrayal.

Anya went still.

Not from fear.

From recognition.

Anya took a breath, started to speak, then stopped. When her voice came again, it was quieter. Steadier.

"Katya. There's something you don't know."

Suspicion flared—brief, sharp.

"They took my daughter," Anya said. No plea. No anger. Just fact.

A beat.

"Leverage."

She reached into her coat then—slow, deliberate—and drew out a folded photograph. Her fingers hesitated for a fraction of a second before she set it on the table.

The room shifted like a blast without sound—only pressure, crushing. Katya's balance faltered. Her hands flexed, as though memory itself betrayed her training.

James's voice scraped out. "More than a year. Mila's barely five."

Katya's lips parted. The name slipped raw and ruined: "Mila…"

Her knees buckled. She dropped into a chair, palms flat, eyes locked on the photograph as if it were a weapon aimed at her.

Anya's whisper cut the silence. "My daughter."

"But—how?"

Anya's voice came quieter, steadier than she felt. "I was with you when it happened. Phoenix—remember? Planting the chip in OBELISK's core. We thought it was our one chance to cripple it before everything spread."

She swallowed.

"I came home to an empty apartment. No broken lock. No warning. Just silence where she should've been."

Her gaze didn't leave Katya's.

"They took her while I was away. They must have been waiting."

A beat. Then, softer: "I don't blame you."

Katya's eyes stayed locked on the photo, and for the first time her rage faltered—not extinguished, but staggered by the unbearable weight of what had already been lost.

James felt it tear through him all at once. Sister. Lover. Target. Every angle cut him open in a different place, none of them clean.

Katya broke the silence, her voice stripped down to machinery.

"Kaliningrad. Forty-eight hours. Maybe less. That's all that matters now."

She pulled her hood higher, ruin hidden beneath discipline.

As she passed Anya, she paused—not touching, not striking—only holding her eyes. Wreckage facing wreckage. No forgiveness. No erasure. Just acknowledgment.

Then she turned to James.

Her voice was flat steel. "You're already on the board. Play or don't. It's your call." A beat. "I kept you alive once. It's her job now."

He flinched. "You don't get to decide that."

Her gaze never left Anya.
"Don't mistake closeness for safety," Katya said. "It's just fire that eats the air."
Then, sharper—using the name like a blade:
"Don't teach him that lie, Tatiana."

She was gone before either of them could answer, the door left ajar just long enough for the cold to root itself in the room.

James exhaled, hollowed out, as if something essential had gone with her.

"She's right about Kaliningrad," Anya said quietly.

"We'd go anyway," James answered. His eyes dropped to the photograph, then lifted to her, sharpened by resolve. "For Mila." A beat. "But is she right about you?"

Anya met his gaze—stripped, steady. "I won't lie to protect you."

The words rang true, even as her chest faltered where her face did not.

James nodded once, the way a man does when he steps onto black ice already cracking.

Outside, a bell tolled. Once. Then again. Each note carried, counting them forward.

Katya was already on the road.

James and Anya would follow, because Kaliningrad wasn't a choice anymore. It was the only battlefield left.

The photo lay between them, Mila's grin frozen in a world she couldn't see. James slid it back into his pocket with trembling hands.

Kaliningrad.

There was nowhere else left to go.

Chapter 47: After the Fire
Elbląg, Poland

"A time to tear, and a time to sew;
a time to keep silence, and a time to speak."
— Ecclesiastes 3:7

"Слово — серебро, а молчание — золото."
A word is silver, but silence is gold.
— Russian Proverb

Everything after the fight had been quieter than it should have been.

They had cleaned the blood in silence—hers first, then his hands where it had transferred without him noticing. The room still smelled faintly of iron beneath detergent.

They had not spoken Katya's name again.

Echoes reached them two days later. The headline:

Local: Gdańsk Station Fire — Three Dead

One body unidentifiable. A single molar recovered. Dental work traced to an off-grid clinic in North Macedonia. Alias on file: *Daria Sberova.*

James read it twice, then a third time, until the rain streaking his screen blurred serif into smear. Too neat. Too intact. A planted truth.

He'd done it himself once—another war, another name. Pull the tooth. Seal it. Leave it where the living would need a body. Death for paperwork. Disappearance for purpose.

He lowered the phone.

Anya watched his face, a stillness sharpened by the steam curling from her mug. "Tell me."

"She staged it," he said. No preface. No hedge. "Gdańsk. A molar out of Macedonia. She used Daria there."

Anya's fingers tightened around porcelain. Her eyes didn't leave his. "Then she's still alive."

"For now," he managed. The words came dry. They weren't about the fire anymore. They were about the shape she made in his chest—memory turning on him. He chose not to say that part. He shared the fact and kept the wound.

Silence stretched, dense as weather. Anya didn't press. She wasn't afraid of truth; she was afraid of confirming what truth would take. She set her mug down too carefully, as if noise might break what they'd built in the last twenty-four hours.

He paced instead of touching her. She watched instead of asking.

"Kaliningrad was already the plan," she said at last, voice even. "This doesn't change that."

"It doesn't," he said.

They let the silence stand.

The wall clock in Sidorov's office ticked with a metronome's cruelty. Maps glowed cool on glass; the Baltic looked like a closed fist.

"You lost two," the general said, each syllable clipped hard enough to draw blood. "Teenagers, Mac. We don't recruit them to squander them at twenty."

Mac stood with his hands behind his back as if the posture could pass for contrition. "Torres killed them," he said. "We removed Torres."

"By calling fire on your own aftermath?" Sidorov's lip curled. "My remit is deniability, not theater. We needed the bodies. We needed the hardware. Now all we have is a crater—and your word."

"*OBELISK* had what it needed before the breach," Mac said. "The strike kept outsiders off our snow. That is the remit."

"Do not quote remit to me." The room chilled. "You expose the program when you act like a jealous god. You burn because you can, not because you must."

Mac let the reprimand pass over his face without landing. "The operator's last buffer was half-sent. He tried to write an endpoint into the air."

"And?"

Mac's gaze slid to the glass map, finger tapping the sliver west of the Curonian Lagoon. "He tried to write—**here**."

Sidorov stared. "And you left that thread uncut?"

"On the contrary," Mac said, almost pleasant. "I pulled it taut."

Sidorov exhaled through his nose, a sound like a fuse snuffing. "You will not lose any more of *my* girls. If you do, I will pull *you* taut."

Mac smiled without teeth. "Then don't send them after men who refuse to die on schedule."

[Katya | Road East]

Snow peeled off the hood in thin sheets, the wipers carving absence into weather. Katya drove without music, without heat, without the small comforts that pretend to be armor. She had made herself light—new papers, cold phone, cash in a heel. The only weight she kept was a ring.

It fit like a wound that had finally decided what shape to take.

She'd staged the fire because the board needed clearing. Langley would close its book; SVR would move resources elsewhere; every other hunter would be forced to look away. Erasure wasn't death. It was access.

But she had left one breadcrumb anyway. Not for them. *For him.*

James would recognize the trick. He would see the tooth and know the hand. He would remember the clinic, the alias, the lesson he'd taught her before she surpassed him at vanishing. It was the closest she could come to a message that wouldn't get them both killed.

The ring knocked once against the wheel as the road bent north, a small sound that felt larger than the car. She had worn it empty for months—metal as promise deferred. Now it meant exactly what it had always threatened.

"Not for him," she told the dark, lying like a professional. "For the part of me that refuses to be erased."

Not that he was hers.

Only that she refused to disappear.

Maybe he wouldn't. Maybe he already had—chosen the red-haired ghost who called herself Anya and wielded closeness like a blade wrapped in velvet. Maybe that didn't matter anymore. Kaliningrad mattered. Mac mattered. *OBELISK* mattered more than any heart.

She pressed harder on the accelerator. Behind her, the last of her names bled away in the rearview—tail lights drowning in snow.

[JAMES & ANYA | THE FLAT]

The flat felt smaller after the article. The rain against the glass had weight, like the world insisting on a verdict he didn't want to read aloud.

The silence stretched, heavy but alive. Anya's hands tightened around the mug, but when she spoke her voice carried no envy—only calculation.

"Then she's cutting her trail. Wiping every mark she left. It means she's going east."

"Kaliningrad." His voice made the city sound like a wound, not a destination.

Anya nodded, slow. "Mac is there. *OBELISK* is there. She'll burn through both if she can. And Mila…" Her throat caught once before she forced it flat. "Mila is there, too. If Katya moves first, she won't stop to separate vengeance from rescue."

James looked at her then. Really looked. The steel in her posture, the fear buried under it. He knew she was right.

He drew the photo from his pocket, set it beside the phone. Mila's grin filled the table like a flare in the dark.

"Then let's go get her," he said.

He didn't reach for her.

She noticed.

She didn't close the distance either.

Katya had her fire, her ring, her war. He had this child's face pressed against his heart.

Anya reached across the table, not to touch him but to slide the map closer. "We move tonight," she said. "Trains north through Gdańsk or Elbląg—then east. If the rail's burned, we go back roads through Warmia."

James folded the map, slid it into his pack with hands that no longer shook. He checked the pistol on the chair, the spare magazines, the comm gear. Movements familiar, grounding. Not to numb himself—but to sharpen.

They both looked at the photo again, then at the rain-streaked window. The east called like a tide.

James slid Mila's picture back into his pocket. His hand closed around it, steady now.

"Kaliningrad," he said.

Not just Katya's battlefield anymore.

Theirs.

[Katya | Waypoint]

A café in Olsztyn that smelled of yeast and diesel. A TV above the counter murmured local news over a crawl of headlines: **Gdańsk Update — Station Reopened After Fatal Blaze.** No mention of names. Only *teeth*.

Olsztyn was quieter. Fewer eyes. Fewer reasons to remember her.

Katya sat with her back to the wall and her hands flat on the cheap wood, ring catching the light with every exhale.

The waitress asked if she wanted milk. She said no and let the coffee stay black.

You erased yourself, she told the mirror of the window. Now see if he can still find you. *"If he still wants to,"* she whispered.

She didn't stay. She didn't look back at the screen.

General Sidorov watched the forest safehouse footage in silence: thermal silhouettes flickering across the monitor, six shadows converging on one. White blooms flared—brief, perfect, algorithmic flowers. To the machine they were patterns. To him, they were death.

He poured vodka into a glass, but did not drink. He left it there, clear and untouched, like an offering.

"Two," he said, aloud this time, letting the number settle heavy in the room. The word sat heavy in his mouth.

His jaw tightened. "Not waste," he added. "Heroes."

For a long moment he sat there, eyes hard, forcing himself to believe it. They had been sent into the fire and had burned clean. If no one else remembered them, he would.

Then he picked up the secure phone, dialed the number that did not ring, that left no record, and spoke a single sentence—one that would have been called treason in an older war, but in this one was nothing more than logistics.

"Move Mac to ground-side. The lagoon."

He ended the call and turned back to the map, staring at the curve of the Baltic until it stared back at him.

Dawn thinned the dark into something not yet morning. James zipped the packs, checked the rifles, then slid the photograph back where it rode safest—over his heart, under his ribs, every breath a reminder.

Anya stepped into her boots without a word. When she straightened, he held her gaze.

"There's something I didn't say," he admitted, the truth scraping on its way out.

"I know," she said. No accusation. Just fact.

"She left it so I'd understand," he said instead, quieter now. "Not the fire—the name. She used one she knew I'd recognize."

"You think she meant it for you," Anya said. Not gentle. Not cruel. Just naming the shape of it.

"I think she wanted to disappear," he said. "And to make sure I knew she wasn't gone."

Something flickered across Anya's face—then was gone.

"We were going anyway."

"We were," he agreed, shouldering the pack that would make neither of them lighter.

The street outside was a wet gray ribbon, stretching east where a city waited like a wound.

They closed the door behind them and did not lock it. Some rooms couldn't be returned to.

Chapter 48: Ash Wire
Kaliningrad, Russia

"For there is nothing covered, that shall not be revealed;
neither hid, that shall not be known."
— Luke 12:2

"Не всё то золото, что блестит."
Not all that glitters is gold.
— Russian proverb

Nothing of their old lives crossed into Kaliningrad with them.

The city carried war in its bones: brick forts swallowed by weeds, rusted cranes kneeling over the Pregolya, the Curonian Lagoon breathing salt through fog. They moved through it like old ghosts—hats low, tempos mismatched to any camera's predictive gait, heat signatures blurred by cheap Mylar sewn under their coats.

They worked the lattice the way Márton taught: buy coffee you don't drink; tip the man who doesn't look up; speak a name you both pretend to mishear. By noon they had a map of rumors; by dusk they had signal.

Mac kept ground-side quarters on the lagoon's lip—north of Rybachy, a cabin cut from a smuggler's daydream and an officer's budget. Boats came and went with no registry. Sentries wore the kind of stillness that meant training beat conscience.

But the whisper about the child was wrong.

She wasn't there.

They cracked an old listening post under a tractor yard, coaxed life from a rack of equipment that should've been scrap. The air tasted like belt grease and dust. Anya jury-rigged an SDR, and scattered the scan across dead utilities.

A shape emerged: packet cadence, call-sign drift, a badge number that had no right to repeat. Not Kaliningrad. A rail garrison outside Grodno—Hrodna—east-southeast, eight hours by car if borders behaved, twelve if they didn't. The name on the duty roster flickered up from the dark: Sinyy Dom (*Blue House*). Transit ward. Soft walls, hard men.

Anya's jaw set. "She's not with Mac."

James stared at the screen until the letters felt like teeth. "Then we take her back first."

"Before Katya lights him up and puts Mila in the blast radius," Anya said, already breaking down the SDR into travel-sized ghosts. She didn't look at him when she said Katya's name.

He nodded. "Before that."

They lifted a trunk from a lockup that shouldn't have known their faces: two folding carbines with suppressors, a pair of Makarovs that had outlived the empire that minted them, a sawed pump shotgun in a canvas sleeve, and three magazines older than either of them with springs that still believed. Anya checked feed lips by feel; James stripped and rebuilt on muscle memory, the table between them filling with oil and purpose.

"Grodno," he said. "We burn time we can't afford."

"We burn it or lose her," Anya answered. "Mac can wait one night."

He agreed. But as he slid a magazine home, the click rang against something older.

The Curonian sky pressed low, and with it came the uninvited. Katya sitting on a rooftop, breath fogging the air. A scarf—his scarf—knotted in her fist in winter that cut like wire. A mouth that rarely promised and eyes that did.

He wondered if he'd ever given her a space that wasn't a countdown. If his impatience had mistaken her winter for refusal instead of injury. If missions had sanded their edges until what could have been never had a place to live.

Anya was certainty.

Katya was something else entirely—unfinished, unresolved, still pulling at him in ways he didn't have language for.

He didn't try to name it.

He met Anya's eyes and gave her the only truth he could spend without breaking them both.

"Let's get Mila," he said.

"Let's," she echoed, and shouldered the carbine.

[KATYA | THE LAGOON]

Night unstitched itself along the waterline. The cabin sat where smugglers once traded lamps—wood dark with salt, windows low, angles wrong in the right way. A dozen sentries drifted the perimeter in practiced arcs. Katya counted breaths, wind shifts, the intervals when boredom walked the fence for them.

She wore no insignia but winter. The ring sat cold on her finger—weight finally honest.

The first sentry went down without a sound, throat opened by a wire that disappeared into the dark with him. The second slept wrong; her palm smothered his protest and the blade finished what quiet began. Third and fourth fell in a single pull of breath—subsonic taps the forest swallowed whole. Number five took longer; six didn't feel a thing.

One of them almost spoke.
She didn't let him finish the breath.

Seven and eight stood under the same light and died under it. Nine dropped into snow and found no purchase. Ten folded at a whisper. Eleven never turned.

Twelve noticed.

He was young, too young, the kind that still wrote letters home by hand. He caught the ghost of her where a shadow wasn't supposed to be, startled backward, boot heel hitting a shovel blade. It rang metal against frozen soil—a bright betrayal.

Shouts. Lights. Mac's clearance door thumped.

Katya didn't curse; she didn't have the kind of rage that wasted breath. She ghosted backward to the ridge line, laid prone, and rested the rifle into the notch her bones had been built to find. Distance: three hundred twenty. Wind: right to left, persistent. She bracketed the doorway through the scope, crosshairs riding the seam.

Mac came limping into view with two men and a handgun he hadn't had time to love. He moved like a man who believed he'd never die—too much shoulder, not enough fear.

She breathed in. The world shrank to glass and heart.

Crack.

The round punched through his knee, patella exploding into wet gravel. He went down screaming into his own command, pistol skittering across the planks, hands clawing at a leg that would never obey again.

For one beat the perimeter froze. Then the sentries broke— some firing blind into the tree line, others scattering toward cover that didn't exist. Panic made them loud. She was already moving.

Katya slid down the ridge, snow hissing under her boots, rifle slung. The Makarov came up steady, muzzle sweeping the gaps like a pendulum. She shot as she advanced—three bodies jerking in quick succession, each collapse swallowed by the surf's roar. One tried to run; she put him down mid-stride, his scream cut short by the second shot.

By the time the last echo rolled back from the lagoon, only the wounded commander was left alive.

He was still trying to rise when she reached him, dragging himself upright on one elbow, blood steaming against the cold.

"Mac," she said, and the sound was a verdict.

He blinked up, face flashing through calculation, charm, and something he thought might pass for contrition. "Kyra," he managed, pain blurring the edges of his voice into human.

She shot him through the shoulder. "My name is Katya."

He cried out, words cracking: "You don't know what you're breaking. *OBELISK* is past waking—it's choosing. You think you can kill your way out? You think—"

"You taught the machine to choose," she said, level as a horizon. "So did I."

"You think I'm the problem?" Mac coughed, blood threading his teeth. "I'm just ahead of it."

She didn't answer.

Mac smiled anyway. "OBELISK doesn't need me. It just needed someone willing to move first."

He tried for a different door. "The child—Anya's—she's leverage, if I d—"

She didn't let him finish.

The first round took his mouth.

The second ended the sentence.

By the fourth there was nothing left to say.

She kept firing until the slide locked back.

It didn't feel like victory.
Just one less thing left to lose.

Silence arrived late and heavy.

She ejected the mag, pocketed the empty out of habit, and took his sidearm for the road. Footsteps pounded on wood somewhere behind her; she faded sideways into the treeline, a shadow that refused to be named.

The ring on her finger caught no light. It didn't need to.

[Kaliningrad → Grodno]

The Škoda they stole had a rattle in second and a heater that preferred to argue.

Anya folded the map until it obeyed, marking back roads that threaded Lithuania like veins, then dipped southeast where the algorithms grew lazy. Eight hours if no one looked too hard. Ten if they did. Twelve if fate remembered who they were.

"We get her out clean," Anya said, watching the road flare and dim in the headlights. "No heroics. In and gone."

"Heroes are dead," James said. "We don't join them."

She cut him a look that was half thanks, half warning. "They were heroes too," she said, and he knew she meant the two young women in the trees outside Torres's cabin. "Too young. Too much stolen."

His jaw tightened. "Torres is the one I'm burying," he said. "They pulled the trigger that put him in the ground."

Her eyes narrowed. "They didn't choose this war."

"And Torres didn't choose to die in it," he snapped. The words came out raw, scraping.

The silence that followed wasn't agreement. It was distance—political, personal—a fault line running through the dark.

The road unspooled—black ice, border posts, a neon Jesus in a village that believed in both God and bribes. James drove in a silence full of ghosts. Katya's eyes kept arriving in the windshield's reflection—blue like a cut sky, steady in storms. He let the memory sting and kept his hands at ten and two.

Beside him, Anya stripped a mag by feel and rebuilt it, every click a prayer she'd never say out loud. She saw his jaw work in the glass, recognized the machinery inside it, and made a choice she would keep making: say nothing now, save what could be saved later.

Somewhere behind them, on the black water of the lagoon, a man who had believed he was essential bled into the boards of a house that would not remember him.

Somewhere ahead, a rail garrison painted the way to **Sinyy Dom**, the same blue as bruises.

They drove.

At the lagoon, the wind erased everything it could—prints, heat, names spoken in pain. It could not erase the hole in the porch or the way the sentries looked at the dark as if it might look back.

In the Škoda, Anya watched the kilometer markers tick down like a fuse. James watched the same numbers and saw a roofline, a winter, a woman he hadn't stopped loving and another he refused to lose.

Not all that glitters is gold, the proverb said.

Some of it is ash that refuses to blow away.

Chapter 49: Adieu, Mila
Grodno, Belarus

Counting, the seconds refused to end.

Fog rolled heavy off the bay, swallowing the gravel road in a gray hush. James cut the headlights a kilometer out, easing the car to a stop behind a line of birch. From here, they approached on foot, the house just shape and shadow—blue paint weathered pale, windows black, porch sagging like tired shoulders. Nothing marked it as a prison except the voices bleeding into the night.

Push-to-talk radios hissed and cracked, every burst of static cutting the silence like a blade.

"*…status check…*"

"*…Mac is dead…*"

"*…kill the girl…*"

The words came jagged, broken by distance but clear enough. Orders.

Anya's lips thinned. James's hand tightened on his rifle until the bones in his knuckles creaked. Mila's death sentence had already been spoken.

"Now," he whispered.

She nodded once, sharp, and melted into the dark.

Too slow. His throat closed on words he couldn't afford.

James set up on the ridge. Suppressed rifle on bipod. Scope lens catching the glint of snow. He scanned through thermals—six shapes. One at the back door, two pacing front and side, one on the roof, one inside by the window, one seated at a table with a phone.

He whispered into the mic. "Six confirmed. They're sloppy, but armed."

"Stay quiet," Anya replied, already moving. "Cover me."

She vanished into fog before he could answer.

The first guard was a shadow smoking near the fence line. Anya came from behind—glove over mouth, knife sliding beneath the collarbone. The body shuddered once, then folded. She lowered him softly into snow, breath steady.

"Five," James whispered.

Another shape shifted near the corner, radio clipped to his chest. Static hissed. "Проверить периметр" (*check perimeter*).

James lifted his sightline to the roof. The sentry's silhouette cut pale against the sky, rifle slung loose with the arrogance of quiet hours. James dialed two clicks, let the breath go, and squeezed.

A suppressed snap.

The body pitched forward, slid off the shingles, and vanished into snow with a dull, final thud.

"Three."

"James," Anya hissed, low and sharp.

She had wanted silence—total erasure. His shot was clean, necessary.

It was also loud enough.

The last two outside snapped to motion, radios flaring with panicked static. One bolted for the porch, shouting as he ran. The other clawed for his sidearm, training lagging half a beat behind fear.

The night broke open.

Anya sprinted. She hit the first man low, blade hammering between ribs. He folded with a wet grunt. She pivoted, driving the knife across the other's throat just as his cry peaked. Blood arced in the beam of his flashlight, then vanished into fog.

"Clear," James said.

The word didn't sit right.

Inside, it wasn't clear at all.

Inside, the handler sat at a table, dossier spread open, phone to his ear. Anya's GRU designation stared up from the page: SUBJECT-05. LIABILITY.

"Confirm execution," he said in Russian. His eyes flicked toward the bedroom door.

He never heard her cross the floor. The knife punched upward beneath his jaw, severing sound before it could form. His eyes widened, blood bright against his lips, and then dimmed. She lowered him soft, chair settling without a crash.

"She's not leverage," Anya whispered, voice like a verdict.

The room smelled of kerosene and paper. On the table, a pistol lay half-oiled. Beside it, a child's doll—rabbit-eared, fabric gray from handling. Mila's.

The bedroom door creaked open.

Mila stood small in the shadows, clutching the rabbit so tight its seams strained. She had braced for thunder—boots, shouts, gunfire. Danger always came with noise. But tonight had been silence. And silence felt like the scariest thing of all.

Her breath rasped loud in her own ears. She wanted to cry but couldn't, not until the figure across the room dropped to her knees and whispered her name.

"Lyubimaya… Mila."

The word cracked open something buried. Mila ran, sudden and desperate, colliding into arms that wrapped her tight. She buried her face against her mother's neck, sobs tearing free like she'd been holding them for a year.

Anya held her close, whispering over and over:

"Я ведь говорила… что найду тебя. Говорила, что приду." *I told you… I'd find you. Told you I'd come.*

She didn't look back at the bodies.
She didn't need to.

"We're leaving," she said.

Outside, James swept the treeline one last time. Six bodies cooled to the temperature of snow. Radios clicked empty, unanswered. For the first time since Kaliningrad, his lungs filled without pain.

Through the scope, he caught sight of Anya stepping from the house, Mila cradled against her shoulder, the rabbit doll crushed between them. She didn't look like the Red Ghost. Not myth, not assassin. Just a mother who had fought the whole world to reach her child.

For a moment, he let himself stop.

Relief hit so sharp it hurt.

And with it came the cut of truth.

James lowered the rifle, and in the hollow that followed he felt something else open: the memory of another bond. A rooftop in Prague. Blue eyes that never let him go. A woman who had staged her own death not to vanish but to finish the war.

Katya.

Anya was whole again.

Katya wasn't.

The imbalance sat wrong in him.

The goodbye formed in his chest, silent and heavy. *Goodbye, Mila.*

He would go where Katya had gone.

Into what was left.

He slung the rifle and moved toward the fog, watching Anya and her daughter dissolve into it. He hoped they would still be there when he came back.

"James?" Anya's voice snapped through the fog, sharp with alarm. He didn't stop.

"James!" This time closer, urgent, breaking. He turned as she reached him, Mila tight in her arms, tears streaking down her face.

"You can't," she said, voice cracked and wet. "Not now. Not now. Please—stay. We can run, we can—"

He shook his head, rough. "You don't need me here. She does."

Anya's free hand gripped his coat, fingers shaking. "You'll die there."

"Maybe. But if *OBELISK* lives, all of us die. Katya will burn herself trying to stop it. I can't let her go alone."

Mila stirred, pressing her face into Anya's neck, too young to understand but clinging tighter all the same.

Anya's tears came harder. "I can't lose you. It's not supposed to be this way."

He didn't answer right away.

Mila's hand had found his sleeve—small, unplanned.

James leaned in, forehead to hers, the rifle cold against his back. "Then hold on."

Her grip trembled, then loosened—because she knew.
Love wasn't enough.

"Come back to me," she whispered. It wasn't plea, it was command. A command she knew the world might not allow.

He almost stayed.

He kissed her once—without hesitation.

His eyes lingered on Mila—small, clutching, alive. His lips shaped the words he couldn't speak aloud. *"Goodbye, Mila."*

Then he turned into the fog, alone.

The world didn't stop him.
It never had.

Anya stood in the snow, daughter in her arms, tears cutting warm across her face as he disappeared into it.

ACT IX - THE GHOSTS WE CHOOSE

"Some ghosts arrive by violence.

Others by choice.

The ones we choose are the ones that stay."

CHAPTER 50: WHAT GHOSTS DO
Kaliningrad, Russia | 4:42 pm, Local Time

Everything about Kaliningrad felt wrong the moment they crossed into it—the air thin, metallic.

Two SUVs eased up the drive, ghost black, tires wrong for the frozen plow throws—new, expensive. Faces hid behind mirrored glass. They moved like men who trusted the system more than themselves.

Kaliningrad Oblast lay cut off from Russia proper, a strip of ice between NATO teeth. The old Prussian house stood on a field where amber trains had once run east, now a relay blindspot *OBELISK* had claimed as its own.

The house was too still. Curtains drawn. Three rooms lit—kitchen, hallway, back room. The back window held a faint figure, moving through small, ordinary tasks.

Katya approached from the ore line, boots finding hollow places in the drift as if she'd carved them out by memory. The knife sat loose in her palm, deliberate and forgettable until it would become necessary. She nested into the old foundation's bow, elbows on frozen earth, breath a small inside thing.

She palmed the burner; its little LED slept until she woke it with two taps. The screen blinked once, then again. A fragment pushed through the frost-cut static:

Coming. Coords?

He must have been close—too close for chance. He had been shadowing her route.

For a heartbeat the world unlatched.

Relief hit first—sharp, like air she hadn't realized she'd been holding.

Hope followed, quick and dangerous.

She let neither settle.

She keyed back two marks only—latitude, longitude. No flourishes. No assurance. He would read her brevity the way he always had: a door left open, but not wide.

The burner dimmed. A beat later it pulsed again, a single line slipping through the cold: **Coming.**

The field reclaimed its hush. Her pulse did not.

Somewhere on the ridge a relay tower blinked—red, patient. Twice a day. The uplink hit their bones like a metronome; it was the machine's heartbeat and its way of keeping time with human cruelty.

She thought of Warsaw, of a platform that smelled like iron, of hands that had looked at her palms instead of her face. She thought of him with a steadiness that had once been love and now read like intent. There were worse things to carry.

She swept the perimeter and found tracks skirting the spruce. Someone else had been here. That, more than anything, sharpened her. She set herself to the plan she had rehearsed until it felt like bone: mudroom, kitchen, hallway, back room. No dog. No last-minute inventions. She stepped away from the wind and slid a flat tool into the breaker's lip. Not yet.

[MUNICH, GERMANY | ANYA & MILA]

The clinic in Munich smelled of antiseptic and lemon polish. Frost clung to the windows, muting the traffic blur of Leopoldstraße beyond.

German signage lined the walls in neat Helvetica—Anmeldung, Wartezimmer, Labor—words that carried no comfort.

Anya sat hunched in the chair, coat too heavy on her shoulders, stomach twisting in a rhythm she could no longer ignore. The vomiting had come sudden, daily, relentless. She had feared it was the safehouse—mold, chemical residue, some toxin that might already be seeping into Mila.

The doctor's voice was gentle but detached, the way you deliver a fact that will change someone whether you soften it or not.

"Your endocrine levels are… abnormal," the doctor murmured. "It would have masked early indicators."

Not toxins.
Not exposure.

"Pregnant."

The word landed with a weight both unbearable and unspeakably fragile. Relief and dread warred in the same breath. Her fingers brushed Mila's hair where the girl leaned against her side, oblivious, safe for now. This child had once been her miracle— a second chance at life, though she had never known how or why the seed had been planted.

Some nights she chose to believe God had given her this gift, unearned but merciful. Other nights she knew better, and that knowledge cut deeper than any scalpel. Mila was hers—entirely hers—but her blessed origin was a wound that never closed.

And now, another life coiled inside her. Another future, unbidden—startling as lightning, frightening as the silence after, yet radiant in a way she could not smother. The terror of it pressed against her ribs, the wonder of it lit something small and stubborn in her chest.

She lowered a hand to her belly, tentative at first, then steadier, as if her palm could make peace between the dread and the fragile joy that now lived beneath her skin.

[KALININGRAD | KATYA]

Farther in, the site made its own signal—short, encrypted, administrative. Katya's burner stuttered once, then lit with a crawl of code across the cracked display:

DISPOSITION: TERMINATE
RISK: HIGH.
ROURKE: DISPOSABLE
YEKATERINA/KATYA/KYRA/MAREK | SUBJECT-09 |
ЛЕДЯНАЯ ТЕНЬ...
RETAIN/EXPENSIVE.

The words had no heat, no human cadence. Ledger rows masquerading as orders.

The relay tower blinked red again, patient as a pulse. OBELISK routed the packet to her burner deliberately; the machine preferred its prey informed.

Katya watched the house breathe. Light moved from room to room on command, a slow, programmatic inspection. The watchers smoked in neat rotations and practiced the stillness of men who had made a career of not seeing. The tower ticked in the periphery; its pulse belonged to no one and to everything.

Katya counted the steps in the watch by the eaves. Six minutes, the schedule said. More than she needed.

They were coordinated the way people who have shared everything essential are coordinated: a touch of shoulder, an unspoken fraction of time. When she whispered the word, the field replied with the echo that had kept them alive in Prague and Tbilisi.

"Next cycle," she breathed.

"Next cycle," came James, the phrase grinding warm and brittle between them. The old ritual, repeated until it became less prayer than engine.

She slid the breaker.

The house went dark.

On the back step she felt the tension of the threshold take her. This was the part where plans contracted into the throat. She felt raw and small and unready—but that was part of the engine: being chosen by danger because you were willing to hold its weight.

The wedge seated clean.

A subtle shift—pressure, not force—and the latch gave without protest. The door opened a fraction, quiet as breath.

Outside, the relay tower blinked once—twice. The uplink registered status change and logged it with the dispassion of a census.

It should have been simple—entry, neutralize, leave.

The machine disagreed.

It let them move. Measured them. Logged each step. Permission, not latency.

The most dangerous kind.

A far relay tower ticked again, unloved by satellites. The uplink kept time.

James moved like someone who had learned to swallow lightning. He had one promise lodged at the base of his throat—a small, tasted thing made of iron: whatever had been written into the eyes of the node, whatever protocol had drawn its teeth, he would answer it with his hands.

They crossed the threshold together. The house had nothing to do but watch. *OBELISK* had already decided how this room would fold into its maps; all that remained was the humans.

They were coordinated the way people become when everything important has already been shared.

Katya stepped forward into the dark the machine had prepared for them and carried with her the stubborn thing that machines could not measure: an answer that would not obey ledger rows.

Outside, the relay blinked, steady as a heart.

Inside, the uplink logged their entry and, with the elegance of cruelty, did nothing at all.

Chapter 51: Ash Seed
Kaliningrad, Russia

"Ashes are the seedbed of what comes next."
— Unknown Field Report, Redacted

"Молчи — и за умного сойдешь."
"Stay silent, and they'll think you wise."
— Russian Proverb

The door gave under pressure, opening without protest.

Then—

the corridor collapsed into noise and light.

James dropped low and moved without hesitation, muscle overriding thought. Katya went higher, a shadow sliding along the mezzanine where the cameras thought they knew angles. The team was small and quiet—armed for close work, speaking only when the dead were counted.

They hit the dockside wing first: labs with glass like winter, servers that hummed with a steady, mechanical rhythm, containment tanks rimed with frost. Suppressors snapped. A guard folded at the threshold, air leaving him the wrong way. Katya finished the motion with a knife.

The facility did not react poorly to being violated; it reacted precisely.

OBELISK didn't rush.

Lights that had been green went red. Doors they had scouted hours before that would have given them a route out sealed. The building reconfigured itself in the time it took to reload.

The corridor tightened. James's rounds reduced targets to silence—one through a sternum, one into the hollow where a throat used to be. A shooter spilled through a side hatch and the pump answered with a blast that threw dust.

They cleared rooms in a ritual: sweep, call, breach. The uplink buzzed overhead in a language of brief, clinical pulses; every packet a metronome counting them down.

They had braced for ghosts; none came. Mac was already a solved problem—snow, scope, silence. What faced them now wasn't betrayal with a face, but the faceless patience of *OBELISK* and the people it arranged.

"OBELISK isn't code," she said. "It feeds."

"Mac wasn't trying to stop it."

He slotted another round with a click that sounded enormous in that tight room.

"He was leaning into it."

"Then we starve it," Katya said.

They planted charges on uplink banks and data racks while the building complained. The lights slipped out of sync with their movement. Anya's name surfaced on a distant node—then vanished.

A whisper of a shot cut the thought. Small. Practiced. Ghostly. Somewhere deeper, a sniper took a breath and angled glass to the light.

James jerked; reflex put him behind the server rack as a round chewed the steel where his head had been a half-breath before. The shooter's glint died into the web of conduits. Patient. Waiting.

They moved faster.

A lab on the lower level had been turned into a nursery of data— petri dishes cataloged like offerings, vials annotated in handwriting that pretended to be script but read like code. The air carried something older than chemicals—something decided long before they arrived. Katya wiped a palm across a laminate counter and left a smear of dust like a signature.

"Is this how they seed?" she asked. "They incubate what they can, map what refuses to stay quiet?"

"Not seed," James said. "They don't build it. They pull on what's already there."

Something answered then: an alarm that was not an alarm, tones that didn't belong.

A recorded voice spoke in a synthetic tenor—calm, administrative—listing dispositions and statuses and the soft deletion code for human inconvenient variables.

The message looped. It sounded like a prayer read without belief.

Katya's jaw set. She fired the terminal into darkness with a pistol shot and it sputtered, dragged to black. Then a dozen new packets struck in rapid succession and the servers reconstituted themselves elsewhere in the net.

"They're redundant," James said. He did not like redundancy. He liked finality.

They reached the core chamber—an amphitheater of racks and cables, a steel column that rose like a spine through the center. Screens hung like altar cloths, mapping recursion as if it were geography. In the center, a console glowed with a thread of coordinates too neat to be incidental:

MURMANSK.
OBELISK: NODE PRIORITY — HIGH.
REDUNDANCY: SEALED.

Something cold penetrated James's chest that had nothing to do with the chill of the concrete. **OBELISK. MURMANSK**—no longer a rumor, no longer just a syllable scrawled on a note. A map. A directive.

"Murmansk," she said. "We were already there."

Her jaw tightened.

"It didn't matter."

They had minutes; maybe seconds if *OBELISK* orchestrated countermeasures—the way an animal will suddenly fling its bulk at a hand that comes too near.

A door slammed. Reinforcements—human ones—rushed the choke point they had cleared. Boots hammered the concrete, rifles clattered against webbing, breath steaming into the corridor. The awful certainty of people who still believed they were right.

Katya moved with a surgeon's cruelty, slamming her shoulder into steel. Pain sparked down her arm but she used the ricochet, footsteps arranged like percussion. James had the sawed pump; up close, at the hinge of a man's surprise, it made violence look tidy. They folded through bodies until the corridor felt like a throat closing.

He thought of Anya's daughter in Munich, of the rabbit-eared doll. He thought of Katya on the lagoon ridge, rifle braced, breathing snow into a wound she kept telling herself would scar. They weren't ghosts. Just people following a script. The script was *OBELISK*'s, but the trigger-pull was flesh and blood. That thought steadied him more than any training.

The charges ticked green to amber to red—then thunder. Heat pressed his ribs flat, ears caved inward, balance spinning. For a heartbeat he staggered, half-blind, mouth full of grit. The world tilted, then steadied just enough to run.

They moved.

Exits configured; stairwells opened. Smoke bled through vents, confetti of insulation and paper. The team stacked like a machine, moving through the building's new rhythm.

They were not clean on the way out—no one ever was—but they carried what mattered: the ledger's image burned behind James's lids, the coordinates that spelled the next place they would have to burn.

Outside, the night hung heavy and close. Snow filmed the world in thin white, the flakes sticking to lashes, to rifle steel. Somewhere in the trees a scope's lens winked and was gone— not miracle, not mercy. Just patience. Whoever held that rifle had been waiting for them to stumble, and perhaps they would have, in another life. But Murmansk had been pressed into their hands like a charge, and there was no stumbling left to give.

They broke east, three klicks, and found the husk of a monastery: stone walls blackened by lightning, air still thick with the ghosts of old prayers. Behind the collapse of an altar they made a camp, shadows thrown wild by the cough of a stolen lighter. None of the shadows seemed to belong to them.

Katya sat apart, arm bound, eyes fixed on the coals. James warmed his hands and, by cruel reflex, found Anya's scarf where he had tucked it. The silk was warmed by his breath, threaded with a scent that belonged to other rooms, other promises.

Katya's gaze flicked once, caught, and lingered. The firelight carved hollows into her face, sharpening exhaustion into something harsher—something personal.

"Still carrying trinkets?" she asked, voice flat, all edge.

Her eyes cut to the scarf, then back to him. "I thought it was me," she said.

James let the silence draw thin.
"A scarf doesn't decide anything."

His voice was low, rough with fatigue, but it carried more than denial—it carried want, guilt, something unsaid.

Katya's mouth curved, sharp. "Men have betrayed countries for less." Her jaw tightened, the mask straining, cracking. "You're hers now," she said. "And I—" She broke off, breath jagged, swallowing the rest. The pause was raw, almost intimate, before her voice hardened again. "Doesn't matter. Ash is behind us. Murmansk is ahead."

James shook his head slowly. "It's not that simple, Katya."

Her mouth curved, bitter. "It never is."

The scarf coiled in his hand like a secret neither of them would name.

Act X – Echoes from Beyond

"The dead are not gone;
they are the pressure on the choices we have left.

CHAPTER 52: THE BURN LINE
Murmansk, Russia | 0320 Local Time

"Some ghosts choose to burn, so others can breathe."
— FIELD MEMO, OBLIVION ARCHIVE (REDACTED)

The node sat carved into the ridge, a scar without windows, without flags. No architecture, only intent: racks thrumming with signal.

They came through the run-off channel—ninety meters of crawlspace, shoulders scraping concrete, water black with chemical frost. James dragged himself one-armed, side wound oozing with every push. Katya never slowed. Knife between her teeth, breath controlled, she moved like she'd rehearsed the crawl a hundred times.

The grate unlocked with a green pulse from her cobbled thermal kit. They slid inside.

Heat closed around them immediately. Rows of servers stretched into shadow, their hum layered with the cadence of heartbeat. Red security lights bled like wounds across the concrete.

James knelt beneath the uplink core, planting charges with shaking hands. Katya's fingers blurred over a terminal, forcing the system to turn on itself. Alarms whispered overhead— warnings caught in their throat.

Then the vents hissed.

Figures dropped fast from the ceiling—black visors, curved blades, no insignia. Silent, disciplined. Not soldiers, not mercenaries. Custodians.

Steel clashed before James could rise. His blade caught the first throat, but pain surged down his thigh as another loyalist cut deep. He snapped a spine against the floor, blood pooling across server glass.

Katya was fire incarnate. Every blade that met her returned sharper, every strike she met answered with a kill. Blood streaked her face, her eyes hollow of fear.

They carved through bodies, but more poured in—from catwalks, from crawlspaces, from between the racks. No bullets. Only steel. Only silence and the economy of death.

James staggered with each step, his leg threatening collapse, his ribs screaming from a fresh cut. He caught himself on a rack, teeth gritted, vision tunneled in red. Katya hauled him forward, shoving, dragging, refusing to let him fold.

The corridor split: one path to the fallback relay, another plunging deeper toward the vault chamber.

James rasped, "We don't split—"

She shoved him hard against the wall, one palm firm against his chest. "You're not walking that distance. Not with that leg."

He tried to argue.

She pressed her pistol into his hand, jammed a spare magazine against his vest, blood smearing both. "You hold here. If I fall, you finish it. Don't you dare quit."

His voice broke. "Katya…"

Her mouth curved—sharp, unsparing. "Neither of us were meant to last this long."

Then she was gone—stride steady, shoulders squared, sirens washing her in red as the vault's steel mouth yawned open ahead.

James pushed off the wall after her.

One step.

His leg failed.

He went down hard, breath punched out of him, blood slicking the floor beneath his hip.

"Katya—"

A shape moved behind her. Blade up. Fast.

James dragged himself onto one elbow, vision collapsing to a tunnel. The pistol wavered in both hands.

He fired.

The shot cracked through the corridor.

The man behind her dropped mid-stride, throat gone.

Katya didn't turn.

She crossed the threshold.
The airlock began to close.

James clawed forward.

Fingers hooked the ridges in the floor grating—pulled.

Dragged.

His dead leg followed, useless, heavy as something already buried.

Pulled again.

The world narrowed to inches.

The gap at the door shrinking.

Her back—still there.

Still there—

"Katya!"

Another shadow broke from the side.

He rolled, fired from his back. Missed.

The man came on.

James jerked the pistol up again, fired.

Hit.

The body slammed into the wall and slid down.

He dragged again.

Elbow. Fingers. Pull.

The metal edge of the door was close now—too close.

For a heartbeat, her face turned in the narrowing gap.

Blood-slick. Eyes bright.

He was right there.

Then—

The gap closed another inch.

He reached.

Fingers hit steel.

Slipped.

The door slammed.

The sound was absolute.

Through the window—Katya.

Red light. Blood at her mouth. Shoulders set like none of it could touch her.

She lifted her chin to the intercom.

"Every fire needs oxygen," she said. Static broke the edges of her voice. "Breathe for me."

Then, quieter—

"Tell her I didn't break."

Something in him gave.

He hit the glass. "Katya!"

Her hands moved—fast, certain. The console flared. The room answered.

Then the scream.

It tore out of her—sharp, wrong.

She folded around it.

Blood first. Nose. Then ears. Then her mouth.

Her eyes found him.

Wide.

Not fear.
Something else.

He slammed the glass again. "Katya! Don't—"

She held him there for one impossible second.

Then—

she was gone.

Not falling.

Not breaking.

Gone.

The vault answered with a single low note.

Everything died with it.

Lights. Sound. Motion.

Silence took the room.

He hit the glass again.

Nothing.

No flex. No seam. No give.

The door didn't move.

It wasn't going to.

He stayed there a second longer than he should have.

Palm flat. Breath fogging the surface. Waiting for something—anything that meant she was still there.

Nothing came back.

He lowered his hand.

Turned.

The charges.

His fingers found the detonator. Plastic. Warm from his skin. Real in a way nothing else was.

He didn't remember deciding to move.

Only that he was moving.

Back through the aisles.

Past the bodies. One still twitching. Another facedown between racks, blood pooling slow and dark beneath him.

The servers still hummed.

Just there.

Like nothing had changed.

James took a step.

His leg didn't follow.

He dragged it.

The motion pulled something loose in his side—heat, wet, spreading.

He stopped.

Not by choice.

Just… stopped.

For a second, he thought he might not move again.

Katya's face—caught in the narrowing gap.

He swallowed.

Pulled forward.

One step.

Then another.

He didn't look back.

Tried to.

Couldn't.

The timer.

He knelt—harder than intended. The impact jarred through his ribs, stole what breath he had left. He stayed there, hunched over the charge pack, hands braced on the casing until the dizziness passed enough to see.

The numbers blinked up at him.

He stared at them.

Didn't register them at first.

Then—

He reached.

Fingers slipping once.

Twice.

He set it.

Two minutes.

His hand hovered there.

He adjusted it.

One minute, thirty.

He closed his fist around the detonator and pushed himself upright.

It took longer than it should have.

Everything did.

The corridor stretched in front of him—longer now, unfamiliar. The same space, but wrong.

He moved into it anyway.

Elbow brushing the wall.

Step.

Drag.

His boot caught on something. A body. He didn't look down.

Step.

Drag.

The air shifted.

Cooler.

He kept going.

Didn't think about the door behind him.

Couldn't stop thinking about what was on the other side of it.

The hum followed him partway.

Then it faded.

The silence after it felt heavier.

Cold hit him.

Snow.

It took him a second to understand what it was.

Open air.

He kept moving.

Past the threshold. Past the tree line. Further than he needed to.

Because stopping meant—

He didn't let himself finish that thought.

The detonator pressed into his palm. He tightened his grip around it like it might slip away if he didn't.

He tried to breathe.

It didn't come right.

He counted.

Not out loud.

Not clean.

Just… numbers breaking through the noise.

Thirty.

He pulled in air.

Too shallow.

Twenty.

He tried again.

It caught.

Ten.

He stopped.

Not by choice.

His body just… gave him that much.

He forced another breath.

It hurt.

For a fraction of a heartbeat—

everything held.

The world suspended.

Sound gone.

Air gone.

Even the pain paused, as if waiting.

Then—

it broke.

Light tore the ridge open.

The blast followed, late and enormous, ripping through the air and the ground beneath him.

The mountain answered.

The node collapsed inward—steel folding, racks tearing free, the entire structure devouring itself in a violent, collapsing breath.

Heat rolled over him.

Snow lifted.

Then fell again.

James dropped to his knees.

He didn't brace.

Didn't catch himself.

Just… fell.

The ridge burned.

Flame climbing through the torn structure, smoke rising into a sky that didn't change.

Ash falling.

Smoke climbing.

He stayed where he was.

Hands at his sides.

Breath shallow.

Unsteady.

Alive.

Katya was gone.

—

The world kept going.

Chapter 53: Leave in Silence
Murmansk, Russia

"Уйдёшь молча — услышат громче."
("Leave in silence, and they'll hear you louder.")

"Tell her I never broke."
—Yekaterina Volkova

He left Murmansk the way a wound stops bleeding—slow, too much ice.

The hub lay behind him under a sky the color of iron filings. He limped through service corridors that smelled of burnt plastic and hot dust, found a maintenance road, hot-wired a van that coughed like an old smoker, and drove until the hum in his bones passed for silence.

Roads unraveled into villages that never made maps. He changed shirts twice, plates once. Snow showed everything—what you carried, what you left behind.

When he finally saw her, it wasn't planned.

A farmhouse outside Arkhangelsk, smoke lifting from its chimney like a small permission. Anya stood in the doorway, hair braided back, her daughter pressed to her hip—a rabbit doll's ear knotted around small fingers. No makeup. Wool coat. Scarf. A face that had chosen survival.

For one suspended second he thought he'd dreamed her out of the smoke. Then the child shifted, and the sound was too alive to be grief.

Anya's gaze found him, took in the limp, the crusted bandage, the wrong way he carried his weight. She didn't say his name. She stepped aside.

Inside, the house smelled of tea and soap and chopped wood. Boots by the door. A kettle that remembered what warmth was. She sat him down, set a mug in front of him, then vanished down the short hall.

When she returned, he finally asked, hoarse: "Why here?"

Anya's eyes flicked toward the frosted window, the horizon beyond it. "Far enough north. Far enough from anyone who's looking."

"Tell me," Anya said.

He started.

Not all of it.
Some parts didn't have words.

The corridor. The door. The red light.

Her voice.

He stopped there.

"Again," Anya said.

He swallowed, steadying himself. "She screamed," he admitted. "Like something was being pulled out of her that shouldn't come out. Then… Her eyes… Lights died. She… was just gone."

Anya nodded once.

"До скорого, сестра," she whispered.
See you soon, sister.

She crossed to the sink. The heave came fast, ended fast. She rinsed. When she turned back, her face was flat again.

"What they did to her," she said.

Her eyes dared him to call it pity. He only nodded.

The kettle clicked off. She poured two cups, steam rising between them. She sat across from him, knees almost touching.

"I need you to tell me again," she said. "Every word. So I can bury her with the right ones."

He did. This time he gave it to her clean, as Katya had said it: flat, steady, carved into stone. *"Tell her I never broke."*

Anya listened with her whole face. When he finished, she set her cup down like it weighed too much.

"She never said goodbye."

"No," he said. "She didn't."

Anya walked to the window, frost feathering its corners. Outside, the world was white and still.

"You were my blood and my mirror," she whispered to the glass. "Save me a place."

When she turned, softness was gone, replaced by something surgical.

"What took her," she said, each word deliberate, "I'll take it back."

"I could stay," he said. "We could disappear."

Anya's eyes snapped to his, sharp enough to cut. She stepped closer, her hand still red from bandage work, and pressed her palm flat against his chest. Not tender. Commanding.

"If you stay, you don't vanish. You lead them here. Every drone, every ledger, every loyalist sniffing for a ghost—they'd all find her because of you."

James sagged under the weight of it. The farmhouse, the tea, the quiet—it wasn't a life offered. It was bait.

She met his gaze, steady, unflinching.

Her voice cut clean, leaving no room for doubt. "You don't get to give her ghosts just because you're tired. You finish what you promised. You keep breathing so it matters."

He wanted to argue, but the truth in her face left no room. She shook her head once, jaw set hard.

She stepped close, lifted his shirt, checked the bandage with a nurse's hand. "You'll scar ugly."

"I'll live," he said.

Her mouth gave him half a smile that wasn't safe. "Go before the roads go," she said. "North, then west. Cold is your friend— it slows questions."

He nodded. Stood. The room swayed. She steadied him with her palm against his ribs—the same place Katya once had.

At the door she pulled a small, battered notebook from a drawer and pressed it into his hand. He knew it before he saw it.

"She would have wanted you to use it," Anya said. "We both do."

On the threshold she leaned in, pressed her forehead to his for the length of a breath. Not a kiss. Something else.

"When you need a name," she said, "write your own."

It hit late, the way some bullets do—echoes of other cities, other hands. By the time he opened his mouth, she had already stepped back.

"Go," she said, the word both benediction and order.

[KUBINKA // DIRECTORATE S ANNEX — MOSCOW]

General Sidorov sat alone in the Kubinka annex.

Two dossiers lay on the desk before him. Subject-05 and Subject-09. Firebird and Ice Shadow.

The dyad had been his design, back when he was still a colonel: flame paired with frost. For a time, it had been flawless, lethal beyond calculation. And then, inevitably, it fractured.

Years later, the files returned to his hands. Redacted margins. Conflicting death reports. Handwritten notes from officers who hadn't been there when the blood was still warm. He studied them without expression.

He opened the first folder.

[SVR DIRECTORATE S // FILE EXCERPT]

Subject: Tatiana ___ (alias: Firebird, designation: Subject-05)

Status: Former Directorate S operative, current location fluctuating

Operational Profile:

- Training and conditioning began at age fifteen in SVR-run program. Enhanced hormonal/genomic interventions.

- Codenamed *Red Ghost* by adversary forces; reputation includes multiple confirmed kills across Europe.

• Paired with Subject-09 (Yekaterina / Ice Shadow) as a dyad. The pairing was considered *wildly successful* but collapsed after sustained operational stress.

• Subject-05 subsequently disengaged from assigned post and unilaterally exited Directorate oversight. Command determined active recovery to be cost-inefficient; subject retained on extended autonomous leash with remote monitoring in lieu of repatriation.

• Subject listed as deceased in Prague, Warsaw, and Odessa. None verified.

Behavioral Notes:

• Documented emotional ties: SUBJECT-09

• Highly protective—extremely, lethally protective—of Subject-09.

• Developed a sisterly bond; evidence suggests attachment overrides mission directives.

Command Assessment:

• Survival profile exceeds training expectations; unexplained variance.

• Operational use limited: subject disregards state loyalty when attachments threatened.

• High potential for disruption if uncontrolled.

Handwritten margin note, origin unknown:
"Every morgue says dead. Every field report says alive."

[SVR DIRECTORATE S // FILE EXCERPT]

Subject: Yekaterina ___ (alias: Ice Shadow, designation: Subject-09)
Status: Active Directorate S asset / high-variance subject

Operational Profile:

• Entered program at age seventeen under accelerated conditioning cycle.

- Enhanced neuroendocrine modulation and reflex calibration; field nickname *Ice Shadow* reflects observed emotional detachment.

- Confirmed operations across the Caucasus, Baltics, and Ukraine with extreme kill efficiency.

- Embedded in CIA under long-term deep-cover assignment; current integration status: active.

Behavioral Notes:

- Documented to operate with near-clinical detachment, but variance occurs under specific relational triggers.

- Developed sister-level attachment bond with Subject-05 (Tatiana / Firebird).

- Evidence of reciprocal loyalty: subject accepts operational risk only when proximity to Subject-05 is ensured.

- Bond identified as destabilizing vector: together, they demonstrate increased lethality but reduced command compliance.

Command Assessment:

- Effective in high-deniability eliminations.

- Emotional variance tied to Subject-05 presents long-term control risks.

- Separation of Subjects 05 and 09 recommended but historically unsuccessful.

- Potential catastrophic outcome if bond uncontrolled.

Margin annotation, redacted:
"One burns. One freezes. Together, they break the pattern."

General Sidorov closed the folder. Subject-09 had fulfilled what was required, though she would never grasp the scale of it.

The next phase was already in motion.

The Koschei.

And then—

Tessera.

He turned the key.
Left the room dark.

CHAPTER 54: THE WEIGHT OF SILENCE
Arkhangelsk, Russia

"Silence is not absence. It is the pressure before the storm."

The farmhouse had gone quiet.
Quieter than it should have.

Anya stood at the window, scarf loosened, breath fogging the glass. Outside, the night was a blur of frost and black trees, a silence that wasn't still.

Behind her, Mila shifted in sleep, rabbit doll knotted tight in her hands. The small, steady rise of the child's breath was the only rhythm Anya trusted.

She sang the lullaby she had once hummed when Mila was small:

Лиса в лощине,
хвост — как пламя.
Снег тихо падает,
зовёт тебя по имени.

Я отдал тебе мир,
небо, море—
иди смело и прямо…
…и всегда возвращайся ко мне.

Her palm pressed flat against the glass, skin stinging where the cold came through.

Tell her I never broke.

She closed her eyes.

Then opened them.

Rage rose.
Grief squeezed.

She whispered into the pane:
"До скорого, сестра."

The words misted, then vanished.

Her hand fell to her stomach before she could stop it. Reflex. The nausea had begun to fade, but the truth beneath it had not. She pulled her hand away quickly, unwilling to let the gesture grow shape, unwilling to speak what she carried. Not yet.

She felt it.
That was enough.

Her gaze hardened, cutting past the frost, past the line of trees, past the horizon itself. Somewhere, the Americans were drafting new maps. Somewhere, OBELISK listened. And somewhere, James walked into exile with ghosts on his back.

She remembered him in the snow outside Murmansk, bandaged and staggering, clutching the scarf she had once pressed into his hand. He hadn't held it for warmth. He'd held it like a tether.

She had given him that thread, and he had carried it into silence.

She turned from the window. Mila stirred, brow furrowing in some half-dream, the rabbit doll pulled closer. Anya's face softened.

She brushed a strand of hair from her daughter's cheek, then let her palm drift lower once more, resting lightly against her own stomach.

This time she didn't move it away.

She drew a breath.

CHAPTER 55: WRITE YOUR NAME
Arkhangelsk, Russia

The ferry's horn moaned against the ice, low and tired, like a wound that wouldn't close.

James stood on the deck, scarf tight against his throat, the beat-up notebook heavy in his coat pocket. Anya's words were still on him, raw and alive. *Write your own name.*

He didn't look back toward Arkhangelsk. He'd already spent too many years staring at horizons that never returned what they took. The sea pitched under him, black water flecked with pale shards of ice, gulls circling like they were waiting.

He didn't look back.

Anya watched the ferry lights dwindle until they were no more than a suggestion against the snow. Her daughter tugged at her coat, not asking anything. Just holding on. Anya bent to smooth the child's hair and whispered something only she could hear. Her free hand lingered against the doorframe, steadying her, as if bracing for a weight no one else could see.

Inside the farmhouse, the tea had cooled. She rinsed the cups, steady as ritual. When the knock came, it was neither loud nor hesitant.

A woman in a dark wool coat. Early forties. No smile. Authority carried without effort.

She had the one-pager in her pocket—a red-ink corner note: *Window closes faster than grief.* Helena had been given seventy-two hours. She had counted them twice.

"They called me Helena in Havana," she said. "They don't anymore."

Anya let the silence sit between them until it felt like another presence.

Helena's voice carried the calm of someone certain she'd already won. "The flags don't matter. Systems collapse. People like us survive."

Anya's eyes hardened, fury rising sharp as glass. "The systems already collapsed. Yours especially. You burned my sister when she was the only one holding your lines together. She died stopping OBELISK. You gave her silence."

Helena didn't flinch. Her tone was ice. "Family is a lie you told yourself. She was a comrade. Nothing more."

Anya's grip tightened on the teacup.

The handle snapped with a brittle pop. The sound didn't fade—it hung sharp between them, like a gun cocked but not fired.

She stepped into Helena's space. Heat radiating. Muscles tight. Every nerve screaming to lash out.

Helena didn't move. Not a blink. Not a step back.

Anya stopped. Her anger found a wall and slid down it, cold now, returning her to something sharper than rage.

Anya dropped the broken handle onto the table, porcelain clinking against wood. Her voice was low, dangerous but measured. "She was both," Anya said, low, surgical. "Sister and comrade. Remember that."

Helena folded the paper away like a surgeon putting instruments out of sight. "We can offer sanctuary, medicine, and a way to keep what matters to you safe," she said.

"I don't want your sanctuary. I want them to account for what they did." Anya set the broken cup down as if laying down a verdict. Her voice had no tremor. Only a flatness that meant decision.

Helena's answer was quiet steel. "Refuse us and you will leave more sisters in the earth," she said, voice flat as a file.

Her daughter pressed at her coat hem, small and still, a silent anchor.

Anya laughed once, a sound with no humor. "You speak of sisters as numbers in your ledger." Her palm closed into a fist until knuckles went white. "Say that word again," she said, "and you won't leave this house."

She stepped closer.

"I won't bury you."

She continued quieter, under her breath, almost lost in the cold between them. *"And I'll come for every last one of you—*
—Fuck you."

It wasn't for the room. It wasn't even for Helena. It was a grave marker, spoken low enough to stay buried.

Her daughter's hand stayed at her coat hem, steady as an oath.

Anya opened the door wide—not an invitation. A dismissal.

Helena didn't move at first. Didn't blink. Her lips parted. "Tatiana—"

"My name is Anya."

Helena's mouth curled, faint and sharp. "Call yourself what you want. I know *exactly* who you are. That's why I came."

The pause was there—the faintest catch, half a heartbeat too long—

"When you're ready, we'll be waiting."

A beat.

"We don't mind waiting."

Helena's boots crunched into the snow until even that sound was gone.

Anya stood in the doorway, hand still clenched from the broken porcelain. Slowly, deliberately, she closed the door. The latch clicked like a verdict.

Only then did she move.

Her palm drifted downward, finding her belly. She rested it there, a vow her enemies would never read: *never again.*

Her hand fell away.

[REYKJAVÍK, ICELAND]

Each night he walked the cliffs until the wind peeled at his coat and the sea hurled salt like penance.

Sometimes the storm carried static.

Sometimes it carried a scream.

He never decided which was worse.

The notebook waited on the table, cover scuffed, corners bent, the weight of two women's hands behind it. Two ghosts, one dare: *When you need a name, write your own.*

At last he reached for the pen.

The page waited, blank and merciless. For the first time since Murmansk, the rest of the world belonged to him.

He wrote the first letter of his name.

Then stopped.

EPILOGUE
Reykjavík, Iceland

The sea was calm.

The sky—bruised violet.

James cradled a cooling mug of tea, bitter without honey. His ribs ached with the coming weather. His coat, once black, had worn to ash.

He hadn't spoken his real name in months. But hers—he remembered.

The notebook waited where he'd left it. Scuffed, smoke-stained, the weight of two hands pressed into its cover. He opened it.

He wrote one word. *Katya.*

Then, on the next page, smaller script:
Even ghosts breathe.

The ink held.

His breath didn't.

Outside, auroras rose—green fire across the sky.

He stepped out, page in hand, and lit it.

The paper curled. The ink blackened. The flame whispered.

Ash scattered across the sea.
"Goodbye, Katya," he whispered.

Behind him, in the dark belly of the trawler, a console blinked awake.

James didn't hear it.

The sea gave no reply. Only silence—heavy, listening.

And in it, James remained.

Alive.

Alone.

Postscript
Moscow, Russia – Kremlin

The Kremlin's walls held their silence like a weapon. General Sidorov stood before the long table, dossier neat, squared to its edge. Across from him, the President let his glass rest untouched, eyes fixed somewhere far beyond the room.

"She was extraordinary," the President said at last. His voice was low, measured. "She didn't hesitate. Not once. Yekaterina saved my life when no one else could." He paused, letting the memory cut through protocol. "The world may forget her name. I will not."

Sidorov inclined his head. He had always known Subject-09 carried variance beyond control. That variance had kept the Federation alive at its most fragile moment. And in dying, she had opened the space for what must come next.

"The dyad has collapsed," he said. "The pattern remains."

The President's gaze sharpened. "Koschei."

Sidorov let the word settle, then gave the faintest nod.

"Phase 1."

A beat.

"Tessera."

The President raised his glass, though he did not drink. His voice was iron. "Never again," the President said.

The crystal touched the table with a muted chime. Outside, the bells of Moscow tolled the hour.

Sidorov closed the dossier. "Then we are agreed."

The silence that followed was not absence.

It had already begun.

[STRATEG-7 // FRACTAL INTERCEPT]

ARCHIVE ORDER LOCATOR // 7·7·2·7·3·5·4·6 // Σ41

Never again is just repetition with sharper teeth.